BAER CHARLTON

DEATH ON A DIME

A SOUTHSIDE HOOKER NOVEL

Death on a Dime
By Baer Charlton
ISBN-13: 9781495489150
ISBN-10: 1495489159

Edited and formatted by
Literary Editor Rogena Mitchell-Jones with
Rogena Mitchell-Jones Manuscript Services
www.rogenamitchell.com

FOR JAMES ALIGO

11/21/1938 – 11/23/2008

OTHER BOOKS BY BAER CHARLTON

The Very Littlest Dragon

Stoneheart

BOX

01

The fork was a burning accusation firmly planted by the steel-like fist through the bony hand with one finger touching the dollar and change tip. The pain seared the rims of the young punk's sunken eyes as his mouth opened slowly in a silent breathless scream. Pinpricks of strain-induced sweat ruptured around his temples, and his body froze against the pain as his brain told him what was happening.

The cold gaze of the gold-flecked green eyes slid slowly from the interrupted book, locking onto the frightened brown eyes twitching on the young street tough. The quiet leather-jacketed avenger slowly swung his face closer to the blanched face of his captured prey. The young man's inner soul was clearly quaking as he took in the fierce scarred face.

"Did you think you worked hard for that dollar?" The chilling voice was barely louder than the young man's breathing.

The eyes on the young man grew even wider as his face started a shudder of denial.

"Did you run your ass ragged all night until the drunks come in to steal your tips because they think you would never miss it?" The vise grip on the fork wavered ever so slightly, grinding the points of the fork, buried in the offending hand along the Formica counter of the all-night diner. "Did you ever think the waitress just might need that dollar more than you do?"

Less than six inches separated the two faces as the tension built. The trapped thief now wondered if his hand was only the beginning of what could happen to him that night. A distinct aroma started to emanate from his lap as he lost any decency of control he may have previously had back when the other dude was still reading his book and eating his dinner.

"Hooker!" The woman screamed from the other end of the counter as she flew out of the kitchen. Rushing to the counter, she tried to stop what she was afraid would happen. "Hooker, stop!" She slid to a stop and placed her hand on the fist and the fork handle. "Stop," she pleaded. "He didn't mean it."

Hooker turned his gaze from the kid to the woman. "He was going to steal your tip, Candy," he rumbled. Slowly, with both of her hands guiding his, he withdrew from the fork.

The mousy blonde's shoulders slumped as she saw the tines of the fork buried fully in the boy's hand. She reached out, grabbed his jaw, and shook it toward her. "Johnny, don't move. I'll be right back, but don't move." She shot Hooker a cold look as he returned to his dinner, borrowing another fork from the place setting on the other side of him. Picking up his book and turning it over, he stole a glance at the now rushing waitress as she pushed through the door to the back. Glancing at the kid, he saw the scared child that hadn't been there when the hand had crept across the counter toward the tip.

"Johnny, huh?" The kid nodded numbly as a tiny bit of drool snuck out of the side of his drooping mouth, still blinking at the blinding sear in his eyes, a low painful moan quietly bubbling up from a deep primal place in his belly.

The scrawny waitress banged through the swinging door and rushed back in as she folded a couple of clean towels. She started and stopped in hesitation, considering what to do next. She gingerly rolled the hand over to see the points of the tines making four pimples along the palm of the hand, bumping out, but not penetrating all the way through.

Hooker reached over without looking, and grabbed the fork. "Hold his hand." Turning the page with his other hand and chewing, he continued to read.

"What are you doing?"

"Hold his hand down tight, or it will hurt worse." Hooker made a mental note of where he had stopped reading and looked up at Candy's face. Despite the freckles, her two decades of hard life lay carved deep. With grim determination, she pushed the hand back down into its original position and pushed down with both of her hands. The fork flashed out of the hand as she reached for the towel to stanch the bleeding.

"What were you thinking, Johnny?" She scolded as she tied the towel in a knot. The white Turkish towel was stark against the long-unwashed skin. "I've told you a hundred times that if you need money, come ask me. We don't steal." She reached out and ran her fingers through his hair trying to straighten out the mess crowning the shrunken boy caved into the chair in front of her. "What am I ever going to do with you until the Navy or somebody takes you?" She fussed.

The kid slowly rolled his shoulders and mumbled, "I don't know."

The waitress mirrored her younger sibling, and then, shaking off the sorrow and resuming her bravado armor of the late night waitress, she turned on the leather-jacketed man quietly reading. "As for you, you're done," she demanded. "Pay the bill, and go back to work."

Hooker looked up, pained. "But I wanted some of that…"

She cut him off. "Not tonight, mister. You're done." She waved the back of her hands at him. "Shoo, you can have apple-pie tomorrow night." Still shooing him, "Tonight, you've done enough damage. You'd better leave a big tip though, because tomorrow I'll have to take him up to the clinic, and I don't have that kind of money."

Hooker withdrew from the counter seat and started to protest, but was shut down by a snap of her head and a single hard glare. Knowing defeat, he fished a twenty-dollar bill out of his wallet, thought about it, added a five for the meal, and then slipped both under the edge of the coffee cup. He caught the kid, Johnny eyeing the largess of tip, and pointed at him as he closed his left eye and sighted down the pointed finger at the kid, who sunk even deeper in the chair.

As he started to walk off, he caught the hurt and stern

look on the face of his favorite waitress. Slapping the kid gently on the shoulder, he parted with a half attempt to make up with the server by saying, "Do what your sister tells ya, Johnny, and stay out of trouble." Turning, he took three steps and pushed through the glass door into the damp chilly night.

Glancing at his watch, he noted the five minutes to midnight as he opened the door and clambered up into the large yellow and blue tow truck. He leaned across to the glove compartment and hit the upper corner to make the door open. Fishing in the large dark maw, he withdrew a half-empty pack of unfiltered cigarettes. Absentmindedly, he tapped a single cigarette on his watch face as he stared across the empty street at the dark shops. His mind was a million miles away. His hand fished the keys out of his leather jacket, and then turned the square silver key in the switch. Hooker listened to the turbo wind up, and then pushed the small silver start button. The largest, fastest tow truck in the five counties of the Bay Area rumbled to life.

Looking in the long side mirror, he smiled and rolled down the window, as the oldest street urchin in the city came drifting along the side of the truck like so much night mist. Delicate fingers, like those of a concert pianist, lightly danced and walked along the edge of the steel working bed of the tow truck. Hooker absently counted the touching pattern. It never changed. Always three, then a skip or hop, then two, a midair twist, a middle finger bounce followed by a midair flare of the whole hand flat and spread, and then dropping into a repeat for the next three feet of the truck. Every night, it was always the same time, always the same Peter, and always the same finger dance of touches working their way along the twenty feet of truck bed.

"Good morning, Peter." Hooker greeted the man who was little more than a walking pillar of filthy rags.

"Oh," the man feigned being startled. "Oh, it's you. Good morning, Hooker." He stopped, but looked back at the restaurant.

Hooker chuckled quietly. He had never seen the street urchin look directly at anyone, or even face them.

"What's the word?"

The bum compulsively washed his face with his right hand as he almost slurred, "Thunderbird."

"Half the price," Hooker recited in the ritual.

"Twice as nice." The man giggled in his pride of having a special connection with this man in his big working truck. "H-h-h-hey H-h-hooker?" Peter stammered. "Do you have a s-s-s-st-stick I could b-b-b-bum?" He looked across the street as his right hand rose above his head, and like an elephant's nose, the hand searched the air and then retreated to the safety of his head, and repeated the ritual.

"Let me look around here, Peter. Maybe somebody left something from the day shift." Hooker would never tell Peter the truck was his and his alone, or he stocked the cigarettes in the boot just for these shared moments, but he thought about the moment as he continued to strike the end of the cigarette on the watch face.

"Well, th-th-that would be g-g-good." The elephant nose rising a little higher was rewarded with the 'cancer stick' and retreated.

"Do you need a light there, Peter?" Hooker pushed in

the as yet unused lighter on his dash. "I have a great lighter right here on the dashboard."

"N-n-no thanks, I-I-I'll use it l-l-la-later," Peter responded, completing the ritual as he wandered off back the way he had come out of the dark.

Hooker watched in the mirror as the migrating heap of rags slowly dissolved into the dark of the night. He reached for the radio's microphone, silently reciting a small prayer for the homeless man. Take care, Peter, and may you sleep without your demons tonight and find peace in the morning. Hooker moved the mic near his mouth and keyed the red talk button.

"Dispatch, this is unit 1-4-1. Show me 10-8," letting them know that he was back in-service.

"10-4, Hooker. All we have hanging is a 1971 white El Dorado with a flat tire, south bound 101, just north of Pearl."

"Sure," Hooker responded. "I'll take it. Show me five minutes out."

"10-4, showing 1-4-1 on call number 0-0-2, ten minutes out at 12:06. And Hooker, no speeding. It's only a flat tire."

"10-4." Hooker hung the auto club yellow microphone over his disused rearview mirror facing the tow mechanism behind him and chuckled at the mother-hen routine. Hooker checked both side mirrors, and down both ways of the empty boulevard. Robotically, he jammed the gears into the first of six gears of the main transmission. His right hand reached slightly back to the second gear shifter, selecting the second gear of the four-gear 'crash box' or transfer gearbox that gave him twenty-four gears in all. Hooker liked to think of the gearing as zero to one-twenty in twenty-four. Slowly, the eleven tons of giant truck nosed out onto Winchester Boulevard and headed for the freeway on-ramp three blocks away.

02

Hooker, born Hieronymus Octavio O'Keller, loved the giant truck as much as he really loved anything. The body of the machine once worked as a Marmon logging truck with an over-sized conventional snout. The snout didn't need to be so long, so Hooker and his uncle had chopped it down to the needed length. The cab was roomy and easily fit the extra radios that were the lifeblood of a gypsy freelance tow-trucker. The engine was a special that had started life as a 900 horse-powered drag line winch on the back of a logging truck that could winch a forty-ton tree trunk up a thousand feet of steep mountain side, until a falling boulder had killed the owner and destroyed the front half of the drag line truck.

Flipping the truck through a few of the twenty-four gears, and winding through the streets to the on-ramp was second nature for Hooker. The roll and rumble of the engine was what he liked to think his blood sounded like rolling and rumbling through his veins. Flipping the blinker, he down shifted and wound the steering wheel as the giant lumbered lazily around the corner and began to drop down onto the I-280.

His right foot feathered back slightly, and as the needle he wasn't watching dropped just under 2,100 rpm, his right hand popped the shifter out of fourth, and he palmed the nob up into fifth and danced his toes on the gas pedal as the giant began to roar down the on-ramp. The now 1,200 horses roared up the twin stack pipes just behind the cab as Hooker bypassed sixth and seventh and jammed the gearbox straight into the eighth and rolled out on the freeway dressed for dancing—empty and under a full moon. Fifteen seconds later, eleven tons of yellow and blue steel was rolling toward Highway 101, twenty-five miles per hour over the limit and still climbing.

"Hooker?" He ignored the sideband radio behind his head.

"Hooker, you had better answer me, or I'll start calling you by a different name." The sweet voice oozed from the speakers directly behind his head and could not be missed.

He rolled his eyes, reaching behind his head where the microphone hung. "Go ahead, momma."

The woman was as much his mother as his uncle Willie was his real uncle. But they were a major half of the only family he ever really had.

"Sugar, there is a little birdy out there that is talking about a big truck which is not obeying the speed limit."

Shit! Sherriff Deputy Podell, hated by 'most everyone. They called him Poodle behind his back. "Is that dog huntin' or leashed to a tree?"

"Running wild in the street, darlin'—just thought you'd want to know, and you still have plenty of time to make that flat tire. Please don't ruin my evening, sweetheart. You know I worry about you." The voice was soft and sweet and sounded like a young Marilyn Monroe, or the best wet dream you could think of. But the voice didn't match the woman as she put down the desk stand microphone and slowly rolled her extra heavy-duty, custom made, over-sized, all steel chair back around to her main desk.

The dark room was punctuated by the small pools of light from the tiny desk lamps. Three women wrangled most of the radios operating in the entire south bay area surrounding San Jose and Santa Clara. The business was simply called 'Dispatch.' Some called it Night Dispatch. Either worked for Dolly, as long as they called her. Even though some traffic came in from plumbers and alarm companies during the day, the bulk of the business came after the sun went down. By three am, even the police radios were handled through the Dispatch. The city and county quite literally went through Dolly's switchboard.

Of the near half-ton of female flesh that occupied the room at that moment, almost half sat behind the large, custom-made black walnut desk. There lay one main adornment on the desk: a large, highly-polish tree limb paperweight that read *The Stick*—meaning, *the stick you stir stuff up with*—and Dolly was the only person allowed to touch it, much less use it.

The buck started and stopped with the giant woman affectionately known as *Momma* by many of the 'homeless waif' young tow-truck drivers who learned fast: at least one person in their world cared about them—Dolly.

"Think he listened?" The voice floated from the

younger dispatcher, Dina, who could still possibly buy her pants at a regular store, if she were lucky. The business of answering service and dispatching is a non-stop eight-hour torture of doing nothing but sitting, talking, and eating. Between calls, Dolly occupied herself in the Dispatch's large kitchen to satisfy her passions for cooking, eating, and feeding the multitudes at her twelve-person table.

"If he knows what's good for him," Dolly growled as she picked up her pen. "Call him for an ETA." Estimated time of arrival was the lifeblood of a defensible dispatch log.

The middle dispatcher keyed her headset microphone, "Unit 1-4-1?"

"1-4-1, go."

"ETA?"

The radio squawked, and then a short bark as Hooker was obviously downshifting with an open keyed mic, "Um, got a little traffic out here, probably will be about another six or eight minutes, over."

"10-4, Hooker, just let us know when you get there."

She side glanced over to Dolly to see the woman nodding her head as if listening to some unheard melody. Confirmation of Hooker behaving himself was music to Dolly's ears like none other. The dispatcher smiled as she flipped another switch and plugged in a line, answering, "South Bay Alarm, how may I help you?"

The dimly lit dispatch room was brighter than the dark along the side of the road where Hooker rolled up behind the Cadillac El Dorado. The flat tire was on the right rear, the one in the mud.

Not thinking, Hooker pulled his personal mic from

behind his head instead of the yellow towing radio's microphone. "1-4-1, show me 10-97. I don't see a member anywhere. Didn't you say this was a club call?"

Dolly looked up at the two dispatchers, then back around at the radio. Spinning her girth around with an unnatural grace, she grabbed the *lollypop,* or desk stand microphone. "Hooker, you stay in the truck. We'll try the call back number." She thought about it a second. After being in the business for so many years, all of her internal alarms were going off at once.

"Hooker?"

"Yes, ma'am."

"Son, why don't you back away from the car until we straighten this out?" She took a large breath. "Just give it about a hundred yards, would you?" She knew there should have been a highway patrol or someone standing by at 12:30 in the morning.

There were two clicks on the radio as Hooker acknowledged by keying the mic with a double tap.

The young dispatcher Patty leaned back, looking at Dolly. She shook her head to confirm the *no answer* to the number she had dialed. Her much larger boss held up her hand with four fingers in the air, as a visual confirmation as she spoke into another microphone. "10-4 unit 7-1-9-Kilo, tow-truck is standing by about one-hundred yards north."

Dolly muttered under her breath the holy prayer of all night dispatchers: *And now we wait.*

The California Highway Patrol car glided past Hooker and eased over to the shoulder as it approached the large white car. The red lights were flashing, casting eerie shadows as another car slid by in the fast lane as far away as it could get from whatever was going on that morning.

Dolly's voice whispered from the speakers, "Hooker, the chip just called ninety-seven. Do you have eyes on him?"

Hooker whispered back, even though his truck's twin pipes and giant engine could never be classified as stealthy, "Be vewy vewy quiet… we're hunting wabbits," he called back in his best Elmer Fudd imitation. He watched as the officer slipped slowly out of his door with his right hand on his service pistol.

Hooker nodded to himself as the officer slowly eased the door almost closed. The dome light was off, the interior of the patrol car dark to prying eyes. Even Hooker could not really tell if a second officer was in the car or not, usually not.

The officer inched along the driver's side of the Cadillac, almost running his butt along the chrome strip presenting the smallest target, and yet getting the best view of the interior. As he reached the back seat window, he rotated and presented his front to the car as he leaned down to get a better look at something in the back seat.

Hooker jumped as the officer buckled in the middle and jerked like a marionette as his back exploded through his highly starched shirt. The rag doll, once a police officer, was thrown six feet out into the traffic lane.

Hooker's right hand slammed down on the large red brake disengage button and dropped the gearshift as his left foot engaged the clutch. As the shifter snicked into the reverse cog, Hooker dumped the clutch and floored the gas pedal. The rear window of the Cadillac exploded into a crazed pattern, and then a large hole appeared. The eleven-ton monster roared backwards up the freeway as all eight drive tires threw dirt and gravel.

Six pits appeared in Hooker's windshield-turned-target. The engine screamed as it hit well into redline, and Hooker still didn't let up on the gas.

Buckshot, or what he thought was buckshot, rattled off the windshield a second time, but left no pits, so Hooker jumped on the brakes, opened the clutch, and whipped the steering wheel a flick to the right and then harder to the left as the giant truck's tires all howled in a ten-part harmony as the truck slewed around and was now faced the wrong way up the freeway. Hooker slammed the gearshift into high second and dumped the clutch, and worked the truck back up toward the *get out of Dodge* gear. He thought he might have heard some more of the heavy buckshot rattle around in the tow rigging, but he also figured it might just be his imagination.

Letting the truck run itself down the main lane of the 101, he reached back with his left hand to grab his personal microphone from behind his head, as his right hand slapped its way through to the last gear in the second tier of gears.

"Dolly, the chip is dead," he called. "Shotgun with double aught buck is my guess. License plate was Charlie Adam X-ray Niner One Five."

"Got it, Hooker. Officers on the way," said the consummate professional, but then the mother took over. "Are you OK?"

"Dings in my windshield, but I'm OK." His hands were starting to shake. "Mom, it was a set-up."

"Doors open, Hooker. Coffee is always on." She knew when a driver had crossed a line of comfort, or worse, tolerance, and she knew the office was a safe haven for Hooker. "The Chips will want to be able to find you soon, and probably the sheriff as well. I'll call the Captain and get him over here. Careful coming down Story, the boys have been out tonight. You don't need a 45 or 9 mm round through your cab, too."

Hooker clicked the mic key twice, downshifting as he surged the wrong way up the long straight ramp. Hard right, back over the over-pass, and he felt the powerful ass-end drift out screaming of hot rubber sliding sideways on the only slightly damp night asphalt. Stomping on the accelerator, he powered back up through the second gear of the third tier and 70 mph. *Let the boys try to hit this moving target*, he thought as he hit the city street's 35 mph speed zone and pushed the truck up through the eighty mark, roaring past a collection of Asian street punks standing gape-mouthed on the corner. Hooker laughed a sardonic deep-throated chuckle as he caught out of the corner of his eye one of the kids reaching under his shirt for what had to be a pistol tucked in his waistband. *Been tried before, buddy.* He pulled the chain for the air horn and gave it two short blasts in salute. The kid was not earnest about shooting the highballing truck—he was just posing for his gang brothers.

Hooker rode the brakes instead of using the noisy air brakes in deference to the neighborhood. As he brought the rig quietly around the corner, he drifted the shifter into eighth gear, or semi-low third, as he pulled up into the large parking lot.

Grabbing the microphone behind his head, he squeezed the key. "Coming in."

As the engine rattled down to silence, and he slipped down out of his door, the heavy steel-plated door swung open and a very large shadow stood backlit, waiting.

As Hooker approached the doorway, Dolly quietly stated, "Plates were on a Ford half ton in Gilroy this afternoon. The guy didn't even know they were gone." She stepped back a few feet then turned on her bare feet and waddled back toward the kitchen. "That sort of thing happens when you're pushing ninety-two, and still driving into town without a license. Daughter he lives with didn't even know he had gone into town." She looked back at Hooker. "That happens when you drink heavy before noon."

Dolly stuck out her left arm and stopped herself on the door jam with her right. She waved the great left wobbling arm and hand toward the two dispatchers huddled in the two pools of dim light. "Patty, Hooker. Hooker, my new girl Patty." She turned to give him a hard look. "And no sniffing her neck until she has gained at least forty pounds. She's my brother-in-law's baby girl, and he has a bad temper and several shotguns."

The young girl plopped her face into her hands.

"Hey, Patty, nice to meet you."

In a good imitation of her aunt, she waved a wobbling but slightly smaller arm at Hooker. The glow of the dim light didn't do much to hide the burn of the blush on her face and ample upper chest.

Dolly moved farther into the kitchen and came to rest in front of the stove as Hooker quietly quick-stepped over to the two dispatchers, and nuzzled into the large neck of the quiet bleached teased blonde in a well-stretched tank-top t-shirt. She quietly giggled as he nuzzled near her ticklish ears.

"And don't you be nuzzling Dina's neck either, young man. She's getting married in two months," Dolly continued from the stove.

"Yes, ma'am, just congratulating her, Dolly." Stepping around to face her, he mouthed, "Really?" She nodded, as she rubbed both hands on her belly then put her finger up to her lips and nodded toward the kitchen. Hooker's eyes went up a notch. As he passed around back of her, he nuzzled back into her neck whispering, "Pregnant women are so very sexy." He danced away from her horrified slap and jumped over to Patty's neck for a quick nuzzle that made her jump, as he whispered, "I just couldn't wait for a whole month."

The young girl had a horrified *I'm so offended* look on her face as he strolled back to pay attention to Dolly. She looked at the older operator, and then they both grabbed at each other as they broke-up into fits of giggles.

Dina leaned over to the younger girl and confided, "He's always that bad, but when you need the shirt off his back, it's in his hand before you can ask." She smiled at the thought of Hooker without his shirt, and then realized the younger gal was having the same thoughts as she watched him walking back to the kitchen. She giggled and playfully slapped the new sister in lust. "You are so bad." The two giggled as they turned back to the large board of holes and lights, and then stole a last glance at the retreating hind end of male, which led to more giggles.

The giggles stopped only when they heard a throat clearing in the kitchen. Dolly did not need to look to know what was going on. She had been doing the job longer than the two girls had been out of diapers.

03

The young man stood behind the large woman stirring the sauce in the pot, and reached around and gave her a soft long hug, almost hanging on for support, his trim bearded jaw resting on her shoulder.

"Are you going to be OK?" She continued to stir so she didn't have to look at him and expose the red wet eyes she had been wiping.

He leaned his head against her head and rested. "I guess." He took a quick large breath and sighed. "I think it was John Senol."

She sagged, and was quiet for a moment, weighing the information. Quietly, she confirmed it with a slow nod.

Hooker's eyes stung at the confirmation as he whispered more to himself, "His little girl just turned two this last month." Dolly just nodded. Turning to the cupboard for a glass, he added, "I don't think I'd want to be the captain this morning."

"Nope." She raised her head and stared at the wall behind the stove, seeing too many other things. She called out, "Dina, any word on Captain Davis?"

"He just passed King and Story, so about two minutes." She plugged in a cord and keyed the boom mike at her jaw. "10-4 3-7-8, we have you 10-8. You'll be looking for a 1978 Gold Pacer with a flat tire. Let me know when you get there, Danny." She looked over at Patty and mouthed the word 'newbie.' The younger girl made large eyes and rolled them as she planted her face in her right hand and began to giggle in a quiet laughter.

Dolly tasted the sauce from the spoon she was blowing on, nodded and put it down, and then headed for the door. As she cleared the kitchen door, she glared at the two dispatchers. "You two better not be making fun of the new kid Danny. He's very sweet, and I want him around for a while."

"Yes, ma'am," they chorused.

Opening the door as the knock came from the outside, she stood there with her left fist buried deep in what was probably her hip. Slowly shaking her head, she backed up and let the Highway Patrol Captain into the hallway. "Sauce is done, and I'll be starting the pasta directly. Coffee is at least four hours old, and Hooker's in the kitchen. Why don't you two go use the office? I'll bring you the coffee."

The officer removed his hat as he crossed the threshold revealing the grey flattop haircut standing ridged from the decades of brushings. His craggy face, abused by teenage acne, softened as he leaned over and gave her a kiss on the cheek. "Thanks," he muttered softly as he kept moving.

She quietly closed the heavy armored steel door that stood between her and her 'girls' and the not so nice world a few feet away. It had not always been that way, but over the years, the neighborhood changed, and after one harrowing night of blazing guns, the steel door was installed. As was her habit, she touched her two right fingers to her lips in a kiss, and then pressed them on an escutcheon directly above the doorknob—a badge with the number 701 on it—the same badge number of the officer who died that night.

Hooker stepped out of the kitchen and took the officer's hand. "There is a juvenile over at county that had a fork in his hand," the Captain greeted him. "Know anything about that?"

Hooker just looked him in the eye and weighed his options. "There's a young officer lying dead on the south bound 101, too. Which one do you really want to talk about?"

"In the office," growled the older man. Looking back over his shoulder at Dolly, "Double the sugar, please." Nodding at Hooker's back, he continued, "It's going to be a long night."

A snap glance over at the dispatchers across the room and he was turning into the office behind the young man in the leather jacket. He was already loosening his tie.

"10-4, Danny. I'm showing you 10-97 on call number November Delta 0-2-1."

The older officer closed the office door slowly as he weighed the young man before him that he had heard about, but had never met. Essentially, he looked like a street tough: curly mop of black hair, tight and trimmed to the jawline beard, and a white t-shirt and raked jeans over the engineer boots favored by most of the hard-core bikers.

With over thirty years as a Highway Patrol officer, he also knew that his background was coloring his perception of the kid. But if Dolly said he was her golden child, then it was her church, and he would just have to tread lightly until he understood the liturgy.

Placing his hat upside down on the table, he lowered himself into the chair across the table from Hooker as Dolly pushed her way through the door.

"Why, it's pitch black in here. Let me turn on some lights," Dolly fussed as she set the large mug of coffee in front of the officer who was trying to wake himself up by washing his face and hair in his hands.

"Please don't," Hooker, responded softly. "The extra light would disturb the girls. It reflects off the notes on the board, and they can't see the right holes for the plugs." Dolly and he both knew it was a bullshit reason, but she nodded and backed out.

"Chet," she added, using his shortened family name, "I have pasta with meat sauce ready when you want it."

"Thanks, Dolly, but let me wake up first," he said as he registered that it was only 2:20in the morning. He groaned inwardly, and looked over at Hooker.

"No, I'm good, Dolly, thanks anyway. It did smell great though. Maybe reruns tomorrow."

She slowly closed the door with a quiet click and padded back to her desk as the yellow pool of light and mounds of paperwork hid the romance novel she knew she would never get to tonight, or any time soon. She looked over at the two girls, the older of which could feel the heat of her look, wagged her head, meaning still no word from the officers at the scene. She creaked down into her custom steel welded chair, and for the first time, regretted making the office sound proof.

The two men sat silently sipping on the steaming thick gutsy coffee, each busy with their own thoughts, and neither much thinking about the events earlier in the night. Dim light glowed through the soundproofed windows from the small lamps in the dispatch room.

Looking for answers in his mug of coffee that he knew were not there, the officer rumbled a low throat-clearing rasp. “You look after people because you really care.” The officer watched the young man with his one eye as the other closed against the steam from the coffee.

The kid shrugged with a roll of his left leathered shoulder. His face was a pure statement of *yeah, so what?* But there was a slight hiccup in the movement of mug to his lips, as if he suddenly realized that it truly was something he had done.

Slowly setting the mug down as if he weren’t sure that he wanted to let go of the security of the warm stoneware handle, Hooker looked up into the eyes of the officer. “And your point would be?” He presented a full press of street tough, with a twenty-mile stare of pure cold steely-green eyes, the heat just below the surface singeing the edges of the eyes and words.

The eyes held for a few seconds before the older acquiesced and passed back a low shrug of his own. “Just saying.” The much older officer knew that you don’t work a lifetime in the gutter without some of that getting on you, even on the relatively clean streets of the Golden State’s highways. But a caring person on the streets was a good thing to have, and even better to know. He had his confirmation about Dolly's *golden child,* and it was good enough for him.

Another sip of coffee and he dove into the debriefing, even as informal as it was. "You were the first there." He put his mug down and folded his hands together on the table in front of him. "What made you back off?"

Hooker started to shrug but thought more about what it was that had warned him. "When you roll up on a member… auto club member," the officer nodded in understanding, "there is always a person who is happy to see you, waving with at least one hand and sometimes two, big smiles, especially in the middle of the night. But tonight, there was nobody there. No one was standing on the side of the road, jumping up and down waving their arms. It was just—I don't know—wrong." He stopped drawing patterns on the table with his finger and looked up. "And, I didn't see the flat tire. They had called it in as a rear right flat. It was in the dirt, but not flat. It looked as if they were ready to drive off."

"Did you see anyone in the car?"

"No, the dome light was off, as were the headlights, but I think the car was still running. I mean, who waits in the pitch black of night, and not put some kind of light on?"

The captain nodded, and scratched the middle of his flattop, nodding as he thought for a moment before he stated, "You're right, they don't."

29

04

Dolly knocked on the door and opened it. In her right hand, she carried a tray with a plate of food and a carafe of more coffee. Placing the tray down on the table, she set the plate in front of the grey haired officer. "I know you won't have time later to get any food, and I remembered you don't like pasta, so I made you an omelet and toast."

Captain Davis looked at the very large omelet. Probably at least four eggs or more, with what looked like Linguica sausage slices, and a white cheese oozing out around the mushrooms that were falling out of the open mouth of the omelet. All smothered with a long-simmered meat sauce. To balance the plate, Dolly had stacked four pieces of wheat toast. "Whoa, Dolly, what about my diet?" he complained half-heartedly.

Pouring the man more coffee with one hand, she reached over to pick up the top piece of toast, took a bite out of it, and replaced the remainder to the stack. Dolly then offered the carafe to Hooker with a twinkle of devil in her eye. "There, now you have the diet platter," she teased with a giggle, as she nudged the older man almost off his chair with a side push of her plentifully padded hip.

"Hooker?" Dina called from her station.

Laughing at Dolly's ideas of *diet*, the young man stiffly unwound himself from the straight chair he had been sitting in for what seemed like hours. "Yeah, baby?" He wandered toward the door with his mug held out to Dolly for a refill.

"I've got Manny on the phone."

Stepping into the larger darker room, he glanced over at the large school clock that hung with its own pool of light on the wall. Calculating distance and time he replied, "Tell him I'll have his jump start at quarter after five. And remind him that he owes me a ten spot," pointing at the dispatcher with his finger as a gun, and snapping his thumb down. Then realizing what he had just done, he apologized.

Turning, he handed the mug of coffee back to Dolly. "Here, finish this for me. I have to go get me some jelly donuts, and don't you dare tell Stella." He kissed her on the cheek and was out the steel door before she could protest or feed him.

She just rolled her eyes and slumped into herself, she quietly mused to herself, "Kids. It's a wonder he has any meat on his bones at all." She looked at the mug of coffee, and kind of snarled like a dog that didn't trust the food in front of it. She raised the mug, took a sip, and cringed. "Needs some cocoa," she muttered to herself, looking back into the office to make sure her other man was still busy with his food. She then shoved off for the kitchen. "Girls, I'm making cocoa."

"Sounds right," followed by, "Ditto," was acknowledged with a nod from the queen bee. Caffeine and calories kept the night shift running.

Humming a senseless tune—one she probably learned in the kitchen from her mother or grandmother—the queen bee was where she loved to be… cooking for others, and being the center of the universe for things going on in the South Bay.

05

The black clad shadow strolled across the parking lot that usually had no more than a few cars in it, except during New Year's Eve, when the lot could be holding upwards of thirty tow-trucks, and a few police squad cars. It's hard to look at the seemingly small puma-brick building and imagine that it could hold over fifty drivers and their wives or girlfriends, or just someone who was riding around with them, but Hooker had seen a packed house before. Two years ago, a call for a tow-truck had come in, and the dispatcher realized that there was not a single truck out in the over four hundred square miles of the greater San Jose area—everyone was at Dolly's.

Unlocking the door, he stood back as the large orange tabby erupted out of the cab, bouncing off the side fuel tank and into the grass. He waited for his partner, as he knew it would only be a minute or two at the most. He turned and saw the beat up one-eyed street tough cat starting to go into a crouch. Whether it was a mouse, bird, or a fight, Hooker didn't have time to indulge his cab mate.

"Come on, Box," he snapped his fingers. "Gotta go

get some jelly donuts for Manny."

At the sound of one of the few humans he could tolerate, the cat broke from the grass and shot over to the truck. Bouncing off the tank, off the door, slipping through Hooker's legs and past the front of his seat, he was in his box before Hooker even had the door closed or the truck fired up, purring the whole way.

Hooker just wagged his head as he turned the key and hit the start button on the side of the dashboard. The giant engine fired back to life and shook the cab. The radios all lit up and the eight-track came to life as Tennessee Ernie Ford moaned about a giant of a man buried in the bottom of a mine. It was almost enough to make Hooker purr. His right hand reached down and scratched the twenty plus pound ball of fur behind what was left of a scarred ear, "Maybe Manny will have something meaty for you this morning, eh, Box old buddy?"

His hand shoved the small shifter into the second range, and moved the large shifter into first, as he eased out the clutch on seventh gear. The large truck rolled forward into the last of the dark night.

Reaching up behind his head, he clicked the key on the microphone twice, as he shifted up to eighth, and the double clicks returned. The traffic light was still glowing cherry red as the big yellow truck slid through the intersection at fifteen over the speed limit, and as Hooker again shifted into the next higher gear, and swept the behemoth up the ramp and onto the 101 headed north toward the only donuts he would allow in his cab.

The night air would have been nice, but there was just a tinge of a morning fog that was putting a bite in the freeway wind, so his window was uncharacteristically rolled up. It was common enough for Hooker to show up at a wreck in the middle of a cold winter night eating an ice cream cone. The many times he had stood looking at bodies smeared through bad wrecks on Blood Alley could have garnered him a nick-name from the officers who work the night shifts, but his name was enough. Mostly, the officers were just glad to see him. Whether he got a tow or not, he was always the first to pop flares, direct traffic or break out his broom and trash can to help clean up the mess. Many times, it netted him tows that were not his, or at least a much-appreciated unopened box of CHP 30-minute flares left on the rear working deck of his truck.

The low rumbling hum of the engine combined with the muted whine of the tires were not enough to drown out the almost whisper of his least used radio—a small ham sideband walkie-talkie that he had reworked into a static radio. "Hooker, are you out there?"

Hooker flipped the switch over his head to engage the same microphone. Reaching back behind him, he grabbed the mic and squeezed the key. "Go ahead, Sweets."

The whisper persisted in an eerie surreal way. "Bad vibes, man, really bad vibes. All night I have been having bad feelings, man. All night I've been seeing things of you."

"I'm fine, Sweet. What did you see?"

"Can't talk about it on the waves, man. Come by the house for breakfast when I wake up. We'll talk then, man." The voice was as smooth on the radio's scratchy little speaker as it was on any stereo that listened to KLIV from midnight until the sun came up with Sweet Sam at the helm.

“Three pm it is, Sweets, three it will be. Get some sleep.” Hooker hung up the microphone and switched the toggle back to its regular setting connecting him directly to the radio on the credenza behind Dolly. That radio link had meant the difference between work and going broke many times. It was probably equal amounts of her having a soft spot for him and she knowing that he could be counted on to do some of the tougher jobs in towing. It also had a lot to do with the fact that on any given day, he spent twenty hours or more in the cab or within earshot of his radios… or told her where she could call him. Either way, she had a direct line to him that rivaled an umbilical cord.

He downshifted for the steep off-ramp turn that would dump him onto the parkway and four blocks from the Whole Donut, as he muttered to himself, “Sweet, sweet Sweets.” Shaking his head, he shifted again and hit the street still about twenty over the limit, but slowing as he bled off speed with the Jake brake, rattling windows in the business district.

Sweets and Hooker went back many years from when Hooker had first started towing with a bogus driver’s license at the age of fourteen. Hooker had rolled up on a jump-start in the early morning at the radio station. It was a 1959 Buick La Sabre with huge wings spreading out and away from a large rear deck. All Hooker could think about at the time was what a great car it would be to take to a drive-in theatre. The back seat was as big and roomy as a queen-sized bed.

The lanky black man had been standing there next to the driver’s side door, and as Hooker got out of the truck and walked over, Sweet had started slowly shaking his head and clicking his tongue. He was dressed in an all-white linen suit with a red tie as if he were going out clubbing up in the city on a Saturday night with a couple of fine ladies on his arms. His appearance was complete with a white linen fedora and dark glasses. As Hooker got closer, the slender black man started humming, "Humm uhn ahh, they do make them younger and younger every day."

Hooker ignored the *younger* remark and asked what the problem was and not really paying any attention to the white cane in the man's hand that was stretched along his body. At fourteen, and trying to appear twenty, who's tallying up the dark glasses and a white cane in the middle of the night and a car that won't start?

"I think it's a dead battery, man," the dapper dude said with his head rolled back almost like he was looking more at the tops of the trees than at Hooker.

Hooker just shrugged, and popped open the hood. With his flashlight, he looked over the battery and checked the connections. Wiggling the cable, he whipped out his small wrench and tightened the connection. "Go ahead," he called.

"Go where, man?"

"Try it."

"Try what?"

Hooker looked around the hood to see the man still standing where he had first met him. He hadn't moved a step. He wasn't even trying to open the door.

"Get in and try to start the car." Hooker explained shortly, if not a little testy.

"No can do, Roger Roo," the guy rhymed.

"Why not?" Hooker asked.

"Don't know how."

"Isn't this your car?" Hooker was now very confused, and was just starting to wonder about the dark glasses and the guy's behavior.

"Sure it is. Paid cash for it three years ago."

"Then why don't you start it?"

"I don't know how."

Just as Hooker was starting to figure he had been played for a sucker, another, much larger black guy came out of the building saying, "Oh great, you're here." Walking over and taking Sweets by the elbow, he started to guide him around the car to the passenger side. "Let me get Sweets in his seat, and we'll be set to start it."

Hooker was stunned and stood there saying nothing.

Sweets turned his head in Hooker's general location. "You didn't know I was blind, did you."

Hooker, now embarrassed, swallowed, "No, no I didn't."

"That's OK, daddy-oh. I didn't know you were white either," and smiled with the classic ten megawatt smile that was his hallmark. "But I did know you're not old enough to drive."

Danny, Sweet's brother, driver and caretaker, helped him in the door so he didn't hit his head or crunch his hat. Danny was the stereotypical linebacker turned bodyguard, with the nice suit pants and a leather jacket for a sport coat. The only difference with Danny was that he had never done anything except take care of his brother since Sweets was in high school when a welding tank in the metal shop had exploded and a large piece of steel had hit Sweets in the head, taking his eyesight, but leaving him with a couple of quirky gifts.

One was the ability to remember every song he had ever listened to—who the artist was, the recording company, how it had done on the charts, and any residual effects the song had on the artist or music in general. With that ability and a deep voice like honey in the summer sun, a very lucrative career in radio had supported him and his brother, along with their mother.

The other gift, if you could call it that, could cause sleepless nights and unidentified anxiety: a quirky gift of seeing things—not necessarily in the future, but just things. Sometimes he just let it go because it didn't mean anything to him, but sometimes he knew whom it was connected to, and that was when he called Hooker.

Sweets never told anybody Hooker's real age, but on his real twenty-first birthday, the three of them had a quiet dinner together to celebrate his majority.

Danny didn't say very much, but when he did, it was important. That night in the parking lot as Danny closed the door behind Sweets, he walked to the front of the Buick and gently lowered the hood until it quietly caught with a dull metallic click. Turning to Hooker, he shared the truth of the night. "My brother told me about you yesterday. There was nothing wrong with the car. We just needed to meet you." Handing him a simple white card with two phone numbers on it, he said, "The top number is the house, the bottom is here, both are unlisted. Don't lose the card."

Hooker nodded as Danny slipped a fifty-dollar bill

into his hand. “Don’t write this call up, you were never here. This call only went through Dolly at the Night Dispatch. If you ever have a problem, talk to Dolly. If you’re ever hungry, go see Dolly. If you need money, come see me.” He turned and walked to the open driver’s door. As he started to fold his towering mass through the doorframe, he paused, “What’s your name?”

“Hooker.”

“Fair enough, Hooker. We’ll be in touch.”

Hooker blew two sharp blasts on the air horn as he pulled in behind the Whole Donut. The rear parking lot was a field of concrete that had random parked tractor-trailers and cars. Out front, there was the obligatory early morning clot of San Jose PD squad cars.

The back screen door screeched as the human form of twisted wire stepped a foot out. “Hey, Hooker, how’s it hanging?”

“Choke and puke, with cream on the side, Ralph. Same as it always is, same as it always will be. How are you and the missus?”

“Fighting like cats and dogs as usual. She’s top dog, and I’m as pussy whipped as I wanna be.” He rubbed the last of his unfiltered Camel straight out between his fingers as he field stripped the butt, a habit left over from his three tours of duty in Vietnam where he had left half of his guts and was forced to come home, bringing home a just turned sixteen-year-old girl that he married on her eighteenth birthday. The two had less than nothing, but by leveraging some help with his Army buddies and the VA, he sunk their life into the Whole Donut, and the community never let them down.

"What can I get for you this morning?" Looking at his watch, he then added, "Oh, at this hour I'm guessing you're picking up a jumpstart for Manny?"

"Yeah, his wife is down south, so he needs his fix."

"Coming right out!" He shuffled back into the kitchen calling out the order to his wife in Vietnamese. The hum of the fans on the roof was a dull massage as the day prepared to wake up and take notice of the sun. The air over the south bay was taking on that special glow that the hanging thin fog would get about an hour or so before dawn.

Hooker's right hand dangled down between the seats and absently twiddled with the larger intact ear as Box's purr echoed the deep quiet rumble of the turning idle of the lopping engine. The eight-track clicked into the next round as the New Riders of the Purple Sage softly harmonized about tumbling tumbleweeds. Hooker let his eyes close and drifted across the desert, and the boys from another time crooned in a bygone way.

The screen door squealed and Mai Lin walked out wiping her left hand in her apron. The shy smile on her face could light up Spartan Stadium in Hooker's opinion. He opened the door and reached down with a five-dollar bill. Mai Lin handed him the box of donuts and pursed her lips with a "pfut" at the money. Smiling she instructed Hooker, "You give Mr. Manny a big hug for me. You tell him, he is no good to not come around here and see his goddaughter, Mai Lin."

"OK, Mai Lin, I'll tell him, but I will leave the hugging thing up to you." Closing the door, he watched her laughing and walking back to work where she would put in an eighteen-hour day and never complain. She was in a good home, with a good husband who worshipped the ground she walked upon—she would tell you she was blessed, and Hooker didn't doubt it, but he knew it was Ralph that was the one who was blessed.

Sticking the transmissions in seventh gear and shoving the box of donuts down deeper in the passenger seat, he let out the clutch and as much to Box as himself said, "Let's go see Manny, Box."

Two blocks over and he took a left that would lead to a right, and another left and would become Almaden Expressway, named after California's first commercial winery—or as the lower life would raise a glass to, the first winery to put out wine in a box.

Hooker chuckled at his old joke and looked down at his constant companion. "Should we get a little Box down in the Almaden Valley, Box?" Hooker was known for a few sips of a beer a couple of times a year, but because he always considered himself to be on duty, he never really drank, so the *Box* was in reference of where he had found his companion—half dead in a box behind the Almaden Winery. It was the only fight Hooker had known Box to lose. He had been one torn up kitty.

The street flowed out into the expressway, and Hooker wound the truck up into a higher gear. Glancing at his watch, he shifted again and laid the hammer down, as the white lines became just a little more solid looking as they blurred together. *Where does the time go these days, where does it go?* Arriving at five-fifteen at Manny's was important, and it was going to be close.

.

06

Just off the Almaden Expressway, deep in the Almaden Valley, the big yellow truck roared around the sweeping curve that led into what Hooker thought of as the *Hill of Stupid.* In homage to California's roots, the developer, or someone equally as stupid, had started naming series of streets 'Calle de' something, so giving directions to places like Manny's home for the last twenty years, which had been as simple as turn left on Sage Road, then left on Rim Drive, and go about a mile, look for the pinkish building on the left with the red tile roof, had turned into right on Calle de Dios, left on Calle de Verde, right on Calle de Verde Gras, right on Calle de Altos, left on Calle de Suenos, right on Calle de Alta Verde, left on Rim and look for the pinkish house that doesn't look like the rubber stamp houses.

Hooker couldn't help but hate the developers who had no idea what the names meant, and the people who bought the ticky-tacky claptrap soon-to-be shacks that encouraged the developers to cross the small valley and start crawling their way up the other side. Some days his favorite fantasy was a horrific wild fire that would scorch and cleanse the earth. But he knew there would be no stopping the rape of the valley. He was just thankful for the few orchards that still lined Blossom Hill Road, as well as the bean fields.

Turning up onto Rim Drive, he let the engine roar for the last quarter mile with the twin pipes rattling the windows of the overpriced wannabe fake Tudor manors, with the two and three car garages poking out like a dog's snout, and two cars parked in the driveways because you know the garage is stuffed full of crap.

The only hand built adobe plastered hacienda in the whole valley came into view. The wheelchair-bound figure waved as Hooker pulled up across the driveway that led down and around to the garage that was out of sight from the street. Only the giant gate in the front pierced the front wall that rose ten feet to the red clay hand and leg formed barrel tiles on the roof. A much younger and able-bodied Manny and his wife Estelle, had gathered the clay, mixed, and shaped the barrels to be dried in the hot summer sun, and then carefully stacked around a bonfire made of wood and coke. They set the fuel ablaze and fed it for ten hours, firing the clay tiles in the traditional way.

As Hooker slid down out of the cab, holding the box of jelly donuts, Box bounced down to the tank and shot out toward the small patch of grass beside the driveway. For not the first or hundredth time, Hooker admired the deep thick walls that he knew contained stacked bales of straw to create the two-foot mass. The concept of the super insulated walls was something that had come from the prairies of Nebraska. Manny had grown up first in a dug out hole in the ground, covered over with two feet of sod cut from the prairie floor, while his father and mother built a house out of straw bales and plaster. They had lived in it for the rest of the forty years of their lives.

"That Box does like my grass," Manny commented.

"Well, it beats pissing in his box in the truck, eh, Box?" Hooker chuckled as Box shook first one hind leg then the other in an attempt to shake off the dew from the taller grass he had just stepped on.

Passing Hooker a disgusted look for his insulting talk, he took two bouncing jumps then into the man's lap with a roaring purr. Settling into a fur ball facing forward, Box was ready to be carried into the house on four wheels instead of something as pedestrian as walking.

Bombastically, Manny rolled his eyes and lolled his head looking at Hooker. "Nah, he's not spoiled at all, is he?" They both chuckled at the running joke about the cat's habit for the last few years of hitching a free ride in the wheelchair, since a bullet in his spine had robbed Manny of his mobility.

As they moved through the thick medieval looking gate, hand-hewn from junipers found on the property twenty years before, their talk was relaxed and causal. The fountain in the center of the inner plaza tinkled with a lazy music that Hooker always found relaxing, but not enough to take up Stella on her offer for him to come live full-time in the north wing of the hacienda. Manny would even pay to have his small lawn turned to a concrete apron to park his truck on, but the thought of cruising up and down The Hill of Stupid, was just too much for Hooker to even contemplate, even as seductive as the offer was. He also knew that in his heart of hearts, he would end up weighing a hundred more pounds with Estelle's great cooking.

"So Stella trusted you and ran off."

"Trust schmust, hell, she just stocked plenty of insulin before she left." He grinned back at Hooker who was still holding the box of forbidden fruit. Well, fruit filling at least.

"That reminds me, your goddaughter gave me hell about you never coming to visit." Hooker pushed open the eight-foot matching doors to the front gate door, running his hand over the adze marks on the iron hard aged Black Walnut.

"Screw them, both of them," Manny said without conviction, as he rolled through the doors onto the honed slate entry floor. "Those two haven't stopped long enough these last three years to come up here for even a late night dinner." Hooker sensed an edge of truth, and even a certain underlying hurt and anger from the man who had sponsored not only Mai Lin's citizenship, but the founding of the Whole Donut. But he also understood the dangers of not taking some down time and being consumed by one's profession.

"Have they ever come up here since the shooting?" Hooker laid the box on the giant granite topped island and looked out the wall of windows over the sink and countertop that ran along the east-facing wall. The sun was just a half ball of fire with streaks of rays caused by the unseen bits of clouds.

"Screw it. I don't want to ruin a perfect morning. Grab the coffee pot, the mugs are out here." The older man grabbed the box of contraband and headed for the adjoining sunroom. Wheeling past Box, who was face down in a bowl of his favorite food, he reached over and scratched the cat's back and gently petted his hand into a cone that ran up with the thick meaty tail that ended shortly in a one-inch crook at the end. His ministrations were greeted with a deep appreciative rumble that sounded more like Hooker's truck than a cat's purring. Manny chuckled as he kept on rolling into his favorite room. The cat was very picky, but when it came to Manny, it was an on-again/off-again relationship that changed with the day.

Two hours later, the sun was well up, Box was snoring in a pool of sunshine on his pad made from old down pillows, and the two men sat lounging around the table with an empty box, and plates that had only tiny traces of omelets that Hooker had whipped up to help counter the sugar shock to the diabetic system. Manny's injection kit with the spent ampule lay on the table among the carnage.

"So you never saw anyone in the car?"

Hooker shook his head. "No, it was as if the shooter were invisible." He cocked his head thinking. "In fact, I don't even remember seeing a muzzle blast either."

"If it was a shotgun, and it was a full choke on a long barrel," Manny scratched his chin by rubbing it between his fingers and thumb. "or maybe it was just below the window or something so you couldn't see it." He looked up into the young man's eyes. "I don't know, but it's curious."

"Even if it were below the window, the muzzle blast would have lit up the interior like a bolt of lightning."

"True," the former police officer acknowledged.

"I know my truck isn't that quiet, but the window was

open, and I also didn't hear any gunshot either." He raised his mug and sipped the last of his coffee.

"Hmm," the mind of the older man churned as he looked out across the valley, and back on over thirty years working a beat solving crimes. It was there, he could feel it, and it frustrated him that he just couldn't see the answer—yet.

He looked over at the young driver, whose hand still held onto the handle of the mug on the table and was slumped just a little more as he had fallen asleep sitting up. Manny's heart ached, as he knew that the boy probably had been in the truck for at least the last twenty-four, if not forty-eight, hours without any real sleep, just a little shut eye here and some closed eyes there. He reached across the table and poked at Hookers hand. "Hey."

The head came up, but the eyes were only at half-mast. "Hmm?"

"Go climb into bed. I'll call Dolly's and let them know you're here." He waved the back of his hand at the young man. "Go on—and I mean get naked under the sheets sleeping. Enough of this fully dressed, just stretching out crap. Your eyes are bleeding out of your head, and you need to stop for some down time." He shooed him some more as Hooker slowly pulled himself up and lumbered off back down toward what was kindly known as 'his room'—a suite with its own living room, master bath and kitchenette.

"Come on, Box."

"No, leave him be. He's already smart enough to be asleep." The old man just shook his head at the closest thing to a son they had ever had. "I'll wake you if you get a call." As he thought to himself, *like hell I will, if it's before maybe dinnertime!*

Turning, he sipped on his coffee, watched Box's side slowly move up and down, and thought about a shotgun blast that had no sound or muzzle blast in the night. In his experience, it was impossible to silence a shotgun, and hiding the muzzle blast on a dark night would be almost impossible, too.

Softly, he muttered more to himself than the cat, "It just can't be done, Box, it just can't be done. But it was." His body was broken, but his mind was better than ever.

He reached down absently and grabbed his large wheels as he slowly moved towards the phone with the coffee mug jammed between his paralyzed legs. Time to make a couple of calls—calls he could never have made when he was an officer, to people who would never speak to a person in uniform. But first, he had to call Dolly. He glanced over his shoulder at the large schoolhouse clock that matched the one in her dispatch room. He pushed a little harder so he wouldn't miss his sister-in-law.

07

Hooker had sat bolt upright at the sound of the silent shotgun as he watched the officer lift off the ground and sit down in the road, slumped like a rag doll. The time telescoped as the body slowly rolled back spinelessly to lay crumpled on the asphalt as Hooker blinked a third time and washed his hands over his face, stretching his eyes out away from the vision that, no matter how much time would pass, would always remain that vivid.

The shadow cast by the fountain in the courtyard was on the wrong side of the patio. His mind tried to make sense of the meaning until it finally gelled that it was already afternoon. Then he remembered his lunch date at Sweets' house.

Throwing the covers to one side, he swung around and looked at the clock—two forty-three pm. He folded over and reached for his jeans, and caught a strong whiff of his body. Quickly he sat back up with his lip curled, thinking. The math came down to well over forty-eight hours since he had last danced in the water locker, and there was no way he would be allowed anywhere near

Sweets smelling like a herd of banded sheep in heat.

As he finally turned off the shower, he heard the distant phone ring. Intermittent with the rubbing of the plush terry towel bath sheet, he could hear Manny arguing with someone on the phone. The one thing you never wanted to do was argue with Manny, especially on the phone. Hooker chuckled as he remembered a time when he had witnessed Manny in the heat of his favorite battle—on the phone.

It had been about the easement that was going to run along the bottom of their property. The conditions of the easement would have prevented Manny from having a barn, or raising chickens or even a single horse. Now, Manny could care less about having livestock. Life in Nebraska in general, and one horrible memory in particular (having to go to school after plucking hundreds of frozen chickens that had died when the power failed the night before), had cured Manny for life about keeping any kind of livestock, even a family dog. Box was a very special case, and Box knew it.

Manny had been bounced from one functionary to the next higher, all not really understanding that Manny had worked longer for the city than they had worn long pants. Manny knew exactly *who* he needed to talk to and who had the authority to rescind the easement. He could have just called his office, and be done with it, but where would the fun be in that? So Manny, writing down every name and asking for exact spelling and job title along with their direct phone number, would once again go through his entire song and dance. The results were always the same—a transfer to someone with more authority.

With each new person, Manny would roll his head with a beaming toothy smile, and wink at Hooker who was relaxed in the warm afternoon sun of the sunroom. Manny was in heaven, his favorite room, his favorite cat sleeping and purring in his lap, and his favorite game of warfare.

Finally, the game came down to the final show down. The county commissioner who had been his former partner when they worked as beat cops. Each knew more about each other than their own wives ever would. They both knew where the bodies were buried, and they knew that the other knew it as well, because they had buried them together. When one had been reprimanded, the other was standing right there getting the same. When they were honored by the Mayor, and eventually the Governor, they were honored side by side. But only one had taken the bullet and that had given him the edge forever more.

As the commissioner had answered, Manny changed his tone. The nice guy was gone. The bad cop was out, and he was stomping through the unmarked graves, kicking the thin dirt covers off all the bones, and doing it in full sunshine. He rampaged for almost exactly five minutes with his partner unsuccessfully trying to wedge in a word. Finally, he stopped. In the middle of a sentence, he just stopped. Winking and smiling at Hooker, he held up his thumb, the one finger, then two, then a third and finally, the forth, and on the other end of the phone was the question.

"Are you done?"

Manny didn't say a word. The silence was deafening, and you knew that his former buddy could taste it along with the bile that was building up in the back of his throat.

Manny in his wheelchair with flaming wheels like the chariot of Apollo had come to call, and he wasn't happy—not one bit.

The commissioner had started the county line of song and dance, which Manny let run for almost thirty seconds before he started pounding the speaker part of the phone on a board he had brought in just for that purpose. Ten whacks, ten seconds, and then he counted to three and quietly said, "Paul, you haven't been listening."

Manny quietly read his list of notes, and the names, titles, phone numbers, and responses that he had been through that afternoon. At the end, he told the commissioner that he had missed his lunch (the remains littered the table between him and Hooker, which required another smile and wink), and that he, the commissioner, should check into this miscarriage of the taxpayers, and especially the staunchest of supporter's personal trust and get back to him in say, about an hour? Then without waiting for an answer, he had quietly hung up, while writing down the time.

The phone had rung about forty-two minutes later. There would be no easement. Manny was free of the county ever annoying him again. Manny's favorite phone sport was winning.

Shaking his head at the memory, Hooker shrugged his leather jacket over his shoulder, and checked the room to make sure there was no real evidence that he had been there, he turned and walked down the hall to the main living space. He was rounding the corner as Manny hung up the phone. Hooker walked over to his favorite chair, and lowered himself in slowly, as he studied Manny's concerned and concentrating face.

Finally, Manny focused on Hooker. “That was a buddy of mine, a weapons expert.” He looked out over the valley as he raised his glass of iced tea and took a slow long pull. Carefully putting the glass back down on the roughhewn table, he looked back at Hooker. “It seems that there is a way that you could shoot a shotgun at night, and hear nothing, as well as see no muzzle flash.”

Hooker’s eyebrows rose.

“It matches the strange things the coroner found in the wound, as well.”

“You spoke to the coroner?”

“We play poker every Wednesday night, and we’ve been masonic brothers for well over twenty-five years, why wouldn’t I talk to him?”

Hooker just shrugged and rolled his eyes wide to look at the floor and Box soaking up the sun. “So what did he find that was strange?”

Manny edged forward, knowing he never had to swear Hooker to confidentiality, because he was now in his element as a detective. “The wound had fibers of stainless steel, and there were fifteen dimes in the body cavity.”

Hooker frowned. The stack of dimes in a twelve-gauge shotgun was on old trick. The sawed-off pump in the cab of his truck was just such a case, but there is only room for fourteen dimes in a standard shell, unless you shaved the wadding the extra dime’s worth. But why? “Who would shave the wadding down, just to have an extra meat cutter?” Shrugging his hands in askance, “I mean, if the first buck forty didn’t get the job done, what’s a cup of coffee extra going to do?”

"Good question," the detective mused. "Good question. And it probably goes to motive," he concluded as he reached for his iced tea, with his mind's eye a hundred miles away.

The two sat thinking as Box rolled over for some more sun on his belly.

"Oh, Karen called. There are a couple of commercial tows waiting for you this afternoon, so when you're ready, give her a whistle."

Hooker smiled and nodded as he pushed himself erect. "Did she mention what or where?"

"She said they're for the Fly, and one was up in Contra at an impound yard, so you can go do that before or after the traffic clears. Maybe it's something for that dead time from seven to nine."

Hooker nodded. "I've got to go over to Sweets' for lunch. He was doing that freaky thing this morning and wants to talk..." he said as he pointed down to Box.

"Oh, sure, leave the mange bucket here. We'll throw together something for him to do." They both looked at the topic of conversation that was ignoring them. "But make sure you pick him up for the night shift, or he will be pissed all night long, and I'll have to get the short stick-end of it all."

"Deal," Hooker nodded as he strode toward the front door.

As if as an afterthought, Manny mentioned, "Oh, your ten-spot is there on the hall table."

Hooker glanced over and saw a wadded up bill with a ten showing just a little too obvious. He nonchalantly grabbed it and shoved it in his pocket feeling that it was more like a couple or three bills wadded together. "Thanks, Manny," and he was out the giant door.

As he walked around the fountain toward the front entry gate, he withdrew his hand from his pocket and peeked at the money. As he suspected, there were two bills wadded in the center, a C-note and a Grant. He shook his head, and looked back at the front door as he slipped out through the gate. *Typical Manny,* he thought, but he also knew that the twin saddle-tanks on the truck were getting low, and Hooker was a strictly cash for fuel kind of guy.

As he fired up the monster, his right hand reached down and back, finding the handle that fit only his hand, that was matched up to eight dollars and change in dimes, stacked in the sawed-off pistol-gripped Mossberg. His thumb rubbed the walnut grip as he thought about the fifteen dimes in the dead highway patrolman's body. *Why the extra dimes?*

The truck eased forward and headed back down The Hill of Stupid, but only going through the back way where there were no houses thus far, but just little orange ribbons tied to stakes that seemed to migrate a bit more with the passing of each Friday night.

Hooker reached behind his head and double keyed the microphone. A few seconds later, there was a return double click. Dolly was back at work, and Hooker would talk to Karen the day dispatcher later, but first fuel and lunch at Sweets or vice versa.

08

Driving through daytime traffic is in a completely different category than driving the empty streets in the middle of the night. Mr. Obvious would point to the hundreds of cars flowing around the big truck, but that's not it. It's the mix of cars, the light, and the many things that are vying for one's attention. The first couple of billboards ever put up got a person's attention, as did the first few neon signs, or red signs, or the kind that the lights jump around; but when you line a street with billboards every hundred feet that are filled with red neon lights that jumps around, then you just have a mass of oddly pulsing color and light. In that universe, the muted small sign that does nothing is the one that stands out glaringly, or is totally missed. Much is the same with the little old lady standing stoically on the side of a busy expressway with no car.

It didn't sink in to Hooker as his reflexes took over. The left ring finger flexed and triggered the right turn signals as Hooker checked his mirrors, clearing the lane change. He would miss the lady, but that meant he would just have to put the truck in reverse, and back-up on the shoulder for a few hundred feet, and as he changed lanes slid and got closer to the lady, his mind caught up to what his eyes were seeing.

About sixty feet off the side of the expressway, parked in the cull de sac of a side street, was a light colored Cadillac de Ville. The lady was wearing a hat with a lace veil, and matching white gloves that held a pump shotgun that was rising to take aim at Hooker. The long dress and flat chest weren't the giveaway, but the black *men's* shoes and the left hand jacking the pump on the shotgun. His mind may have even missed the first muzzle blast, and because Hooker was engaging all ten sets of brakes, the shooter had misjudged the lead, and the dollar and change of dimes had twirled away across the high hood of the truck. But at point blank range, the next shot would be different.

A normal person would probably try to swerve away from the pending danger, but Hooker was more a part of the mass he was herding like an elephant down the road, and swung even harder toward the shooter. The sudden change in the demeanor caught the shooter off guard and the flurry of dimes rattled noisily in and around the towing structure on the back bed as the figure in the dress still holding the shotgun became unbalanced and tumbled backwards down the small embankment. Hooker stomped harder on the gas pedal and roared away, as he grabbed at the second microphone that hung lower and unused under the dashboard — the microphone that he would never have touched under any other circumstances.

"All units in the area of Almaden Expressway and

Seneca Street, be on the lookout for a light colored late model Cadillac de Ville. Driver was last seen wearing a hat with white lace veil, long dark grayish granny print dress, white gloves, and men's black shoes. The shooter is also packing and using a pump shotgun. I repeat: the driver is armed with a twelve-gauge shotgun and is using it. Armed and very dangerous; approach with caution. And do NOT approach alone, get back-up." Hooker let go of the key on the microphone as he shifted into the next higher gear.

The radio squawked. "10-4 units Adam 12 and Bravo Zero-4 . . . Hey, who is this? Unit, identify yourself."

Hooker grimly slowly wagged his head and gave the illegal radio a cold stink-eye as he muttered to himself, "Not on your life, dude."

"Reporting unit, identify yourself." Hooker just kept driving.

As he pulled into the truck stop, he thought more about the coincidence of the shooter. Was he the target? If so, how had the shooter known to be there at that random time of day? Or was it just a cop they were looking for? Or just anybody that would pull over for an old lady on the side of the road, same as Hooker had? And, more importantly, was this the same six-bit killer from this morning, but five miles away from the original kill zone?

Hooker stuck nozzles into the two saddle tanks and climbed up onto the working deck of his truck. Slowly going over every inch of the lift rigging that had been exposed to the shotgun blast, Hooker checked for paint chips or dimes. There were a few old chips that he made note to do some touch-up paint on later, but no obvious new chips, but several white or silver marks where the soft silver dimes had rattled around among the uprights, boom and cables. Looking around, Hooker almost missed the tiny edge of the little silver disk peeking out from under the edge of a bolted flange.

Taking the point of his pocketknife, he teased the dime out into the open. The trademark icon of the burning torch stared back at him—a 1960 Mercury head dime.

"Hey, Hooker, your tanks are full."

Jerking erect, he looked at the attendant in the door of the control doghouse. "Hey, Billy, do you have an envelope or something like it that I can have?"

"How big do you need?" The lanky kid leaned against the door jam, with both hands jammed down in the pockets of his one-piece uniform with the cuffs rolled back almost to the elbows, his only allowable nod to looking cool and pumping gas at the pimple-riddled age of twenty.

Hooker, looking down at the evidence on the deck floor replied, "Big enough to hold a dime."

Smiling a little too big, the kid withdrew his right hand and held a tiny piece of paper folded into an envelope the size of a thumbprint. "I can finish this off and let you have the paper."

Hooker looked up and realized that what the kid was holding would also contain trace amounts of some kind of illegal drugs. "That's a perfect size man, but could you make me a fresh one?"

Ducking into the doghouse shed, the kid called back. "Sure. Just give me a minute."

True to his word, he walked out with a fresh yellow envelope made from a legal pad. "Your total comes to ninety-three dollars and sixty-four centavos senor. The envelope is on the house."

Hooker traded the Benjamin Manny had given him earlier for the envelope. Carefully unfolding the envelope, he reached down with his knife and tried to lift the dime, which he only just skated around the bed of the truck.

Seeing that he was having trouble, the kid reached out toward the dime. "Here, I'll get that for you Hooker."

"Stop! Don't touch that."

The kid froze.

"Thanks, Billy, but there might be some fingerprints on there that we need." The kid backed off. Finally getting the dime against a welded foot flange, Hooker got the blade and paper under the dime and refolded it back into the needed envelope.

Securing the knife blade and stowing the knife in his front pocket, Hooker pulled out his wallet that was chained to his belt. Opening the zipper pocket, he stuffed the bindle in and secured it all back into his rear pocket. Taking the receipt from Johnny's hand, he looked at the change, knowing that it would soon be a white powder in the kid's nose. Hooker ignored something that was not his business. "Keep the change, man. Today you earned it."

The kid was confused, but smiled and stashed the money in his overalls. "Thanks, Hooker, you're the best."

Hooker gave one last glance around the working deck, and then jumped down. Reaching into a welded cup of a recess, he withdrew the lead hammer he kept there. Bouncing the hammer on all ten tires, Hooker checked the air pressure. He made his way around his rig as he visually checked the condition of the tread, mentally making a note that if he were lucky, the expensive set of tires might make it to the end of summer.

Returning the tire hammer to its hole, he traced his way back to the nose of the truck. The hood was a split affair with a continuous hinge running the length. Unlatching the one side, Hooker raised the hood, which folded and lay back on the top of the other side. With a grease rag in his left hand, he withdrew the long spring steel rod that measured the life's blood of the beast, the oil. Wiping the oil off the rod, he reinserted then withdrew the rod and examined the level and color of the oil. Again wiping the oil from the rod, he restored it cleanly to its hole. With deft fingers, and an eye for the unique truck engine, Hooker went about his daily engine check.

"Billy," Hooker called to the kid now back to reading the paper in the doghouse, "put me down for two cases of oil for next week."

"You got it, big daddy," the kid called out. "Are you going to need some new filters this time?"

Hooker thought a moment. "Nah, I still have some of that last case left." Stepping over to the door, and looking in, Hooker saw the nudie magazine the kid was hiding in the newspaper. "You'll go blind reading those magazines," he said softly, startling the kid.

Snapping the paper shut around the magazine, with the horror of being caught, he jerked his head around and looked at Hooker with his mouth hanging open. Seeing Hooker with his silly sidelong smile, he knew his secret was safe, and Hooker was just funning with him.

"Can I just read them till I need glasses?" he asked goofily as he pushed the thick-glassed offenders back up his nose.

Hooker laughed. “Too late.” They both chuckled as the kid waved his fist in front of his crotch and made a squinty buck-toothed face.

Hooker turned to go with a roll of his eyes. “Put me down for a case of air filters, though. I’ve got an itchy feeling I may be doing more work down in Gilroy or somewhere as screwed up hot and dusty as Salinas this summer.” As he walked back around his truck, he thought about the summer heat in Salinas as he shuddered and stuck his tongue out with a *blaah*. Hooker hated the heat, and San Jose was bad enough, without the extra rotting vegetable smell that reeked in Salinas and Hollister through the planting and growing seasons.

Firing up the monster, he eased out of the truck stop, blipped his air horn, and was vapor in the wind as the kid returned his attention to the naked girls that he would only ever dream about.

09

For as dapper a dresser, and as nice a car as Sweets ran around in, the neighborhood he lived in confirmed his blindness. Modest mid-century homes, the hallmark tacky look of hasty post-World War II construction, lined the quiet streets of the Willow Glen neighborhood where mostly both parents had to work to make ends meet. Hooker pulled up in front of the primped and trimmed, model home of the neighborhood with an immaculate charcoal gray 1968 Lincoln Continental with suicide doors, parked in the curved driveway at the front door. The front door opened as Hooker walked up the drive, and the mass of Danny filled the doorway.

"You're late" he growled. "I was forced to eat your share so Sweets wouldn't know you never showed up."

"Yeah," Hooker teased back, "otherwise, you would have probably starved to death and looked like the poster child for Biafra." He cocked his head and made huge eyes as he then lolled his head around on his neck.

Danny laughed through his nose as he tried to maintain his stern body-guard/bouncer look, grabbing the much smaller man and enveloping him in an almost acceptable shoulder man hug. Squeezing him through the doorway, he groped the iron-hard six-pack body and chided Hooker about being underfed with his oversized clothes hanging off his coat hanger frame of a body, an accusation belied by Hooker's bulky muscles gained from pushing more than his weight around in the garage gym at Manny's. Neither man looked like he had missed a meal, and both had nothing to do with looking like a poster child for a starving country or a coat hanger.

There was a loud squeal from the kitchen and a pleasantly padded good-looking older black woman came rushing around the corner wiping her hands in her apron. A palm width shock of white hair waved through a still massive headdress of salt and pepper that was more like a lion's mane than the lioness. Her eyes were crinkled over a megawatt smile of large beautiful teeth. The spray of darker freckles folded into the warm reassuring laugh-lines pressed into her face from a lifetime of joyful celebration of life as the mother of two boys she was proud to call her own.

Her arms flew open as she reached to fold Hooker into her bosom. "Oh, my ghost child has finally returned." She giggled as Hooker nuzzled in her neck, as was his signature in making larger women giggle and squirm.

Deep in her neck he muttered for only her to hear, "You are keeping yourself pure for me, aren't you, Tilly?"

Giggling until she jiggled all over, she pushed him back and gently slapped his chest. "Why child, of course I am… But you can't keep me waiting too much longer." She pushed up on her mass of hair with the flat of her hand, and posed with her other hand on her out-thrust hip that was bouncing. "After all, a girl in her prime of life is a much sought after commodity."

Laughing and squealing she spun her arm into his and guided him into the large kitchen and family room combination. "Come on in, and let's get you fed before my other babies die of starvation."

Danny snorted softly through his nose and followed them deeper into the house.

Sweets lounged in his large chair near the sliding glass door, with his signature two-toned patent leather shoes crossed on the leather ottoman. On his head was a pair of professional grade headphones as he listened to something on the large reel-to-reel tape recorder. His face was slightly furrowed in concentration as he listened.

"Sweets!" Danny barked, then continuing the now running joke, "Hooker is finally here, the famine is over."

The slender hand with long musical fingers slowly reached over to the machine. The body flowed forward as the man sat up. Hovering over the buttons, there was a pause, and then a single finger made the choice and depressed the lever, stopping the tape from scrolling. The other hand reached up and whipped the headphones off his head as the feet popped off the ottoman and Sweets stood up. "Hooker," he started toward them as his right hand came up as if to shake. "How good to see you, my man," he gushed as he moved across the empty room.

Watching Sweets move about his familiar territory, one would not know he was blind, other than that, his eyes were perpetually closed, and he held his head as if he were always watching the ceiling above you or slightly behind you. Hooker detected the soft little ticking that Sweets made with his tongue, like a bat locating his surroundings. Discounted in America as nonsense, Sweets had taken the family to Switzerland for a year while he had learned the echolocation system. It wasn't infallible, but it was impressive to watch Sweets do it.

Looking back at Tilly working at the cooking island, Hooker smiled and played the theme song. "Sweets, good to see you man, and I'd love to talk to you, but I'm starved. Can we just eat first?"

A small bit of celery hit Hooker in the back of the head as Tilly softly laughed and reached over with the long French knife and poked Danny in the behind as he stood before the open door of the refrigerator, sneaking a drink of milk straight from the gallon jug. "Hey, mister," she cried, "what do you think I am, blind?"

Chagrined, Danny put the jug back and closed the door. Turning, he whined like a pre-teen caught with his hand in the cookie jar, "Mama, I was thirsty."

"Then get some class, and get a glass." She waved the knife in his face, and then lowered it to below his belt, "Or next time I may just do more than poke."

Turning on Hooker, she asked, "Are your hands clean, young man?" Pointing the knife at the sink, she sniffed the air and scowled as if offended. "You can wash that diesel I smell off them before you carry some of *my* dishes into the table." Ever the queen of the castle and the Sweets Empire, Tilly Sweets trucked no back talk or accepted any contradiction to her velvet covered iron fist.

An hour or so later, the shards of a traditional Tilly meal lay scattered about the table like bodies on a battlefield. Danny picked at the remains like a vulture. A peck here, a peck there, and after a while, clean bones and a happy grown boy named Danny. Sweets didn't have to see to know what his brother was doing, as he had been doing it all his life. Tilly sat quietly, but inwardly was in horror at what Hooker took so coolly as just part of his day, or so he seemed to project.

"I didn't see her or him in a dress, just all black except the throat." Sweets continued. "The throat was definitely white. Like it was missing on a photograph or something. It was also strange that I saw the rage of the gun, but not the fire." Sweets picked at his own plate with slender piano player's fingers that seemed to sense where the little bits of food were still hiding as they played around and across his place setting.

Putting his mug of coffee down, Hooker stared at the table as if the answers would be written in the grain of the wood. "Manny was confused about that too, but he has some theory about some kind of silencer over the end of the gun that would suppress the muzzle flash as well as the noise. But this afternoon, there was just a raw naked shotgun and it was barking just fine."

Even without sight, Sweets looked toward where he knew his brother to be.

The older brother simply said, "I'll check around."

Nodding acknowledgement, Sweets looked back toward Hooker, as he asked, "But the cars were either the same or similar?" He scratched his left palm in a nervous habit of thinking. "Sounds like the shooter is either stupid, or has a fixation on that car and color."

Hooker shrugged and leaned back in his chair, and with his one eyebrow arched, he fiddled with his empty coffee mug and stared. "Yeah, well, it is a very common color for that year or a couple years in the De Ville line."

As they all sat in a post lunch torpor thinking about the shooting, or not, the phone rang, and Tilly got up to answer it as Danny turned to Hooker and quietly asked, "Now what?"

"I don't know." Hooker shrugged as he still stared at the mug. "I'm just the tow driver." There was something there, and he just couldn't put his finger on it. "But I'm not going to go into hiding." Looking up at Danny, he then looked further up at Tilly, who stood there with her hand covering the phone.

"You just may want to do that." She held the phone out for Hooker as she finished with a concerned look on her face. "It's for you—and she is all kinds of pissed off."

Hooker's eyes went big as they rolled in to the look of shame. What now?

Taking the phone from Tilly's out stretched hand, he hesitated to answer. "This is…"

"Yes."

"Yes, ma'am."

"No, Dolly, I didn't mean to…"

"Yes, ma'am. Right this second, ma'am."

"Yes, ma'am?"

"Did they say how much?"

"Just a moment." He covered the mouthpiece and looked at Danny. *"$400?"*

The large guy just scoffed, snarling the one side of his lip that flared that nostril and nodded, as if to say that Hooker was talking about chump change.

"Yes, ma'am, I'll be in the truck in five minutes…"

"No, ma'am!" he snapped.

"Yes, ma'am, I've got my foot out the door as we speak."

As he hung up the phone, Danny had a wad out and was peeling off Benjamins. Tilly saw her chance and stuck her hand out, too. There was only one heartbeat of hesitation, and she was holding two more of the Bennies.

Hooker snatched his jacket with one hand and the bills in the other. "Tilly, hug Danny for me." And true to his word, he was out the door as he cleared his last command. "And Danny, give Tilly a kiss."

Tilly stared at the doorway, then out the window with wide eyes. Turning back and blinking at Danny, she asked in a stunned voice, "Did you know he could move that fast?"

Danny and Sweets both chuckled as Danny stood and started to clear the dishes as he had done since the job had fallen to him in high school, and after the great experiment of Sweets learning how to do so with the fine China they no longer had.

Tilly stopped the large man with a hand that was dwarfed on the giant chest. "Hey, mister, you heard the man." She turned her cheek and opened her arms wide.

"Ah, mama," the embarrassed little boy whined as Sweets just steepled his hands to cover his silent laugh at his brother's discomfort.

The sound of the monster truck vibrated into life and then faded off down the street, and the sounds of birds and afternoon lawnmowers returned to the quiet neighborhood.

10

Valley Medical Center, known locally as Valley Med, hulked in the waning afternoon sun, crouching like a vulture overlooking the freeway. Occasionally, the vulture's pickings were slim, but most days, when people forget how to drive, the freeway turned into a human smorgasbord. The 280 Freeway was the hallmark of insanity of state or county highway planners who lived elsewhere. Planners who didn't understand the impacted nature of the area were responsible for designing a lack of off-ramps with direct access to the Medical Center, the final destination of the many ex-drivers and walking brain donors who tended to park creatively on or around the network of the southern Bay area freeways. The nearest off-ramp to the Medical Center and emergency treatment was half a mile away from the door to the ER.

Parking his rig in the larger lot fenced off for county vehicle use only, Hooker locked the door, and took a deep breath as he hung from the key in the door, gaining inner strength. Resolved, he slowly pulled the key and turned to face the music.

A *normal* hospital's emergency room at its busiest is

quietly filled with those with broken arms or bodies that can't wait to see their family doctor in the morning. The patients sit in quiet stupors waiting for their names to be called as the system slowly makes its way through the caring of those in medical distress. Triage is performed on those who walked in from the bus stop, those who drove themselves, those who somebody drove, and those who were admitted directly through the large double doors by two uniformed medics who drove them there with a very loud obnoxious noise maker and pretty flashing lights on the front of a one-ton van with extra headroom; usually, these are not the brain and organ donors from the freeways—those go directly to Valley Med.

The ER at Valley Med, is on the other channel of the TV steeped in the reality shows of man's stupidity to himself, man's cruelty to others, and man's incestuous flirtation with his own mortality or those close enough to be infected with or by the same stupidity. If there were one summation of all the carnage and semi-breathing cordwood that was shoveled into the county emergency hopper, it would bear the honest title of operator error. Rare was the case of a non-provoked, or a non-self-inflicted wound in the county grinder.

The blonde, cute in a cowboy/horsy sort of way, with her ponytail down past her seat cushion, looked up and slumped back relaxed in her chair. "Well, if it isn't Hooker." She smiled a sarcastic yet friendly exhausted smile. "And look, he doesn't have something wrapped up in a greasy rag that needs stitches."

Hooker stood leaning against the intake secretaries' cubical wall, knowing that he would never be able to get past the friendly ration of crap that he so well deserved for the seeming nonstop summer of not-so-minor gashes and lacerations he had brought into the ER, not all on his own body. He also knew that 'Cynthia Eye Candy' was just getting warmed up, and she would never cut Hooker any slack for his onetime slip of his nickname for her to one of the EMTs.

"Connie, come look," she called her best friend and head nurse. "It's Hooker, and he doesn't have a box with ice and body parts in it." She cackled her throaty high smoker's laugh. "So, what can we do for you, slick?" She rolled forward toward her armament of an IBM Selectric II typewriter she could fire faster than Al Capone's Tommy gun could go through a barrel of bullets on a Valentine night. "And, no, I won't go out with you, so don't ask."

Hooker considered a few sarcastically funny responses, but none that would be appropriate or conducive to getting what he needed, so he just played it straight. "I understand you have a young kid named Johnny that came in last night with a fork in his hand, and you're holding him for ransom."

Hooker couldn't have gotten a more stunned wide-eyed response from the secretary if he had slapped her face. Slowly she rose with her mouth pursed in an open oval the size of a dime. Her blue eyes were like hot daggers as she examined his soul through his eyes and kicked it down the rotting stairs of purgatory. "You… you're the one who…" she drew the words out in a long breathy whisper. "You…" Her mouth snapped shut and she spun around. "Connie," she called into the nurse's office with her sarcasm freezing hot as dry ice, "the child stabber is here. And I'm taking my break." She stormed off, looking back twice, scandalized, with hot daggers for eyes, at Hooker.

The stocky older nurse stepped sternly out of the small office and surveyed first the retreating secretary and then Hooker. Her face was a motionless tableau of concrete, all mixed up, and set for life, making her unreadable to Hooker. Silently weighing the balance of the circumstance, she stepped over to the folders on the duty shelf. Pulling one, she glanced at it, and looked up at Hooker. "You are here to pay for this?"

Hooker looked down the hall where the secretary had gone, thinking, then returning the nurses gaze, "Yeah," he sighed. "I sure am." He reached deep in his jean's front pocket.

The nurse held up her hand in a sign of stop. "Oh no. I'll give you the bill, but you have to go pay up at accounting." She withdrew the triplicate form from the folder and gave it to Hooker. "I believe you know where it is?"

Hooker nodded. Looking back down the hall again, he knew he would be *paying for it* for a very long time to come.

"When they are finished with you, come on back here, because we aren't done with you yet."

Hooker looked at her stern face, weighing the intent, nodded, and turned toward the hall to the elevators. Silently, he thought to himself, *I'm sure you aren't... not by a long shot.*

As he stood waiting, a familiar dark specter, accompanied by an adjunct figure, wandered down the hall toward the elevators and Hooker. The standard uniform was a little rumpled as if it had been a long night or day spent sitting uncomfortably at the bedside of someone in need of a kind voice, a warm hand, and an attentive set of ears. As long as Hooker had been stopping by Valley Med, the man clad in black from shoes to neck was a familiar and warm sight, who had always been topped with a massive head of wavy, but now thinning, snow-white hair matching his huge pearly white smile. His green eyes were always sparkling.

"Father McBride," Hooker greeted him as he also nodded to the nun that walked with the older priest. "You look like you've had a long day already."

"I think, Hooker, at eighty-seven, I may be getting too old for this duty," the smile widened. "So, it's probably a good thing that I'm only eighty-five." Taking Hooker's extended hand and shaking it as vigorously as a scared young teen trying to impress his date's father.

"Well, Father," Hooker looked him up and down, "You don't look a day over eighty-three to me."

They both laughed as the elevator dinged and the doors opened to let a family out before they stepped in. The nun that had been with the priest touched him on the elbow with her hand that was bound excessively with a very long rosary. "Father, I'll meet you later to take you back to your parish in time for Vespers."

The priest jerked up his head and looked at her as if she had just appeared. "Oh… oh, yes. Thank you, sister," then he remembered social protocol and introduced the nun to Hooker. "Ah, sister, I'd like you to meet my good friend Hooker. Hooker, this is Sister Mary Michael Frances.

She's over at Holy Redeemer," turning for confirmation, "Am I right?"

The sister nodded but offered no hand. "Yes, I believe I have seen you before, but we weren't introduced." Nodding to the older priest, she confirmed his memory. "Yes, I've been in Sanctuary for the last two years now."

As she turned to go, she nodded again to Hooker as her hands wound even more vigorously about the binding rosary. "Nice meeting you, Hooker. I'm sure we will be seeing more of each other."

Something about the extra-long rosary was familiar, and it bothered him at the back of his memory as he watched her walk away. He marveled, not for the first time, how a nun was able to seemingly blend or disappear in a busy hallway, much like a chameleon on a branch.

Turning to poke at the numbers as they stepped into the open elevator, the priest grew sober, and with downcast eyes, shook his head. "You know, Hooker, it's a sad world this has become." He raised his eyes up to the ceiling and crossed himself slowly and dramatically, then looked back down as if studying the floor for answers. "I've just spent the better part of the night and morning with a poor young fellow that was brutally attacked over a single dollar bill."

Without thinking, Hooker commiserated, "Father, that's terrible."

The elder's right eye slide sideways and looked at Hooker through the shaggy bramble of his bushy eyebrows. "Aye, 'tis now and the saddest part is that if the young man had asked for the dollar, explaining his plight, the attacker would have probably given him that dollar and maybe even more." He shook his head again as he eyed the floor counter, blowing out his breath as the elevator came to stop at the third floor and the doors whooshed open.

As Hooker moved to the door to leave, the priest dropped the other shoe. “At least he wouldn’t have gotten the four tines of a fork through his left hand.”

Hooker froze, and slowly turned and looked at the priest whose lower lip was furled up against his upper lip and nose, with his left eyebrow arched high over the mischievously twinkling eyes. “It wasn’t the kindest of things to do, Hooker. Not kind at all.”

Hooker stepped his black engineer boot into the opening to stop the automatic door from closing. He thought a few seconds, and then asked, “Is there anyone left in this building that doesn’t know about what happened at Bob’s last night?” His shoulders sagging as the wind was rapidly leaving his sails. His head slowly cocked to one side.

The priest suddenly jerked and held up his index finger. “Oh, thank you, young Hooker, I nearly forgot,” as he reached out and pushed a low button on the panel, “Walt! Walt doesn’t know, but he will in a few minutes.”

“Walt? Walt the janitor in the basement?” Hooker was horrified as the doors slid shut on the priest’s enormous smile and a wave from the tip of his brow with his right hand.

The seconds ticked as Hooker stood looking at the stainless steel panels of the elevator doors. A blurry visage stared back. *What did I ever do to deserve this?* he thought, knowing that there were some events and actions that could never be recalled, no matter how much a person wished or wanted to recant or make new. Finally turning, he looked across the hall, directly into the billing and cashier department. There standing was not one, but five women behind the counter, glaring at him, trying oh, so hard not to laugh at the squirming familiar friend.

As he slowly staggered across the hall, as if to the gallows, he began to hear the low humming of a disapproving Claretta Nightingale Johnson. "Um mmm um um ummm," she mouthed as she wagged her large head and larger afro. This was a woman not to be trifled with, but to be reckoned with, especially now with the fierce back-up squad at her side.

"Mis-ter Hook-er," She stated, enunciating every syllable to its fullest.

"Yes, Miz Johnson?" Contrite, Hooker bowed his head.

"Don't be tryin' no sweet talk on me, young man. This one is going to cost you." Her puffy fists were buried in the bum-rolls of her hips.

Hooker thought a second. "French chocolate pie or Black Forest cake?"

She looked to her posse, and they nodded. They turned to face the young man and laid down the rules, "Both. One tomorrow, the other on Friday," she started. "Better make the cake on Friday, and it better be large, because we have a couple of birthdays this week."

"Yes, ma'am," Hooker saluted. "Cake on Friday, it is."

"And," she stuck her scolding single finger-facing palm out toward Hooker, "no nuzzling necks for a week."

Hooker collapsed for dramatic effect into the plastic chair and the posse all feigned horror at the tough sentence laid down by their leader. Reconsidering the harshness, and the joy it brought the entire five, "Well, maybe not until Friday with the cake."

Hooker and the posse wiped their brows, as the girls giggled and went back to their work answering the phones that had been buzzing the entire time.

As Claretta jockeyed her ample body into her business chair, she reached out and slammed her right hand down hard on Hooker's left hand on the low counter. Her eyes were all business and steel cased. Low and quiet, she clenched out her edict. "What you did was wrong. No matter what your gut was telling you that you were protecting, it was still wrong. That boy is scarred for life. You may as well have pulled that shotgun of yours and taken his life. It would have been more merciful. Now he has to live out his life with four little scars the size of his conscience, forever reminded of that night." She gently shook his hand. "And that, young man, is just wrong."

Hooker just sat looking into her eyes. She was not telling him anything new, or anything he did not know. It was just one of those bits of the universe giving you feedback that you really didn't want to hear. His nod would have been nothing more than a light breeze ruffling a few of his hairs, but she noticed, and the subject was now closed, almost.

Swiveling the chair in a high-pitched squeal that she did not seem to hear or just ignored, she deliberately walked her fingers over the hanging charts in the stack-rack in front of her. Each finger step was an excruciating eternity for Hooker. "Humph." The large black woman's face scrunched up in consternation and confusion. She glanced over at Hooker who was all but squirming at the delay. Looking at the side counter, she glanced back at Hooker and then picked up the manila folder as if to say, "Oh look what I found!" It couldn't have looked any more contrived.

Without even glancing in the folder, she pronounced his sentence. "You owe us $382.25. The extra $17.75 will go toward the uninsured children's fund." She reached out her left hand toward Hooker as he rose up on his left butt check and fished into his front pocket withdrawing the four Benjamins Danny had given him earlier. There was nothing Hooker could say or do; he had been neatly backed into his own corner.

Finally opening the folder, she withdrew the bill marked "PAID" and handed it to Hooker. "You go show that to Connie. And while you're at it, let her know you are bringing cake on Friday." The large dark brown eyes were orbs of steel—warm steel, but steel nonetheless.

"Yes, ma'am." Hooker rose to leave. "Thank you Miz Johnson. I'll see you tomorrow with that chocolate pie."

She waved her hand dismissively. "Oh, forget the pie!" Her hand turned into an index finger gun of vengeance. "But you best not forget those *two* cakes on Friday."

"Yes, ma'am. I will order them today, and have them hand delivered or bring them myself on Friday." He saluted as the elevator door opened, and he made his escape. Thinking about the current tone of the medical staff, he knew he would have those cakes delivered. It was just safer that way.

11

The Emergency Room had gotten much busier with the end of the school day and other injuries. The bedlam was palpable as Hooker swung out of the elevator and headed toward the intake area. The blonde's anger was still smoldering as she looked past the old man with the bloody towel held to his forehead. Hooker knew that it would take weeks or months to mend the woman's attitude.

Connie stepped out of her glassed-in office, pointing to a phone on the counter. "Line five."

Hooker frowned in confusion, picked up the phone, and poked at the blinking button of line five as directed. "This is Hooker."

"Don't say a word." Dolly's voice had an edge that Hooker rarely heard. "You know you screwed up, and I don't even want to talk with you right now, but I have to. So shut up and listen. The boy—what's his name?"

"Johnny?"

"Johnny. And I said shut up, and I meant it. The boy, Johnny, is there at the ER. and Connie will show you. You take him with you, and you watch out for him. If you get the chance, you can go drop him off with Manny, but if it's getting close to seven before you can drop him off, you better feed him. And I don't mean some kind of shit burger on State Street. You go get him something that is good for him." Stopping to think, she continued. "In fact, just swing by Togo's now, get some dinner, and then call Dina. She's holding a call for you and it's already five away." The five she was referring to was that the call was already five out of the twenty minutes allowed for a driver to respond to an auto club call for roadside assistance. "So get moving, mister!"

Hooker hung up the phone as he looked to Connie for directions. She was pointing behind him, and the young boy was rising as Hooker turned. The entire left hand was wrapped in gauze, and it looked more like the hand of a snowman. He kid was obviously gun-shy with Hooker, and Hooker gave him some distance. He waved for the kid to follow. "Come on, let's get you fed," as he turned to Connie waving and mouthing a "Thank you", as he knew she had gone a lot easier on him then he deserved. The blonde followed him with an icy glare that sent shivers down his spine as the men left. *A very long time,* Hooker thought.

Arriving at the truck, Hooker unlocked the passenger door and watched protectively as the boy climbed up clumsily into the high cab. Hooker had seen older women in high heels and tight skirts make the entry with more grace. He shook his head as the side of his mouth pulled back in wonderment and amazement mixed with disgust. Gently closing the door, he walked completely around the truck with the bang hammer checking his tires. Even with the time ticking, there were habits that could save your life that you never shorted. He was aware of the set of eyes watching in the mirror as he performed the curious ritual.

Finally climbing into the cab, Hooker fired up the giant engine and waited out the radio tubes to warm up as he fiddled in the box without Box, touch-stoned the shotgun and reached behind his head, keying the mic twice. He didn't expect the two return clicks, but reassuringly they were there. Some rituals transcend even a pissed-off woman.

Jamming the gears into first over second, he eased out the clutch, checking the mirrors all around as he oozed the yellow monster truck out of the lot and onto the side street. Reaching for the radio with the yellow microphone, he pulled the mic, shifted up twice and keying the mic calling the regular auto club daytime dispatcher. "1-4-1, show me 10-8 at Valley Med."

"10-4, 1-4-1, be advised I have a T-3 'can't start' on a 1968 blue Chevy Nova, on Eighth Street. Member is in front of the Togo's sub-shop. Call is now fourteen minutes old." The crisp tenor voice of Randy had just the hint of being in on the 'Let's mess with bad-boy Hooker day' joke.

Hooker smiled at being toyed with. "Ten-four, 1-4-1 out." Turning to the young kid he asked, "You up for a foot of a Togo's sandwich and some chocolate milk?" Re-keying the mic, Hooker ordered meals for the two of them. "Dispatch, could you double my usual on eighth?" The yellow radio just stutter-sparked with the answer. The auto club favored shorthand acknowledgement was just a swift-key double tap.

The kid just blinked, as Hooker shoved the gears up, and around into the higher transfer case and back to the bottom of the main transmission. The old system of a four-gear transmission, backed with a four-speed transfer box gave a truck a lot of pull at different speeds and conditions with the result of sixteen gears. But not being satisfied with just pulling power, Hooker and his uncle had found a rare 6-speed transmission that worked with the engine and the transfer case. This resulted in a set of gears left over at the top for speeds that could take the enormous former Marmon logging truck turned tow-truck roaring down the night black-top faster than most standard police cars. Hooker frequently arrived at crash sites even before the fire or medical first responders.

This resulted in Hooker being given tows that weren't supposed to be his, but were issued for expedience sake to clear a street, road, or freeway. This also caused much consternation among the ranks of his slower competition. They coupled his moniker to that of a prostitute and hung the term *Southside Hooker* on him as a name of shame—until he had the Fly and his paint shop letter both sides of the truck with the signature name. Additionally, the lettering ran up the large giant booms of the largest Holmes towing rig you could have installed on a truck of any size. The subtext was Hooker's proudest addition: *When you need a quickie.*

Turning right down Eighth Street, Hooker started looking for the blue Nova that needed the jump-start. Looking for the darker B5 blue, he almost passed the custom powder blue car with the jacked up rear-end, large meat tires, and tiny kiddy wheels in the front. Hooker looked for a zit faced know-nothing rich kid of an owner, and was surprised as a greying husky bearded guy in a Grateful Dead t-shirt waved from the porch of the Togo's among the co-eds standing in line.

Hooker fished a ten-dollar bill out of his pocket and handed it to Johnny. "They probably already have our sandwiches and cows ready." As they opened the two doors, sliding out, Hooker flicked on the unneeded but required strobes and flashing lights.

As he came around the rumbling nose of his rig and approached the auto club member, he couldn't help but notice the stacked six-pack of carburetors poking through the hood and topped with a mechanical blower ram scoop. The hood was up, which had camouflaged the large mill and true hot-rod stack on the labor-intensive engine of a true muscle car.

As the member stepped off the curb and joined Hooker, he held out his card, which Hooker absently took as he examined every inch of the spectacular engine. "You put in a lot of late nights under this hood." Turning to the guy, who now was smiling at the well-deserved knowledgeable compliment he took in the unassuming nature.

"It sounds like you have a few of those nights under the hood of your truck, as well." The man leaned back to look around Hooker who was leaning in to look closer at the header system. "What is that, about a 1956 Diamond Reo cab?"

Hooker looked up and smirked in camaraderie, "Close, but no cigar. It started life as a 1959 Marmon hauling logs in Oregon, but we shortened the nose about four inches to bring the dual radiator closer to the fan."

"That isn't a stock Detroit in there, either."

With the pissing on the backside of the barn and measuring of manly parts, Hooker continued. "The mill was a wild-cat Marmon engine used as a logging pony on a high wire show in Oregon, but we pumped about 300 more ponies in her when we went through it and worked her over for power and speed." Hooker was having fun talking in the shorthand of gear heads but forgetting that not all gearheads also knew the shorthand of the loggers in Oregon, but the guy got the gist and nodded.

"So," Hooker got back to business, handing back the member's card, with the name Roth not lost on Hooker, pointing to the line on the form for him to sign, "…what could ever go wrong under your hood, that you would need a jump start?"

Signing and handing back the clipboard and form, he said, "Nothing, and you were never here." The man laughed. "So I will never have to admit I stuck an underweight battery in her." He smiled conspiratorially at Hooker, who noticed the folded bill peeking out from under the form on the clipboard.

Tearing off the receipt part and handing it to the now fully recognized man, Hooker turned to the jumper cables wound above the large push bumper. "Works for me… Mr. Smith." Hooker smiled and clipped the cables to the battery as he also held the cables off the custom paint job. He admired the probably several pounds of mother of pearl that was a dying talent to paint just right. The *rat* engine rumbled to life. Standing and admiring the engine and hard work, Hooker waited a few minutes before unclipping the cables, knowing his rig would do more toward recharging the small battery than the guy's car would do with an hour of driving.

Winding the cables back up, Hooker noticed the kid climbing back into the cab as the man gently lowered and then pressed his hood closed with an unheard click. "You probably want to either charge that battery, or just get a properly sized one or two installed."

Slipping Hooker another tip, "I hadn't thought of using a dual battery, but I guess it would make a lot of sense. I think I'll look into it. Thanks for the jump."

"No problem." Hooker pocketed the extra tip. "If you want the dual, you might stop by and see the Fly on San Jose Avenue. He puts them in the highway pursuit cars all the time. Those beefed up Magnum four-forty engines matched up to the Torque Flight and three-ninety-one limited-slip Posy rear-end just chew up batteries as well as tires."

"Thanks for the tip," the man waved and smiled as he eased himself back into the hot rod. Revving it a couple of times, then pulling out and rumbling down Eighth Street, Hooker followed the sound and sight as he felt sorry that his uncle hadn't seen the engine or the *man.* He would have really enjoyed talking steel and iron for hours.

Shaking his head, Hooker turned and walked around the truck and climbed into the cab to find Johnny halfway through a sandwich and one dead brown cow lying in his lap. Hooker snorted and looked for his sack as he reached for the yellow microphone.

"1-4-1, show me 10-98 at Togo's."

"10-4, Hooker, call your base."

"10-4, 1-4-1." Hooker switched to his commercial radio and checked in. "Base, 1-4-1."

There was a few moments hesitation, as Hooker knew that this time of day was a busy time for police, plumbers, and other tow companies. "10-4, 1-4-1, stand-by." The gentle static of a half keyed mic, or one that was shared, softly filled the cab as Hooker turned right and settled down alongside a naked shady stretch of curb. Opening his sack and withdrawing one of the twin six-inch torpedo sandwiches, he unpeeled the paper and took a large bite into the beef, turkey, and Provolone cheese with salad and balsamic vinegar, and a dusting of raisins. Opening the small shaken carton of chocolate milk, Hooker took a pull on the brown cow as the radio squawked back to life.

"Thanks for holding, 1-4-1. We have a multi-car pile-up, Southbound 101 at Coozer Road, CHP standing by. Fire and ambulance are on their way. You are requested to see the CHP officer, Larson, for your tow. I'm showing you 10-8 at 17:27."

"10-4, 101 and Coozer Road, 1-4-1 out."

The sandwich hit the sack, as the last half of the brown cow hit the back of his throat, and the carton landed in the same sack. Jamming the truck into gear, Hooker cleared his left mirror and left about twenty feet of black rubber at the curb as he headed for the on-ramp eight blocks away.

Flipping on all of his rotating lights, he glanced at the kid who had gone somewhat white and had stopped eating. "Put your seat belt on." Hooker didn't even want to watch as the kid fumbled even that procedure, as the truck ground its way through the city street traffic and finally roared up the on-ramp onto the 280 headed for the commute jammed 101. Hooker swore his usual silent tirade about those few hours he worked during the daylight hours where it was traffic, not the work that tried his soul.

True to form, the 101 was at a standstill, probably because of the accident nine miles away.

Reaching under the dashboard, he flipped a hidden switch, and a multiple bank of red and blue strobe lights flashed from inside the grill at the right height to be seen in rear-view mirrors.

If he thought he could get away with a siren, Hooker would have installed that too, but the lights would just have to do for now. Hooker maneuvered onto the shoulder. The combination of flashing lights and the monster truck's scary front bumper with its grill looking like the mouth of a chromed shark did the trick. He inched past the nine-mile clot of cars along the south county's only artery. On any given day, a quarter million cars and trucks passed over any mile of this freeway.

As the giant yellow truck glided past the same spot where Hooker had witnessed the Highway Patrol officer being killed, his mouth froze with the last bit of sandwich stuffed halfway in. The vivid image replayed in a snapshot of time that sent a chill down Hooker's spine and caused him to twitch enough to shake the wheel.

Johnny looked over, "Are you all right?"

"Yeah." Hooker passed it off as he checked his side mirrors. He also scanned the field beside the road. Shoving the last wad of sandwich in his mouth, "Just something that happened last night," glancing over at the kid's hand, "after I was finished with you."

The kid raised his left hand and large mitten of white gauze. Looking at it, he slowly turned it examining the wrapping. Softly, he commented, as much to himself as to Hooker, "Yeah, that was a bit scary there."

Hooker felt like the ass that he wasn't going to admit to. Again clearing his mirrors to see an ambulance about a mile back slowly making the same slow trek, he glanced over at the kid with the still unkempt hair. He thought about not saying anything, but as it was his nature, he prodded anyway. "Well, I hope you learned your lesson of asking if you need something, instead of just stealing it." The kid nodded slightly and looked out the window as Hooker continued. "I bet you caught hell from stealing stuff out of your mother's purse as a kid, too."

The young man, turning an even more childlike face to Hooker, admitted quietly, "I never really knew my mother. She left us when I was three." He blinked back the sting in his eyes as he kicked the dam of his life open a little more. "Our dad couldn't take it and left on a ship two years later. Candy and I have been on our own since she was fifteen." Staring blankly out of the front windshield, the kid blinked back tears and wiped them with the large bandaged mitt. "I try to help," he sighed. "But I just don't know how to do anything, so nobody will hire me."

Hooker shifted into the higher gears as the shoulder widened and flattened out where the valley spread into more traditional farmland. Hooker knew that very soon the smell of freshly harvested garlic and onions would fill the valley air and push its way as far north as Fremont and Menlo Park. It was Hooker's favorite time of year, but it wasn't starting out well.

"Holy crap!" the kid exclaimed as they crested over the last low rise. They could see the mass of fire engines, ambulances, and police vehicles that had already arrived on the scene from San Martine and Gilroy from the south.

Hooker quickly surveyed the scene from his professional perspective. Pointing with his right hand and finger, "You see that larger fire truck near the right side? Not the farthest, but like the third over from the right—the one with the door open?"

The kid nodded. "The one with the guy just getting in?"

"That's it," Hooker continued. "I'm going to park right behind him. In the very back of the truck is a ten-gallon tin pail, a broom, and a shovel. I want you to get them and meet me at the front of our truck, got that?"

"In the back of the fire truck?"

Hooker shot the kid a frown.

"The pail and shovel—they're in the back of the fire truck?"

Hooker was stunned at the lack of understanding in the kid. "No—*my* truck." Slowing and working into the mass of the disjointed parking lot of emergency vehicles, Hooker continued. "You'll have to keep up, but I just need you to follow me as I sweep the glass, plastic, and guts."

The kid was horror struck.

Hooker didn't have to look over, because he could sense it. "If you have to throw up… you run for the grass. Don't you dare throw up on any of the fire trucks, cop cars, or most of all, this truck, and just in case it's a crime scene, not on the highway. You got that?" Hooker pulled to a stop and looked at the now blanched face of the kid.

The kid only nodded with big eyes, afraid to trust his stomach by opening his mouth.

"It's not so bad, kid, you'll get used to it." Opening the door, "Now come on, time is ticking. Get the pail, broom, and shovel, and meet me right over there." He pointed.

The kid fumbled with the door, and getting out, he found the pail, broom, and shovel, arriving at the back of the fire truck only seconds after Hooker showed up with his two brooms from his side panel that contained everything else he might need.

The CHP officer turned as Hooker and the kid walked up. Jerking his chin at the kid, he asked, "Hey, Hooker. Is he with you?"

"Yeah, for this accident at least. His name is Johnny, but you can call him Squirt." They both eyed the large white billboard of the wrapped hand. Hooker blushed slightly. "He stuck it where it wasn't supposed to be, but he won't bleed on your scene."

The officer thought about it, but thought better about a snide remark. Glancing one more time at the hand and kid, he turned to Hooker and pointed out the scope of the accident. "The car is still pinned in the side of the jack-knifed truck, but fire is getting the driver out, and then they will see if the passenger is even alive." He pointed along the innermost lane. "We want to clear number one as soon as you can jerk the truck back off the side, but we have to wait out the fire guys. So, the sooner you and the Squirt can start scraping the crap up, the sooner we can clear this mess."

A fire crew in turnouts came over on his way to the

truck. "We're about five away from getting the passenger, and then we'll know about the other."

"Ok, we'll have Hooker pull the rig when you guys give the OK." The officer turned to confirm with Hooker, but only addressed empty air as the fireman jerked his thumb back over his shoulder toward the two moving out into the fast lane. The fireman just chuckled as the officer muttered, "Damn, he's fast."

"OK. I'm going to sweep the crap into small piles with the push broom," as Hooker started. "All you have to do is shovel it into the bucket. Use the whiskbroom to get the last pieces. It has to be entirely clean, or they will never let you work another accident. Got me?"

The kid nodded as Hooker shoved the handle of the whiskbroom into the kid's back pocket. "Keep up."

The two swept and shoveled like the devil was behind them. There was not a lot of accident detritus on the highway, but combined with the usual small stones, washers, a nut or bolt here or there it all added up. Soon the pail wasn't the light tin pail anymore, but a weight that tipped the scrawny kid as he moved it from rapidly appearing pile to two more, as Hooker wielded the broom across and around the contaminated area.

A sharp whistle split the air from the direction of the pinned car under the truck's trailer. Hooker's head popped up to see one of the firemen circling his finger in the air. Hooker waved, and turned on the kid. "Squirt! Leave it, get to the truck now." Seeing him struggle with the can, Hooker stepped over, handed the broom to the kid, and grabbed the now heavy can as they ran to the truck. Stowing the can and throwing the brooms on to the back of the truck, Hooker pointed to a fence post. "I want you to go stand there, and don't move until I call for you."

Hooker's left foot hit the step on the large 100-gallon saddle fuel tank as he rocketed into the cab. Hitting the large red three-inch button that released the air brakes, he jammed the truck into gear as he closed his door. As he slowly wound his way along the scene, he eyed the trailer and tractor to see how he wanted to position his rig to pull them out of the hot lane and over to where he could hook up and then tow them. But first, he would have to turn the tractor back over onto its tires.

Leaning out of the cab window, he called to one of the firemen standing by. "Do you know if the trailer is loaded?"

The fireman nodded, and held up four fingers meaning it was a full load or four quarters. Hooker groaned and wheeled the giant truck for a straight shot from the back end at the tractor.

Setting his brakes, he jumped down and headed for the rear towing deck. Dropping one of the many doors on the side, he reached into the now exposed controls. As he flicked at the main switch, he could hear the truck's engine increase by the needed hundred RPM's he would need to drive all of the hydraulic pumps on his towing deck.

Pulling out one of the levers, he actuated his outrigger legs as they slowly slid out from just in front of the rear sets of tires. Pushing down, the legs extended and planted on the asphalt, pushing the rear end of the truck off the ground. The truck now couldn't roll, and would be a dead 22,000-pound anchor for his winches.

Setting another lever to neutral, Hooker watched as

the thirty-pound hook slowly dropped from its own weight. Grabbing the hook, he fed the line into a pulley assembly called a 'snatch block', which he attached to an iron ring on the back of the deck. Walking over to the wrecked truck tractor, he carried the hook as he spooled out the five-eighths inch winch cable of stranded steel rope.

The frame of the wrecked truck was twisted, but Hooker knew from experience that the twist could be taken out and the rig salvaged, but the kink where the left front end had folded during the process of jack-knifing, was another story. Hooker knew he didn't have to be careful with this rig; it was now just scrap iron. But he still had to get it out from under the trailer in such a way as the trailer could be also towed.

He kneeled down and looked at what was left of the fifth-wheel connection on the bottom of the trailer. There was a gaping hole where a round tongue should be sticking down. The trailer was, essentially, un-towable. It would have to be loaded onto a flatbed trailer. Not his problem. Hooker didn't do flatbed work.

Standing, he spotted the CHP officer in charge. "Hey, Mike," he called.

The officer turned. "Yeah, Hooker. What have we got?"

"Dead trailer and it's full." Hooker dragged his index finger across his throat. "You can put that call into the Brothers. It's going to need their flatbed and a crane, but I'll jerk the tractor. It's toast, but the Fly can strip it for the insurance."

Nodding, the officer started to turn, and then looked back. "By the way, just so you know, there is something wrong with your front grill that the watch commander coming up from Gilroy wouldn't like."

Hooker thought a moment then grimaced as he headed back to the cab to turn off the emergency lights that were completely illegal.

Letting down the landing gear of the trailer would help stabilize the trailer once Hooker jerked the tractor out from under the leading end. It couldn't be towed by the gear, but it would stand on the gear statically until Hooker could get his sling under the nose to coax it to the side of the highway where it would have to be unloaded into another trailer, then pulled up onto a flatbed lowboy trailer, and hauled away.

Hooker looked south down the highway as the flashing yellow lights on two approaching trucks caught his eye over the mass of the first five cars that had started the entire mess. Hooker's mouth pulled back to one side in a sardonic grin of self-satisfaction knowing it was never unnoticed when he was first on an accident by many minutes. In this case, almost a half hour had passed.

Turning back to the tow buckles that were common in rigging sea-going barges to each other, but only Hooker used in towing and recovering wrecks, he worked the clasping buckle to the lower frame as the cable passed up and over the higher frame. In the initial pulling of the cable, the entire tractor would be pulled out from under the trailer, but once free, the buckle would create leverage, and flip the tractor back up-right. In theory, that is.

Hooker waved to the other tow truck drivers as they began the ugly and low-paying task of sorting out the cars that were mangled. Hooker could tell, that unless the lower ends of the two cars were put on dollies, (a small low-laying on-site constructed rig with four wheels that made the wreck roll straight), the towed cars would be wobbling down the highway side-ways; expedient, but not a professional sight to display in front of officers who may just choose someone else the next time, with or without a rotational system in place.

Hooker, watching how the other driver worked, cranked down the landing gear on the trailer. Slowly, it lifted the weight somewhat off the tires of the tractor. Returning to the controls on his truck, Hooker began to take up the slack on the cable, then watching the flipped rig as he increased the tension, he increased the load until he saw the truck begin to slide. After about a foot, he stopped and walked over to check the trailer. Satisfied that the truck would slide out smoothly from under the trailer, he continued pulling the tractor out. As the hind end of the tractor cleared, the trailer clunked down the last few inches and rocked back and forth, but sat solidly on the tires and metal landing gear.

Stopping the pull, Hooker ran another cable out and buckled it to the truck's front bumper, which was trying to swing away from the pull. This stabilized the front, and he went over to the rear set of tires lying on the asphalt and kicked what looked like an over-sized doorstop called a chock between the lower tire and the highway to stop the back end from swinging. Returning to the controls, he slowly took up the tension one last time and was rewarded with the truck slowly flipping back into an upright position with a sick squishy crash with chunks of the fiberglass fenders and front hood shattering into shards and crumbling down onto the engine and highway.

A couple of the firemen standing around watching clapped in an unsolicited show of appreciation for the performance. Hooker smiled shyly and gave a mock bow. Assured that the trailer and tractor were now safe, he turned and whistled, waving the kid over. “Grab the broom and shovel, don’t worry about the can,” he directed. “Sweep it as best you can with that gimp burger of yours into a pile near the front end of the trailer.

Turning back to the controls, he started dragging the rear end of the tractor around as he reached over and whipped the stay cable out of the way. Running the stay cable back into its small hidden spool under the bed, he let the main winch gradually drag the tractor back toward the tow truck, and out of the way.

One of the Garcia brothers walked over from his truck. “Hey, Hooker, where you at?” he greeted. Hooker never understood the question of *where he was at*, but understood it meant the same as *how are you?* or *What’s going on?*, but it didn’t stop him from verbally kicking the older Garcia brother in the mental shin.

“I’m right here in front of you, Joe.” He smiled stupidly as the man became a little flustered for probably a fifth dozen time. They just never learn.

“No, I mean… oh, never mind.” The tow driver caught himself and half-heartedly mock swung his big meaty fist at Hooker’s shoulder. “Hey,” as if he just thought of it, “if I sling a dolly and lift balloon under that trailer, do you think you could pull it out of the fast lane at least?”

Hooker looked at him with the still goofy face. “Sure.

Let me hook them both up, and I'll even haul 'em all the way to Gilroy for you." Sarcasm was the trade money between the two drivers, but Hooker knew that it was only logical that as he was already in position to pull the trailer and clear the lane, and it would also build cache with the highway patrol.

Joe shot him a snap double-take look, and then started off toward his two trucks. "Thanks, Hooker, we'll get it set up."

Hooker dug in a little more. "Just hurry it up. I have a date tonight, you know."

The giant of a man just waved with all five fingers, which hinted at becoming less. "I know, I know—with my skank sister," the man called over his shoulder. The non-existent sister was an old joke that went back to the older Garcia's high school days, long before Hooker had ever heard the joke and started in on the now ineffective teasing. It was just now a running joke among most of the drivers who towed the south end of the Santa Clara valley.

Thirty minutes later, with a 'case of toast' hanging off the back end of Hooker's truck, he turned right onto the narrow rural highway that would lead the back way to the lower Almaden Valley. The kid was kind of quiet as Hooker sat chewing on the last of the second half of his sandwich.

Shoving the wad of sandwich to one cheek, he looked over at the kid. "What's wrong Squirt?"

The kid gave him a hard look, and finally replied, "That."

"That? That what?" Hooker went back to chewing and driving.

"Squirt." The kid sighed. "Where the heck did you get that for a nickname?"

Hooker thought about it as he chewed. He swallowed and downshifted for a sweeping curve then upshifted as the road straightened back up. "I don't know, but I bet I was just being preemptive."

"What's that?"

"What?"

"That pre-whatever it was."

"Preemptive? It just means I did it before someone else does." He took another bite of his sandwich and washed it down with more milk from the second carton of brown cow. Looking back over at the kid watching him, he chuckled. "That just means that before day is out, someone else will probably be calling you that also."

"Won't neither," the kid defied.

"They will not either," Hooker corrected his grammar, "and, yes they will."

"Nobody even knows me."

"It doesn't matter." Hooker pulled the turn indicator and downshifted twice. "I'll make you a bet—nobody calls you Squirt in the next five hours, and I'll pay you double. But, if you get called Squirt, you work the next few weeks for me, for free."

"You can't tell anyone."

"Deal?" The truck eased into the back road that lead up to Rim Road. Hooker smiled, knowing he was stacking the deck unfairly in his favor.

"Deal." The kid leaned back in satisfaction that he might have just gotten a job.

Ten minutes later, they walked through the massive

twelve-foot tall doors of the hacienda. As they crossed the patio, the kid's eyes were the size of baseballs as he marveled at the large hand-hewn beams protruding from the stucco walls, the fountain completely set with colorful tile, and the repeat of the massive double five-foot wide and twelve-foot tall doors letting into the house.

"You're too late," Manny called from the sunroom as they stepped into the clay-tiled entry and gently closed the door.

They walked in through the kitchen toward the sound of the small TV playing in the corner and the older man lying on the large leather couch with a lap and stomach covered in a purring orange fur rug. Looking up over his reading glasses, he took in Hooker then noticed the young man standing behind him.

"Who's the squirt?" the old man caustically called out.

Hooker gave the now dejected kid a knowing smile. Slowly turning back to Manny, he jerked his left thumb back over his shoulder. "He's my new free worker for the next few weeks while his hand heals and he stays out of trouble."

Manny turned his attention back to the TV and a commercial he could care less about, that was turned too low for anyone to make heads or tails about what was being said. "So, you got a name, Squirt?" he asked seeming to only be paying half attention.

The kid started to answer then closed his mouth, twice. Manny finally looked over at him from over his glasses. "Well?" he asked softer.

Quiet in resolve, the kid's shoulders slumped as he

answered, “Squirt, I guess.”

Manny studied him, looked at Hooker who was half-smiling and shrugged with his face as he turned toward the kitchen. “Yeah,” Manny stated, looking back at the TV. “Good name, it suits you pretty good.” The old habits of a cop holding a straight face, and delivering an even straighter line, were evident to only those around the person a long time. Hooker was beating a fast retreat and hiding his quiet laugh in the lower section of the freezer.

“You leave that orange sherbet alone in there, Hooker.”

“Just looking for the Rocky Road, Manny.” The on-going joke was that there was no Rocky Road, and Manny wasn’t allowed any sweets, but would sneak little balls of sherbet that were kept there by Manny’s wife ‘in case Hooker might want some.’

Hooker pulled out the sherbet and got down three bowls. In the small bowl, he place about as much as two melon balls worth.

Handing a larger bowl and spoon to the kid, they walked back out into the sunroom where Hooker placed the small bowl down on Manny’s chest in front of Box. “Don’t gorge yourself, Box. Leave a lick or two for Manny.” Turning, he sat down and watched the last vestiges of the sundown leave the sky before Manny reached up and turned on the lamp behind him.

“Slow day.” Manny observed, as he indeed shared the dish with the cat.

“Yeah, picked up a commercial rig down in Blood Ally. It’s out on the hook. We’ll go drop it at the Fly in a few minutes.”

"I heard it on the scanner." Manny ran his finger in the bowl and stuck it in his mouth, looking over at Squirt. "Any guts?"

"I saw two tarps in the cars that were out front." Hooker glanced at the kid. "But I didn't let him near it." As he pushed the last bit up onto his spoon, "I figured I'd break him in slow."

Manny nodded as he put the bowl down on the side table. Box stretched then jumped down headed for the dog door that was just big enough for him. "What did Sweets have to say?" He pulled his legs over the edge of the couch and sat up.

"Not much." Hooker stood and collected the bowls and handed them to his new employee. Johnny headed back into the kitchen.

"He said that he saw the person, dressed all in black. All in black except the throat and that was white."

"Hmm." The detective rubbed his chin then washed his face with his palms. "That would account for not seeing the shooter at night."

"Yeah, but I know what the SOB looks like in a dress." Hooker remembered that afternoon, and was amazed how it seemed like weeks ago.

Manny looked up, frowning, with a question on his face.

"I was shot at from the side of the Expressway just up from Blossom Hill." Hooker continued to relay the events of the afternoon, and fished the dime out of his pocket in its envelope.

As Hooker continued telling about things in the hospital, and picking up Johnny, Manny carefully picked out the dime with a pair of tweezers and examined it with a magnifying glass he got from his side table by the couch. Looking at an oblique light, he was looking for possible fingerprints.

As Hooker admitted to the conversation in the elevator, Manny stopped and looked up at Hooker. The ever-present detective gears were grinding away.

"What?" Hooker asked as Johnny rushed back into the sunroom.

"I think there is someone outside, messing with the truck."

Hookers chair was empty as the front door swung open and he ran outside. Six long strides across the ten-stride piazza, and Hooker's warning sense slowed him down and he veered left and stopped just behind the closed half of the thick oak front gate. Peeking around the corner, he saw the front blossom of the muzzle blast as a buck and change slammed into the two doors just missing his head.

As Manny wheeled out the front door, hell bent for leather, and armed with both of his nine millimeter pistols, they heard the squealing of tires as a car left in a hurry. Hooker looked around the corner and he saw a light shadow, but no taillights, as the car crested over the first slope and was gone. "Damn!" he spat.

Turning back to Manny and the kid, he was seething, and Manny read his mind and put it into words. "It just became personal." They all turned and strode out to check the truck over.

"What exactly did you see, Squirt?" the detective asked.

The kid thought. "It was more of a moving shadow."

He struggled for an explanation. “I kind of felt it more than saw anything.” He looked back at the kitchen window and back through the front gate. “I know!” snapping his good fingers and pointing at the gates. “It was that this side of the gate was closed. It was open when we got here.”

Deep in thought, Hooker raised an eyebrow. “Good memory, kid. I don’t know if I would have caught that.” He looked at Manny as he sat thinking.

Turning, Hooker reached up under the seat of his truck and pulled out the large flashlight that was police issue for a reason. Switching on the bright light he began to examine the truck in close detail, while Manny and the kid stood watch.

Finally returning to the house, Manny was quiet and pensive. There was something that was just hiding behind the curtains of his mind, and he couldn’t draw them back. Frustrated, he wheeled past Box as the cat came out to see where everyone else was.

Hooker headed for the bathroom as Box watched after his buddy, and his usually free lap ride around the house. He was now ignored. Miffed, Box looked past the wheeled meal ticket and turned his attention to the new person standing in front of him.

Johnny didn’t know what to do with a cat that was almost as big as some medium sized dogs. He stood frozen.

Box, sensing this uncertainty, casually walked over for a good sniffing session. Finding nothing truly offensive, he decided that ignoring this person until he went away would be a good enough tactic. Besides, it was time to hit the streets and log some *box time*.

Hooker came around the corner and was slightly amused at the sight of the kid being cornered by Box. "Careful, he can take that hand off in a heartbeat." He smiled as Johnny responded with an appropriate blanching as he slowly drew up both hands to his chest.

Hooker opened the door, and Box shot through first, followed with trepidation by the kid as Hooker called out over his shoulder, "See you in the morning, Manny, I'm locking the door."

The detective responded with a distracted grunt and wave. His mind was grinding and it wasn't looking good.

12

Hooker keyed his mic twice as he turned down the dark street and pulled into the large parking lot in front of Night Dispatch. Setting the air brakes, Box was already under his feet waiting for him to open the door. Hooker chuckled as he opened the door, and the orange streak flew from the cab, hit the asphalt maybe four times in the twenty yards to the door, and with a last bound, he was nestling in the large chest of his truest affection in the world. For all of her cooking, Dolly was the one person who never fed Box a single thing. She didn't have to.

Hooker slapped the back of his hand gently on Johnny's arm and pointed at the two in the large doorway. "Box only pays me attention because I feed him and haul his ass over to see his girlfriend." He laughed a low evil chuckle, as he got close enough to Dolly to nuzzle his nose in her rolls of heated neck.

Dolly pushed him away, laughing in mock disgust, as she turned on her bare feet and padded back down the short hallway. "You are such a slut, Hooker. You'd stick your nose in any fat woman's neck just to make her giggle." She lifted Box to her face and nuzzled the purring mass of orange, and adding over her mound of a shoulder, "Who's the Squirt?"

Hooker turned back to smile at the kid who was standing in the open doorway with a gaping mouth of indignation. Hooker rolled his eyes as if to say, *What can I say?* but told the kid, "Shut the door. You'll let the bullets in."

The kid sneered at what he took as a joke until he spotted the five slugs buried in the outside steel plate of the door. His eyes popped and his butt poked forward as he pushed the heavy door closed behind him. "Really?"

Hooker nodded and proceeded into the dark room punctuated by the pools of dim light. He walked toward the dispatchers, asking about the second commercial tow they were holding, but when he got close, he got the giggles he was looking for as he nuzzled their necks.

Dolly sat and leaned back so she could apply both hands on the large cat nestled between her ample breasts. Watching Hooker, she grumped in mock disgust, and turned her attention to the kid. "Do you have a real name, Squirt?"

The kid hesitated and looked to Hooker for guidance. Dolly noted the subjugation and told the kid it was her house, and to just ignore Hooker. Besides, he was busy.

"Johnny," he told her quietly as he slicked back his hair with his large white gauze mitten.

The penny dropped, and Dolly dove in predatorily to catch it. "So you're Candy's little brother."

"You know my sister?"

Dolly snickered in one breath—pay dirt! "No son, I

truly don't." Glancing toward the figure bent over into the other small pools of light. "He doesn't respect me enough to bring her by."

Standing, Hooker smirked, "I heard that." Walking over, he placed his hand on Johnny's shoulder. "Johnny, this is Dolly, she runs the city and county by night, then loans it back to other people during the day." He patted the shoulder lightly. "If you ever get in a bind, you tell them you need to talk to Dolly Dispatch, and they will bend over backwards to help you not be pissed enough to talk to Dolly."

The kid stood looking at Hooker just soaking it up. Turning to the large woman and cat, "Is that true? What he said about getting in a bind and all?"

Dolly quietly examined the kid then asked, "Do you have a wallet?"

Confused, he nodded, fishing the wallet out of his jeans.

She held out one hand and took it. Her other hand fished in one of the drawers as the fur chest warmer complained about the movement and lack of attention. Finally, she withdrew three business cards, and held them up for him to see. "Don't ever lose these. One is mine, and the other two belong to the Police Chief and the District Attorney… with mine being the most important."

The kid just nodded, and with that *bunny in the headlights* look on his face, returned the black leather wallet to his hind pocket. "When are you here?" He looked around the gloom of the cavern-like room trying to squint into the dark recesses. "Don't you have any real lights?"

Hooker laughed as he turned toward the kitchen to see

what was on the stove or in the refrigerator that he could grab a mouthful of before he got his hand slapped. "She does," he called back as his head got lost in the lower section of the large commercial refrigerator. "She actually uses them." He poked open a large Tupperware container with a smile. "New Year's Eve the place is lit up blindingly with all two of the sixty-watt bulbs she keeps in her bottom…" as he stepped back out into the main room, and handed the kid a couple of sticks of homemade beef or elk or deer jerky, "…drawer." Smiling with a self-satisfying smirk at his crude joke, he looked down at the oversized woman as she slowly, lovingly stroking the deep purring chest of a very contented cat, searing the air between her and Hooker with her scowl.

The kid chewed hesitantly on the dried meat as he looked from the one dangerous person to the other, and wondering if either were having an effect on the other, or whether they were really even dangerous. Deciding that food was a better topic of conversation, he held up the now half-chewed stick of jerky. He glanced in Hooker's direction. "This is good, what kind of meat?"

The large woman shook from the poke of mirth that started somewhere from deep inside, as she and Hooker both said 'road kill' at the same time. The kid's head snapped around and his eyes the size of hubcaps fixed in disbelief that it please not be so. "Yup," she continued. "Best not to ask the gift horses in their mouths. They carry *big* guns." Her body was now quivering and rolling from her captured laughter that was now enough to disturb her chest heater. Box almost stopped purring as he complained with a mouth full of white teeth and a silent cry. She petted him back into supplication and just kept jiggling silently with a twisted smile.

Hooker took over with rolling eyes. "The Chip's bribe her with the stuff they clean off the highways." He jerked his head at her while enjoying the view of the kid's squirming war between being repulsed and the addicting flavor and finished with, "They figure with her Southern background, she would love to get fifty pounds of dried possum or raccoon, so the regular road kill is as close as it gets." He laughed as he ripped another chunk off in the side of his mouth. "The joke is, she hates the stuff, but keeps it for the tow truck drivers who are so starved we don't care anyway, as long as it wasn't once human or dog—that we know of."

The kid blanched from white to almost transparent, as both of the dispatch gals had to release their microphones and stop talking before they broke the cardinal Dolly rule of no laughing over the radios. Never!

Hooker deadpanned the kid as he watched him near his stomach's limit. The young hand began to shake and quiver as the fingers all but let go of the offending meat. Hooker stood quietly chewing and slurping with relish on the hunk in his mouth. Slowly in a classic John Wayne voice, Hooker told the kid, "Suck it up, Squirt, this is some of the best that the street has to offer. From here on out, it's all downhill." The tip of his tongue slowly traced his lips as he finished the swallow and readied himself for the next bite, if only to keep his face straight, as he twisted the knife a little harder into the young kid's mind.

Dolly, who normally enjoys a little mischievous humor of her own, took pity on the kid. "OK, Hooker, enough. It's all right Johnny, he's just pulling your leg. They buy several bags of Grumpy's Jerky from the mini-mart around the corner, take it out of the bags, and stick it in the Tupperware, just to see if it will get a rise out of me." She waved the back of her hand at the jerky in his hand as she tried to reassure the kid. "It's all good and safe, go ahead, and enjoy it."

Returning to petting the cat, "The only reason I don't eat it is because Hooker keeps putting the container on the bottom shelf of the reefer where I can't get it, and he isn't gentleman enough to bring me some." She smiled innocently as she batted her eyes at Hooker.

Slowly the kid moved the meat back toward his mouth. Hooker leaned over and placed a stick of jerky directly in front of the woman. She shoved one eyelid half shut in heated distain and glared at Hooker, which caused him to smile sweetly back at her—the line of bullshit busted.

"Come on, Box, it's time to go." Hooker turned to head for the door.

The cat slowly opened one disinterested eye and snuggled down even deeper into the large billowy-soft bosom. "Pick my boy up on the way back, Hooker," Dolly growled as she snuggled Box deeper on her chest. "He needs some time with class."

Hooker rolled his eyes and put his hand on the large door's knob. Dolly looked over at the small black & white TV that had a seemingly static view of a parking lot and the large tow truck sitting there. Thinking as she looked, she finally looked back at Hooker and nodded. He opened the door and waved the kid out with his sticks of jerky.

As the door was closing, Dolly leveled with one last shot of the running joke about the jerky in her care. "If it were human or dog, you wouldn't be able to tell by taste, because it all tastes like beef anyway." The heavy door clicked shut with a rumble that concealed her outburst of laughter. Hooker was having more trouble controlling his.

As they neared thc truck, Hooker snuck a peek at the kid, and as he raised the jerky into his mouth, Hooker looked away saying, "She's right, you know, about the taste. You can't really tell because the pepper and stuff is all you can taste." The kid's mouth hung open around the slowly retracting jerky. While the kid was thinking, Hooker continued. "The Cannibals call it long pig, but only because they've never tasted beef or deer," grinding the blade a little deeper.

As they climbed into the cab, Hooker was proud of the kid, as he noticed the last of the jerky was still in his hand, and he was chewing—thoughtfully, but still chewing.

13

Hooker jumped in the truck and looked at the kid. "What do you think kid, should we go north?" Silently, the kid just nodded and kept chewing as he closed the door and rolled down his window. Then he went back to staring strangely at the jerky in his hand, still undecided whether it really was road kill or not, or if he should even care.

Pushing the small silver button that lit up the monster with his left hand, Hooker's right hit the air brake release. Jamming the truck into gear, they slowly rolled out of the parking lot. In the gathering gloom, the giant yellow truck slowly loafed its way down the streets as the street punks looked on. Picking up speed, Hooker turned onto the highway roaring up the on-ramp and dropping down onto the northbound 101. The longer stroke gave the heart of the beast the throaty slow growl, but the custom oversized pistons gave it the bark that was unique and distinct as Hooker started skipping gears, and leap-frogging into lower edges of the higher power bands, as the giant mill made full use of its longer stroke and hulking torque and the unladen truck.

Mae West was nothing more than a yellow streak passing an over-confident red Corvette in the second lane as they roared passed in the *slow* lane. Snapping his fingers, Hooker remembered that he needed to stop in at the restaurant. Shooting a quick glance at the kid, he took the northbound 280 transition ramp toward Winchester Boulevard. The kid gave him a strong look, not sure of where they were really going. As far as he knew, they were headed north and inland of Fremont, not toward San Francisco. Hooker just shrugged and said he had something to do first.

By nine o'clock, San Jose normally half-asleep, traffic on the 280 northbound was light and dry, and Hooker just rolled along letting himself mentally drift over the day's events. Less than twenty-four hours had passed but it seemed like two weeks. Something someone had said knocked on the back of Hooker's head—not quite remembered, but not forgotten either. It frustrated Hooker that he couldn't pinpoint it. Whatever it was hadn't been important at the time, but now maybe it could be. He mauled the road kill of his memories, searching for that tasty morsel that would fulfill his need.

The small square of a dirty yellowish-white Toyota or Datsun car drifted right, languidly across the front of the truck and slowly made its way up the dark off-ramp. Something about the small cubic spot of light color in the dark of the night worked on Hooker's mind, but it wouldn't come. Shrugging, Hooker down shifted the truck and slowed for the next off-ramp. Double clutching, his two feet worked back and forth in the synchronized dance of teamwork as his right hand worked, blurring back and forth between the two gearshifts as he transferred the main transmission to the lower tier of street gears. Some days, the possession of twenty-four gears spread through two transmissions could be a headache, but generally, it was just so second nature for Hooker that he never gave it much thought.

Hitting the top of the ramp, Hooker drifted his left foot across to the brake pedal in-between the dance of the clutch and gears. The yellow hulk loomed up off the freeway just as the light turned green for his left turn, and Hooker left the last downshift undone as he manhandled the large steering wheel, swinging onto Winchester Boulevard faced west toward the creepy tourist attraction of the Sarah Winchester house. Hooker was convinced that it was the color of the house that had influenced the florid choice of yellow and blue as the California choice for the auto club trucks.

At least with his uncle, and some creative thinking and exceptional paint job, the converted monster former 1959 Marmon logging truck was barely in the realm of the vapid scheme of the other trucks in California. The sixteen pounds of crushed reddish-pink mother of pearl had just happened to fall into their possession when they were thinking of what to do to the primed grey hulk parked under the army of long florescent lights in his uncle's barn. The 1932 deuce coupe hot rod in the corner under the tarp with the sixty-eight layers of hand rubbed lacquer in Candy Apple blue had provided the other half of the equation.

After six long weeks and many sleepless nights of sanding, the yellow truck shimmered in waves of pearl, pink, and red with the nose on fire with cold-hot candy apple and blue flames reaching back to lick at Mae West on the driver's side. A WWII score board of five Volkswagen bugs, two Toyota Corollas, one deer, and three rabbits gracing the passenger side. Under the scoreboard was the ribbon saying, 'Caution: You may be next', and under the much-revered Ms. West was the old railroad slogan, 'It's what's up front that counts, everything else is behind.'

Mae West waved at the rest of Winchester Boulevard and the Winchester house a few blocks farther on as Hooker swung the massive truck into the back driveway to the parking lot of the diner. Pulling to a stop in the empty area of the lot, he looked at the kid. "You can come or stay, it's your choice," he said as he opened his door and started out. The kid rolled his eyes and slid out his side and caught up to Hooker at the door. Mae West purred in the lot with a husky heavy drinking and smoking kind of throat as the two men walked past the large fiberglass statue, and his ever-present plastic smile. Hooker pulled open the glass doors and walked into the bright lights of a twenty-four hour restaurant in its slow 'catch a breath' period of the late evening.

A couple of regulars took up the pews at the altar of mediocre coffee and food. But unlike other discerning diners, many of these had no other choice other than to return to something heated over a tenement hot plate. At least with the counter, there was usually Candy, who was not only gentle on the eyes, but also had a kind heart, if not a soft spot, for the less fortunate in the world — something for which Hooker had a whole new understanding and respect.

The two men stood half way down the long counter as they waited for Johnny's sister to finally finish with the small deuce table and see them. The smile faltered as she turned and saw whom it was. The pause was telling as she weighed the possible meaning of Hooker bringing her brother into the restaurant. Slowly she came toward the two with a deadpan 'I can take anything' face.

"What?" She asked the two quietly, looking like a stern mother from Hooker to Johnny to Hooker again.

"I just wanted you to know that the Squirt will be with me for the next couple of weeks, so I can keep an eye on his hand." Hooker ignored her stare and attitude.

"Would you stop calling me that," the kid protested under his breath as he hung his head looking around to see if anyone had heard.

"Shut up, Squirt!" his sister snapped quietly. His head jerked to look in horror at the betrayal from his own flesh and blood as she gave him a hard look before refocusing on Hooker as he was nonchalantly finger-combing his waves of dark curly hair — something she down deep wished she was doing instead.

"Is that going to be OK?" she asked as if the kid wasn't even there.

Hooker glanced at the object of the discussion. "Yeah, I'll feed him, and we'll pick up some more clothes later, but he lost a bet and now Johnny has to work for free for a couple of weeks." He nodded his head at the white mitten that was now a little soiled. "Besides, I've got a lot invested in his hand healing right." He was smiling the silly smile that was more goofy than self-satisfied. "So it stays where it belongs and away from other people's property."

The older sister weighed the value of the offering as her eyes slowly slid through a blink into looking hard at her little brother who was now looking anywhere but at his sister. Quietly she asked, "Are you going to behave?"

The now very red face nodded and mumbled acquiescence, "As long as he stops calling me that."

She looked silently at her troubled brother and took a deep breath, sighing out, "Shut up, Squirt." Turning to Hooker, she glanced at her watch. "A little early for lunch."

Hooker quietly snorted his acknowledgement of the new treaty. "I just wanted you to know that I had him and that he wasn't lying dead up some alley. I have to jerk a truck up north, but we'll be back for lunch. I need to ask Peter some stuff when he comes around for his midnight cigarette."

"Where's Squirt going to sleep? In the truck with you?" She watched the kid squirm at the new name, but it appeared that he was getting used to it for some reason.

"We'll hole up out at Manny and Estelle's place, and I'll give you the phone number when we get back for lunch, but you always have Dolly's number at dispatch. Or worst case, you can just tell any cop you need to get ahold of me." He backed out of the restaurant dragging his new charge.

Candy laughed and waved them to leave as she turned to grab a fresh pot of coffee and restart her rounds of the sparsely occupied booths and counter. "Hey, Hooker," she called out.

He stuck his head back in the closing door.

"Bring me a donut."

He shot her with his right hand finger gun and a wink, and was gone.

14

Running loose up the 680 on the backside of Fremont, Hooker let the monster get out and breathe. Some days it just seemed like the 1,200-horsepower that finally arrived at the twin axles was somehow restrained by the slow chugging around from jumpstart, to flat tire and the occasional tow.

The original engine had started life as a Wildcat towing winch of a different type in the wild woods of Oregon logging. As steam engines and trains were pushed out of the great forests of the Pacific Northwest, gas and diesel powered machines took over many of the jobs. And as companies became more about the owners and shareholders in the east, instead of the wood-wise loggers in the forest, newer and wilder machines and techniques were tried until something went wrong and one or more died. So was the story of the 1,200-hp engine now hidden under the large nose of the monster truck, nicknamed Mae West.

One of the more crazy reckless forms of logging was reaching down into draws and valleys and pulling the logs up the hill or mountainside to the logging road and staging area above. With much of the timber ranging in butt spreads or girth, the size of a man's height or larger logs could commonly weigh into the many tons in a single lift. This load required a lot of bulk power, but also needed speed. Three speed slip gears driven by huge engines seemed to be the answer.

The story goes that the *High Wire* on the *Show* (logging company) was over a mile long and as thick as a good woman's wrist, (one who could milk eight or ten cows twice a day and run a bunkhouse of a hundred loggers.) The rip-line rode up and down the High Wire with a hundred pound pulley and at the end had a set of collars that would strap onto or choke the end of the sixteen to twenty-four foot-long log. When the rigger blew his whistle that the log was choked, the high-top man at the *donkey* engine would pull on the accelerator, slip the brake on the take-up reel, and the log would lift from the forest floor and fly up the hill at a speed approaching eighty miles per hour. Lighter logs had a nasty habit of completely leaving the ground and indiscriminately whipping about in the air over the logged off mountainside. Standing or walking anywhere within a hundred yards of a High Wire was known suicide. But then standing at the top of a High Wire with five tons of log flying at you at four times faster than you can run, isn't always a guarantee for a long life either, and that was how the donkey ended up in a salvage yard, sitting next to a 1959 Marmon conventional tractor. They were two castoffs of a changing world, both in need of a loving home.

Hooker was working on his third year towing, and

was finally a legal age to go get a real driver's license and it might as well be a commercial towing license. So they looked around, and they found a Holmes 950 extendable split-boom towing rig and began building the custom working bed.

Uncle Willy wasn't really Hooker's uncle, but more of the guy who grabbed him by the ear one night, hauled him home, and kept his nose somewhat clean since Hooker was fourteen. Having this home kept Hooker out of the system and off the streets as a runaway from the ninth foster home in six years. William Hollister was a man caught in a time and at an age when you were supposed to marry a woman and build a family—not shack up with another man, at least not if you are a high ranking officer in the Naval Intelligence. The occasional houseguests of his 'uncle' never bothered Hooker, as all of the men were nice and respected the law that Hooker was off limits and would one day find a nice girl to 'make him happy.' Sadly, Hooker observed that happy was something eluding Willy except when he was black with grease to his elbows, skinned knuckles, and listening to the hum of a perfectly running engine. Even if it was only a lawnmower, it did not stay stock past its first winter.

Hooker could not stand the silence of having a living, breathing person in his cab, one who could talk, but did not. Not that he wanted a non-stop chatterbox, but just some talk. "So where did you two live after your old man bailed on you?" He grabbed a glance at the kid with his head against the window watching the night go by. He was not the first, as everyone got the *stare* the first time they rode ten feet above the highway.

The kid had a kind of dreamy far off look to his eyes when he finally focused forward. "I remember living in a garage for a while, and then there was a guy that took us in when I was in the fourth grade. He was nice enough to me, and helped me with homework, but I think he was, you know, with Candy. So when summer came, we left. Candy got a job in Turlock waiting tables in a breakfast diner, and we did laundry at night. I ran back and forth with dimes keeping the machines going, and Candy would iron the sheets and stuff."

"How did you end up in San Jose?"

The kid just looked out the window, chewing on what he could or shouldn't tell. Looking down at his hand, and bandages, he kind of shuddered. "One night the owner cornered Candy in the back room of the Laundromat and was starting to…" the kid's eyes glistened and reflected the oncoming lights. He chewed as he sucked both of his lips in working on pain to stop from crying. He probably had never really faced the scene he was replaying in his mind.

"Hey," Hooker offered quietly. "It's OK, you don't have to…"

"No." The kid shook and wiped his face. "It's OK. If Candy goes out with you, it's something you have to understand. She's not… she's, um… things haven't been very nice for her." He took in a huge breath and slowly let it out. "And you might be something good in her life finally."

"She's a nice lady, Squirt. You could have gotten a lot worse." Hooker grabbed the mic from behind his head and pulled it around as he keyed the red button. "Dolly?"

He waited in the silence that was a volume of the

monster engine and the whine of the giant tires in the night air. Hooker looked to the left as he caught the last sight of the bay lights before they were cut off by the hills as he dove into the rolling hills to Pleasanton.

"Go ahead, Hooker," the radio squawked.

"10-4, sweetie. Can you please call Contra yard and tell them I'm about thirty minutes out and ask them in that Dolly-by-golly way you have to get that truck ready to roll?" Releasing the key, he smiled with the knowledge that she had her ways of getting people to do things, and he had his way of asking her for that help.

"You mean you don't have a phone in that super truck of yours? The girls tell me you have everything else."

"None of your girls have been in my truck, Dolly. The bed is too small." Out of the corner of his eye, he saw the kid looking back into the single sleeper, which was a very comfortable thirty-two inches wide.

"And you better keep it that way, mister." The thud of the microphone key was followed by silence. Hooker knew there was nothing but mock-offended giggling going on at the dispatch. The silence was broken with a terse "Stand by."

Hooker turned toward the kid, who was laid up against the window that was rolled down to just above his ear, so the longish hair was whipping around in the open air. Hooker knew that look, he had felt it hundreds of times—the edge of despair where it just aches, no thought, just the ache.

"You going to be alright?" he asked.

"I stabbed him." The small voice drifted mournfully in the buffeting wind and was gone.

"What?"

The kid sat up and leaned his head back over the top of the seat. "He had his hand up her uniform and was pulling her panties down." The horror that he was reliving was written all over his face. "There was an old knife, like a kitchen knife or boning knife that they used for opening boxes. I grabbed it." His eyes were big and wild, his mind almost out of control as that night seared in his veins, unrelenting. "I stabbed him." He looked to Hooker. "I stabbed him in the back."

Hooker glanced at the kid, and then just stared down the highway as his vision tunneled for a few seconds. So much was just too close to home that Hooker had to take a couple of breaths. He felt his heart climb back down his ribs and retake its proper seat.

"Hard?" Hooker croaked, "I mean—did you stab him very hard?" He glanced over, and then checked the gauges and meters on the dash and cleared his mirrors.

"I buried the blade till it stopped at the handle." He took a sharp breath and slowly let it out as he tried for a better grip on his life. "We didn't know if I killed him or not, so we ran." He looked over at Hooker. "That's when we came here."

Hooker thought about the impact of such an event, and not knowing the extent of what you had done. "How old were you then?"

The kid's head flopped forward as he resumed looking down the highway. "Twelve. We had celebrated my birthday the night before. Candy had bought two cupcakes and we rolled up some paper to look like candles and lit them." He looked out the side window as they crossed the bridge over a dry riverbed. "It was the first birthday I had ever got any kind of cake."

The silence stretched on as the big truck wound its way through the hills and up the backside of the east bay. The moon was just coming up over Livermore as Hooker turned left and started the back way into the Contra Costa Impound Yard where a stolen 1975 Peterbilt waited to be hauled back to the San Jose Police yard for processing.

15

The towing yard was like most others — bright stadium lights in the front, but not so well lit near the rear where the dogs usually hung out. It was one of the few things Hooker hated about the job, the dogs. You never knew if the owner was just seeing if you were stupid enough to test the yard and the free running dog, or if the dog was really trained enough to be completely on off-leash command. Contra Costa was the latter. Hooker even knew the two dogs Mutt and Jeff, and more importantly, they knew him. They also liked him because he kept Box in the truck so Box couldn't come tear them up as he did the first time they met.

As Hooker squatted down to look at the undercarriage of the diesel truck, Mutt came around the backside of the truck and nuzzled up under Hookers arm. "Hello, buddy." Hooker grabbed the head and shoulders of the large Rottweiler with his right arm and gave the head and ears a rough rubbing down with his left. The dog's hind end wiggled wildly as his rear feet lost traction. "What do you think of this piece of shit truck? Huh? Should I tow it on out of here?" The dog backed out and away from too much affection as he heard his yard mate returning from doing his business out in the darkest part of their fenced world. Hooker went back to looking at the condition of the rig he was going to tow, and he wasn't pleased.

Standing up he looked at the huge man in the grease splattered one-piece jump suit. "Jesus Mike, what the heck did they hit with that front end? Those tie rods must be at least fifteen degrees out of whack." He shook his head.

"The police said they left the highway doing about seventy and the riprap, those great big rocks along the stream bed, was what stopped them." The towheaded, goofball looking guy with one crossed eye said as he reamed his left ear with his pinky, while his right hand was busy scratching his butt through the jump suit. For once, Hooker was thankful for the man's uniform. He didn't want to think what the guy would have been doing with easier access that regular pants would afford.

Hooker looked back at the twin driver sets of wheels. "Well, I'll have to pull her with the ass down, and I didn't bring anything to pull the axles." Returning his gaze to the large man, he found him examining the interesting artifact he had found in one end or the other, and Hooker didn't want to know which. "Can you pull those, Mike?"

The man looked up with a startled look as if Hooker and his truck had just materialized in front of him. "Huh? Oh… uh, yeah. Sure, Hooker, I can do that. But it will cost you extra." The guy kind of sidestepped and kicked the dirt. Hooker knew that 'extra' wasn't an extra charge that would be on the bill.

Lowering his voice, Hooker looked around the empty yard like a conspirator. “What do you need, Mike?” He slumped down on the truck’s tire with one hip as if he were bored already.

“While I pull those axles,” the man nodded and pointed at the obvious, “maybe you could run into town and get me some dinner?”

Hooker looked at the man well past the 300-pound setting on the scales. It didn’t take a genius to figure out what was going on. “She still has you on that diet, does she?” The man just caved inside of himself and nodded.

“Would a couple of bean burritos with extra cheese do it for you?” Hooker sympathized with the guy. The man had fought the battle all of his life. Now his wife was determined to hold him to a thousand calories a day. And for her, that meant driving him everywhere so he couldn’t stop for extra food.

The man’s face brightened into a gratifying smile. “That would be great, Hooker. You’re my hero, and I’ll have those axles out by the time you get back.” The man turned toward the small mechanics shop he maintained behind the office.

Hooker let himself out of the gate and climbed up into the big truck. Gently closing the door, he sat quiet for a moment with Johnny watching him. It was like a ritual of prayer. He took a couple of slow deep breaths and finished with a soft ‘thank you.’ Looking over at the kid, he reached forward as he laid the gears in the right alignment and pushed on the big red parking break button to release it. The air hissed loudly in the night as he flicked his head at the kid. “What?”

"You just . . . sitting there," the kid waved his finger at Hooker's seat, "are you OK?"

Hooker chuckled as he let out the clutch and the truck lurched into the street. "Oh, yeah. Just keeping clean by being dirty, is all." The monster 1,200 horse-powered engine loafed down the street toward the local Pup & Taco with bean burritos the size of a large cat's head. Hooker's mouth folded up in a wince as he remembered that Box was not in his box where his idle right hand was feeling for an ear to scratch.

The light changed to green and Hooker shifted back up the gears as he continued on his mission. Back in the yard, he knew the large man was swiftly getting greasy and dirty without a care, except for the reward that was coming back with Hooker. In a way, it just wasn't a fair trade. Hooker knew he was the winner, because it's a disgusting job pulling the axles on all four of the drivers, but he also knew that Mike would say that he was the winner, as he buried his face into the warm bean burritos as if they were manna from heaven.

The low-sodium stadium lights turned the parking lot around the eatery into day, except unlike the warm sunlight, these lights turned make-up into garish Halloween war paint leaving attractive young girls looking more like vampires, ghouls, or zombies, which of course they found unacceptable so they stayed away. And without the girls, the boys didn't hang out either. With the parking lot not full of teens hanging around, it cut down on the criminal activities and made it a lot more attractive for the straighter elements of society to frequent the twenty-four hour establishment in the middle of the night. Knowing he could never fit the Marmon through the drive-through, he parked out in the far corner and set the truck into a stable idle as the giant motor loped in a deep throated rumble. “Just hit the lock button, as you get out.” he nodded at the door to the kid. “I need some coffee and we may as well wait inside.” The two doors clicked shut and they walked across the tarmac.

Uncomfortable with constant companionship, Hooker fidgeted with the conversation. He looked at the kid. “So what do you want to be when you grow up?”

To the kid’s credit, he didn’t answer fast, but kept walking. Finally, he looked up at the night sky just above the burrito shack. “I haven’t thought much about it, but it’s more like what can I do?” He looked over at Hooker. “I didn’t finish high school, so someone like the cops won’t take me.”

“Does that appeal to you?” Hooker held the door open. “Being a cop?”

The kid shrugged. “They kind of get respect, they make good money, and they help people.” The kid stood for a second waiting for Hooker to laugh at his simplistic view of the world, but when no laughter came, he continued into the restaurant.

Hooker looked back at the truck waiting like a hulking behemoth in the night under the sodium lights as he thought of his own choice and of the Manny that he had met seven years before, and the Manny of today in his wheelchair with a wife he could never take dancing again. “There is that respect thing,” he said softly. “There is that.” Turning, he followed the kid into the restaurant, resizing his opinion of the conflicted young man.

The Peterbilt rode behind the Marmon like a pregnant salmon, large but docile on the hook, as they wound their way back down the backside of the east bay. The crescent moon was a rusted orange sliver coming in from the central valley above the inner coastal hills behind Livermore, as the large yellow and blue-flamed nose of the giant Marmon pushed through the gathering moisture of the night air. Hooker listened more to the heartbeat sound of the throbbing oversized engine, and then he paid much attention to the several dials that were meant to monitor the life of the stroked and bored out engine—an engine that had started life as the biggest most powerful engine that came stock in any truck, even before his uncle Willie and he had first stripped it down to parts of bare metal.

Hooker flexed the fingers of his right hand, remembering his fifteenth birthday. He had never seen inside the large bore of a diesel engine before, and he was totally captured by the size of the bore, as he stuck his hand with fingers spread loose down into the port to the top of the piston. That was the moment that he knew that he was destined to be the master of the monster, and if it could be made even fiercer, he wanted it. And so the research had begun.

The research nature of Willie had forced the young Hooker to get a library card and sift through hundreds of books, searching out the engineering that would justify the machining and sizing of the engine's basic body, commonly referred to as the *mill* — the working core. At first, Hooker rebelled at what he thought was some kind of weird punishment and resisted really reading the books or taking the time searching the bibliographies. He felt that the way to build the engine was just make things as big as you could buy them, and it would all work out.

He had silently chuckled at the tiny sweater-clad librarian with the tight bun of newspaper gray hair coming over and sitting down at the table across from him. She looked at him with the eyes of a teacher that he was trying to lie to. She studied him for almost a full minute before she snapped quietly, as only a librarian could, “You don’t deserve this opportunity.” Her eyes burned, stone cold, through his.

“Excuse me?”

“God knows you may or may not deserve it, but you have been given an opportunity that many other people would give a left leg to be even allowed to glimpse. And here you sit pissing it away.”

“What do you know?” The defiant street-forged tough surged to the surface.

“I know you have someone who loves you, and cares about you, like the son he thought he would never have. I know that when that man does his research he has ten times as many books, real books.” She dithered her finger at the few books scattered on the table. “Not these kiddy books. I know that if you don’t square away your research, you will end up building a monster that will eat you alive and blow up in your face.” She started to rise. “Get squared away, or quit wasting your time.”

“You’re just a stupid old woman who doesn’t know squat!” He lashed out from a place of being caught doing exactly what she said… and it hurt.

Her head snapped back at him, the eyes burning, as she slowly sat back down. “Do you know what it feels like to drive a 1932 deuce coupe with a 380 horse flat head Lincoln motor, at a hundred thirty miles per hour across a salt flat? No. Have you ever held onto the handlebars of an oversized Indian Chief doing over a hundred miles an hour down the coast highway on a moonlit night, and you have no lights? Do you know what it feels like when a piston pulls out of the bore, and punches out the side of your fresh engine because you may or may not have built it wrong? No, because you're just a kid with more sperm and little boy bravado in your pants than experience." She rose back up with seething indignity and fired her parting shot. "When you can tell me why you need a new transmission in that truck instead of a wider bore, I'll respect you and tell you the four books you need to read cover to cover. Until then, you don't need to come back in here."

Hooker had watched as the tiny woman walked away with a certain pained bowlegged wobble that implied some of the past that she had hinted at. He thought about what she had said, and even more importantly, had hinted at, as he replaced the books on the shelf, and then he left the library, wrapped in his battered pride.

He had finally asked his uncle about the little bird lady at the library and then sat transfixed, as Willie had spewed forth the longest string of stories about her father and three brothers who were the biggest rogue racers along the central coast.

The *little sister*, Madeline, was barely distinguishable as such, as she had been drawn into their world of gas, grease, and hot metal without a mother to provide any alternative rearing. She had been the first woman to drive over two-hundred miles an hour at the Bonneville Salt

Flats in Nevada, and had an oversized Indian Chief Motorcycle engine blow-up during a drag race, sending her to the hospital for most of that summer. They put her legs and body back into some kind of useable order. She had gone to college and tried to teach auto shop, but the men of the world wouldn't allow it, so she resigned herself to the library, where she guided those who would listen to the education they wanted or needed. That is where a young Willie had found her, and learned of their mutual affliction or addiction to metal and grease.

Hooker eventually learned his answers, and even came to the revelation about the new transmission on his own. Long before he had the nerve to go back to that branch of the library, he had made friends with the diesel mechanic at the Fly's truck repair, who, to his surprise, handed him a few books from a shelf that Hooker hadn't noticed before, and referred him to many books for the answers to his questions.

Finally armed with an expanded knowledge and understanding of the huge torque power band, and lack of ability to rev to high revolutions because of the mass of metal being moved in the engine, he walked into the library and up to the desk of the seemingly distracted and very busy librarian. He stood silently waiting his turn as she shuffled papers and books, while making notes.

After a few minutes, as he started shifting his weight from leg to leg, she looked up over her half glasses. "And what kind of transmission have you decided you need?" she asked flatly, as if the conversation of seven months earlier had never ended.

"A six speed Torque Master."

She thought about it with a twisted turn to her pursed lips. "Hmm," she decided. "And is that going to match up to the Bell transfer box?"

"With an adapter ring we are going to mill."

"And, so I would assume that Willie is in agreement with this choice?"

"Yes."

"Anything else?" She drilled him with her intensity.

"We're going to expand the range in the primary for a wider range, that is possible with the eight extra gears." He recited with a bit of attempted self-satisfaction.

"Which, Mr. Hooker, the word is 'which', not 'that'… is possible," she corrected, nodding. "And what do you plan to gain by the new added and adapted gears?"

"We've got all the bottom end pull and muscle we will ever need, so the change will all go into expanding the top end. The truck as it is, would probably top out at seventy, but with the change it should be capable of a hundred and fifteen to a hundred and twenty miles per hour."

"And why would you want to ever drive such a huge CHP target at those kinds of speeds?" She slowly removed her glasses and began to polish the lens with a fold of her dress. "Is there a race track that I don't know about?"

Hooker laughed, understanding that they were now reading from the same book. "I drive tow trucks for a living. Sometimes in a wreck, a wrecker is a critical piece in saving lives, especially a large recovery wrecker that can pull a tractor trailer off a car."

She nodded, as she reached low under the counter and retrieved a small stack of books. "I believe these are yours now to check out." She pushed the stack toward the young man with a small smile of pride.

He quickly reviewed the titles and handed one of them back. "I read that one, and then bought it last month." He smiled with well-deserved satisfaction. "I think these others are on Uncle Willie's shelf. I'll check tonight, and if they are, I'll return them tomorrow."

Ever the librarian, she admonished, "You may want to check the publish date of your uncle's books, and the revision date of these before you so hastily return them." She reached up and pulled the half-glasses from the end of her nose, letting them hang from the chain about her neck. Looking up warmly at the much taller young man, she shared her wisdom of the book. "Just because you are talking about 300 cubic inches of 1930 and 300 of today, doesn't mean you are talking about the same dynamics of energy."

Understanding that he had overstepped just a bit, Hooker backtracked into the line of grace. "Yes ma'am, I will bear that in mind in the future."

"You are welcome here anytime, Hooker, to do research or to even just say hello and keep me appraised of the project truck."

Turning to leave, the young man ran his fingers through a much-needed haircut. "Yes, ma'am."

Just before he touched the door, she called out one last admonishment. "And Hooker…" He looked back. "I do plan to get a ride in the new Speedwagon when it's finished."

"It's a Marmon, ma'am, not a Reo."

"Yes, Mr. Hooker, but I suspect between you and

Willie, it will most definitely be a "Speed" wagon of a truck." She smiled, with a slight pull of stiff skin to one side of her face.

He nodded as he now understood and smiled broadly as he pushed through the glass door, thinking of an old line in a Mae West movie—*it's what's up front that counts.*

What was up front protested as his reminiscing had caused his attention to drift and the pyro-meter was registering near the danger zone. Quickly he backed off the throttle, but also shifted to the higher gear, dropping the RPMs, which would let the engine relax back to a cooler running temperature. He looked over at the passenger who was leaned against the window napping from exhaustion. A small trace of drool ran down his chin, reflecting like a Christmas tree the many lights of the dashboard and its many dials and radios. What Hooker had misheard as Box purring, was a low quiet snore coming from the young man.

Hooker smiled as the slow sweeping curve brought them out of the hills, and for a brief moment, into an expansive view of the south bay area. The lights of Moffett Field, twenty miles across the back-bay mud flats, twinkled as a small red light lifted off the ground. The P-3 Sub-chaser airplane ascended to its flight duty for the next long day over the Pacific Ocean. On top of Hanger One, the giant former dirigible hanger, red lights slowly strobing on and off, were both a warning to aircraft and the pulsing heart of the south bay.

Hooker slowly reached for the radio behind his head to report to Dolly. Thinking, and then looking back over at the kid, he relaxed, letting his hand fall. The kid needed sleep and Hooker would call her in about a half hour when they dropped the truck off at the San Jose Police impound yard.

16

"Hey, Hooker," the first cop said as the two slid down next to him at the counter. "Who's the squirt?" The two officers smiled with big goofy smiles.

Hooker looked over as he chewed on his sandwich. He swallowed and turned to the kid, waving his sandwich at the two cops. "Johnny, I'd like you to meet Officers Asshole, and his partner Dickhead." Looking back at the two now laughing officers, he prepared to take another languid bite. "Who let you two out together?"

Sobering, the taller redhead offered, "Until they solve this cop killer stuff, every car in the south bay is on doubles now. This is why we stopped in to talk to you. You were there when the Chip got it, right?"

Hooker nodded as he chewed.

The second of the twin brothers asked, "Is it true you couldn't see the shooter? That it was all just black?"

Again, Hooker nodded confirmation.

"When the shooter shot at you, there was no muzzle blast?" The slightly taller brother, beefier by at least fifty pounds, was trying to get his mind around a night firing with no muzzle flare.

Hooker, reliving the scene, laid down his sandwich and wiped his hands on the paper napkin in his lap. Looking with a squint at the pie cupboard, but seeing that night again in vivid detail, he spoke, "No… no, that wasn't totally right. From head on, the flare was that of maybe a twenty-two or a thirty-eight, but definitely not a shotgun." Shaking, he looked back at the twin Irish cops. Walking stereotypes, even down to the fact that they were fourth generation cops, but two of the smarter street cops in the city. They were the same two that had busted him for stealing a car when he was fourteen and told him he should be driving for a living, but only legally. When he showed up driving a tow truck three months later, they turned a blind, but friendly eye to the fact that they knew his true age, not the twenty years that was on the totally fabricated driver's license in his jeans.

They were looking at each other in that silent communication that was exclusive to twins. Hooker raised the cup of coffee and sipped while he waited his turn in the silence. The kid, not understanding any of it, just quietly ate his sandwich and fries.

"So it's probably what Manny was thinking," the larger one said turning back to Hooker. "A two-liter coke bottle stuffed with steel wool, taped to the end of the barrel."

"It makes a lot of sense," the other continued the train of thought. "It would suppress the noise and the muzzle flare at the same time, and then it's totally a throw away."

"So," Hooker swallowed, "a smart shooter, but not a professional who is going to do this on an on-going basis."

The two cops nodded. "And they found nothing on the car they recovered?"

"Wiped clean with white gas." The two shrugged with wide eyes and contorted faces at Hooker's furrowed brow, as if to say *Who knows?*

Hooker looked back at the pie case as Candy came down the counter with more coffee. "Are you gentlemen here to harass customers, or just arrest Hooker and his squirt to put me out of my misery?" The squirt flinched and didn't even look up at his sister.

"Special duty tonight, ma'am," the smaller, and married one chimed in. "Harass and to lust after the most beautiful coffee packer in the three counties." His brother looked at him askance. In his defense, he whined back at him, "What? A guy can't even flirt?"

Candy leaned over, and in a voice reserved for a small baby or adored puppy, she patted him on the cheek saying, "It's OK, little wubby, we wuves you any way Puddin'."

He flushed bright red but returned, "I'm Cup Cake," pointing his thumb at his brother, "and he's Puddin'."

The larger just rolled his eyes in mock horror and slowly planted his face in his open hand.

Returning to business, she started to turn a mug over. "Coffee?"

They both shook their heads. "No, we just needed to check in with the mayor here," jerking a thumb in Hooker's direction.

She nodded and turned to Hooker and giving no options just poured, as she dropped the check on the counter. Nodding toward her sibling. "Is he behaving, at least?"

Hooker frowned as one side of his face pulled back, deliberately drawing out his answer, "I'm afraid not." Wagging his head. "He goes to wrecks and just stands there."

The kid looked up in horror, coming to his own defense, "You told me…"

Ignoring the kid, the waitress turned and quipped as she wandered off down the long counter, "Then don't stab him this time. It didn't work before. This time just shoot him." She didn't laugh, and everyone but the kid was amused. He just collapsed more into himself as a tiny rivulet of catsup ran truant at the corner of his mouth.

Hooker reached over and patted him on the shoulder. "Relax, kid. You have thirteen days more to redeem yourself. And wipe your mouth," pointing at the corner of his own mouth. The two cops quietly snickered at the kid's expense.

Pivoting back to the cops, Hooker turned serious. "So what about the guy in the granny dress that shot at me on Almaden Expressway?"

"When was that?"

The day was rapidly running into a week's worth of memories. Hooker had to stop and think what day it was. "This afternoon, as I was coming up from Manny's, where the two bean fields are split by the street that cul-de-sac at the embankment. A little old lady was just standing there, just watching the cars go by, and then as I approached, I saw a raised shotgun, which pumped out about two or three shots as I hammered it and flew by. The shooter was knocked ass over teakettle, too. The car in the cul-de-sac was cream colored and was either a Cadillac or a Cordoba.

The jerk also showed up at Manny's place about sundown, and if it hadn't been for Squirt here, would have probably gotten a fair piece of me."

"You say the berm at the cul-de-sac between the bean fields?"

"Yeah, I called it in."

The two cops did that twin look thing and then turned to Hooker as they rose. "We've got to go," the one started. "We'll find you tomorrow," the other finished as they were out the door.

"Clear it first through Dolly."

The twins smirked knowingly and waved as they pushed out through the glass door.

Hooker turned back around to the kid, who was still blinking at the door where the cops had been, processing things a little slowly, or too much, so Hooker asked him, "Did you fart?" The kid looked horror struck, and then realized that Hooker was joking with him and began to laugh uncontrollably.

Candy stepped around the corner from the manager's station and gave him a stern look. "Hey! No laughing in here." Which of course, made the kid giggle all the harder. She rolled her eyes. "Hooker," as she held the phone out to him.

Hooker got up and snapped the kid on the top of his head. "Knock it off, or you'll get us kicked out." Looking at his watch, he saw that it was five of midnight—must be Dolly. He took the phone from the waitress. "Thanks."

"This is Hooker." The voice was not the one he expected.

"Stella's home, and she said to come now, not in the

morning."

"Yes, sir. We were just walking out the door." Hanging the phone, Hooker fished in his pocket for a ten-dollar bill and a one. Handing them to Candy, he told her they had to go. Gathering the kid on his way, they were walking across the parking lot as Hooker thought about how Manny had sounded, very distant and very serious. But it was almost midnight.

As Hooker sat in the quiet cab, the kid didn't say a word as he fished the pack of cigarettes out of the glove box, tapped out one, and threw the remainder back in as he shut the box. Hooker stared out the rear side mirrors as he tamped the tobacco stick on the large white Bakelite steering wheel turned ivory and brown with age. Very low, the AM radio played country western rock music that was almost more of a white noise than it was music. Sweets wouldn't be on for another thirty minutes, and then the tone of the music would change.

Hooker looked out at the left side mirror and watched as a smudge of the night moved and materialized again alongside the truck. When he opened the door and stuck his foot out, the smudge stopped, and then stood wearied and still. Speaking softly in a soothing, casual tone, Hooker said, "Hello Peter." The smudge was torn between the confrontation, and the offering of a cigarette. The ritual had changed.

"Hooker?" The sound was like a wisp of fog off the bay that had lost its way and rasped along the rocks of the Santa Clara fields.

"Peter, I need to talk to someone." His right hand was fishing back and pointing to the glove box he had just closed. Snapping his fingers and pointing until he heard Johnny move and open the box. "Peter, I have two cigarettes, if that makes it OK." He held up one finger and he felt the kid slip one more cigarette into his hand.

"I… I don't know Ho… Hooker." The man was out past the edge of where he was comfortable. "I just don't know… I've never had two cigarettes before Hooker."

"It's OK, Peter. I'm not going to make you take it. I was just offering it."

Relieved, the man sighed and took another small step as he felt along the edge of the familiar truck bed. The torn dirty fingers were street thin and as sensitive as a surgeon or concert pianist. The man *felt* his way as much as he saw his way. Everything was a touchstone in his life as routine ruled his being.

Quietly, Hooker cajoled him forward. "I'm not getting out, Peter. I just need my other foot here in the door," as he moved his foot. In the small fisheye mirror he had installed months before on the inside of the door, he saw the shadow of a man hesitate, so Hooker offered out the routine cigarette. He saw the shadow resume, and a lighter colored patch of smoke snaked out and the cigarette was gone from Hooker's hand.

"Peter?"

"Hooker?" the night-shaded smoke whispered back as the cigarette was slowly passed directly under the man's nose.

"I need to talk to the Mouse."

Silence.

"Peter?" Hooker restarted the slow dance with the street urchin grown old.

A moment of silence then the whisper. "Hooker?"

"Peter, I need to talk to the Mouse. Do you know where she is?"

The man was in conflict now and it upset his world. "The… the Mou… Mouse isn't very… very nice." Peter and the Mouse had history, and Hooker knew that, but it was why he knew that Peter would know where the Mouse was at all times, just to avoid her.

"Peter, I know she isn't very nice to you. Peter, I know that, but I have to talk to her. I have to see her. Peter, I need her help."

"Hoo… Hook… you need help?"

Hooker was amazed that the deranged street waste was actually grasping the concept. "Yes, Peter, I need help. Help that only the Mouse can help me with." He let that concept rest a moment.

"The… the rock." He stumbled. "The rock."

Hooker thought about what rocks, and which one could be *the* one. "You mean the rock near the big church, Peter, or the one between the college and the stream?"

The mist looked back toward his safety zone of the dark, "Hoo… Hooker?" He was torn between his friendship and his need to be only a part of the fabric of night—friend or flight.

"The church or the stream, Peter, and then you can go." Hooker watched the mirror.

The words choked in his mouth, "The stream…"And the mist was a vapor and the vapor was air.

Hooker slowly pulled his feet in closing the door, looked at the kid, shook his head scowling, and shooed the pack of cigarettes to be put back in the glove box. Turning the key, he listened to the turbo turn as the starter whined up to speed until he hit the start button firing the glow plug that ignited the monster engine into life. Thinking about the rock and the stream, he absently stuck the truck in seventh gear and rolled out of the driveway, heading south on Winchester Boulevard toward the back-way into the Almaden Valley.

Shifting up into tenth, he looked over at the kid who had a look on his face as if he wanted answers but was afraid to ask. “Peter?”

The kid nodded. “He’s not all there, is he?”

Hooker had to think about that, and he wondered if Peter had ever been *all there*, but maybe in another time or place with people that cared for him. Hooker thought that he would like to believe that—that at one time, life was better for the man that now walked the streets at night dressed in only rags. “No, no, he’s not.” He thought about what Peter would occasionally say. “But some days, he has more.”

They rode along in silence, each man thinking about his own realities. The asphalt drummed against the tires as the lights clicked by and the gears changed up and down as the night wore on.

Half way down the long boulevard, Hooker glanced over at his passenger. “A cop, eh?”

The kid nodded absently. “If I could.”

Hooker thought about it as he shifted down approaching a flashing signal light. To his right he could see headlights coming, and he knew they had a flashing yellow, so he eased on the brakes and dropped the truck into the lower ranges, but not choosing a specific gear, he just let it drift. A little white Toyota wandered across the midnight intersection, and the driver turned and looked at the large truck slowly rumbling his way still a hundred feet or more away. Hooker could see the guy's eyes get larger and his mouth make an "O" of surprise. Even from the nearly half a block away, Hooker could plainly see the man's face. *So why couldn't I see the shooter's face from the same distance away?*

Hooker glided across the intersection and looked down the street as he watched the white square box of the Toyota become just a patch of light in the dark of the night. Something about that square bothered him, something about *something* that someone had said. The big truck had almost glided to a stop before the kid dug Hooker out of his thoughts with a short stage cough.

Embarrassed, Hooker glanced at the kid. "Umm, sorry. I was just thinking, I guess." He jammed the shift into eighth gear and ramped up the speed. As he swiftly passed through the next four gears, he continued to sort through the various things he knew… or didn't know.

"Can I ask a question?"

Hooker looked over at the kid, stunned that he had initiated conversation. "Sure, any time."

"Everyone we have run into today has asked you the same thing, everyone."

"Yeah. So what's the question?"

"What is it with everyone and the name Squirt?"

Hooker looked at him and started to laugh.

"I'm serious," the kid whined. "Every single one of them—we walk up and they asked you 'What's with the squirt?'"

This made Hooker laugh even more. It was so pitiful it was hilarious, and it became funnier because the more Hooker thought about it, the more he couldn't explain it because he was laughing. Finally, he pulled the truck over, and got out to take a walk. Finally, the kid slid down from the cab and joined him.

Hooker stood on the edge of the hill looking northeast across the lower southern half of San Jose. The twinkling lights represented all the people who were snug in their beds, peacefully sleeping, and staying out of Hooker's way. It was a dark bucolic scene that Hooker never got tired of. Without looking at the kid, for fear he would just start laughing again, he told him that the word 'Squirt' was more of a term for the new guy, instead of a name. The 'Squirt' in a patrol car was the newbie, except the term FNG wasn't for nice company, especially as there were more new officers that were female, so the term Squirt, meaning the small guy on the pecking order was more acceptable.

"So, are we good now?"

The kid hung his head. "Yeah, we're good."

"Ok, then, because we need to fly like the wind. We're late, Squirt!" Hooker reached out, tousled the kid's hair, and jumped back as the big white mitten waved threateningly. Sobering, Hooker thought about the kid and what it must be like to be outside of the know, only looking at the curtain, and never getting to sit in the theater and seeing the show, even though he bought the ticket. He looked at the kid. "Sometime when we have time, I'll tell you about Peter."

Hooker looked at his watch as he ran the truck up

through the ninth gear. 12:38—perfect. Reaching back behind his head, he grabbed the microphone and keyed the mic as he brought it past his face. “Sweets, you got your ears on?” He reached down with the mic in his hand and pulled the shifter out of twelfth gear into neutral, double clutched and shifted the transfer case from second to third, clutched again as he revved the engine, and pushed the main up into thirteenth gear as the radio squawked.

“Danny, Hooker. Sweets is OTA (on the air).” The voice could have been a professional DJ as well, but Hooker knew that Danny was the kind of guy that had only about seventy words a day in him. They hit that limit, and that is all you’ll get out of him until the next day.

Hooker thought about it for a moment, and then keyed the mic. “Danny, I’m about five out from Manny and Stella’s place. So have Sweets call me there. But first, the question is ‘Who dresses in all black?’ You got that? Who dresses in all black? Have him call me at Manny’s.” He let go of the microphone and waited. It wasn’t that Danny was dumb, far from it. It just took him time to process things back into words.

“Four,” came back the reply. Hooker knew that Danny hadn’t ‘swallowed’ the ‘ten’ that should be in front of the four, but that it was just Danny’s shorthand.

“Thanks, Danny. Dolly, I know you heard that, I’ll be 10-7 in two.” He re-hung the mic as the radio clicked twice. Some nights Dolly was as talkative as Danny was, but he was surprised that she didn’t remind him to come get his *mangy partner.* But he was pulling up the hill, and started working down through the gears, before he remembered to actuate the mufflers, which were actually just a set of baffled chambers that he could divert the exhaust through, therefore quieting the thunder from the giant engine.

As the two men were climbing out of the truck, the radio squawked, "Hooker, don't forget that you left a demanding package of mange lying around here." Hooker laughed and closed the door, then opened it back up and reached up to push the lock button down. He looked over and saw that the kid had remembered, too. *There might be some hope for him yet,* Hooker thought as he headed for the house and the kid followed.

17

"Sweets, honey, I just heard the truck pull up. So let me put Manny on. You two can brainstorm while I go hug my baby." She nodded and listened. "I love you too, baby, here's Manny." As she handed her husband the phone she kissed him on the top of his head.

"Sweets!" Manny bellowed. "It's been way too long since you boys brought your mother out for Sunday dinner. Stella is home now, so we won't take no for an answer."

Stella chided, "Manny, he's blind, not deaf." As she reached the front door, she called back, "She can bring desert, anything she wants to dream up." The door opened, and she was rushing across the plaza for the front gate.

"Yeah, that's what she said, anything Tilly wants to dream up," he laughed. "I for one hope she dreams in raspberry and chocolate, they're kosher, you know. Well, in this house at least." He smiled as he missed the free loving energy that Stella always brought to the house or wherever she was.

"We'll be there, and I'll make Danny wash the car, so it doesn't stink up the neighborhood." Sweets' voice oozed through the phone. "But listen, my man, I've got to hop out for a moment and spin up another record. I wish I were throwing down rock. I could spin out that Iron Butterfly and go for a walk in the park, and be right back."

Manny leaned back into the wheelchair as the country music came on the line as the hold music. He thought about how different his life had turned out from what he had thought it would be as the only Jewish boy growing up in a cow town in Montana. His father was the government appointed doctor for the Indian reservation, and by proxy the only doctor in the small town.

His father had been a joyous man who wasn't what anyone would have called a devoutly religious man, except that he loved his holiday confections. Like Stella, his mother was an amazing cook, and could care less about keeping kosher except when their parents would come to stay. She would do crazy things, like set up a kitchen in the ranch's guesthouse, and then run back and forth to serve the dinner. Finally one year when both sets of parents were visiting for Passover, and they sat down for the Seder dinner, his mother's father-in-law had asked his mother for a large glass of her buttermilk that he had heard so much about. Then her father, looking at the meat, said that sounded splendid and that it would help settle the whiskey he planned to have later with a nice cigar.

Manny chuckled to himself thinking that just might have been the last strictly kosher dinner he would have had, until he married his Stella. She was the only woman who could cook kosher so good that even a cowboy would ask for seconds.

Outside, Stella stood in the gate under the light with

her arms akimbo as she watched with a mother hawk's set of eyes the young man who had become so special in their lives. She thought back to that night that Hooker had been the knight in shining armor for her and her best friend, Claire in the middle of the night on Christmas morning. As she watched, the two men climbed out of the truck and lock it up. Hooker called softly for the new kid to do something on that side of the truck.

Finally, they started across the front yard. "This must be the squirt," she called.

"Yes, ma'am." The kid didn't hesitate to answer. "The fun new guy."

Stella laughed and shook her head. "Oh good lord, you've already spent too much time with Hooker." She grabbed Hooker and squeezed as if she were afraid to let go. "You weren't hit anywhere, were you?" She nuzzled in his neck so the Squirt couldn't hear her being a baby or a fussing mother.

"No, ma'am, but I can't say the same for Mae. She might need some new glass, and some touch-up paint." He nuzzled back, still hugging the zaftig woman with the bottle blonde hair.

She pushed him back, more to get a good look at him but also to tease. "I'm hugging you and you're talking about that other woman. I never…" Turning to the kid, she put her arms out and moved a large-chested hug on the much confused and embarrassed boy. "It's good to meet you, Johnny. Don't let my Hooker work you too hard, you hear?"

The kid felt sort of strange about the older woman, but it did make his tummy feel good, as well as deeper inside where he hadn't been touched for a long time.

Sensing his unease, she turned and hooked her arm in both men's arms, and started through the gate. "Sweets is on the phone, and they will be here for Sunday supper, and so will you two." The matter was settled before the subject was discussed. Hooker smiled deeply that *his* Stella was home.

They busted through the front door bubbling with laughter. "Just a minute, Sweets. They just walked in." Manny covered the phone as he barked, "Hooker! Sweets is waiting."

Hooker strode into the kitchen, taking the phone, "Where you at, Sweets?"

Stunned, Sweets was at a loss for words for a second, "I'm… I'm at work. Where did you think I was?" Hooker could hear the consternation in the man's voice at being thrown for a loop by a slang usage that he never heard from Hooker. Hooker smiled at getting the older friend.

"Now you know why I hate that greeting. It just sounds stupid." The two laughed in agreement.

"Danny told me what you were thinking. But man, you forget I told you about the figure being all in black." Hooker could hear the edge of indignation creeping into Sweets voice. "But I know you remembered, but had something else in mind."

"Very perceptive, my good brother, very perceptive." Hooker eased over the ruffled feathers. "And with that, I'm assuming you came up with a list?"

"The man is hot tonight. But I have to jump out and do some work with our sponsors for a bit and earn our keep, so I'll call you back in about fifteen or twenty minutes," and hung up with no more dismissal. Hooker, used to the working ways of Sweets, hung up the phone without thinking anything more.

Turning, he found the soft brown eyes of Stella boring into his soul through his eyes. "You know, Stella, you're just a bit creepy when you do that to me."

Manny laughed from the archway as he rolled into the sunroom. "Hah, try being married to her and rolling over in the middle of the night, only to find out she wants something." He picked up the TV remote control. "Go ahead, and ask her what she wants… if you have the guts."

The object of his derision, and his undying affection, slid her eyes sideways as the lids lowered to the hooded eyes of a hunter. She harrumphed as she slid her eyes back to Hooker, quietly starting to confide in him, and then seeing Johnny, she stopped. "Squirt, why don't you go watch a little television with the cranky old man. It'll probably do you both some good."

The kid knew when it was in his best interest to become vapor, and in the clearing wisps of his presence, Stella turned her attention to Hooker. Putting her hands on his shoulders, she moved in closer. "I just wanted to hear from you that you were all right. I don't just take Manny's word for things. He's still a cop. Even though they took the man off the force, the macho stuff is still in his belly, and they will never be able to pull the detective badge out of his pants—it's attached." She smirked at her slightly crude joke.

"I'm fine, Stell," nodding his head. "Really, I'm OK. Well, other than I have a kid to drag around for a while." He rolled his eyes with a little too much drama.

"Yah, and Squirt is another thing." She looked with a sudden hardness in her face. "Really? Putting a fork through a kid's hand?" The fact that the two sisters talked about everything had stopped surprising Hooker a long time ago.

"It wasn't all the way." He shrugged. "Just most of the way." His face looked up at her from a sideways boyish half smile that showed he knew that punishment would come, but knew it would be bearable and just maybe he could weasel out of it.

Her finger flashed up into his face as her nose came within two inches of his. Her whisper had bite as well as bark. "Don't you dare try to give me those big weaseling green eyes. This time it won't work." She poked his chest, driving home the guilt that she had no reason to inflict. "You had better pay for his doctor bills!" she whipped around to the sink. "Doing some foolish street punk thing like that. What were you thinking?"

He opened his mouth, and she jumped right back into his face with finger and all. "Shut it." She glared hard, and a lesser man would have wet himself. "Anything you thought you were going to say, you better think about for a day or so."

The phone rang and Manny picked it up in the sunroom as Stella just stood with silent eyes locked on her knight in shining armor, and the child they never had. Every bit of motherhood was being used up in heaps and loads far beyond mortal woman, and Hooker was the beneficiary and he knew it.

"Hooker!" Manny called.

She poked her finger one last time for emphasis and

let him go. Hooker slid from between the stone island and an even harder object.

"Yeah, Manny?" he asked as he walked into the sunroom. The kid was staring at Manny who was drained of all color and still listening as he wrote on one of the legal pads that were always within reach of Manny, as well as not one but three pens in his shirt pocket, and even his t-shirts were pocketed. Hooker thought, *once a detective, always a detective—it's attached.*

"OK, here's Hooker," he said, handing over the phone. "It's Captain Davis."

"Yeah, Captain, what can I do for you?"

"Hooker, we have another officer down. I want you to handle the tow, but you're going to need a flatbed."

"I don't have one, but I can get one. Where's it at?" The officer told him as he looked and saw that Manny already had it written down.

"I need you to bring Manny out with you, can you do that, or should I send a patrol car?"

"No, I can handle that." He looked at the small man in the chair. "But why Manny?"

"He knows more about what we're up against. Just bring him and fast. This one is going to be hard to keep a lid on."

"We're in the truck, sir." Hanging up and then picking the phone back up again, and dialing a number from memory, he turned to Manny. "You need anything else?" The man nodded and headed into his office that he almost never used anymore.

From the office, he called out, "Hey Squirt, can you give me a hand in here?" The kid was last night's vapor as he reappeared on the way to a place he was needed.

The ringing on the other end of the phone stopped and a groggy voice answered. “Si, this is Jose.”

Hooker’s head snapped around at the sound of the older Garcia answering. “Jesus, Joe! You sound like shit.”

“Miguel is in worse condition. He’s been throwing up since last night. Hooker, I tell him to go to the medico, but he is one giant pendejo. What I gonna do with such a stupid brother?” The older brother was now starting to sound almost alive. “What you call for, Hooker? It’s the middle of the night, you know? Not every peoples be a vampire like you.”

“Joe,” Hooker didn’t know how to phrase his request. “I need a flatbed right now.”

“You no have one, senor.”

“Joe, I know that. You didn’t get this call, but I’m going to give you the whole tamale. But I don’t know where the tow is going, and you probably never saw it, but I need your ass up here, and don’t worry about a ticket. There isn’t a cop between you and this address, trust me.”

“Where you need it, man?”

Hooker gave him the address and then told him what was there. The man gave a low whistle and told him fifteen minutes. Hooker hung up knowing the man lied because with his trucks, it would take him at least thirty, and the clock was ticking.

Walking out into the entry vestibule he called for Manny and the man rolled out of the office. “Hey, Squirt. There are those two black bags in there, too. Can you go place them… not throw them like Hooker would, into the back of the truck?”

The kid slid by confidently. “Sure, Manny.” Then he saw the *bags*. “Do you have dead bodies in these coffins?” He started lifting the large black crime scene bags.

Hooker glanced in and saw the bags. “Good gosh, Manny, I thought they took those away from you when you got your ticket clipped.”

“Shut up!” the man barked. “The less you see and know, the better.”

Stella, the guardian, stood by the door and kissed each on the top of the head or cheek as it was presented in passing. As Hooker followed up the rear, she rolled her eyes and hissed. “Retired my aunt Sarah’s behind!” She kissed his cheek. “You’re still on my shit list, but you watch out for the old battle axe. I still might want to have him around.”

“You’ve got it. Don’t wait up.”

She stood stoic in the doorway watching the three traverse the courtyard as the watery lights cast giant shadows along the walls. Four decades of marriage had tempered her steel, but only that which was visible on the outside. The young girl, quaking on the inside was about to go call her little sister who was busy pampering a battle-worn fur-ball on her chest, purring contently with the smell of pure white Albacore tuna on his breath. Spoiled would be too mild of a word when it came to the relationship of Box and Dolly.

The kid hoisted each of the large squared-off black ballistic nylon bags up onto the back of the truck. Each got its own grunt from the young man. Finished, he came around the right side of the truck to see Hooker with Manny slung over his shoulder, climbing up into the cabin.

As he flipped Manny down onto the seat, he looked down at the kid. "Go get up through my side and climb into the sleeper." Climbing down, he collapsed the wheelchair, placed it effortlessly on the back work-deck of the truck, and strapped it down with bungee cords.

Climbing into the cab, he looked at Manny in the passenger seat. "What do you think, back route or down Blossom Hill?" He fired up the monster and stuck it in seventh gear.

Manny leaned over and felt for the hidden switch he knew was there as he sighed. "Why waste time, lets fly." The flashing red and blue lights lit up the neighborhood as the truck began to roll down the road. "At this hour, you won't need a siren." He smiled over at the man he always thought of as *the kid,* but then looked back at the very young face of the new squirt.

The asphalt stretched out and was consumed by the giant Marmon truck and the oversized engine as it slung the monster down the road like a Corvette in a tail wind. The denizens of the night and drunks coming out of the closing bar of the steakhouse could see the yellow swirling lights on top and the alternating blue-red hiding in the oversized grill from many blocks away. The street itself was all but empty as the three men rolled across the bottom of the valley to the other side.

Reaching back, Hooker grabbed the mic and keyed in. "10-8."

The radio squelched and then cleared. "About time. You left the house seven and a half minutes ago." Hooker could hear the constant purring of Box through the radio.

"Box must not be massaging you in the right places,

because you sound like your panties are in a twist, Dolly. What's up?" Hooker was actually concerned.

"It's not going to be a pretty sight when you get out there, Hooker. You keep Squirt away from it, you hear?"

Hooker looked over at Manny, and the man nodded in understanding and agreement. Hooker just double clicked the mic and hung it back up. He cleared his mirrors and looked back over at Manny as he downshifted for the red light at Snell, but instead of stopping, merely turned right. "Was there something you were going to tell me?"

The former detective glanced and nodded back at the kid in the sleeper.

Hooker glanced back and gave Manny a look of exasperation. "He's a grown-up, for god sake. What can be so bad?"

Thinking for a moment, Manny finally spoke. "They think it was a flame thrower, both officers were killed, but it wasn't instant." The older man looked out the forward window. "Captain Davis said it likely won't be very pretty."

Hooker weighed what the man was saying and started downshifting to turn left. Across the broken fields a half mile away, Hooker could see the flashing and rotating lights of police and fire trucks. He manhandled the large truck around the corner and reached over and down under the dashboard to switch off the highly illegal red and blue lights.

Parking Lot B came up first as they slowed and made the turn into the giant lot where you could park four aircraft carriers while leaving a lot of room between the ships, or two thousand cars and trucks. But, at two o'clock in the morning, there were just police and fire department vehicles with one burned out car in the middle, all under one of the larger flood light poles that dotted the parking lot.

Hooker nosed in as close as he could without being intrusive. He'd leave that department for Manny to handle later. Unloading the wheelchair while the kid clambered out of the sleeper and unstrapped the large crime scene bags, Hooker climbed up to catch Manny as the man literally rolled out of the seat seven feet above the asphalt.

"Holy moly, Hooker. Any slower, and I'd be picking myself up off the grinder by myself."

"Here, let me put you back. This I want to see." Hooker gave just as he received the friendly caustic sarcasm from the man that he loved deeply, and who had been like a father or favorite uncle to him.

"Just try to get me in the chair without sticking the back-rest up my butt."

Hooker smudged a bad imitation of Mae West as he slowly lowered the older man—"Excuse me, but is this seat taken or just filled." The two shook with the bad old line that they relished anytime Hooker helped him with a transfer to his chair.

Hooker straightened to find an officer standing at a casual parade rest, waiting for the center of attention to be readied. "Officer Aligo, how good of you to join us." Hooker joked, but got no rise to levity from the usually humorous or near to humorous large Filipino.

"Sorry, Hooker, but there is no humor here tonight." Looking from the driver to his passenger, he asked, "Do you have everything you need, sir?"

"I think so, James. If you could help carry the bags, I think Squirt would appreciate it." As the officer started to turn to the bags, Manny cautioned, "But first I want the lay of the land. I take it that you were the first responder?" He caught himself. "I mean, of course, after the other two."

"Yes, sir. Basically, what you will see, other than some parts still with bits of fire still present, is exactly what I rolled up on."

"Did you deploy any fire extinguishers?"

"No, the small flames were already guttering, and I wanted the scene as uncontaminated as possible, sir." He looked over his shoulder, and thought aloud. "There was one thing, though."

"What?"

"While it was settling down, a round cooked off and punched a very large hole in the front windshield, sir."

"About the size of a dime?" Hooker injected.

The officer thought about it as he looked at his fingers. "No, but close, more like the size of a nickel or quarter."

Manny looked back at Hooker. "The close range would be also capturing the energy of the explosive wave. Therefore, I would expect it to be a little larger."

Hooker nodded. "That's why you have the higher pay grade."

Manny's head snapped back toward Hooker with his most 'nail them to the wall' look. Then turning back to the uniform, he asked, "Did you hear anything landing?"

"Dimes, sir. Marked them all, I think. How did you know?" His face became a mass of confusion.

Manny gave him a side-stare as he began to push

toward the scene that was stinking up the neighborhood like a luau gone horribly wrong. “It’s what I get paid the big bucks for.” Throwing a call in Johnny’s general direction, “Punjab, bags,” he rolled away, consummately taking command of the scene. “Officer Aligo, where’s my path in?”

The officer pointed out the two small cones, “Straight in to the driver’s door.”

As he cleared the vehicles and came to view the entire scene, he noted the small yellow cones on the asphalt. He thought a moment and spun the chair. “Officer Aligo?”

“Sir.” The man hustled over hauling one of the large heavy bags.

“How many dimes did you find?”

“Twelve.”

“Hmm…” Manny spun his chair back to look at the yellow cones standing like little soldiers. Something was wrong, and then he saw the pattern.

“Hooker?”

“Yeah, Manny, right here.”

“What is the farthest you have shot a dime load and hit anything?”

The young man looked at the officer of the law and hesitated only a moment. “When Betsy was Betsy Ross McWhole, it would be the day you and I shot that barn. That would be almost what, a hundred feet? But as she is now, about fifty or sixty feet at the most.”

“What if you shot it almost straight up and through a windshield?”

Hooker looked out across the parking lot and now understood what the little yellow cones were. “I would guess that there are probably one or two more dimes lying under those two cars and the fire truck."

Turning his chair back to the officer, he agreed. "My thinking exactly." Pointing to the three vehicles and a couple of others, he told the officer how to back them away from the scene. "Everyone is to be in latex gloves. I want no chance of getting someone's fingerprint or jelly donut leftovers. I want an officer on each tire, as the vehicle backs out in creep mode. I want four hands floating on those tires. If they feel or see a dime, they call a halt. We'll place the dime, and mark it, and then keep going. But in the end, I want all five of those vehicles backed off about one hundred feet."

"You've got it, sir." The officer took off jogging toward the cluster of other officers, both San Jose PD and CHP.

Soon the three stood watching a slow painful process unfold which, in the end, yielded four more dimes. Manny looked up at Hooker with a question on his face. Then looked back at the scene. "What's wrong here, Hooker?"

"Too many dimes, Manny, too many dimes." The young man stood slowly shaking his head trying to make it understand the evidence.

Johnny cleared his throat, and Hooker looked over jerking his head as if to ask what was on the kid's mind. The kid cleared his throat again. "Why is sixteen dimes too many?"

Hooker stared at the scene with his eyes twitching taking in the information more than they were swiveling with surveillance. Finally turning to the kid he asked, "Do you know anything about how a shotgun shell is put together?”

The kid nodded. “Yeah, kind of. There is a metal back end and plastic front. There is the powder and little BB’s in it.”

Hooker took over the simplistic explanation. “Once you put the powder in, you pack it with a small disk of felt, and then there is a thicker felt pad called the compression pad, and then a plastic cup with the shot in it. All of that has to sit at such a point that the top can get crimped over and formed into place.” The kid was nodding along, until Hooker added, “Take out the cup, and a standard two and three-quarter-inch shell only holds fourteen dimes, not sixteen,” as he extended his arm and waved it across the now expanded crime scene.

Manny was slowly rolling into the scene, yelling for the officer. “Aligo! Have them look for the wadding and plastic cup also. I seriously doubt that they’ll find any, but it’s worth a look.” As he rolled up to the side of the car and the open driver’s door, he viewed what he could of the interior. Everything appeared charred, but was really just smoke blackened. Manny’s nose was working overtime as once again he was back in the middle of what had been an inferno.

As he looked across the dashboard, his eyes stopped. Even if he had been a religious man, he would have stopped when his brain caught up to what the eyes were seeing. “Hooker?”

“Yeah, Manny?” Hooker called back from over a hundred feet away. “Got your back, you need your bag?”

“Come in slow, straight at me. Oh, yeah, and bring the smaller bag.” Manny was still focused on the interior, trying to make heads or tails of the object on the dashboard.

Hooker kneeled down to Manny's height. "What am I looking at?"

"Look along the dash for two things, one the condition, and two, what the hell is standing in the middle—because it sure as hell isn't a Virgin Mary."

Hooker studied the dashboard and its strange swirling of burn marks. Thinking about what could have caused the pattern, he also started putting himself in the place of the shooter turned fire bomber. He stood and looked at the almost untouched backseat. And other than the smoke damage, and secondary, the front seat was all but pristine.

"What do you see?" Manny, in educator mode, stirred the pot.

"When they pull the residuals, my guess is the dashboard was wiped down with gasoline, but why?"

"What is on the dash?"

Hooker now stepped around the man in the wheelchair and crouched in the doorway. He then stood over the windshield, and then walked around the car trying to get a better look but to no avail. Finally, he arrived back standing next to Manny, who handed him some rubber gloves and some stick swabs. "Go ahead and climb in, there is nothing on the seat or anything you might touch, but I want a swab of the residue just down from that object."

Hooker obeyed and climbed in. As he got close to the object, he could see what it was.

"It's the brass butt of a 12-gauge shell, isn't it?" Manny swore.

Hooker nodded.

"Get the swab, and then here is a bag."

Hooker poked at the remains of the shell and it moved. Taking the swab, he wiped it along the area just below the shell. Retracting the swabs into the protectors, he traded Manny for the baggie and removed the shell.

"How did you know it wasn't glued down?

Manny focused on writing the pertinent data on the containers and baggie they went in. "I didn't, but I know you would have found a way to give it to me."

Hooker climbed out of the car and handed the baggie to Manny, who slapped the prepared tape on it that sealed over the top. Slipping the baggie into the container in the one bag, he looked up, saying, "Are you up to this?"

Hooker just stared at him thinking a moment. "I saw my first dead body at fourteen, and my first dismemberment that same summer. Shake and bake, I didn't get until that nine-car in Blood Alley the next spring when IBM laid off all of those whack engineers who decided crossing the center line was better than going home to the wife and kids." He slowed the recitation of his resume in gore as he remembered whose parking lot they were standing in. "So, does anybody ever get to the point of being *up to it*?"

The man stared up at the angry young man from his wheelchair. Manny had forgotten just how much Hooker had seen and never brought home with him. Personally, he didn't know why the boy never suffered from nightmares. Only Stella knew that Manny, after six years off the force, still woke more nights than not in cold sweats that she had to wipe down with the towels that were always handy by the bed. He nodded, "Good point," and as he turned toward the back of the car, he caught sight of the young boy thirty feet away, standing ready with the other bag, the one he would need now. "Hooker?" he asked softly.

Hooker looked toward the kid. "Yeah, I know. I was thinking about that." He stepped in front of the wheelchair. "But there is something you might want to consider."

"What? He's a kid."

"Yes. But he's a confused kid who has never found a place to fit in. Today, he has busted his hump, and in his own way, managed to fit in." Hooker didn't know why he was riding to the kid's defense so hard, but he had decided that it really didn't matter, because the kid deserved a break, white mitten hand and all. "Besides, he thinks he wants to be a cop." Hooker's shoulders sagged with the weight of sharing something he didn't know if it was his to share.

Manny thought more about what he was seeing in Hooker, and then what he said. He turned and whistled, waving the kid forward. "Bring the bag. Watch where you walk, and follow where Hooker came in," he instructed the kid. "And walk slowly, for Christ's sake."

They watched as the kid performed an exact duplicate of Hooker's path and approach. Manny looked at Hooker, who just looked away so Manny couldn't see the growing smile of pride. The three moved to the rear of the car.

The two officer's bodies were draped with yellow tarps. Manny looked at the lumps and back at the trunk lid. He rolled close to the bumper and looked into the deep trunk where he saw the remains of two mangled five-gallon cans with blown off lids. Manny thought he knew what he was looking at, but wasn't sure. The paint on the inside of the trunk was blistered across the entire trunk-lid. There were no hot spots. The bottoms of the cans had been blown apart, most likely, Manny thought, by det-cord (detonation cord used as a fuse and igniter because it burned at 700 mph.) The cord probably was used to first cut the bottom off from the sides of the cans, creating a plunger. Then there would be a larger charge in the center of the can bottom to push both the can bottom and the contents out. A last trailing bit of the explosion would ignite what was probably home-made napalm as it hit the trunk lid and splashed out onto the two officers in a wave of sticky gelatinized gasoline that first robbed them of oxygen, then cremated them alive as they fell screaming in silence from the lack of air and their bodies melted from the extreme heat. Manny had seen it before as a liaison officer in a country known as Vietnam. Only, there it was called Foo Gas, and it came usually in fifty-five gallon drums instead of five-gallon cans.

"Squirt," he asked quietly. "Look on the top of the trunk lid. Don't touch it, just look." Manny turned to see the kid staring at the bodies under the tarps. "Johnny, I need you here with me now." The kid kind of shook. "Johnny!"

The kid snapped out of it, and turned toward Manny, "Sorry, I was just…" he looked back at the tarps. "They didn't know what hit them, did they?"

Manny's shoulders caved-in, ever so slightly. "No," he said sadly. "They had no idea what they were up against."

The kid, turning to the requested task, spat out almost

sub-vocal, “We really need to nail this asshole to the ice-house wall.” Looking at the top of the lid, he scanned the wide expanse of scorched and blistered paint. “What am I looking for?”

“What do you see?”

“It’s scorched.”

“How? In one spot, all over? Is it sunburned or seared like a steak on the Fourth of July? Look at it, and just tell me what you are seeing. Don’t tell me what you think you see.”

The kid backed off and looked at Manny for a moment as if he were crazy and could do some serious damage to a few million brain cells, and then he eased back over and started looking at the lid with a more critical eye.

“At first glance, it just looks burned all the way across, but then if you look at the top at an angle, you see that there are two areas that are kind of round, and the metal is a little more rippled, like it got more heat or something.”

“Good, Johnny, go on. Tell me about the colors.” He sat with his eyes closed, seeing through the kid’s eyes.

The rings are full black metal, there is no paint there, but there is like an outer ring that is white, like a chalk. Maybe the paint burned up and…”

“STOP!” snapped Manny. “Don’t do that.”

“Do what?” The kid was only a little defensive, and more wanting to do it right.

“Don’t think. Don’t conjecture about what could or couldn’t have possibly happened. Just tell me what you are seeing. OK?”

Hooker stepped over to the other side of the car and

looked at the lid, also.

"Ok," the kid resumed. "There is about a two inch ring of white chalky substance where the deformed metal ends."

"Good, that's good. Keep going."

"There are some small red areas, but they don't appear to have anything to do with the initial burn areas. In fact… just a moment." He leaned into the trunk before Manny could stop him. The kid looked up under the rear deck for a moment then stepped over and took the flashlight away from Manny and leaned back into the trunk's more intimate reaches up under the back panel. Looking about for a moment, he gave a grunt and withdrew, and handing the flashlight back to Manny, he said, "The red is from the iron oxide undercoating they primed it with." Pointing back into the trunk, he explained, "When they shoot the final color, they always skimp, and so the final paint doesn't really cover the primer."

Manny sat with his mouth open.

The kid was offended. "Hey, I know things, OK? I worked in a body shop for a short time, and they are always cutting corners." He stood with his arms somewhere between fists on his hips and fists in the air.

Manny held up both of his hands. "Peace, peace. No, I'm impressed. I would have never thought to look under there. How about you, Hooker?"

Hooker came around the edge of the car. "Hey, I'm sitting in your chair."

Manny considered the new information, and slowly spun his chair around. Looking at the slain officers and the trunk lid back and forth. "Guys, do me a favor and peel back the tarps, go easy though, they may be stuck to the burned flesh. But I want you to start from this end—feet first."

The remains, Hooker was thinking, because from about mid-thigh up, there wasn't enough left to call them corpses, were seared into a tableau of horror and surprise. "They must have died almost instantly," he sighed.

"One would hope." Ever professional, Manny leaned in close to look at the cremation.

Johnny stepped around the end of the car, careful not to touch anything and staring at the two still somewhat smoldering cenotaphs of a pair of cops who gave their all to protect and serve the citizens of San Jose. Gently he asked, "What am I looking at, Manny?"

The older detective looked up at the kid and saw that he was serious in his request. Nodding, he turned back to the evidence. Pointing to the thighs, he indicated the burned edges. "If this had been just gasoline, the splash would have at least taken the entire pants from the knees up. But what we have here is napalm. It's a gelatin and very sticky so where it landed is where it burned."

He looked back up at the kid. "What we probably have is homemade napalm, which is not much more than a bunch of Styrofoam or polystyrene mixed into gasoline. The gas melts the foam, but the foam changes the gas, and eventually, it thickens or gels until you have napalm." Seeing if the kid was following, and seeing that his eyes were clear, and his head was nodding, he continued. "The nasty thing about napalm is that the foam chemicals mixed with the gas form a hydrocarbon that burns much, much hotter than gas alone. In fact, gasoline doesn't burn, just the fumes. But with napalm, the heat quickly reaches an intensity that allows the liquid itself to ignite, and when that happens, the burning temperature turns left and goes straight up and burns at temperatures approaching five-thousand degrees. Because it is so sticky, it's very hard to get it off you," turning to indicate the former officers, "but these guys were ambushed, and I'm willing to bet a steak dinner at the Bold Knight that when the flaming mass came at them, they took a very large suck of air, drawing the flame right down into their lungs, searing off any oxygen exchange after that."

"They didn't even have a chance." The kid sagged.

"No, no, they didn't." Manny grimaced and turned back toward the kid. "It sucks, but that's kind of the way the job is. You get the test, and if you're lucky, you pass well enough to then learn the lesson."

They worked for another thirty minutes taking samples and lots of pictures, until the Medical Examiner showed up to take over. The ME that walked up to the perimeter was an old friend of Manny's, and he guided him down the already known pathway to the car.

They shook hands. "Hello, Frank. I bet they got you up from a sound sleep."

"Manny," the man grumped. "It was supposed to be my night off. They can't seem to find my understudy, for some reason." Looking about, he asked in the shorthand that comes with working close together for years. "Run it down, will you?"

"Two officers, my guess seeing the open door on the empty car, they come to investigate. They see the trunk lid cracked maybe an inch or so, and open it. Inside are two five-gallon cans full of napalm, and rigged with det-cord. Opening the lid, pulls that wire that triggers the mechanism. The napalm is ejected from the cans, straight up, hitting the lid and forcing it fully open. The napalm is ignited by now, and starting to hit temperature as it hits the stops on the lid and bounces out hitting the two officers. The initial strike is down the bronchial, searing the membrane into Saturday night's steak. They are dead standing at twelve-thirteen A.M."

The ME is still nodding as he follows the pattern as Manny describes it. "Um hum, yes, yes. How did you get the twelve-thirteen? Why not twelve-fifteen?"

"Because *that,*" pointing to the all metal dive watch on what was left of a wrist, "is when the guy's watch stopped."

The ME leaned over and examined the watch. Standing, he dusted off his hands. "I don't know why they even called me."

Manny turned to the Squirt. "Pull the small plastic box out of the smaller bag and give him the evidence, and give me the paperwork right beside it, would you please?" Turning to the ME as he pointed at the cops walking a grid, "Frank, those officers are looking for a 12-gauge shot cup, some dimes, and the wadding. I rather doubt that they will find the cup. I don't think he used one. There are sixteen dimes out there. But I'm very curious about the wadding. Let me know what you find. If you could call me later this morning, I'd like a full rundown. You have my phone number. Just so you know, I'll be running a board of my own at the house. I'd appreciate it if you would call me with any info before you kick it upstairs."

"Are you on the clock now, Manny?"

"No. Chet called, and this is personal," he jerked his head in Hooker's direction. "They shot at my boy—twice." He started rolling around toward the pathway. "Bags, boys. We're going home. We still have a beating from Stella coming. I smelt pineapple upside down cake earlier."

Hooker put the bag down on the working bed of the truck, and turned to the kid. "Strap these down, Squirt, and if you're feeling strong, you can stow Manny and strap his chair down, too." Turning to Manny, "I need to go arrange things with Jose, and I'll be back in a few minutes. Don't do anything stupid while I'm gone." He reached into the cab and grabbed his leather jacket against the chill of the early morning air.

Manny watched as the young man walked away like the man he had become. Manny thought about the night that he and Stella had met such a young kid. For a Jewish couple, it had been quite the Christmas present, even though they hadn't known it at the time; but then, a lot can change in a decade or so. He just shook his head and looked over at the new kid. Maybe not so fresh scrubbed, but he definitely had that hot and eager look in his eye.

"Don't even think about it, Squirt. I'd crush you like a June bug on a two-step line dance floor in Gilroy on a Saturday night." The two laughed at the funny saying, but more as a relief from the horror that they had just spent nearly three hours with. "I've got to say, kid, you handled yourself well out there. There are plenty of rookie cops, and some older ones too, that see something like that and just start puking their last Sunday's dinner all over the crime scene." He nodded and watched the kid turn darker in the dark, but Manny knew that the kid could tell that he wasn't just blowing smoke up his skirt. The kid really did have potential.

"So, are you going to tell me about that hand, or do I have to have Stella beat it out of you?"

The kid passed the now dirty gauze mitten back around behind him, and the night darkened even a shade deeper around his ears. "It's nothing," he lied quietly.

Manny looked at him for a full minute, and when he realized the story wasn't forthcoming, he looked away where Hooker was arranging the tow with the flatbed truck. "That's OK. When we get home, I'll just loan Stella my belt, and she can beat the story out of you." He could feel the horror in the kid's eyes on the back of his neck and smiled inwardly as he watched Hooker direct the action that needed to happen in scraping up the mess.

Hooker pointed out the alignment for getting the car. "We'll have to use the inflate bladder to get the back part up high enough to slide the dolly under those rims." He looked at the melted tires, and turned back to the large Mexican-American with graying at the one temple where he had been hit by a wreck recovery gone bad. Other than that, he was a handsome man, if you liked gold teeth. "Do you have some heavy plastic or Visqueen? Because we're going to want to line those tires, or you'll never get that gooey rubber off your dolly."

"My dolly?" The man slurred in one of his favorite movie lines… "We don't need no stinking dollies!"

"OK," Hooker pointed out, "My dolly. And I don't want it all covered with fung." He made a face at the larger driver. "But my point is, the ass-end of the car is toast, so you can't jerk from it, or it would fall apart, and if you snatch from the front, the car will just break up, and there goes the crime scene, and then we're both out of business. So we have to dolly the butt, and pull the dolly from the front. Comprende, amigo?"

"Si, si, si, si." The man nodded then jerked his head as he saw the cop approaching.

Hooker turned. "Ready for us, Aligo?"

"About five minutes. The ME is done, but we need to figure out how to scoop the bodies and still have them hold together."

"Sure, no problem." Hooker nodded as the officer strode off to arrange a few last details on his crime scene, like the three news reporters who had shown up in the last thirty minutes.

Turning back to the larger Garcia brother, he finished going over where the tow would go, and how to deliver it and who got the bill. "The Captain requested it, and he knows what the bill should be, so don't be bashful, but don't slam them either, or I'll come after you." Hooker hiked up his left eyebrow for emphasis, and the driver got the message.

"No problem, jefe, I do the tow, drop it and bill it. No hard skin on my back, but what about the dollies?"

"Don't worry. I'll pick them up tomorr…" Hooker caught himself and looked at his watch, "…later today. Don't even bother with them, because they will need the bladder to get them off anyway. So I'll just do it all at once." Turning toward his truck, he waved at the officer who was circling his hand in the air for the sign to circle the wagons and get things done. Dancing backwards, he pointed at the burned out hulk. "Go ahead and back into it for a front snatch, and we'll be right over with the dollies and bladder." He then turned and jogged for the giant truck, and smiled at seeing Manny still sitting in his chair. He chuckled and thought *smart kid.*

As the first pink tinged the grey of the last night air, the tall nose of the big truck followed the flatbed truck up to Blossom Hill. Then as the smaller truck continued to the forensic lab's barn of a garage, Hooker flicked his blinkers, and turned left across the south end of the valley and the smell of rich loam soil turned to plant beans and strawberries. Hooker always thought that he had the best territory in the South Bay area basin. Just along Blossom Hill Boulevard itself, there were orange, apple, and cherry orchards, and then there were the back reaches that stretched down through San Martine, and onto the Garlic Capital of the world, Gilroy. And if that wasn't enough food, there were truck farms that ran all the way down to King City until they stopped at the great expanse of Fort Hunter Leggett.

The sun was searing the frothy wisps of clouds as Hooker pulled Manny out of the truck, and they all headed toward the end of the very long day that felt more like a week. Even the woman, standing with arms akimbo in the front gate doors, would not have a shot at them until about three pm and a pot or two of coffee.

18

The phone wouldn't stop ringing. The answering machine should have picked up, or at least some other person in the house, but the phone kept ringing. Then it stopped. Silence. Then broken again by the jangling ring of the phone that continued.

Hooker didn't care what time it was, but he felt like someone on the other end of the phone needed a piece of his mind. Rolling out of bed, he stuck his stocking feet in the boots captured at the side of the bed by his pants legs. Grabbing the belt, he pulled them up and buttoned the fly as he expanded his eyes to make them focus.

Shuffling across the room, he opened the door that allowed the strong midday sun into the darkened room, and semi blinding him as he made his way to the still incessantly ringing phone. Waking up amicable was not one of Hooker's strong suits. "Hello," he answered curtly.

"Hello, princess," the voice oozed.

"Oh, hi, Willie."

"My, we are so chipper this morning. Did you have a

lousy night last night?"

"Yeah, we were out on a burn job till sun-up. What do you need?" He started looking around for a note or something that would explain Stella or Manny not answering their phone. Distracted, he missed his uncle's statement. "Wait. What did you say?"

"I said it was all over the front page of the Star this morning. Imagine my shock to see not only you, but also Manny at a crime scene. I thought that old fart retired and got a life."

"At seventy-four, I would be careful who you called 'old', you old fart."

"Stop it. I'm only seventy… one." The silence was palatable as Willie waited for a reassuring compliment that he all too well knew wasn't coming. "Speaking of the child, why isn't he answering his phone?"

"I don't know, Willie. Stella came home last night, then we rolled on the fire call… what does it say in the paper?"

"Oh, plenty, but you know newspapers. They always get things wrong then they have to retract them the next day, except it takes them a week. But they think they are still right, until they say their wrong, so they put that off as long as they…"

"Willie!" Hooker grabbed his forehead with his whole hand in an effort to stop the coming headache. He loved his uncle dearly, but there were days…

Quieter and calmer he asked the now silent phone, "Willie, what does the paper say?"

"Well," ignoring being yelled at, "Hmm… responded to a call from security… blah, blah, blah… two officers…

found a 1968 Coupe de Ville… anda, anda… oh, here it is, and it appeared a fire bomb killed the two officers on contact." Hooker could hear the man put the paper down in quiet exasperation. He asked softly, "Hooker, is it true? About two officers killed?"

Hooker sunk against the kitchen island and the cold granite felt good across his upper buttocks. He sighed. "Yeah, Willie. Unfortunately, this time they got it right." The headache wasn't going to stop today. "Did it say anything about them finding anything else?"

"Oh, yeah, they are calling him the 'Dime-Load Killer'."

"Oh, Christ on a crutch—who is?" Hooker looked out the window into the courtyard.

"The Star, silly," the man exclaimed. "The police would never use such a stupid name."

As his uncle had broken him of swearing out loud, Hooker swore under his breath.

"I heard that, Hooker. That will be a nickel in the jar when you get home, you naughty boy."

Hooker rolled his eyes. "Anything else, Willie? I've got to get some more sleep."

"No, just checking in. And letting you know about the article."

"Great, thanks." He started to hang up, and then remembered. "Hey, Willie, would you make up the bed in the guest room, please?"

"Male or female?"

"What?"

"Is our guest a male or a female?"

"What's it matter what sex the person is?"

"It matters, trust me. If it's a female, I need to use the nice sheets and some throw pillows. If it's just one of your tow truck buddies whose wife threw him out for being drunk or farting in the fresh sheets…"

"Male."

"Who-ooo?" he sing-songed tauntingly at Hooker.

"My new employee, and be straight with him, he's only eighteen, I think."

"Spoil sport. When are you coming home?"

Sniffing his t-shirt and twisting his face up. "Sooner than you think."

"OK, Big Stuff, I'll make up the guest bed and lay out some towels and such. See you later."

"Bye." Hooker placed the phone in the cradle. Now it was really bugging him that nobody was there, and no note.

As he shuffled back toward his room, he noticed Manny's office door was closed. He opened it quietly and saw why Manny hadn't answered the phone. He couldn't hear it. The man sat in his wheel chair staring at two large pin boards with photos and cards tacked to them. On his head was a pair of commercial recording headphones that covered most of each side of his head. Hooker looked at the twelve-inch commercial reel-to-reel tape deck Sweets had gotten for him years before, slowly turning. Hooker's guess was Vivaldi or Brahms.

Manny noticed a shift in the light and turned his chair around, and raising the headphones to the top of his head so he could hear Hooker. "Stella went to the grocery to restock the fridge and should be back soon. The kid is in the sunroom, and when I last checked on him, he was curled around Box."

Hooker snapped his fingers and silently swore. "Bean burritos on a stick!"

"It's OK. Dolly figured we were coming straight home and dropped him off around seven this morning, but he probably won't be talking to you for a few days, so you may as well leave him here for Stella to chase around, or vice-versa."

Hooker was looking at the boards. "When did you do all of this?" Then he realized. "You haven't been to bed at all, have you?"

Manny waved the back of his hand. "Blah, sleep is overrated."

Hooker yawned, and thought about the time. "Well, I'm not as old, so I need more sleep. Wake me about two or so, would you?"

"Sure," the detective was already turned around and looking at his board. Vivaldi softly filtered from the top of his head.

Hooker shuffled back to his dark chamber, and closed out the light. Dropping his pants down around his boots, he slipped out of the boots and fell back into the bed.

Not working set hours and being on-call 24/7 had put craters the size of New Jersey in his internal circadian clock, but did make it easy to drop into a deep sleep before his wavy head of hair hit the pillow. This time was no exception. The only thing that caused a few seconds hesitation was the tiny spot of white amongst the complete background of black. The white had meaning, and a part of Hooker knew he knew what that was.

But old habits took over, and Hooker was dead to the

world until a shotgun blast would rip his sleep apart a few hours later.

19

The shotgun blasts were silent and in very slow motion. Hooker woke because of too many. When they should have stopped at five or six, they kept exploding out of the dark from a light colored car. Shotgun flash after shotgun flash silently ripped through the dark of night, and then the last one made sound—the sound of terracotta plates landing on a granite island.

Hooker rolled over and looked at blurry red numbers that made no sense. There were three blobs of red, and he could have sworn that when he had laid down, a few moments before, there were four. The light tap on the door confirmed that there were really three and it was two in the afternoon.

"Thanks, Stella," he mumbled, wondering if he had really even said that.

The ocean waves roared in his head and ears as he slung his legs over the edge of the bed and sat up with his eyes closed. Washing his face and eyes with his palms, he raised erect and silently stumbled toward his bathroom. Flicking on the shower faucet, he walked past and sat on the throne while the water warmed up, trying to remember what it was that was so important when he lay down. The fog was thick and he was unsuccessful. Flushing, he counted to five and got up, grabbing a towel as he shuffled into the shower room that was big enough for a party of four to eight, or a caretaker and a wheelchair.

Hooker sat on the cedar bench under the water as he filled the wooden bucket with some water, squirted liquid Castile soap into the bucket, and stirred it with the long handled brush. Absently, he thought of the design features that Manny and Estelle had incorporated into their dream home… back when Manny was a virile police detective with his legs working under him. Two months, seventeen days and three hours remained until his retirement. No one ever thinks that they will be the one needing extra wide doors or bathrooms large enough for a wheelchair and a caregiver — no one. But it had not been very long after they had finally moved out of the trailer at the bottom of the driveway and into the house, when a drug bust gone wrong left Manny in the wheelchair that he had only thought his father would need. Forty-three weeks later, Manny had left the hospital for the first of five times over the next two years, and came home to a loving, carefully thought out home that would be fully supportive of his needs. Life is funny that way sometimes.

Starting with his feet, he began to scrub his entire body with the Japanese scrubbing brush. He chuckled as he wondered how it now seemed so natural for him to sit in a Jewish couple's home that was built like a Mexican hacienda, taking a shower in this huge room, scrubbing down with a traditional Japanese cleaning tool. It is so natural to adapt to things that are outside of our nature, and in so adapting, making them our nature. Even though people on the outside make assumptions about only what they see on the surface, like the neighbor across the street for years assumed that Manny and Estelle were Mexicans, he was surprised when Stella whipped up some killer latkes and kugel after they finished the building and held an open house that first Christmas. Maybe it was Manny's Italian name of Romero that threw them off.

Hooker smirked under the foaming head of bubbles and then his hand froze on the handle of the water control. The deck of information and conversations over the last few days suddenly shuffled, and Hooker's dealt hand was a full house flush of black knaves.

The chill that ran down his spine had nothing to do with the hot water now flooding over his head, and then a flash as he rinsed his body: he knew who the ninja in black was… or could be.

Grabbing the large bath sheet, flipping the water lever off, Hooker toweled down as he stepped over to the door and yelled for Manny. The clock was now ticking and a very large train wreck was headed toward San Jose. "Manny!"

"Coming, I said," as he wheeled out of the office toward the glassed hall down the guest wing.

Hooker pulled his pants up, ignoring their four-day filth on his clean skin. Grabbing his t-shirt, he caught a strong whiff of his odor, once again wishing he packed a small bag of spares in the truck.

The wheelchair appeared in the doorway. "What?" The headphones hung about his neck impotently as the wire and jack-plug dangled down his chest to his lap.

"Sweets said ninjas wear all black. You said they make napalm different ways, but you thought our napalm smelled like the kind used in Foo Gas." Hooker was pounding out the words to match his racing heart, "A dollar sixty in dimes… The dimes are the only coin that fits in the shotgun. It's not about the dimes. It's about how many. We know only fourteen fit in a cup, but they found sixteen and no cup."

The man looked at him with stone hard eyes, the mind running faster than the eyes could keep up. Hooker knew the look was one not of stupidity but just the opposite. "So… ?"

Hooker jammed the bottom of the starched t-shirt into his jeans. "So, if the killer uses sixteen, the carrier for the dimes is specially adapted. The focus is on sixteen for some reason, not the dimes."

Manny's mind was now catching up and running at top detective level. "Or maybe, it is about the dimes, *and* how many."

Stella called from the kitchen. "If you boys don't come now, I'm giving it to Box and the Squirt."

All of a sudden, hunger overtook Hooker and Manny at the same time and they moved to the kitchen, both lost in thought. Manny had long ago taught Hooker the power of pushing out thoughts to a group and watch for the answers that take shape from the collective. He could never imagine what kind of collective group Hooker could or would create. Sometimes the kid flat-out amazed him.

As the large terracotta dishes sat in front of the four humans and one content cat in Manny's lap, Johnny tippy-toed into the idea pool. "So, if the message is about the dimes and how many, could the dates or mint mark have any meaning, too?"

"Sure," mused Manny as he morphed into teaching mode. "Let's say you were killing people who did you wrong in 1970. So to get your message across, but you are the only one who understands the message, you load the rounds full of 1970 dimes. Also, let's say this happened in Philadelphia, so you use all dimes that are minted in Philadelphia in 1970."

Hooker sat looking in the coffee mug only inches away from his mouth. Then looking up, he furrowed his brow and looked over at Manny. "Do we know if the dates or mint are all the same?" His eyebrows raised and his eyes rolled. "I mean it is a pretty 'out there' kind of idea."

Manny just sat and stared at Hooker.

Finally, Hooker asked, "What?" shoving his hand out palm up.

Manny just stared, and then said quietly, "That's just it. I don't know."

Hooker now stared at him then held up his hands and shrugging, asked, "And?"

Stella rolled her eyes as she got up and looked at the kid. "Would you please clear the plates, Squirt? I need to get my husband his tools." Giving Manny a look, which he knew all too well, she turned toward his office. "Anything else you need besides your cordless phone, legal pad and a pen?"

"No, dear." He flashed Hooker the wounded husband goofy face, and then called after her, "You are not only my hero, but the love of my shortened life."

She scoffed as she sauntered into the other room to retrieve the items.

Manny quietly planted his face into his right hand as Hooker began to chuckle. Manny muttered into his hand as he slowly shook his head, “I’m so very glad I didn’t marry that fine little Italian girl, Virginia Pipeline.” Referring to a very bad old joke about three octogenarian Italian men, which made Hooker laugh even harder as he rolled over and buried his face in a throw pillow.

Several minutes later, he thanked the medical examiner and hung up the phone. He sat staring at Johnny, who silently started to fidget and blush. Quietly, Manny bounced the back of the pen off the legal pad. “How old did you say you were?” Manny asked.

“Twenty.”

“Hmm.” Manny closed his eyes and laid his head back thinking. The music of Stella’s humming in the kitchen was soothing, but Hooker was getting a little impatient. Manny opened his eyes, and looked at Hooker and Johnny. “The ME said he was just about to call me. All of the dimes that they had recovered from both scenes were dated 1958… and minted in San Francisco.”

Hooker looked at the Squirt and smiled at the kid whose mouth was gaping open.

“He also said that they were all in mint or uncirculated condition. So they were probably, or at least possibly, bought as a collector’s roll.”

Johnny added quietly, “Or bought as new rolls of dimes at a bank in 1958.”

Manny smiled as he turned to the kid. “How does it feel to have cracked a major break in a high stakes case, kid?"

The kid was trying to breathe or catch his breath. "Pretty cool, but do you think it really means anything?" Looking from Manny to Hooker and back, "I mean, like Hooker said, it really is pretty far out there."

Manny thought about what the kid was really asking, and what he really needed. "I think it is the kind of thinking that could lead to cracking the case."

The kid just sat looking at Manny with a stunned look on his face. Box jumped up on the couch, ignoring everyone, crawled into the kid's lap, and curled up for a nap. Hooker's eyes grew big and looked at Stella who had just walked back in as she was wiping her hands on her apron.

Stella looked over at Box and the kid, then back at Hooker. "Oh, that is nothing. They were curled up together all night and Box never stopped purring, even when he was snoring." She chuckled. "It was really quit adorable."

Box cracked open one eye and gave Stella an unappreciative look. *Adorable* was not a Box kind of word.

Hooker, reading the cat's look as a great time to escape, stood up. "Manny, we're out of here, but if you can keep working that angle on the dimes, I'm sure something is there. Later, I'm going to try and get some heartbeat from the street, if she's there." Raising his T-shirt's armpit closer to his nose, he winced. "And we are both going to get some fresh clothes."

Stella caught the slight wince out of the corner of her eye as Johnny stood up and had a suspicion of her own that she decided she was going to act upon. *And things were going to change around here,* she thought.

As the kid walked past, she reached out and grabbed him by the back of the belt. "Hold on there, cowboy. I'm a checking your brand." As she turned down the belt to reveal the label and the size of the pants, then she let him go.

It was only a half second, but it made him jump, "Wha… what brand?"

Hooker slapped him gently on the back of the head, "Don't ever ask a woman what she's doing." He leaned over and gave her a buzz on her neck. Even though she wasn't one of his plump gals, he still liked the reaction he got as she melted into his sideways hug.

Her finger reached over and poked him in the chest with each of her words. "You behave, and be careful out there." Looking after the kid who was making his escape with the orange fur-ball alongside, she added, "And you take care of him."

Hooker broke the seriousness with a tease. "Box can look after himself."

She slapped his chest and shook out her greying red hair. "You know who I mean, jerk." As he slipped out of her arms, she thought of something else and she checked his brand, also. "Make sure you give your uncle the same kiss, and remind him that he is supposed to come help cook on Sunday… and he can bring that blonde friend of his who *really* knows how to cook."

Hooker laughed. "I'll kiss him, I'll tell him, and I'll even tell Hank he has to drag Willie over here, but if Willie touches the brisket, I'm not eating. He would use too much axle grease." Waving at the office door, he yelled at the man with headphones on, "Later, Manny!" but there was no response. Closing the door gently behind him he could hear Stella laughing about Willie, and it put a big smile on his face that matched the sunny day.

As he walked out of the gate, he smiled even harder as he watched Johnny checking the oil on Mae West, knowing that he wouldn't stop until he knew everything he needed to check on the rig before starting her up. The kid *was* a fast learner.

Jamming his hand into his pants, looking for his keys, he felt a small envelope. "Shi . . .eets of rain on the freeway!" He turned back to the house to leave the found dime with Manny. Opening the small packet, he looked at the mintmark—San Francisco 1958. The hairs stood up on the back of his neck and an icy chill shot down his spine. Too close—too, too close.

20

Box jumped out the door before the truck engine finished shuddering to silence. Striding to the middle of the large lawn, he looked around to make sure any and all were paying attention, and then peed standing straight legged. None of that sissy squat-sit for the Box, he was a full-on *man.* Hooker would be the last to remind him of the little 'sleepy time event' that had occurred in the early days of their relationship.

As Box finished and started kicking the grass, he looked over at the neighbor's yard a hundred feet away and the large bulldog that lay in the sun. Box's grass kicking changed ever so slightly until Hooker called from the truck, "Box, leave Coco alone. You already beat him up this year, and once a year is enough." The cat looked offended and turned his gaze to the street like he was thinking, and to make it clear, he was completely ignoring any derisive noise that might have come from the truck that was out of his line of sight. Sighing, he kicked one last grass tuft in Hooker's direction as he strolled off to see if there might be any fresh food in his dish in the very large garage barn where he heard Willie rummaging around banging metal.

"Wait a minute," Hooker stopped Johnny from getting out.

"Yeah?"

Hooker curled his lower lip in against his teeth, and then looked over at the kid. "Have you ever had any dealings with queers?" This was a tough thing to cover for Hooker. For him, it was just everyday living, but he understood that other people had different feelings.

"Once." The kid thought. "I think, why?"

"They aren't called queers, they prefer the term gay. The irony of that term, and the life that many have been beaten up or killed over, is not lost on them. But it is the way they are." Hooker looked through the window into the dark of the shop and watched a small very bright light spring into being accompanied by the static snarling of the welding. Turning back to the kid, "Some, you would never know they were gay, others are... well, let's just say, a bit more flamboyant." The enormity of introducing someone to one of the most important people in his life had caused his mouth to go dry.

"Willie is the greatest man in the world to have in your corner when the chips are down. If I ever had to choose between Willie and Manny & Stella, I think I would rather just shoot myself." Hooker fidgeted with the key ring in his hand. "Manny and Stella are like the folks I never had, but Willie... well, Willie is the kind of uncle you can talk to about everything. You have a question about cars or trucks? He's your man. You have a question about understanding girls? Well, he's your girl. He's not the best cook, but we're still alive, so he's not going to kill us."

"OK," Johnny stated as he blinked a few times.

Hooker looked over at the tense young man and realized just how on the edge of becoming a good-looking man he actually was, or at least he could clean up good. Reassuring, "It's OK, he won't touch you, unless you tell him you're gay and you want him to touch you. He's kind of in a new relationship right now with a very nice guy."

Hooker was relieved as he watched the tension wash out of the kid's shoulders, and the rigidity disappear in the set of his jaw. "OK," the kid started with a sigh, and then his eyes flashed big with horror. "I mean, it's not OK. I mean, I'm not that way, so it's OK that he is, but I'm not so it's not OK for… oh shit." He collapsed against the door. "I'm just screwing this up, aren't I?"

"Naw, you're doing fine." Some movement caught his eye in the large shop as the man walked across one of the columns of light from the skylights. "Oh shit." It was Hooker's turn to slump. Turning to the kid, he shared the last secret. "Just so you know—he sometimes wears a dress around the house."

The kid looked at him, and then a smile tugged at one corner of his mouth. "He's wearing one now, isn't he?" Hooker rolled his eyes down and twisted his mouth as he nodded his head. Johnny continued, "It's not a pretty one, is it?"

Hooker looked out of the side of his eye at the kid and grimaced in a gimpy smile. "Not on your life. It's the ugliest rag he owns, but hopefully, he will light it on fire from the welder." As they laughed a mutual laugh of camaraderie, they rolled out of the respective doors and strolled into the unavoidable.

"Uncle Willie, I've told you a hundred times not to wear your good dress when you're welding," Hooker called out at the man working halfway into the very large barn of a garage shop that was strewn with trucks and cars in various conditions of assembly or disassembly.

"Hooker, damn it all! Its laundry day, so what's a girl to do?" The man in the long granny dress so popular with young ladies a quarter his age, walked toward them as he worked his hands out of the large welding gloves and pushed the large mask deeper back on his head.

Extending his firm mechanic's hand, trying hard to keep the Nancy suppressed while he stood in a flowered dress, combat boots with no laces, and a large black leather smithy's apron with decorative studs arranged in a heart shape in the crotch area, he lisped ever so slightly, "William Nest, but just call me Willie."

The kid engaged him firmly and shook. "Johnny, but everyone is calling me Squirt."

"So good to meet you, John," giving Hooker an evil look. "Ignore the Cretans. They can be horribly cruel."

Hooker leaned over and gave him one of his signature big kisses on his neck. "Stella sends her love, even if you are an ass sometimes. Which reminds me, Sunday dinner is at the Hacienda."

The older man leaned over and sniffed, "Eww, good thing I'm doing laundry. And stop doing that, I'm not one of your fat ladies."

Hooker leaned back and looked at the somewhat overweight, but very much in shape older man in the dress, as he raised his eyebrow. "Really?"

Willie slapped at Hooker's chest with his gloves, "Stop it! You'll embarrass your young man here." Then realizing what he had said, he fumbled. "That's not what I meant," as he put a hand out toward Johnny. "I didn't mean to offend you. I mean I just…"

Johnny smiled and clapped the man on the shoulder. "It's OK, and there was no offense taken." Patting him on the shoulder, he started off to follow the way Hooker had taken. "And it may just be my opinion, but really?" He held out his hand palm up as he moved it up and down at the dress while screwing up his face in a disgusted grimace. "The floral pattern is just wrong with the leather. I think that maybe a nice patchwork quilted jean dress would be so much more 'go to town.' And, it *is* a more slimming look." Turning before he busted up laughing, he stepped through the doorway into the hall-breezeway leading into the house, catching up with Hooker.

Just inside the door leading into the giant playpen of pure testosterone, with its mix of steel, grease, and gasoline, was the only thing adorning the walls of what Johnny could see to be a sparely appointed living quarters. The kid stopped to look at the photograph and document placed side by side in a simple reddish wood frame. The black and white photo had been taken in a hospital. President LBJ was laying some kind of medal with a long ribbon on the chest of what Johnny assumed was a younger unconscious Willie. The tubes and bandages made it kind of difficult to tell for sure.

Hooker looked up from the open door of the white refrigerator. Seeing the intent concentration on the young man's face, he anticipated the questions. "Manny says the medal is a Congressional Medal of Honor, but Willie won't talk about it. He just says it's his three pieces of silver. The document is a DD-214, his separation papers from the Navy. He calls them his 'slave papers of freedom.' Those two things mean he never has to be anybody but himself, and he never has to answer to another person for who he is.

"One of his longtime friends up at the Navy yards made the cherry frame for me. I had a picture framer in Willow Glen do the rest. The cherry is because of the old story about not telling lies and chopping down the cherry tree. I hung it there to remind him every day to be honest and proud about the man he is."

The silence fell as Hooker felt a rising stiffness in his throat. He realized that this was the first time he had ever really vocalized how he felt about his adoptive uncle, and how really proud of him that he was. Not for his past heroic service for his country, but the man he was today, and every day. The weight of the story hanging on the wall wasn't lost on the kid.

A few minutes later, as they stood in the kitchen draining the gallon container of milk, and the last of a bag of cookies, Hooker stared at the kid. The mischief in his eyes he couldn't hide, so he just let it play. Finally, it was too much and he started to chuckle. "Really?" He made a goofy face at the chuckling kid. "More slimming?"

"Well?" The kid laughed with his palm up. "Wouldn't it?"

Hooker rolled his eyes to the side and lolled his head over to one side. "Umm, maybe. But, come on, 'more go to town'? I'm trying to discourage him from flaunting it about down town."

The kid just sliced his head in a sweep as he looked at Hooker. "I don't know, but I do kind of think it's his life, and he should do what makes *him* happy."

"The guy used to get the snot beat out of him for wearing a satin jacket and talking different. What do you think his wearing a dress at Safeway would get him?"

"Probably not a discount, but he might get some better melons." Hooker saw that the kid was having fun, but was also serious. "Look, I'm just a kid, but this isn't the 1940s or 50s when you couldn't be different. They used to beat a black guy to death for even whistling at a white lady, but now we have marriages. This is the 1970s. We've been through the Flower Power and the Summer of Love. Who says an old guy can't wear a dress — the Scottish guys do."

"Well said." The man in the dress now stood there in just his white boxers with red hearts.

Hooker almost lost a mouthful of milk and cookies back up his nose. Swallowing, he choked out, "Where's your dress?"

Jamming a thumb back over his shoulder Willie responded, "Out there in the shop, probably still burning." Turning to the kid he asked, "Newer darker denim, or that faded look with some colored patches?"

Now it was the kid's turn to almost lose his food, but chuckling as he recovered. "The darker would be more slimming, but the faded with patches would be more funky, and compliment your hair." He gave the man a serious look. "Besides, with the patches you could do a red bandana heart where it counts and drive Hooker nuts." Blinking, he waited for the man to step up to the plate, but he wasn't going to flinch.

Finally smiling, the man clapped him on the shoulder and turned to Hooker. "You found a good kid, and you can bring him around more often. But you really need to do something about that one white mitten. In a neighborhood like this, it could give people something to talk about." Pointing at the offending hand, the Nancy came out just a bit too much. "It is supposed to be white, isn't it?" Turning, he scratched at the words on the backside of his boxers as he walked back down the hall, past the framed photo and document. Hooker could just make out the words *Kiss Me Hard.*

"Oh, and Stella said to remind you that you're helping cook this Sunday, and just so you don't poison us, bring Hank."

The man called back from the hall as he continued to walk out the door, "Yes, dear. Hanky Panky it is, and I'll wear my new jean dress." Waving his hand in a loose wavy kind of flounce as the industrial fire door closed softly behind him.

Hooker leaned over and planted his face in his palms, shuddering. Looking out with one eye between his fingers at the kid, he mumbled into his hands, "See what you started?" His hands dropped to his sides and his head bounced off his chest and then just hung there as he sniffed and snarled in disgust. "Laundry, I need to do laundry."

Looking up at Johnny, he pointed toward the large adjoining room. "Living room, TV, magazines, but they're all car stuff, and books which are more car stuff, or just hang out with Box. I'll just go change and we can get over to your place and get you changed."

"Can't."

"Can't what?"

"Can't get changed," the kid slumped against the large island as he nibbled at the last cookie.

"Why not?"

"The only other pair of jeans I have are ratty and the knees are blown out." Looking in the direction where the older man had gone, "Torn, I meant to say ripped out." He smiled shyly. "You don't want me working for you looking that way."

"Then buy another pair." Hooker was having a little trouble getting his mind around the concept of only one real pair of jeans.

The kid said it all by pulling his pockets out and palming the three pennies and a nickel.

Hooker was going to get a headache. Finally, he waved at the kid. "OK, come on. What size do you wear?"

"Twenty-eight waist and a thirty-two leg."

Reaching into the drawer, he pulled out the only two pair of jeans that were in the drawer. Too many foster homes, and always a fist swing away from the next, Hooker wasn't big on having a lot of clothes to pack. He handed one pair to the kid. "Thirty – thirty-six. You can pull them in with the belt and cuff them up inside the leg."

Reaching into the closet, he pulled out two white t-shirts that were pressed to the flatness of a linoleum floor. "Large is large." Pointing across the hall, "Towels on the towel bar are clean and for you. Use anything you see, except my toothbrush. There should be a new brush in the drawer to the right of the left sink. When you're done, just hang the towel on the bar, that's yours. Then come on out. My office is off the living room."

The kid looked at the clothes and turned a half shade of red. Quietly he nodded. "Thanks."

"They're only for today or so. We'll work things out. Willie did more for me than a cheap pair of jeans and a white shirt." Turning to walk away, he added, "I'll see you in a bit. There is plenty of hot water, so take your time and relax."

Hooker walked into the large garage and looked around. The welder was shut down. Willie was nowhere to be seen, so Hooker strolled out to the one place he knew the old man couldn't resist—Mae West.

The bright sunshine did nothing but stir up the fire in the radiant red pearl over the yellow paint and candy-apple blue flames. Willie had the right hood up, and Hooker figured he was sniffing the oil to see if the driver had highballed the rig into hard-on-the-engine territory. Hooker smirked as he rounded the huge chrome front bumper. The old man had his head buried deep down in the front of the engine compartment. "You got lucky this time, junior." Pulling back out and jumping down to face Hooker, Hooker was at once glad the dress was a long dress, because on a warm day like this, he suspected the old guy probably was going commando underneath. The fact that he had been wearing boxers a few minutes before meant nothing.

"The oil is ready to change, but you haven't been scorching it." The old man wiped his hands on the red grease rag.

"Then why am I lucky?"

The old guy eyed him with his good eye, as the other was squinting against the glare from the sun. "Dolly called."

"Oh shit," Hooker muttered as he walked back around the truck to go call her on the radio.

"It's OK," Willie stopped him. "I talked her down off her pity party. It's a slow day. There wasn't anything out there, but Stella stopped in, and so she knew you were up and out, but didn't call in." The old man leaned against the bumper as he absently rubbed the chrome.

"So what did you tell her?" Hooker looked off down the valley to where he knew the dispatcher was sitting.

The old man shrugged with a conspiratorial smile. "I told her the truth."

Hooker gave him a hard look that the old man ducked. "I told her I needed to change the oil and fix a few other things, but that I would have you down in her loving arms by six this evening when your shift starts."

"What other things?"

"A couple of things come to mind." Hooker, watched as the usual uncle Willie slipped smoothly back into the career officer of Naval Intelligence and spy. Willie had a jagged scar running from below his left ear, down his throat and hooking out to the end of his chin where the meat hook used on him as a POW in North Korea had stopped and caught hold of the jawbone before it ripped out four days later. Never invisible, the scar was now shining extra white from lack of blood. Hooker knew that meant his blood pressure was up about whatever came out of his mouth next.

"What's on your mind right now, sir?" Hooker stood a little straighter out of respect for the man.

"Maddie also called. Your paper was due yesterday."

Hooker sank mentally into the depths of the well of I-screwed-the-pooch. "Yes, sir, it was," knowing there were results and then there were stories. He knew that neither his uncle nor the librarian would be willing to listen to stories.

"I explained you've worked hard lately, precluding you from logging some time with the history books. She agreed with me about rounding out the discussion to include the piston shape of the side draft flathead, you could give a better understanding of the dynamics for an early muscle car. We assumed you can get it done in twenty pages instead of a cheap note of twelve." The white brush cut hair stood stiff as the man's stare. The muscles rippled along his jawline, daring the least whine or complaint from his ward.

"When would she want the paper, sir?"

The soldier softened some as he turned back to the truck and knelt to look under her. "I'm sure that Sunday would be the most appropriate time."

"Before or after the barbecue, sir?"

Muffled as he looked along the length of the undercarriage, "I'm sure that when you get there, you two can find a few minutes to review the merits of your continuing education, Mr. Hooker."

"Yes, sir."

Standing and cleaning his hands in the grease rag, the calm softer uncle had returned, within reason. "You have a leak, tiny, but a leak in the lower radiator hose," and bending over, pointing under the truck, "and I know that spot of oil wasn't there this morning."

Standing up he looked hard at Hooker and let his jealous girly side slip out a tiny bit. "Just what have you been up to with my girl, young man?" A father with a sixteen-year-old girl couldn't act more protectively. His rag filled fist rested on the now out-slung hip as he raised one eyebrow.

Hooker's eyelids slowly lowered in that challenging look of the old teenager… the sure-fire way to knock the old man off his game.

Willie struck out with the rag as he softly waved it across Hookers chest and quietly giggled. "Oh, just never mind. I'm sure it is something that a girl in my delicate years shouldn't even want to hear." Moving off toward the large barn doors, he swayed his hips in an exaggerated flounce. Dropping his voice back into the deep serious register of his mechanic's voice, he directed Hooker. "I'll move the Speedwagon out of the way and you bring Mae all the way back and over the pit."

Hooker swung up into the cab, and as he turned the engine over, he reached left-handed for the microphone. "Dolly, sorry about the no call, but as Willie told you, I'm down for maintenance this afternoon."

"10-4, Hooker, just wanted to know where you were."

"If you need me for something small, I've got the Ford here."

"10-4. Just take care of Mae and we'll see you for lunch. We are expecting two of you correct?"

"Negative. Box will be with us too… set the table for three."

"I meant Johnny."

"10-4. He's my slave for twelve more days."

"10-4. Get your money's worth."

Hooker double clicked, and hung the mic, as he eased the beast through the large barn doors. Slowly creeping down the glass smooth shop floor, the giant truck was more like a dutiful puppy following the flour-sack dress over lace-less army boots. As the old man walked down the stairs into the grease pit, Hooker drove on over the top of him until the windshield just touched a tennis ball hanging on a cord from a rafter thirty feet above.

Mae West shuddered to silence as Hooker set the brakes and arranged all the gears to neutral. The voice that giggled up from under the truck was partially amused and half-nervous. "Oh dear, you are not going to believe this." Hooker slid out of the cab and walked to the set of stairs at the front end of the pit.

Looking up at the large radiator hose, Hooker eyed the slight nick, and then the oil pan where the maker of the nick had come to be buried. The dime had punctured halfway into the large front face of the pan. Completely in awe of the amazing trajectory that dime must have taken to nick the heavy hose, and still have energy to bury itself that deep into the heavy steel pan, he turned to the older man and wailed in a whiney voice, "My… my baby is… is… WOUNDED!"

The two could laugh now, but both knew that this was not really a laughing matter. The older man carried five major scars that he had acquired during his thirty years in Naval Intelligence, and Hooker's mind was still replaying the other night's event overlaid with helping Manny process the crime scene that night and morning. Hooker remembered his times with Manny. "Don't touch it." To which the man just raised his palms up next to his face in a *stick-'em-up* formation of submission.

Hooker climbed back up into the cab and grabbed the mic, "Dolly?"

"Go, honey."

"Can you find Captain Davis and have him bring an evidence kit up here to the house?"

"Is someone shooting at you up there?" Her voice immediately took on the protective edge of someone in control of calling out first responders.

"Negative. We just found some evidence from the other night that Mae wants to give up. He also needs to bring a camera."

"10-4. I'll find him.'

Hooker double tapped the mic and left it lying on the seat.

Walking back under the truck, he found Willie looking up at the front of the giant radiator. Hooker walked over and looked up. The silver flame on the tails side of the Mercury-head dime was just peeking out of the fins in the radiator.

Hooker clapped the man on the back. "Great work, Unc, great work." He then held him out at arm's length and looked him up and down. "You might want to go change. There should be a CHP captain pulling in the driveway in a little bit."

"Is he cute?"

Hooker gave him a stern look.

"I'm going, I'm going!" he said as he waved his hands

above his shoulders. “Just asking, just asking.”

Hooker chuckled silently and shook his head as he looked back up at the dime buried in the fins.

21

"Hey, Hooker!" The fresh scrubbed kid called down from where he was busying himself by polishing every piece of chrome he could find. "Do you have any fingernail polish?"

Willie froze, and then looked longingly at Hooker. Mouthing the words, "This is the stuff fantasies are made of," with a huge smile as he batted his eyes.

"Stop that!" Hooker mouthed back. Turning toward the front of the truck where both men could see the young man's spread legs straddling the concrete stairwell, Willie elbowed Hooker and nodded toward the kid as if to say 'see, see'.

Hooker rolled his eyes closed, then buried his face in his right palm, saying, "No, but I know a nasty old man that should be acting his age. Why?"

The legs straightened and the kid bent down to look at the two men dressed in identical white T-shirts, jeans and dirty sneakers. He ignored the goofy lascivious moon-dog look on the old man's face as he blandly explained, "There is a good sized gouge here in the face of the bumper, and it looks to be down to the steel. I thought maybe some nail polish would keep it from rusting."

Hooker screwed up his face in askance at Willie muttering incredulously, "A gouge? In the bumper?" The two scrambled out of the dark hole to look at the wonder that had occurred in the armor plate steel custom made bumper. Unlike most bendable modern piece of shit bumpers that Willie and Hooker had considered when they were building Mae West, the chrome beauty that graced the intimidatingly massive front end was made entirely from the same armor plated steel used to make battleships, courtesy of the local Navy repair yard. The steel had been chrome plated to a military 'work' thickness and maybe a squidgy point beyond. As Willie always said, "It pays to know people who know you."

"Huh?" Hooker looked at the narrow divot that was no longer than a half-inch where a dime had given its useful life. Turning to the older and wiser man. "Got any better ideas?"

Willie stared at the dime edge mark. "Heck no, it would have just rusted on me." Turning to the kid, he gently slugged him in the shoulder. "You're worth keeping around here, Squirt." Stepping over the open stairwell, he headed toward his boudoir stating, "I'll go get you some nice pearl pink I have been dying to get rid of."

Hooker shot him a glaring look, knowing full well that the man was joking. Taunting the old friend, Hooker shot back as the man reached the door, "Knowing you, if you have wanted to get rid of it, then it must be 'pussy pink'." The old man responded by scratching the back of his head with his middle finger. Hooker and the kid laughed as they also heard a car pull up and into the barn.

Rounding the nose of the large truck, Hooker saw the captain standing up out of the California Highway Patrol cruiser. Hooker grabbed a fresh red grease rag off the large commercial bundle, and wiped his hands in the cloth as he sauntered across the rest of the 10,000 square foot car barn. "Any trouble finding the place, Captain Davis?"

The man reached into the open trunk, withdrawing a large black case that was a field exam kit. "No, Hooker, it was a piece of cake. Dolly brought me up here a number of years ago for your uncle to fix my truck." Looking around at the size of the barn and the height of the unsupported arched roof, he marveled and wondered. "Of course, the little three car garage has kind of grown since then." Turning a full three-hundred sixty degrees, "I understand having all the real estate, but why the air space?"

Hooker snorted a laugh, remembering his second summer with Willie. "Willie bought it from the Navy as surplus. It was a smaller 'Battle Balloon' repair barn that they never erected, and it was just sitting up at Moffett Field, so they sold it to him." Hooker was kind of proud of the building, too. "When they brought it up, Willie looked at the piles and piles of materials, and then told the commander that they forgot to include the directions for assembly. I guess it was slow at the base that summer, so they sent a crew along with four cranes, and the building was up on the five foot deep footing foundation in less than two months." He winked. "Of course, it was summer, and with the swimming pool and all, there were many details that dragged on for the next three months."

"But how do you heat something like this?"

"Hot water," Hooker started, "The first well Willie drilled hit water that was 140°F. The second well went almost horizontally into the mountain and hit an artesian aquifer, but it is very cold water for drinking."

"Aquifer?"

Hooker stopped, never realizing that he might know something others didn't.

"Actually, it's called a 'confined aquifer', which means water that is under pressure… about a hundred pounds constant to be more exact," Willie explained as he walked up, sticking his hand out. "Good to see you again, Chet." They shook, "It is Chet, if I remember right?"

"Nobody but Dolly and family calls me that anymore, but sure, you're close enough to family." The Captain smiled, remembering his real family.

"Still have that 1952 Chevy Step-side with the straight six?"

The officer chuckled sadly, putting down his case as if it were just another heavy burden. "Nah, I sold her paying off the cancer bills, along with the fishing gear."

Willie waved off the sad memories with a loose hand. "Pah, we don't have any fishing gear around here, but I'm sure that anytime you need a truck and or a beer, we can rustle up something."

The officer weighed the offer.

Willie quickly added to put the man at ease, "You can even bring a lady friend up, if you want. Hell, we even let Dolly come up on some occasions, when she promises to behave herself."

Agreeing to the now specified terms of the offer, the officer relaxed. "That sounds good. In fact, I'm having some troubles with my new car."

"I hate new cars!" Willie snapped.

"1955 MG TD."

Willie softened. "Well, in that case…" smiling then snapping his fingers, "as long as you let me rip out all that Lucas electrical crap."

"Done!" Chet smiled broadly sardonic with the side of his mouth. "That is the problem I'm having—electrical." And just to solidify their friendship, he threw in, "And maybe we can look at how to stick a small block in it?"

Smiling at Willie's 'gone-goofy-in-lust smile', he picked up the case again and asked, "What am I processing here?"

Hooker scooped the air with his hand as he turned. "It's in the truck, over here."

The two older men followed. "So how do you heat with the hot water?"

Willie pointed at the glassy floor they were walking on. "We run it through a series of copper pipes that are buried in the sixteen inch thick concrete floor. I change the mix to heat about the middle of September. By October, when it starts to get cold, then the floor is radiating about ninety degrees. That keeps everything in the building about seventy-three to seventy-five degrees in here, just right for t-shirts or a dress." He looked over for a reaction, but there was none. "Best of all, every tool or piece of steel is all the same temperature. So it makes it a real pleasure to work out here all year long."

"But what about when the summer is over a hundred?"

Willie reached out and stopped the man, and kneeling

down, he placed his palm flat on the floor. "Feel." The officer did, and his eyes arched. "Fifty-one degree water, straight out of the mountain; but right now I'm throwing a mixed temperature of about sixty degrees to match the nice weather, but I'll go straight cold by the end of the month."

They rose and continued toward the truck. "So, what about the house?"

"Oh, there too," he continued. "I actually tore down the shack that was here and started over. So by then I knew about the hot water and buried the pipes in the house pad, too."

"How did you ever figure this system out?"

Willie waved his loose hand. "Wasn't me. The Romans did it two thousand years ago, and they learned it from the Chinese." He pointed at the divot in the chrome bumper. "After World War II, they built a whole community in New York called Levittown, and every house is radiant heat."

The captain leaned in closer to the divot. "Holy cat fish! That is one hell of a dime load." Looking up at Hooker, "I'm assuming that one of the dimes did that."

"I think it may have been when I was a lot closer on the Almaden Expressway and those two or three shots came from the side."

"There are two more," Willie added.

"Dings?"

"Nope. These two stuck around." The older man giggled at his little joke. Then he remembered something more, and turned to Hooker. "I guess I have to date Jeff for a pair of dimes."

Hooker rolled his eyes. "I think Mae can forego your

suffering with Jeff for a couple of simple dimes painted on her side," in reference to the tote board of 'kills' on the truck's side. The drama of Willie and Jeff's breaking up was what drove Hooker to seek refuge in one of Manny and Stella's guest rooms.

The other room had become the 'catch all' as everything not in use was moved into the room at the end of the hall and farthest away from the kitchen. Stella had joked off and on that it was where she should store Manny on most days. Then she would snuggle down on his lap, as he would explain that there really was a defining difference between abuse and use. Hooker had never heard them having even a half-heartedly angry word for each other, even though they referred to each other in such terms as *useless old man, good for a doorstop,* and *old woman.*

Willie, on the other hand, had been in a few relationships that were less than good for him or anyone around him, but he was learning. His recent lover was a more staid plodding kind of guy who would just lean back in his chair and chuckle at Willie's blustering and cackling, and it was having a very good settling effect on the old warhorse. He was finally sleeping more nights than not, and his high blood pressure was coming down into some semblance of control. He had even finally started going up and talking to a shrink at the VA about his years as a spy.

"Maybe after everything is done, they will give us the dimes back, and we can just epoxy them on," concluded Hooker.

Johnny eyed the tote board, and quietly remarked, "Candy could paint a pair of dimes better than that Volkswagen."

"Really? Candy paints?" Hooker's antennas were twitching at the mention of the kid's sister. "Well, maybe someday when she has time..."

The two older men were under the truck with the Captain taking photos before they could pull the dimes out. Hooker looked out the rear barn doors at the large lawn that needed mowing now that the spring was encouraging it to grow. A klaxon horn sounded from one of the timbers that ran like soldiers along the wall separating the house from the garage—the phone was ringing. Hooker looked at his watch. "Willie, don't start pulling the oil yet. I've got a bad feeling about this," as he ran to the phone.

They finished the photos, and took some measurements as Hooker talked on the phone. "Got it, Dolly." Hooker started to step away toward the truck. "Yeah, he's here. I'll let him know. Love you," he concluded as he slammed the handset down on the receiver.

Running for the truck, Johnny saw him and responded by throwing the rag and polish in the bucket and heading for the passenger door. "Box! Go time!" Hooker called. "Chief, we have a nineteen pileup at Blossom Hill and 101 northbound. A flipped fuel tanker gushing its guts onto the 101."

He hit the side of the truck, bounced through the door as he scooped up the microphone, and keyed it left-handed as his right turned the switch, hitting the start button without waiting for the turbo to wind up. The still-warm engine fired into life as he slung the gears into reverse then looked in the mirror. Seeing the captain struggling to run with the case for his car that blocked the front door,

Hooker shifted into seventh and yelled out the window, "Willie! Down!" The giant truck rocketed forward over the grease trench and Willie's head as Hooker roared out of the rear doors and wheeled through and across the rear lawn. Cutting deep trenches in the soft spring turf, out around the swimming pool, throwing sod and any small animals caught in the grass, as he cleared the end of the house and dropped down the old access dirt road that led out to the street.

As he fishtailed onto the street, headed down the hill, he peeked at his large rear-view mirrors, and saw the patrol car swerving out on the street behind as the light bar and siren erupted to aid their rush down the quiet mountain street. Hooker threw on his legal set of flashing emergency lights and kept the lead, even though in theory, the Pontiac should have been able to overtake the large truck, except Hooker skipped gears, and he used all 1,200 horses, as the hill provided. The accident was still almost two miles away.

Realizing he still had the microphone keyed open to talk, he simply called "1-4-1, show me 10-8 in route, ETA two minutes."

Moments later, the speaker from the main radio confirmed as Karen's voice was all business, "10-4: 1-4-1, we have fire and police in route with an ETA of an additional five. CHP unit is on site, and advises 5-Delta-Bravo, 1-2-3-4-5-Delta-Bravo. There is fuel from the tanker that is in the entrance of the transition from North bound 101, they have asked for you to come in from Coyote Road or Silver Creek and snatch roll it back. The rupture is near the top."

"10-4. We are on Silver, and I can see it. They are about to lose some fence."

Turning to the kid, he checked his seat belt, as he hit a short straight away and snapped his, pulling it tight. "Box, get in the sleeper." The cat didn't hesitate. The orange streak shot for the only safe and secure padded hole in the truck.

Hooker hit the Jake brake and flooded the giant engine with air, creating backpressure, and providing a warning horn of sorts as they approached the accident and the backed up traffic. The truck eased into the empty oncoming lane and continued the approach at about fifty miles per hour as Hooker let off the fuel pedal, allowing air pressure again into the engine, which provided backpressure, and the Jake brake slowed the rig.

By the time they got close to the berm of the off-ramp, they were down to twenty and Hooker swung the wheel as they hit the scrub desert along the backside of the berm. The mass of the truck and its custom front bumper peeled about sixty feet of freeway marker fence like a banana. Bouncing along the top of the berm, Hooker watched the tanker and figured how best to set the truck up for a snatch to roll the trailer back over onto its wheels.

The 22,000 pounds of bucking steel and rubber jumped and slew all over the sand berm. The only thing the truck had going for it over the sand was the talent of the driver. Even when a lesser man would have had his hands full with just the steering wheel, Hooker, working the *dance of the two levers,* dropped the rig down through the bottom of the second tier of gears into the bottom end as he slowed to the last crawl along the top of the berm.

"I can't see that side of the berm. Open the door and swing out and tell me how steep it is."

Without hesitation, the kid pulled the handle and with his right arm in the window hole, pushed out and hung over the edge, then swung back in. Holding his arm at an angle of about thirty degrees, he showed Hooker what he needed to know.

Hooker laid the hammer down and the truck vaulted forward as he whipped the wheel right and then spun it hard left as he revved the motor into the red, the ass end slewing around. When the truck came to a stop, it was straddling the berm with the working deck pointed directly at the middle of the tank. Hooker set the brakes as the kid jumped back out of the truck.

They met at the back as Hooker pulled the working deck's control panel open and jerked the releases to let the lines free-feed. The weight of the sling pulled the two snatch hooks down from the twin booms. Hooker unhooked the sling and fed the lines through the snatch-tag ring hooks welded to the back of the deck. Handing one of the hooks to the kid, they ran down the face of the berm and crossed over to the belly of the tank trailer.

The stench of the spilled fuel burned their eyes with creosote acidity. "From here on out, do not rub or touch your face, no matter what, you got me?" Johnny nodded. "Ok, now pull an extra twenty-thirty feet of cable and lay it in a loop like this." Showing him the large six-foot wide loop on the ground. "Good, now all I want you to do is throw the hook as far as you can over that tank."

The kid had a good arm, and Hooker wasn't about to admit it, but he might have thrown the hook and cable a good two or three yards farther than Hooker. “Great, now on your side of the deck, the second box back from the cab, there are two short brass chains with funny looking hooks on each end,” showing the length with his two hands held about as wide as his shoulders. “I want you to bring me one on the other side and drop the second one here.”

There was a loud whistle, and Hooker looked up to see an officer pointing toward the fuel. Turning to the kid, “Hurry, we need to turn this before some idiot lights up a cigarette in San Jose and blows us to Gilroy.”

Johnny ran for the rig, and Hooker hustled over to the officer. “About ten minutes and we can start pulling the trailer. How are we doing on the spill?”

“I wish the fire guys would hurry up and get here. They’re sending a foam truck up from San Martine, maybe in ten, but if we wait much longer, it’s going to get to that grey car, and there is a woman trapped in there.”

Hooker looked over the carnage of vehicles. “Am I the only one here?”

“Yeah, and am I ever glad to see you.” The officer leaned back and looked past Hooker. “Oh great, the Captain is here.” Hooker could hear the dread in the young officer’s voice.

“It’s OK, he’s with me.” Looking back north up the freeway he could see yellow lights flashing. He slapped the officer lightly on the chest to get his attention, and then realized the man’s shirt had blood soaking out from under his protective vest. “How did you get here?”

The officer pointed to the middle of the mass of twisted metal. With the four tires of his cruiser getting some unneeded sunshine, Hooker understood the blood.

“Great, an eye witness.” Pointing back north, toward the still approaching tow-truck, he snapped, “When that tow-truck gets here, have him drag that car and woman over to the center grass.” The officer nodded and winced at the effort, Hooker gave him a look of two counts, then, when the officer waved him off, headed for the snatch hooks as Johnny came running with the short chains. The fuel was everywhere, and Hooker had to walk slowly and carefully.

As Johnny approached, he held up the short chain with a question on his face. Hooker reassured him. “Yup, those are the right ones. The brass won’t cause a spark and ignite the fuel. There is nothing we can do about the snatch hooks and cable.” Grabbing the short chain, Hooker wound the pigtail hook onto the one cable and then the other end onto the second cable. “Here.” He held the chain. “Hold this here while I secure the hooks.”

The kid took the chain as Hooker grabbed the first snatch-block hook and walked to the one end of the trailer. Feeding the cable under the edge, he reached and looped cable around part of the undercarriage of the trailer. Finishing doing the same at the other end with the other cable, he went back to the kid.

“I want you to hold that chain until the cable draws it up to about as high as your head, then let it go and get the heck back to the truck. Just don’t slip in this shit, and don’t wipe your face.” The kid had just tried to wipe the sweat from his forehead on his shirt. “Your shirt is now soaked with the fumes of the fuel, and will burn your eyes until you are blind.” He slapped him on the back. “Got that?” Johnny nodded as Hooker nodded and walked back around the end of the trailer.

At the end of the trailer, Hooker met back up with the captain. Looking back, he saw that the other officer was telling the small truck to pull the car away from the fuel. Turning back toward the captain, he assessed the situation. "I'd rather wait for the foam truck before I lift, but there is already about a thousand gallons on the road, and with every minute, that tank is bleeding another hundred or more."

"Go ahead and pull it. Hopefully, by the time you get her up, the cavalry will be here."

Pointing toward the grey car and tow truck, Hooker asked for the officer's help. "I won't be able to see him, so signal me when he starts pulling her. Once she's safe, I'll go ahead and pull the trailer up." The captain gave him thumbs up and Hooker headed back to the truck.

Dancing with the two levers that controlled the twin pulley winches, Hooker carefully took up the slack on the towing cables. As the bronze chain that Hooker could see began to pull taut, the kid came back around the trailer. Taking one last look, he turned and shook the captain's hand then started back toward the truck.

"That other tow truck was just finishing setting the hooks in the car and should be pulling her away about now." A low whistle from the captain and a spin of his finger in a circle above his head, confirmed the kid's report. Hooker tightened the cables until they were straight as rods.

"Watch our rear tires. Let me know if we slip more than six inches." He continued the dance as the tanker started to twitch. Hooker was relieved to see the captain moving off to a safe distance in case the fuel ignited.

Slowly, the trailer shifted into a roll and stopped sliding its metal along the asphalt, which was the most dangerous part of this kind of situation. As the trailer tipped closer to upright, Hooker slowed the progress to let the fuel settle into the new attitude, but then he noticed the one thing he didn't want to happen — the rubber tires started to slip in the fuel.

"Johnny, grab those wood chocks and bring them," as he lowered the trailer back down until the metal touched and stopped the sliding. Hooker reached over and grabbed the tin pail used for picking up glass and wreckage, and stopping long enough to scoop up a bucket full of the decomposed granite sand that made up the berm, he ran for the trailer.

Throwing sand all over the fuel-soaked road, and up on the tires themselves, he began soaking up fuel and providing a base for traction. Taking the first two chocks from the kid, he kicked the thin end of the wedge under the tires touching the ground. Then stomping on the asphalt about eight feet away, he instructed the kid. "Go get the shovel, and take that sand dirt there on the shoulder, and make a pile about two feet high, here and here." Johnny took off for the truck and Hooker turned toward the other end of the trailer.

The trailer had 'airport' legs that could be cranked down for the trailer to stand by itself without a tractor. Jumping up on the trailer, Hooker grabbed the crank and turned it. Turning easily, he continued until the lower foot was almost touching the asphalt. Throwing the rest of the sand in the bucket in a pile at the contact point, he was assured that there would be some kind of traction, but not a height that could off balance the trailer when it finally tipped upright.

Looking back to where Johnny was piling his second pile, Hooker smiled. The kid was shoveling at a fevered pitch, and the left mitten that had been white gauze looked more like something a zombie would wear to the prom. “Good enough, Squirt. Clear out.” And they both headed back to Mae West and the working deck.

“Is that so the tanker won’t just continue to roll our way when she comes over?”

“Yeah,” Hooker smiled. “The sand will crush, but absorb the blow enough to stop the rocking. I’ll still be able to pull her off there, but at least we don’t get a back flop.” Johnny put the shovel in its holder, and Hooker pitched the can into its respective hole and grabbed the levers to start the pull. “If that happens, the tank will rupture from one end to the other, and we are ground zero for the wave of fuel, so don’t light a cigarette.”

They watched as the trailer shuddered and slowly began to rise. Hooker watched the airport landing gear for any slipping, but they followed the lead of the tires and held steady in place as the weight began to transfer onto the balance of two tire edges and the half-inch wide edge of the steel foot.

Not taking his eyes off the tanker, he warned the kid, “Squirt, if you see the tanker start to double over, you run south as fast as you can. You hear me?”

“Got it! Make like a bunny.”

The tanker groaned as the stress of the steel tank and its contents, in relation to their connection to the trailer frame, transferred weight. Hooker watched the landing gear to see if it were threatening to buckle, or if it would hold. In his peripheral vision, a part of his mind registered that the Garcia brother's trucks had arrived and were hooking up or pulling cars from the south end. The rig from Central Tow had pulled the woman's car out of the fuel patch, and the fire crew was setting up a Jaws of Life to take off the car's top and door to free the woman. The warm sun overhead could have been a lulling factor in a lazy snooze in the hammock out by the pool, but right now, it was just manufacturing hot steel and slippery sweat.

The one cable started to lose its tension, and Hooker squeezed the lever controlling that winch, causing it to turn slightly faster than its twin. The cable tightened to match the other. Hooker watched the bronze chain holding the two cables and the draw point it created about twenty feet from the tanker.

"Pay attention, Squirt!" He could feel the kid's head that had been scanning the southern area of the carnage now snap back to the cables. "Watch the bronze chain, and when you see it stop being a hard bar between the cables, it means the tanker has reached the balance point." Hooker slowed the winches to a crawl. "See it?"

"Yeah, the links in the middle just came back together."

"Get ready to run. She's coming over now." Hooker let go of the controls, and with his eyes on the tanker, turned his feet into a running position. The kid, also paranoid, looked more like a baseball player ready to steal to second base with a ten-foot leadoff.

Slowly, with a drawn-out groan and a shriek of

complaining steel, the tanker rolled upright and as the tires hit the sand, crushed it to a flat cushion. The top rocked side to side with a bit of lift-off the tires on the far side, but then the trailer settled back and Hooker relaxed.

From somewhere behind the tanker, an arch of white foam laced into the air and fell into a blanket covering the tanker and the giant pool of spilled fuel. The foam contained tri-sodium phosphate to break down the slippery oil of the fuel, and nitrogen to stop any ignition of flames. Hooker thought about the very green grass at Willie's that was thanks to a couple of well-placed BBQs for the fire crews that resulted in a demonstration of the foam. The soap breaks down the surface tension in the soil, and the grass loves the nitrogen and turns an unrealistic green, but then you have to start mowing the yard twice a week. Driving the small tractor around the three acres was more fun for the man than work.

Hooker pointed at the foam and noted to the kid, "Grass along the side of the off-ramp is going to grow like crazy until the summer heat kills it."

Slipping around the ends of the tanker, they unhooked the cables and pulled everything back to the up side to wind it back onto the spools. "Here, put these gloves on and use the rags to clean the cables as I draw them up. Just let the cables run loose in the rags and wipe the worst off." Hooker knew that a true full cleaning and re-application of white lithium would come later. "We'll clean it up later. Right now, we need to rock and roll."

Grabbing the bronze chains, Hooker went back to the rig. Stowing the chains in the second side box, he thought about the last time he cleaned all the gear and boxes. It would be a great job for the kid to do while Willie worked on the engine and Hooker touched up some paint. Maintaining a large tow rig was a full time job. From just the daily washing to cable and equipment cleaning, Hooker really understood what firemen in a firehouse really did for a living, and it wasn't putting out fires.

Hooker jockeyed the giant truck down off the berm and brought it back around to conventionally tow the trailer and tractor. "Are we going to pull the tractor and trailer at the same time?"

Looking at the kid with a smile, "I wish, but no, even if it were legal." Pointing with a thumb jerk, "That tractor can't safely re-hook anything on its fifth wheel until it's been reapproved." Pointing to a large flat space of dirt about mid-way up the off-ramp, Hooker explained the process. "We'll drag the tractor out of the way, over there and haul it up to the Fly later, but we need to get this," indicating with a jaw nod toward the trailer, "to the county yard so they can safely drain the fuel that's left."

"Why the county yard?"

"Because of the crack. Some of the foam might have gotten in and contaminated the fuel. So, right now, it's just considered to be 10,000 gallons or so of toxic waste."

The tractor they had been pulling back upright finally flipped and rocked on its tires. "It won't go to waste. All of the fuel will get used by the county, cleaned up and run through lawn mowers, used in weed burners, or used in their burners for torching asphalt and striping." Resetting the hooks on the sling, "Nothing goes to waste anymore—not with fuel at sixty-nine cents a gallon." Pointing at the tanker. "That right there, the fuel companies insurance will pay them for the loss, and we taxpayers get about eight thousand dollars relief on our county taxes." Heading for the cab, "Everything helps these days."

Later, as they cleaned up for an early lunch at six PM, Willie dropped a stack of clean jeans and freshly ironed t-shirts in Hooker's room. "I've got gauze and stuff out in the first aid kit in the shop." Addressing the kid, he asked, "How's the hand?"

The kid looked at the stitches as he flexed his now clean hand. "It feels kind of silly to wrap it up in a bunch of cloth," as he brought the fingers into a fist and then back flat several times.

Willie stepped over and looked at the stitches. "Hmm, maybe just a jumbo patch will do for now." He looked up at the kid in the eye. "But don't pull a Hooker and go without cover on it for at least a few more days."

The kid held his gaze, and then slowly broke into a smile and a chuckle from the insight into the enigmatic, seemingly together, older young man, "Got it."

Hooker turned into the room followed closely by Box. "You ready? We need to get down the hill or Dolly will be hell on wheels that we were late for dinner," as he looked at his watch.

The kid nodded, but the older man interceded. "He needs a square patch and some ointment first." He gave Hooker a stern look that just looked funny on the old drag queen, back in a pink flowered muumuu and bunny slippers this time. "I'll deal with Dolly, but first things first."

"Come on," he waved at the kid. "We'll grab several patches, and you can put them in the truck as spares."

The old man shot Hooker a hard look. "Maybe you're getting old enough to start packing a First Aid Kit in the rig."

As they clambered into the truck with some added oil at least, Box jumped into Johnny's lap and settled down with a purr. Hooker gave him a stern look as he turned the key then pushed the small silver start button. "Traitor."

Shifting into reverse, they glided out of the barn with the kid and Hooker both laughing at the fickleness of the large cat. Petting the lap-full of fur, Johnny observed, "I take it Box is pretty selective?"

"Fickle is more like it." Hooker swapped gears and they began to roll down the hill. "Almost becoming a slut." The kid laughed and Box changed position so his back was to Hooker, which made the two men laugh even harder. "He almost took Stella's hand off the first time they met." Hooker danced the gears to the next tier. "Even today, she can feed him, but not pet him."

They chuckled and purred, respectively, down the hill as they headed to dinner at Dolly's place.

22

The home-baked sourdough rolls hadn't quite mopped up all of the evidence. Reddish smears remained on the plates, the last traces of the *Dolly made* fresh spaghetti with hand-made Sicilian style sausage from Chiaramonte's on North 13th Street. Everyone around the table sat back with satisfied expressions as well as tummies. Mike, the diminutive driver from Fremont, who had made the stop on North 13th for the sausage and other things on Dolly's standing order at Chiaramonte's, burped quietly, and said it all, "As usual, Dolly, it was terrible." And with a slightly louder burp, "Luckily, there were just enough of us to hide all of the evidence."

"Good thing I brought Squirt," Hooker jibed the older driver. "Otherwise, you might have had to let out your belt some more." They all laughed at the gentle ribbing that went on around Dolly's Wednesday night dinner tables, open by invitation only to tow drivers, officers, the occasional fireman, and a rare county official.

Hooker's presence at the head of the table was mandatory. All other chairs cycled through the county based on a priority that was secret to all but the queen of the county. It was rumored that more promotions, jobs, contracts, political alliances, and elections were formed or destroyed around her table than in any county office. Only Dolly and Hooker knew its truthfulness.

"Well, I'm sure glad you boys could come to this girl's rescue." Barefooted, she hovered around her table tending to the men of her world, with coffee, hair tousles, and the occasional hug.

Getting serious, the small driver leaned forward with his elbows on the table straddling his clean plate, "Any word on the funerals yet?" The table sobered.

Dolly stopped and looked back toward Dina unplugging a wire and hanging up on a call at the switchboard. Without turning around Dina acknowledged the question, "The CHP will be on Saturday at two PM. Services are closed to all but family and CHP. The procession will be open for law enforcement only. Interment will be on the hill at about four PM. I haven't heard on the second officer, but the one PD was Jewish and kosher, so he was quietly laid to rest this afternoon."

The table, as a whole, stared at things in front of them that were many miles away. Over the years, everyone had accumulated the ghosts that haunt them. Some lost friends, while others, well, are 'others'.

Hooker looked over at the walnut colored face of his long time CHP friend Micha Jawolinski as the 'not so young any more' officer looked up from picking at the small red stain on his *Fishermen Don't Lie* T-shirt. The two shared a common ghost from the night they first met. There were no smiles between the two. Just that flat look acknowledging to each other that they were thinking about the same night; it had been a bad night, in a rare soft drizzle on the 101, under the 'Altars.'

It was one of those freak October nights, when the humidity from the bay meets the cold air pushed over the Santa Cruz mountains. It wasn't enough to even call a rain, but drivers react to what is on their front window long before the squirm of their tires, so most had ignored the thin layer of wetting on the summer's built-up oil on the southbound 101 Freeway.

In the prosperous times under Governor Reagan, many highway construction projects had been started. A very large and high Los Angeles style interchange of the three freeways of 101, 280, and the 680 had begun construction. First raised were the over-passing exchange stands. Then another election cycle had swept the new junior Jerry Brown into office. The very large infrastructure war chest had evaporated in a matter of weeks. The shrine-to-Moonbeam Brown was a stack of two four-lane transitions, one on top of the other. Hovering thirty feet above the 101, where the 280 would become the 680, was a northbound 101 transition overpass to northbound 280 capping it all forty feet higher.

Besides being the butt of every joke known to transportation about being an *altar, still looking for a virgin to sacrifice*, the structures were also the source for many wrecks on the 101. Some involved gawkers or the occasional idiot who tried to take a picture while driving, but more wrecks happened as the dangerous rain season started.

Under the stacked altars, the surface is protected,; so

the oil that builds up throughout the summer is the last to dissipate or be washed away. More specifically, on that fateful night, the already wet tires of many cars ran over the oil at speed and starting slipping. Emerging from the underpass onto the truly slick entertainment field of four lanes of water over oil, the hydroplaning tires never stood a chance. What should have been an orderly progression of cars ended up looking more like a yard sale on a late Saturday afternoon. CHP called out seven tow trucks for seven cars. By the time they arrived, there were fourteen to be towed.

Hooker hadn't been called out, but he had simply been returning to his territory when he saw the mess. A tall CHP officer had been standing along the side, waved him over, and pointed at a creative cluster that may have started as three or four cars, but was by then just a mass of mangled colored steel and rubber. Not knowing what else to do, and not having been called out, he began sweeping the traffic lanes while the other drivers hooked up in a ceaseless leapfrog of blow-and-go. As things cleared out, and his pail got heavier, Hooker just dumped it in the others' pails and kept sweeping. His service in the wet, cold, dark night did not go unnoticed.

Mike, one of the older and more observant drivers brought down from up north, had stashed two cars in a parking lot within a mile. He was hooking up his third as he slipped Hooker the keys to an AMC Pacer and told him where it was. It was a *dead bone* or worthless, but it was at least a tow.

As Hooker was pulling out so the Chip could clear the scene, he noticed a red 1952 Chevy pickup with baby-moon hubcaps and an expensive paintjob. The truck was over in the shoulder, facing up the small berm. It didn't seem to have been part of the massacre. Hooker had watched the red truck as his wipers clacked an ominous counting of time, as time suspended. Something about the truck tied itself to Hooker, and he felt it was worth pointing out to the officer, and who knew? He might even throw Hooker the tow.

The officer had told Hooker to go over and check it out to see if it was part of the night's mess, or if someone had just parked a break-down at a strange angle. As Micha cleared the traffic, he was only seconds behind when Hooker opened the driver side door.

As Hooker approached the truck, he had seen the driver, a young blonde. She was the kind of girl that any red-blooded American boy with a pulse would have been proud to take to the prom and who, he later discovered, had been the prom queen just the year before. She turned her face toward him. "Are you alright?" he asked as he reached over and opened the door.

The gorgeous beauty blinked her powder blue eyes once, and then slumped out of the truck and into Hooker's arms. He barely caught her as she sighed, "Don't let me die." Then, she was gone.

Stunned, neither Hooker nor Micha moved. It was all just too overwhelmingly surreal for either to think about performing CPR. The wet turned to rain as the two soaked men stood on the side of the highway, washed in the red and blue flashing lights, and wept. It would be many minutes before the last paramedic came to check on the two standing off in a dark corner. Nothing was ever really said after that, but the two men knew that they shared a commonality that went far beyond anything they could ever say to each other. Several years later, Micha had bought Hooker a shot of whiskey in the bar at the Bold Knight on Monterey Highway. Hooker didn't understand the unwarranted gesture until the man had clicked their two shot glasses and said quietly, "Here is to beauty queens in pickup trucks. May they always be remembered for their laughs, smiles and the way they make their daddies proud, and may there always be many more."

Hooker looked down Dolly's table at that older CHP officer, then raised his water glass to the man, who returned the subtle toast, and they sipped their water, and drank deeply once again their shared brotherhood. Since that night, both had seen more than their share of bodies, but you never forget your first.

Dina's voice broke the revelry. "Mike, your boss just called, and she said if you're not back in your territory in half an hour, you can find another couch to be in trouble on." The men all started chuckling about the driver who had married the boss, after she had gotten the company in a divorce.

"Ace, you just had a T-1 go live in Willow Glen, I'll give that to you in the truck." She continued, "Hooker, I'm still holding that commercial reefer that needs to go down to Monterey, and if you want it, they have a service truck that needs to be in Santa Cruz and will drop you a couple of twenties to get it there. Micha, you were 'on call' as of fifteen minutes ago… Go home and sleep. The rest of you, tonight I need you to clear the dishes and wash them. I need Dolly at her desk." Turning back around to her desk of slips of paper, lights, and corded plugs that needed to be inserted into magical sequences, she galvanized the group. “Jump to it before I hold you all ten minutes on your next calls.” Minutes were everything to a driver, and when it came to whether you run clean or run late, Dina, and the other dispatchers, had the power of a god over your life.

Chair legs scraped as the men rose from the table. They shuffled into their orders of doing as Dina’s added command bumped the group into smiles and a detour. “I’m getting married next month. I’m pregnant and expect extra hugs and kisses. So nobody has any excuse for not giving me presents or being at my wedding.”

The men responded by lining up for hugs and kisses as they headed for the door or to clean up the dinner. Dolly stood command at the door after checking the security TV. As Hooker and Johnny passed review, she stopped them. “Do the loop, and then head for Stella’s. You two need the sleep. And in case I forget in the morning, there are twenty pounds of Chiaramonte’s sausages in the fridge that you need to take to her for Sunday’s dinner.” She kissed both on the cheek.

“Yes, ma’am,” they responded in unison. She swung at Johnny’s behind but missed by an inch. The kid looked back with a smile and laughed. It was the best thank you she could get. She loved her men well fed and happy.

Box stood in the window as Hooker climbed up into the truck and started the beast. Thinking a moment, he turned Mae back off.

“What’s wrong?”

Extending his left leg out of the now open door, Hooker looked back at Squirt. “I think I want to check the oil before we haul a heavy refrigerated truck down to Monterey." Climbing out, he grabbed a fresh rag out of the side box.

"What do you think?" Johnny asked as Hooker looked at the long spring steel dipstick.

"We're fine, but I think we'll swing by and pick up a few quarts extra. I also forgot my jacket," Slipping the tongue back in the tube and closing the hood, he turned on the kid, and questioned "Speaking of which, don't you have a jacket?"

Turning a little red, the kid lied, "Sure, at my house."

Hooker gave him a hard look of a few extra seconds, and when he saw the kid start to squirm, he broke and walked back around the truck. As he got on the other side, he swore under his breath, *fucking kid is just like me at that age.* He failed to realize that he truly had never been *that age*.

It was a long, silent, dark ride back up to Willie's and the garage, and Hooker was not going to be the first to blink. The kid needed to learn not to lie to him. When you are spending almost twenty-four of the twenty-four hours each day together, you have to be as honest as Box with each other.

23

"What did you forget this time?" The disembodied question came out of the dark. Hooker looked around the black volume of space. No work lights burned under any number of hoods of vehicles to be worked on. The fact that the moon had set almost an hour before didn't help seeing into the tar-black shop area.

The voice was definitely Willie's, so Hooker simply stated, "I have a tow down to Monterey, and then up through Santa Cruz and back to Manny and Stella's, so I figured I'd pack an extra gallon of oil, at least till we patch the oil pan."

There was some low muttering in the dark, so Hooker figured that Willie had company, probably Hanky Panky. If so, with them out here in the garage, who knew what games they were up to in the dark, so he was glad there were no lights.

"Good thinking. That's why I left you two one-gallon cans there by the door, to your right." There was more muttering in the dark, but with a very feminine giggle at the end. "We were wondering if you would figure that much out."

Hooker was almost afraid to ask, but his curiosity was up, and about to get the best of him when Johnny stepped through the door, and asked, "We?"

Hooker stiffened, and his shoulders sunk in on themselves as he felt more than heard the small click. A small 60-watt work light went on near the rust red REO Speed Wagon with its hood completely off from work being done. Hooker was afraid to look.

Willie and the female with him were sitting in the padded chaise lounges, fully clothed. "Madeline, I'd like you to meet a very nice young man. Madeline, this is Johnny," pointing to the kid. "Johnny, this is Madeline, or Maddie to her family and friends."

She raised a pint-canning jar half-full of clear liquid, "Nice to meet you, Squirt."

Hooker chuckled, more at the fact that Willie and the librarian were nine-sheets to the wind, than her pegging the kid and the nickname he hated. He turned and smiled at the kid's face.

The kid looked at him in disgust. "That isn't *even* funny anymore."

Hooker pointed with his open hand at the librarian, as if to say, *she's a guest, and you should answer her.* He arched his eyebrows and nodded his head at the older couple. "Well?"

The kid's shoulders slumped in resolve. "Very nice to meet you, Madeline." He reached out with his right fist and almost connected a solid punch to Hooker's arm.

"Oh please, call me Maddie," she slurred back. Looking at Willie with a short giggle, "We're all among friends here. I mean, we're not naked, or nothin', but we are… we'll, otherwise in-car-pass…erated." She hiccupped and then ripped out a definitive belch that could have come from a man twice her size. Her hand came up to almost hide the self-satisfied smile, but then she quietly said, "Oh, my. Excuse me, if that was rude… unless you have one hiding that is better?" She then broke down laughing as she rolled on to Willie's lap as he tried to belch but just farted.

Hooker looked at Johnny and rolled his eyes, saying quietly, "The good news is, one, she won't remember any of this in the morning, and two, we won't be here to remind her." Pointing at the two cans of oil, he told the kid, "Grab those, and stick them in the second side-box on my side. I think there should be enough room. Then open my door and call for Box so he can hit the lawn." Starting toward the door to the house, he added, "I'll just grab the jackets."

The kid picked up the two cans and headed back out to the truck. Securing them in the second side-box, he turned to the driver's door. As he opened the door, the orange streak slipped out and passed him. He turned back to look at the garage, scowling in curiosity, "Jackets?"

He watched Box do his manly evening constitutional. It was more of a ritual a dog might do than a cat. The stance was definitely not that of a cat. As he thought, *but who am I to understand what a cat wants to do.* Box was almost the sum total of his experience of cats, and up until now, he felt it was kind of a nice experience. Little did he know how *chosen* he was, but then, he had yet to experience the tattered, one-eyed street warrior take apart a 150-pound dog like a three year old kid ripping into presents on Christmas morning.

"Box! Go time!" Hooker called as he walked back out of the dark garage interior, calling back over his shoulder at the dark, "Willie, Stella said she would castrate you if you even thought about not showing up Sunday for dinner. Make sure you bring Hank. He can help with the cooking. And Maddie can be my guest. So twist her arm." Heading for the truck, he carried a large fist-full of leather that sort of matched the newer jacket he was wearing over his fresh white t-shirt. Throwing the extra eight pounds of leather at the kid, he instructed, "Here, see if this doesn't keep you warm while we eat some ice-cream."

The kid didn't question it, but slipped it on. The leather was some of the softest he had ever felt, much less worn. It fit him almost like a custom made, which is exactly what it had been for Hooker almost ten years before when he laid down two crisp Benjamins at the Just Leather store up on Steven's Creek. Hooker watched as he walked around the front of the truck, and smiled. He had been pretty sure it would fit. Maybe, if anything, it was about an inch too long for the slightly shorter kid, but then if he got a motorcycle, the fit would be perfect on those cold winter nights.

"Thanks," the kid acknowledged, climbing into the cab. "It fits almost like it was made for me, except a little loose," as he rolled his arms, feeling the fit.

"It's loose like that," Hooker started the truck and set it in seventh, "so you can wear a sweatshirt or heavy Pendleton flannel shirt under it." Glancing at the side mirrors, he let out the clutch and rolled down the driveway.

Smiling as he looked back at the kid's mock horror on

his face. The Squirt threw his hands out and asked in mock sarcasm, "What, and spoil the look?"

Hooker rolled his eyes back into his head with a mock pained look. "Just don't start wearing penny-loafers." He jumped the gear box from eighth to eleventh and let the truck drift down the hill that he had let-her-roll down at least a few thousand times. He knew every twist and bump of a turn so well that one very dark night that he had bet Willie he could take it all the way down to Coyote Road without any lights. They never spoke about hitting the family of raccoons.

Where the kid thought they would go straight out to the freeway, Hooker turned right, and headed west. As he looked at Hooker with a question mark carved in his face, Hooker turned a couple of head snaps to give him a goofy look. "What? Are you going to tell me you don't even like ice cream?"

"Sure, I like ice cream, but what's that got to do with going to Monterey?"

Hooker's eyes got real big as he stared out of the front window. "Everything!" he exploded. Looking over at the kid, the older and wiser street-tough explained with a lascivious smile, "It means we can have triple cones. It doesn't get much better than that." At the kid's confused face, Hooker frowned languidly and smacked his lips flatly as if he were bored. "You'll see."

Fifteen minutes later, they were climbing back into the truck with two triple cones and a little red dish, stored in the truck for just such occasions, with a scoop of French vanilla for Box. The kid's tongue swirled around the top plug of ice-cold delight. Frozen tongued as they rolled down Monterey Highway to pick up the new freeway extension near San Martine, the kid said, "Who would have guessed that there was ice cream available at every hour of the night." With the windows wide open to the still cold spring night air, the crooning of the Texas Boys' Choir gently swirling around the cab, the giant homage to Mae West rolled effortlessly southward.

Nodding his head as he licked his lips clean, Hooker agreed, "Yup, best thing Thrifty did besides those dumb Twin-Pics and dumb ads." As they drifted up onto the freeway, Hooker took a quick lick and reached back for the microphone behind his head.

"Hooker, base?"

There was a minute of hesitation, and then Dolly's voice cut through the night. "I thought you would be in Monterey by now. Well, at least as far as Prunedale." Hooker could hear the laughter just behind the scolding.

Rolling his eyes as he keyed the mic, "I felt it would be prudent to pack an extra gallon of oil or two, so I stopped up the hill."

The silence was longer this time as Dolly was either laughing or busy. Finally checking back, the digging voice was even deeper and sharper. Hooker could feel her eyes on him. "Uh huh, right. You know when you eat that ice cream your voice gets deeper and bed-roomy and drives Dina crazy." She had to stop to laugh. "And you better have thought of that mange bucket with some French vanilla."

Hooker glanced down at the topic of conversation that was already finished and settled back in with a deep purr that would last all the way to Monterey. As he slowly reached for the yellow microphone on the dashboard, Dolly fired her final shot. "And—don't you dare even think about calling Dina right now. She's busy, and I need her concentrating on real things. Besides, she's pregnant and it's not yours. And she's getting married."

"Yes, Momma," Hooker chuckled. "We're clearing Gilroy, and you're all broken up, 1-4-1."

Lowering his voice in an even deeper register, he keyed the yellow microphone, "1-4-1, south bound to the deep loins of Monterey."

The regular auto club dispatcher, Jake, startled Hooker and replied with a laugh, "10-4, 1-4-1, showing you out of area until tomorrow. I will advise night dispatch in 5-4-3-2- I'm gone."

Dina's voice, ever professional, filled the space between Jake's laughter and Hooker's, "Dispatch showing 1-4-1 Zero-Zero-Alpha, deep in the loins." Laughing, Hooker knew he would be paying for it on Sunday with Dolly teaming up with her unstoppable sister Stella, but sometimes, it's just worth it to stir the pot.

Hanging up the mic, he looked at his watch and realized what stretch of road was coming up. Getting the most evil wide-eyed maniacal look on his face, he looked at the kid and asked in a cackling crazy voice, "What's the fastest you've ever ridden in a truck before?" He danced the clutch and sticks, shifting into the top tier of gears as he slid north of eighty.

Johnny thought about it a moment as he watched Hooker slip the truck into its twentieth gear, with four more to go. Looking out at the night ahead, he weighed how much he trusted the person he was with—"Probably not nearly as fast as I think we will be going tonight."

Hooker laughed as he shifted through the last four gears of the giant truck. Eleven tons of rolling stock highballing down a dark moonless highway—these were the nights Hooker lived for, these were the times for which this truck was built. Smiling, he glanced down at his street-tested partner. "Hang on, Box—we are headed for Dead Man's Curve."

He glanced over to see if he had any effect on Johnny, but the kid was just snuggling in to his new jacket and enjoying the ride. His head turned toward the window as he watched the night fly by. He didn't have to look at the speedometer to know that they were well north of the 100 mph mark on the dial that went to 140 mph. Well past.

The five ton refrigerated truck just followed along like a happy little puppy behind its momma in the scintillating starlight as the boys from Texas crooned about tumble weeds and scudding clouds on the dusty trails. These were the moments that Hooker lived for; the defining moments of calm with activity, and the reasons he worked the night, instead of day.

24

"You didn't have to slip me that forty," Johnny half complained as they slid out of the truck, now ticking as it began to cool from the hard run over Highway 17 and the Santa Cruz pass. "It's not like you haven't been feeding me or anything."

Hooker smiled, thinking how he had probably said something similar in that first year or four living with Willie. Looking across the working deck as they each locked up their side panels and boxes, securing for the night. "I'll tell you what, you buy breakfast."

Snorting from the last turn of the key, Squirt just nodded. "Sure, and how exactly was I supposed to pay Estella for cooking breakfast… clear the table and wash the dishes?"

Hooker pursed his lips and lolled his head to one side with a shrug. "It's a start." Reaching out and slapping a hand on the kid's shoulder. "It's a start."

"Hardly seems like enough." The kid mumbled as he opened the large portico gate door. "Jeez Mareez," he stood looking at every light in the house turned on.

"Oh, shit!" Hooker pushed past him, and strode quickly toward the front door. The door opened as he touched the knob.

Stella stood in the way, then stepped aside, her face a swirl of worry, anger, and sorrow. Nodding her head at the office, "A deputy has been killed, down at Calero Dam, at the boat ramp." Her lower lip quivered almost imperceptibly, something Hooker had only seen once before, when Manny had been shot. Then, as now, it was only for a second before the iron and steel renewed and she was her usual self again. She sucked in a deep breath. "He's in talking to the Sheriff himself."

"How are you holding up?" Hooker looked deep into her face.

She hesitated a moment. "We don't know many deputies anymore, but they are all family." She sucked her lips in hard against her teeth then nodded as if to change the subject. Turning to the kid, she patted Johnny on the chest and asked in a too casual tone for the hour, "How was your day today, dear?"

The kid started to talk, but froze with his mouth open, looking to Hooker for guidance.

"Don't look at me." Hooker short-laughed. "Answer the lady." Kissing her on the top of her head, he squeezed Stella's arm. "I'll be in listening to the master when you run out of places to beat the kid." She slapped at his butt, which he bent forward out of the way.

She turned back to the kid still standing open-mouthed. "Come on, I've got some things you need to see, while you think about it." She pulled him through and closed the door. Taking him by the arm, she started him down the hallway of the guest wing. "Did I ever tell you about when Hooker came to camp with us?"

The kid just smartly shut his mouth, wagged his head, and allowed himself to be towed down her memory lane. "Well, it was several years ago…" She wound her arm in his and they walked slowly down the guest wing hall, toward the end room.

Hooker slumped into the large soft leather easy chair in the darkest corner of the office. As he listened to Manny work his favorite tool, the phone, Hooker carefully scanned the boards for the new details that hadn't been there the day before. Each of the new pictures had at least one or three 3x5 cards next to them with details and questions. It was always the questions with Manny. As long as Hooker had known Manny, a question or a picture or a piece of a puzzle had always poked Manny to spew out at least as many questions. He called it his 'Solving Problems with Socrates and Sherlock', his two most favorite people to read or read about.

"Listen, Ted, Hooker just got home, and there are a few things I want to go over with him before we all go to bed." Manny held up his other hand with his index finger extended, "Sure, give me a call in the late afternoon about four. Sure, that would be even better. We'll see you for dinner. Goodnight, Ted." He dropped the phone in his lap as he thumbed the button to hang up.

Turning toward Hooker, he studied the young man's face and body language. "Boy, did you ever need this early night, you look like something that Box was finished with."

Hooker's face rolled into a deep tired smile that pulled

up along his right side. "I think that *something* would be looking better than I feel. It's been a long week." He rested his head back along the chair as he softly blew out his breath. Waiting a three count, he nodded forward and looked at Manny. "A deputy, this time." The small statement carried more weight than the words.

The tip of Manny's tongue snuck forward and licked the center of his lower lip. Then as his lips drew back like steel bars, the tongue tip slid into retreat. "I heard Stella fill you in." He swiveled the chair back around to face the boards. He pointed to the new section. "He was ambushed at the boat ramp down at the dam." Manny slumped back into his chair. "He was supposed to have a partner, but the guy was sick, and the only other person for right seat was a fresh cadet who didn't have his weapon clearance yet." The retired detective's head kept scanning back and forth as he talked—almost as if the talking wasn't connected to the head. "They found all sixteen dimes this time—the four in the door, and the twelve in the deputy."

The two men sat silently, staring at the large roll-around pin boards with writing, pictures, and lines drawn where the battle raged, and there were no answers coming as fast as they were wanted.

Deliberately, Manny rolled back around to face Hooker, quiet in his thoughts. He morosely watched the young man's face as the eyelids caught up with the slouched body in the soft comforting chair. "On your way to your room, you might want to go see the end room."

Hooker looked up with leaded lids. "Hmm?" The message slowly pin-balled around his brain and came to rest in the pocket labeled *We Have a Winner*. He rose and waved good night to Manny who was just chuckling.

Shuffling down the hall, he noticed the light on in the back room. As he turned the corner he saw a cleared out room that was now semi-squared away as a sleeping room. Johnny sat on a bed that Hooker had never even seen before. The kid looked like a fresh poleaxed steer.

"Did you know about this?" The kid could barely control his quivering voice.

Hooker just shook his head no. "Looks good. Goodnight." Turning, he left the kid to his new digs. Hooker figured it would all be sorted out in the morning. If Stella wanted another waif in their lives, far be it for him to stand in their way. His mouth stretched in a small smile as he laid his head down on the pillow. Hooker had been there before, and he knew the kid would be all right.

Moments later, the large diesel engine rumbling in his ear was not Mae. The sun was shining but it was night, and the engine needed a tune-up something fierce, as the lope in its idle was very erratic, and then Box stuck his ice-cold nose into Hooker's right ear.

Blankets and sheets exploded about the room as Hooker turned inside out with the shock. Box, who was used to even more violent reactions than this, just sat purring and staring at Hooker with his one good eye. Something told Hooker that it was late, and either Box needed to be fed or let out.

Giving the tough cat a cold look, that only a close partner could and did ignore, Hooker shoved his legs into his pants, bypassing the boots as he pulled the jeans together around his waist and buttoned the fly closed before cinching the belt. Box, now satisfied that things were going his way, slithered down from the low bed and marched with his bent-tipped tail standing proud, through the doorway that was now being held open by Stella.

"Sorry about that," she reached out and hugged Hooker with a kiss on his neck. "I told him to let you sleep in, but you know how the mange bucket can be." They both looked at the closed door at the end of the hall as they cleared Hooker's room.

She looked back at Hooker and pulled on his arm as she nodded at the kitchen. "Let's give him some time to get used to it." She didn't have to remind Hooker of his first week of unease with his new room that was every bit as much a sanctuary as his room at Willie's house was… until the screaming and tempers that went with a very serious and emotional break-up of Willie and his long-time boyfriend. It wasn't until a year later that Hooker found out that it was really about the friend dying, and that he was breaking up with Willie because he didn't want to be a burden on Willie and Hooker. If Hooker had known that then, he would have stayed and fought to keep the men together, but he hadn't known. Instead, he found his other half of the family.

As the two of them turned the corner into the foyer area, Hooker took one last glance back down the hall and stole the opportunity to kiss Stella's cheek. "Thanks." She just squeezed him a little harder and nodded her head. She knew she couldn't trust herself to talk at that moment.

"Jesus, Mary, Joseph, and Rex!" Manny loudly started from the sunroom, "I thought you were going to sleep the clock around."

"Love you too, Manny." Hooker and Stella veered off

for a stop at the large coffee pot before Hooker had to engage more torment at Manny's mouth. Hooker squinted at the clock to make sure it was still running, because the time was way out of whack.

Stella just nodded as she grabbed a set of hot pads and opened the upper oven. "Brunch is in about forty or fifty minutes. So if you're going to horse play with the frisky old fart and get a shower, I'm going to vote for the water locker first."

Still a bit foggy, Hooker nodded as he medicated his coffee with sugar and cream. "Has the kid even made any noise yet?" Sipping from the large mug, Hooker's eyes slowly slid closed in that *first sip of coffee* ecstasy.

Dusting her hands with the pestle-ground rosemary over the chickens for dinner later that day, she shook her head. "You might want to kick his door and get him moving, too."

"OK." Stepping into the archway to the sunroom on his way to the shower, Hooker took a glancing stab at the man relaxing on the couch with a large book in his lap. "Sorry, Manny, but Stella says I either have to take you out and hose you down along with Box, or take a shower myself. I voted for me in the water. You lose." Looking about, he spotted the orange topic of derision waiting impatiently at the door. "I'm coming, I'm coming."

Opening the door, the orange doorstop became a bullet across the plaza. Hooker sipped on his coffee as he watched the big cat hit the grass, do his thing, and then begin to look for something to beat up. "Come on, Box, no fights today. Not on the Sabbath." Hooker could hear the dual snorts of laughter from the kitchen and sunroom. The furry ball of macho stalked back across the plaza and through the closing door.

Slipping his way to the far door, Hooker knocked. “Squirt, dinner is in thirty minutes, be showered and don’t be late or you have to answer to Stella.” Listening, he heard movement then a groan, so he headed for his shower room and ritual. Sundays could be a total relaxing bust, business-wise, or Hooker could be back up at the crack of noon and run himself ragged until well past midnight or beyond. Sometimes, it was nice to wake up and find out you’re eleven-plus hours into the day, and only having to look forward to a shower and dinner with loved ones.

25

Hooker padded back down the hall and tapped on the still closed door listening to Johnny respond that he would be out in a few minutes. Hooker threw back the last of the coffee in the large mug and headed for a refill. As he walked past the open office door, he saw the pin boards as he remembered the news from last night about the Sherriff's deputy. He scowled at the thought of another cop taken down in his prime, because only the prime work the street—even the ones that are only days away from retirement.

Manny was at the large table going over some notes. Estella's dining table was sacrosanct: for eating and talking – no radio, TV, newspaper or books. Manny was allowed notes, but only if he were working on a case, and only if he was alone. Hooker poured himself some more coffee and stayed away from the table until Manny put down the notes, stacked them in a neat pile, and looked up.

"Another week and you're standing up-right." Manny rolled out their old standby joke as Hooker brought over the coffee carafe to fill the other man's oversized mug. The joke was the evolution of Hooker's first comment to the detective when he woke-up in the hospital paralyzed from the waist down. 'How are you supposed to be an up-standing guy if you're just laying around all day?' had become a myriad of comments to each other about standing and up—but mostly it became about still standing after a grueling week, as well as standing this side of a dirt blanket.

"At least I'm standing on this side of the dirt," Hooker mumbled with a slur that matched his still blurry eyes.

Returning to the long counter, he plugged the carafe back into the wall cord. Hooker turned and leaned his lower back against the cool stone and asked his friend, "Anything new?" As to what he was asking about was completely unnecessary. There had been only one thing consuming Manny's attention night and day.

Grabbing his own large mug, Hooker returned to the table and took a seat at the other end. He closed his eyes and sipped the nectar of morning as if it were mother's milk fresh from the breast.

Manny shook his head, his mind still many miles away from the table. "They thought they had a partial print on one of the dimes, but it was just some grease or something that had a print off a latex glove. Not much help, unless the grease is unique." Slowly coming back to the reality around him, he noticed some movement in the window through to one of the hall windows in the guest wing. "The Squirt's up," he commented.

Hooker didn't even have to look as he could hear the slight squeak of bare feet on the red terracotta tiles of the entryway. "Mugs are above the coffee pot, choose any but the black one or the flowered one, those are Dolly's and Stella's respectively." Smiling as he added, "Only Sweets can get away with saying he didn't know."

The kid grabbed an oversized stone mug, and as he poured, asked with a muffled voice, "Sweets? There is someone I haven't met yet?"

Hooker raised his eyes to look at Manny as they shared a large smile, "Yeah, and trust me, he won't call you Squirt." Manny pursed his lips as he sipped his coffee, and nodded in agreement. "In fact, you're going to like him a whole bunch. But if he doesn't like you, then… well, we'll just have to take you out and shoot you… leave your body for the wolves."

The kid slid into one of the side chairs. "Now I know you're fibbing, cuz there ain't no wolves around here."

Manny's left eyebrow slid up into an arch. "You sure about that?"

The kid looked the man in the eye. "Yeah."

Hooker continued with the mutual digging on the unsuspecting victim. "Would you bet your life on that?"

The voice of reason was issued from the sunroom. "You boys leave the kid alone."

The two men chuckled and sipped their coffee, wisely not willing to risk any comment that may cross the queen of the house, especially on a Sunday morning.

Johnny ventured a bit of humor that played well with the playful nature of their morning. "Stella," he whined in a drawn-out child's voice, "they… they're picking on me."

"Shut up, and drink your coffee," the reply came, as there was also an irritated shake-ruffle of the Sunday paper as she shook out the turned page, and to reinforce the information that the men were messing with the sanctity of her *Sunday morning paper time.*

The kid tucked his chin back into his chest and stared with huge chastised eyes at Hooker, then Manny, as they nodded their heads knowingly and quietly sipped their coffee. As the kid started to say something, Manny held up his right index finger into the air between them to stop him from vocalizing. The paper shook one more time, and then there was a smoothing out and a final flip of paper folded length-wise, the silence of the woman sipping her own coffee, and the click of the matched flower mug clicking down on the glass-topped end table.

Manny, withdrew his finger and looked at the kid. "You were saying?"

The kid just shook his head. "Wasn't important."

Hooker put down his mug and stretched his lanky legs under the table as his arms reached for air behind his head. Yawning, he asked, "So, how was your new bed?"

Snickering, the kid put down his empty mug. "It was great, until I had to share it with Box." Looking over at Hooker. "Did you know that he likes to steal blankets?"

Hooker, unsure if he should feel betrayed by his partner or enjoy sharing the cat, chuckled silently. "What part of my door being closed did you not understand?" He looked down the table and rolled his eyes at Manny in a knowing manner. "You either learn, or you learn to suffer, but I can guarantee you this—Box isn't going to be changing anytime soon."

The kitchen timer dinged. The paper only ruffled a tiny bit, and the two men knew that she was turning down the one corner as she assessed the next movement in the house.

The gentle commanding voice carried from the sunny morning room, any other day, the sole bastion of Manny. "Hooker, show John where the place settings are, so he can learn to set the table. Then take the baked French toast out of the upper oven. The quiche needs about five more minutes. I can't smell it yet." She flipped the corner of paper back and resumed reading the morning horror stories, or as other people called them, the obituaries. "There is a new bottle of berry syrup in the pantry, as well as the standard. Get them both, please." She shook the paper to enforce her will, and the two younger men rose from the table.

Hooker turned to the kid. "Stick with me, I'll teach you everything you need to know about Sundays around this house." As they moved into the kitchen, he added, "If you ever end up at Willie's on Sunday… just start pouring the cold cereal in anything you can find that is clean."

An hour later, the two were standing at the sink, Hooker washing as the kid dried and stacked the colorful Fiestaware pottery dishes, as well as all the rest of the large cupboard full of dishes—every shape and size fulfilling several full sets.

"How many people are coming to this barbecue?"

Hooker cocked his jaw as he chuffed a deep laugh. "Let see, there are about twenty pounds of Chiaramonte's Sicilian sausage, about three gallons of marinated chicken breasts in the bottom of the fridge, what looked to be about three or four gallons of different salads, and that doesn't even start to include what Dolly and Tilly will be bringing. So just off the top of my head, I would say about a good hundred humans, and then there is Danny and Box."

The back of Hooker's head stung as the tips of Stella's fingers snapped off the back of his scalp where it was most sensitive. "Don't you dare be inferring that Danny is an animal, he's just a growing boy who likes to eat… and I like watching him enjoy himself." Winking at the kid, "That mange bucket, on the other hand…" She rolled her eyes as she lolled her head to her shoulder, stuck out her tongue, and hung her head back in her *Zombie* pose.

Once Hooker was cleaned up and as squared away as the morning's kitchen, he sat down with Manny and Johnny for a chalk talk. Manny was not happy, but understood, but the kid was just upset.

"Why can't I come?" The nonplussed youth paced with exaggerated hands, well, hand and arms. "Who's going to have your back?"

"Box," Hooker shrugged.

The kid was incredulous. "A cat?" It stopped him dead in the center of the office with arms at both extremes. "A cat is going to have your back? What's he got, an Uzi?"

Manny's lips were a grimaced taut line, and slowly raised his eyes to engage the kid standing above him. "Don't count Box out. Where Hooker is going, he'll be more than enough." Manny thought for a moment before he continued. "Probably more than the shorty 12-gauge he'll be carrying." He looked at Hooker for confirmation.

"Look, Johnny," Hooker confided adult to adult, "These people are like Peter, spooky and superstitious. They semi-understand the shotgun, but the fact that it's loaded with silver makes it very scary to them. Box isn't like a regular cat. He comes when I call, he is larger than most." The kid's eyes got big with expression as he nodded. "And most of all, he has my back. Anybody tries to sneak up on me, Box will bushwhack them. He's done it before with this group.'

"But…"

"No," Hooker finished as he stood up. He looked to Manny. "I'll check in through Dolly as soon as I get there, and when I clear."

Manny nodded agreement. "And we'll find something around here for Squirt to do on his day off." Turning his chair to look squarely at the beaten kid, he continued. "I think it might be time to clean out the office area in the garage level."

"Yeah, right. Like you have a garage level," bracketing the *garage level* with quoting fingers that he could now use, and a heavy sluicing of sarcasm.

Hooker snorted. "You're going to wish you had said that with a lot more respect when you see his cars… that you now don't get to drive." Grabbing up his leather jacket, he turned for the door. "Keep him working, Manny. I'll check in and be home by dinner."

As he stepped into the foyer, there was a toll to pay, and he gave the best he could of a reassuring hug and smile. Stella ran her warm hand down along the side of his face. "Don't let your sister get to you. She's gone to this world, and there is no redemption that will ever put that genie back in the little sister you knew."

Hooker's face pulled back in a grim frown. "I know. I just miss her, and knowing that she's out there still doesn't make it any easier."

"Both of you made choices when you ran from that foster home. You turned out, and she, well, just turned…"

"I had a lot of help, she didn't." He studied her eyes of concern.

"You offered, just like Willie did, and like we did. Beyond that, it's all up to the person being offered the hand as to whether they take it or not."

Hooker settled into silence and just looked at her face. For a brief moment, he thought that if he had been looking into it all his life, things might have turned out differently, and then again, maybe not. He kissed her on the cheek and turned the doorknob.

Turning back, he called to the sunroom, "Box. Go time." The streak was almost to the front gate by the time Hooker closed the house door. Some things, you just didn't have to tell the cat a second time. Picking a fight, Hooker knew, was another.

The road out to the rock wasn't exactly much of a road as much as it was an ignored or abused track in the South Bay scrub and sand marsh pan. From his advantage of ten feet above the pan, Hooker could see almost anything moving within a half mile—but the operative term was *moving*.

Hooker knew, and could feel, the small army of creatures that *The Mouse* had gathered around her, now out across the pan, watching his slow approach. Although, their mothers had thought at their births that they were all humans, time, and the warping nature of mental illness, had created changelings that only the most creative 'things that go bump in the night' storytellers could even begin to imagine. And mostly, they would be sorry to have imagined. And more beyond that… something that even the most creative would never get close to imagining in this universe.

Even The Mouse had been 'human' at one time. Even though the times weren't the best, she had occasionally worn a dress, gone to school, and talked about 'when she grew up'.

Then there was the change in the foster homes, from purgatory to nothing less than perdition itself. The incarnate was not another foster child, but the foster family themselves. The same family that Hooker had beaten on his way out the door at age fourteen, two very long months after The Mouse had taken a razor blade to the couple as they had proceeded to rape her one more time before they turned her over to their even more sadistic mentally retarded forty-three year old son to 'play with for the night'.

Even in the heat of the day, on the flat pan with the sun reflecting back from the brackish waters of the muds and the back bay, the thoughts of their childhood made Hooker's spine sub-zero and froze his resolve to see her. As he drove closer to the distant wavering knot of dark clay rising from the pan, his usual green hazel eyes slowly drained of color on their way to aqua-white ash. This would not be a day of emotion. This would be a day of pure nerves—and the cold of blue-white steel was his only way to stay alive.

The truck nudged up within fifty feet of the large rock of clay that towered close to the forty feet of telephone poles in the distance. The giant motor rattled and shook in protest, on its way to silence. Box stood as tense as strained cord on a war bow drawn tight with an arrow—all anticipation and potential of death. If the large deep dashboard had been anything softer than steel, his claws would have dug in as the experienced paws of death extended and retracted in anticipation and reflex.

"Ready for this, buddy?" Hooker asked quietly as his eyes scanned the dead scrub, barren of any signs of life.

The tip of the cat's tail kinked, and then the whole swept in an expressive arc of *'Let's go.'*

Checking his side mirrors, where he had thought he had seen a flash of movement, there was nothing there. He reached for the door handle and released the chrome lever, silently swinging out the door as his left foot slipped out and sought the step on top of the saddle tank.

Leaning back and twisting right to reach the shotgun in its wall-mounted holster, Hooker felt the cat hit his left shoulder for a brief second as he catapulted through the open door. The resulting scream, animal as it was, was not Box, but Box's prey. Hooker jacked the action on the pump shotgun and spun out of the door to face any other idiot that didn't understand who they were dealing with.

Out of the corner of his eye, Hooker could see a large chimera of rags, that may or may not be a man, writhing in the dust dealing with over twenty pounds of orange hell-hound in a cat's body. The face and two hands were rapidly losing the battle. "Mouse?" Hooker called out to the rock and pan, "Your dutifully stupid underling is rapidly losing his face and hands." He collected his thoughts. "In a minute or less, the only recourse will be for me to put an ounce of silver through his brain."

"Call off your beast!" The diminutive woman stepped

out away from the bush where she had been hiding. "Call it off. He was only doing what he thought would make me happy."

Hooker stood his ground and after a slow count of three, called softly. "Box, come."

The cat stood up on the man's face and took tearing swipes at the offending hands hovering around him, flaying the palms, and calling forth a fresh scream of anguish and pain from the form under him. One last deep shearing sweep of the quad swords of pain and the man's nose was a spread deck of cards. Turning, Box sprayed his way slowly off the hunter-turned-catch, marking his kill, or at least establishing grounds for territory.

The cat passed behind Hooker's legs, rubbing to let him know he was there, and then settled down and cleaned his paws as he sat next to Hooker and acted as if he were uncaring or even unnoticing of any minor stuff happening around him. Hooker could feel the slow rhythmic breathing as the cat leaned against his leg. The twenty-plus pound cat wasn't even breathing hard, having just taken out a 140 pound man—a tough act to follow.

The small woman calmly walked forward as other entities began to materialize out of the dirt and brush, her cold blue eyes never leaving the matching steel of Hooker's. As she reached within ten feet, her eyes slowly drooped. She broke eye contact and looked at the man holding his destroyed face in his wounded hands.

She looked toward someone off to one side that was out of Hooker's vision, but probably not Box's vision, or at least attention. She flicked her head and made a subtle sign of her hand and two came forward to collect the suffering sacrificial mound of flesh.

Hooker didn't have to look. "You didn't have to test me that way, Sissy."

The woman reared back and hissed silently like a vampire that Hooker had just tossed holy water on. "That name is not used anymore, Hooker."

"Too bad. Those were better days, for both of us."

"Maybe because only you think so." She still circled around like a large wary cat.

"At least you slept in a bed with a roof over your head."

"Some beds are better left unmade," she shot back. "Some look better, but are wastelands of pain and suffering, or just worse than hell itself.

Hooker sighed. "Mouse, we can argue this until we are both old and dead, but that is not why I came here to see you."

"You didn't come to just be neighborly, Hooker." She pointed at the shotgun at his side. "You bring the viper of silver, and the beast of hell. What happened to the trust of a brother?"

"It disappeared with the knife through my back, and the five broken ribs your tribe gave me many years ago."

"You shouldn't have come." She fidgeted, trying to see where Box was without being obvious.

"I need your help." He knew he had the upper hand as long as he didn't stop to look around, as more of her minions slithered out from under the cover where they had been hiding. As long as she was the one that was worried, he could get what he wanted, or at least needed.

The heat of the pan beat harsh on the denizens who

usually only moved about in the cool of darkness. The constant buzz of marsh flies and sand fleas intensified the perception of an intense heat, which Hooker experienced as mild. Hooker knew the sun on the thin milky skin of his redheaded, borderline-albino, foster sister, must be searing and painful. She would pay for days for the few minutes she had been exposed today.

"There have been killings…"

"There are always killings!" she snapped, now impatient.

"These have to do," Hooker lifted his shotgun by the barrel, "with a weapon like this." A sharp intake of breath hissed from the unseen collective. These hidden denizens knew of the silver the gun contained.

The Mouse weighed her options and the value of information. "We have heard."

"I need to know what you have heard, so that I can stop this killer." He studied, from the dozen or so feet away, the flush of heat along her right cheek.

"What is it worth, this information?"

Hooker had been thinking about this for most of the previous day, knowing that this meeting would come down to what she was going to get out of it. It had to have a certain tangible value to her, and yet be an intangible item that he would not have to produce or carry back to her. But instead, it would have to raise her standing as a leader.

"Who is the killer killing?" he asked.

"Pigs," she hissed.

"Police," he corrected.

"Pigs. Pigs—those who harass us and stop us because we are not like them, and who prevent us from going where we need to go for food and clothing. Pigs, who force us to live in this hell, because the people in their washed clean city are offended by seeing someone who must climb through their garbage because they don't want to give us their leftover garbage—their rotting fruit and vegetables or bread that is already molding. Pigs." She picked at her arms in an old habit of irritation that had garnered the nickname of Mouse, the grey dead skin that covered her arms and hung like fur.

"Don't pick, Sissy," Hooker said very quietly, almost to himself, an old habit of his own from better times, or not.

Her head snapped up, unsure if she had heard the name she now could not tolerate, a name that could denote a connection that would belie her position of supreme leader. She glared at Hooker, and she slowly withdrew her hand from her somewhat furry arm.

"OK, but they are still the police. They are my people. I can talk to them. Maybe some kind of accommodations can be made. A blind eye turned, as it were—but only if you can truly help me." For the first time, Hooker allowed himself to slowly look about at some of the now visible walking wounded of the night. She was right, they lacked from any decent food—or any food at all. "I'll also see what I can do about getting you some food, before it's rotten. I don't know what I can do, but I will try. And maybe some kind of medical help…" His voice trailed off as he knew that they would never trust another doctor in their short lifetimes.

She thought for a moment. "Sanctuary and redemption."

"I don't know where they could give you that..." Hooker started.

"No, stupid. Not for us, the killer. The killer is in the Sanctuary and has eaten the meal of redemption and salvation."

"I'm not sure I understand, Mouse. I need for you to talk to me in plain talk, not riddles. We aren't ten years old anymore." He could see that she was at the end of what she could stand. "Please, my time is up, and I have to go. What are you trying to tell me?"

"The person you seek is one of the blessed and forgiven of *His* army. But the person you seek is not the person you think you seek. Look to the killers of nature, and you will find your answer in the garden."

"Mouse, you're not being..."

"Your time is past. Now take your beast of evil and go." She violently fluffed the rags of her clothing like they were a multitude of wings, and the fine dust filled the air enough to obscure her passing to under, behind or into one of the bushes, or even somewhere else. For all Hooker cared or understood, she could have successfully disappeared, and as he turned around, there were no others but him standing on the pan next to the giant truck. The heat and the flies were the only sound.

Hooker slowly raised his right hand up to the grab-hold beside his door, still looking about across the pan. Hoping that what she had said would have some meaning for someone—and soon. He turned up into the cab. "Box, go." The orange streak tore from the lower brush, into the cab through the small space under his feet, and into his box.

Stowing Betsy in her holster, he sat in the silence thinking, his right hand hanging and finding the one almost whole ear to slide between his fingers. He gently massaged his knuckle in the cat's ear and was rewarded with a deep contented purr. All around a good day when you can take on an advisory ten times your size and come away the untouched victor.

Turning the silver key, and pushing the small silver button, the massive engine matched the purr in the cab. Hooker had a lot to think about, but with a quick glance at his watch, knew he would have no time to casually drive and think. Pushing the gears into reverse, he checked his side mirrors as he began the half mile of backing out of the Mouse's domain. Hooker had no idea where her people were, or slept and he didn't want to find out that a three-point turn-around had been a three-person kill as he ran over them. So for future's sake and out of respect for his sister, he could do a little backing up.

The alkali-dusted tires were just starting to spin back to black on the asphalt as Hooker keyed the mic behind his head. "Hooker, 10-98, and safely heading home. Please make the call and advise Dolly and Stella that their chubby little neck nuzzles are safe."

The radio squelched from being picked up too fast and over modulating with a mouth too close to the sensitive lollypop microphone. "You had better be safe, young man."

"I am, Dolly." *Shift on a biscuit,* Hooker thought, *what the heck is she still doing there?* "I would have thought you would be out helping your sister already."

"Nice try. But now we can both go on out. Oh, and

Hooker… I'll take the sausage you forgot."

"Shi…ift in deep sand," he thought. "Thank you Dolly. See you there."

"10-4, base out."

Hooker looked down at his companion who was now sound asleep. "Careful when we get home, Box, your girlfriend is in one of those rare moods." He meant *motherhood.* A small warm smile washed his face as he pushed south into the top of the city, clearing his side mirrors and looking at the sparkle of the last visible vestiges of the San Francisco Bay sparkling in the late afternoon sunlight that was unique to the bay area in the late spring.

Over the years, people had told him about Paris in the spring, and how over there, the evening light was different and magical like nowhere else. He had heard stories about London, New York, and even Los Angeles and San Diego, but for Hooker, he would rather have the spring light in his hometown that bounces off the bay, or the ultra-glow that lit up the sailboats. This was to Hooker like the sprinkles on a cupcake—one of life's little quiet pleasures. He was a simple man who took his real pleasures in the little things.

His right hand hung down along his seat in the off chance that Box might just sit up and stick an ear in twiddling range. The smile seemed stuck on the left side of Hooker's face as the hulking truck dropped down the last slide onto the Almaden Expressway, the yellow brick road to home.

The large flashes of emerald green, mixed with the lines of golden-brown, crept back in over the powder-gray in his eyes. The closer to home, the more there were, and the larger the flashes of green would appear. Purring deeply, Box rose up and stuck his ear in between the proffered fingers. Box would purr for the two of them, as the large engine harmonized and carried the tune.

26

Johnny stood beside Stella as they rewashed already clean dishes. The two were looking at the growing crowd. Both were futzing around, but with different motives—the kid was intimidated by the growing mass of people he didn't know, and Stella was waiting for it to be just the right amount of people for her entrance. Inside, she was worried sick about Hooker, and she wouldn't be able to settle down until both he and her sister had walked through the gate.

Johnny was admiring how good Willie looked in his new patchwork jean bib-overalls, a consideration to convention, and that others might just be a little uncomfortable around a white-haired man in a long dress. A small self-satisfied smile crept across his lower face.

"Did you make that suggestion, too?"

He looked over at Stella with confusion then understood that she was talking about the same thing he was looking at. "Naw—that is pure Willie. I suggested that he would look better in faded denim instead of the flower dress he was wearing the other day." He shot her a shy side-glance. "I was talking about another dress. The bibbies were something he found."

"Or had sewn." She bumped her hip into his. "Don't count the old man out—he has amazing connections."

Thinking a moment as he dried another plate, he asked, "How did he and Hooker meet?"

Stella laughed a low rolling chuckle that came from deep and far away. "That story, you should hear first-hand from Willie. Hooker tells a decent rendition, but the better telling is from William himself."

The kid dried another plate, stacked it, and reached for another. "I guess that will just be a story I'll never hear then." He looked back out at the man standing near the giant open grill as he watched his friend play the fire and steel like it was a violin. "It just sounds too personal of a story for me to ask to hear."

"Pffut," Stella chided. "Nothing that personal."

The kid just shrugged one shoulder and reached for another plate.

"OK, wimp," she shot him a motherly indulging look, "but like I said, this isn't nearly as much fun as when Willie tells it," nodding her jaw toward the window, "especially when he's gone past the second beer and a shot of moonshine or two. Because then he slips a little and his Nancy comes sliding out..." She giggled. "First time I heard him tell the story, I wet myself just listening to him."

"I'll settle for a version that I don't have to change my pants."

"Version of what?" Hooker asked as he strolled out of the pantry, having used the secret stairway up from the garage.

"Well, it's about time!" Stella turned on him with her arms up for a hug.

"I had to park in the lower pasture. There's no room up here." He nuzzled in her neck in a perfunctorily distracted buzz. "Dolly here yet?"

"No, honey, but I expect her along any time now."

"She's probably out circling around looking for a parking place. I'll go find her."

"No, I'll go whistle my little sister up. You tell Squirt how you met Willie."

Hooker looked at the kid who was trying to act busy at the sink. Hooker smirked. He knew that the kid deserved to know the story. It was all part of becoming one with the family. As Stella moved through the plaza like a winter tornado, Hooker clamped his right hand on the Johnny's left shoulder, making the kid jump.

"Don't worry, kid, I'm not going to bore you to tears." He stepped closer to the counter and looked out at his uncle. "Willie will be primed and perfect by about seven tonight, and by midnight, you might have recovered." He chuckled at the wide-eyed look the kid now wore. "For now, you're off the hook. I need to talk to Manny."

The kid turned his head, facing Hooker. "You got something?"

As Hooker moved toward the office, he called back, "Maybe."

Johnny wiped his hands in the dishtowel, and then on his new jeans as he followed Hooker into the office in search for the detective.

Forty minutes later, Stella knocked and opened the office door. "Hank says you men have only five more minutes for your man bonding thing. So beat your drums faster."

Sweets being the fastest with the mind and lips, answered for the eight men. "Thank you, my love, we were just wrapping up the details and preparing ourselves to partake in the radiance of your beauty and hospitality."

"Awe, thanks, Sweets. That is just so sweet for you to say that, but it doesn't mean you're clear of slinging bullshit. Hustle them along." Giggling, she quietly closed the door, and then called through the thick wood. "You now have four minutes."

Manny rolled his eyes. "So if all of the saved, redeemed, forgiven, and sanctuary stuff is about a priest, why are we looking for the wrong guy?"

"I'm not so sure we are." Hooker scratched at the back of his left ear. "I think Sissy was being obtuse, but I also think she tried to direct me, but not to appear so in front of her clan."

Danny grunted and shifted uncomfortably, giving Hooker the eye.

Hooker looked at him a second, and then asked, "What?" with his hands out and shoulders in a shrug to say, "What did I do wrong?"

Danny half rolled his eyes. "She's right. You need to stop using it."

"What?"

"Sissy. It's demeaning and doesn't help her or you."

"It's short for Lucinda, her middle name. Claire is her first. It's the only name she went by for years."

"No, it's about being a sissy. It's not who she is. She is not your sister anymore, nor a Lucinda or a sissy. She is a commander of an army. If they catch a whiff of weakness, they will turn on her and eat her alive, man."

Sweets perfunctorily stood up and raised a hand. "Danny is right. Hooker, you need to respect the Mouse's right to be the Mouse, even if she is surrounded by rats." Lowering his hand as he aimed his open palm in the direction of the doorway in which Stella had appeared. "Gentlemen, our time is up. The ladies, and a gentleman, await our presence."

The remainder, grousing, rose from the places they had come to roost on in the office. Danny, ever being Danny, groused the loudest. "There better still be some food left."

Hooker grabbed at the big man's tummy and shook it. "Mihito, tus flaco." (Little one, you're skinny.) The three laughed as they walked out of the office pushing Manny—Danny being one of the few people who had ever been allowed to push him.

The roar of the ongoing conversations flowing about the large patio was a wash of topics with varying levels of mirth and merriment. It was a much-needed salve for Hooker and most of the rest in the crowd who were all somehow connected to the law enforcement industry. Manny held court from his massive *special* table, the large round one he had built even before they started raising the adobe walls.

Manny and Stella had known, even before going into this house, that they wanted a place where many could gather, or just a few for an intimate dinner. The patio that spread out from the house was larger than the footprint of the large sprawling hacienda, fully taking advantage of the nine months of outdoor entertainment weather enjoyed by the trapped heat in the Almaden Valley. It was the main reason for originally buying the land—other than the knoll being their favorite picnic spot for many years.

Manny looked around the several tables where many still picked at the remains of a food orgy which would have made the ancient Romans proud. Others, who had reached their limits, were merely in resting or relaxing as they enjoyed the group dynamics. Seeing the tell-tale signs, he quietly touched Stella's hand and minutely jutted his jaw towards the other over-sized table containing Willie, Hank, and Johnny, as well as other unsuspecting members who were about to receive 'the story,' as it had come to be known.

Johnny needed a point cleared up. "Wait, wait… why, was he stealing your car in the first place?" He wanted to make sure he wasn't getting only the partial story, but his loud question stopped many conversations at other tables. Some wondered what was going on about a stolen car, and others who knew the story and the storyteller had quieted the rest so that they could hear it, too.

"Well, silly," Willie's hand flopped languidly out in the air as the many shots of Madeline's family moonshine worked its magic on his inner Nancy, "because he was hungry, of course." The final 's' was drawn out into a little giggle that needed a wee bit more moonshine.

"But who was he going to sell it to?"

Hank laughed as Willie sipped. "That's the best part—the kid didn't have a buyer."

Willie put down his half-pint canning jar and reinserted himself back into his proper role as the storyteller. "He hadn't thought that far. Little Hooker had only thought up the idea the moment he saw my unlocked car." Waving his hand about to wash the air in front of him and his stage as he winked. "We'll just forget about it being a convertible with the top down."

Pulling himself up to show up-rightness and respect, he would imbue in the character of the *young* Hooker. "I'm sure he's been able to break into many tougher cars since then." He got the much reached for laugh, from almost the whole crowd, as he now raised his voice in the knowledge that he was the entertainment for the entire large patio.

"So, as I came back out of the hardware store with my purchase, I'm greeted with a tiny little butt, wiggling in the air as he's trying his hand at figuring out which wires to pull and cross to hotwire my car." Full into his Nancy now, he waved his spread right hand across the stage in the air above his face, so that everyone could see his panorama he was seeing.

"As delightful as it was at the moment, I knew he was about to start ripping into wires that would take me a full day or two to reinstate. So I popped him one on that cute bottom!" Willie was giggling in his own fantasy.

Hooker growled from a distant table. "Will-ie."

"Spoil sport," Willie stage muttered under his breath. "Well, as much as I wanted to—I just cleared my throat instead. I said in my deepest cop voice I could, *'I've got a 357 here that wants to know what the hell you think you are doing in my car.'* Well, you have never seen a kid flip over and get so big-eyed in your life."

Danny elbowed Sweets in the arm, and quietly muttered, "Except when mom caught you stealing those cupcakes she had baked for the church bazaar." The two men chuckled at the common memory as their mother gave them a stern look from two tables away.

"Now, Hooker is a pretty quick thinker, and on occasion, he's even smart." He sipped as he milked the chuckles from the crowd that almost all knew the man being roasted, and he returned the jar of moonshine to the table with his two smallest fingers stretched slightly out. "So he looks at my hand, and says, *'You don't have a gun.'* My Hooker… so quick. He figured that out all on his own. So I told him never to bet his life on it, and told him to scoot his ass over," motioning with his fingers and two hands. *"'We're going to lunch,'* I told him, because obviously he was hungry. Of course, it never hurts to use a situation to your advantage, and turn it into a teachable moment, so I did."

He leaned back as if he were driving the 1952 DeSoto Sportsman. With his right arm stretched out, and his wrist draped over the large French ivory steering wheel, and moving lazily back and forth as he steered, he turned his head to look at Johnny. "The first thing you need to know about stealing a car is that you don't hotwire the radio first."

The eruption of laughter at Hooker's expense carried out across the valley to the very tips of the hills barely lit by the setting sun. With good food and good friends, Stella and Manny sat back and took it all in as this was their entire intent when they had first sat on a knoll in the dry stub-grass overlooking a then sparsely populated little valley. Someday, they would have friends to come and enjoy the same view, and plenty of good food for all to share.

As the evening dimmed, and the talking quieted, Johnny busied himself by carrying in dishes to the sink. Some of the guests had left, begging early shifts or pressing business, but the general mass was talking over coffee.

With one load, he found Dolly already at the sink absently washing the colorful heavy dishes, looking out at the crowd that were as much members of her fiefdom as they were her sister and Manny's.

As Johnny set the stack down on the sideboard, he noticed her watching Hooker making rounds among the guests. He stopped briefly to kiss Stella on the top of the head as he smoothed his hand across her shoulders. Her right hand caught his and gave it a small squeeze, as she never broke eye contact with the young couple that she was listening to.

"So I know how Hooker met Willie, and I think I understand that knowing you just came with the job, but how did he meet Stella and Manny?"

Dolly stopped washing, but kept watching her sister and the young man. Thinking, she heaved a deep breath. "That would have started Christmas Eve, 1942, at the Alameda air station." She pushed softly to turn and lean her backside against the counter. Her mind and sight were many miles and years away.

Johnny started to protest that Hooker wasn't that old when her finger rose to silence him.

"They were just a couple of crazy kids. Manny was fresh out of the police academy and had even taken a few tours of downtown as a foot patrol squirt. But the war was the war, and when Pearl Harbor was hit, it was everybody in. But by December 7th, Manny was already in San Diego learning how to chip paint on a destroyer expecting to go kill Germans.

After his weeks of boot camp, he had five days of leave before shipping out to Pearl. He called Stella and said he was catching a train up the coast and they could take the bus over to Reno to meet his folks who were coming down from Montana. That long ride over to Nevada was enough to convince her that she would never find anyone else. On the way back, he asked her to marry him. But they were out of time, so they got the base Chaplin to marry them there on the tarmac with forty other sailors waiting to ship out.

Stella had called when the bus stopped in Sacramento, and asked her best friend Ruth to come be her bridesmaid. Somewhere, Ruth had even found some fresh flowers. So there they were married for all of five minutes, and Manny got on the plane. Some wedding night. He didn't come home for two years."

"But…?"

Up came the finger again, as she turned to pour a mug of fresh coffee. Sipping, her eyes closed languidly, either enjoying the drink, or remembering. The mug hovered a moment at her lips as she continued. "Well, it was war time, Christmas Eve, and two young girls. They coaxed the coxswain on a Navy man-boat to ferry them across the bay to the Tenderloin in San Francisco where they had dinner and danced with any and every sailor. By the end of the night, Stella and Ruth had a fist full of men's names and addresses. I think, by the end of the war, they were writing about a hundred letters a month between the two of them.

"But back to Hooker—so by the time Manny gets back, Ruth and Stella have celebrated not only that wedding night, but two anniversaries while Manny was away. So, being the smart man that he was, and is, Manny sends them off to San Francisco every Christmas Eve to light up the town. Except the night they met Hooker, they didn't make it back so easily. Their car broke down on the 101 in a rather unsavory section of Santa Clara.

"Hooker was on his second or third year of driving then, and could have even had the night off. But Hooker being Hooker, took the backup position because he and Willie had baked chocolate chip cookies, and whipped up gallons of hot chocolate.

"He'd just headed out with a big batch of warm cookies and coco to give to all of the other drivers working the night shift, when Manny called me at two in the morning. He explained where the girls were, and how they were dressed to the nines. So I called Hooker. He always had the fastest truck and was near that area anyway.

"Hooker found them, but I didn't tell him who they were. I kept checking in with him like a mother hen. He couldn't get the car running, so he needed to tow it back to the dealer which was way up in Palo Alto."

Taking a sip of the coffee, she shook her head. "It wasn't an easy thing like now. No freeway then. So he had to drag it back up the 101, and then back into the Camino Real. Meanwhile, he has to put up with me on his case, asking where he is, how Mrs. Romero and Mrs. Steinberger are doing, are they hungry, or need something to drink—anything to keep his mic open so Manny, on the line with me, could get a kick out of this kid, too."

Danny brought in a huge stack of the remaining plates, and put them on the counter, nodded and headed for the bathroom. Stella and Johnny just watched the silent juggernaut move with the grace and silence of a cat. Dolly quietly observed more to herself than the kid— "If I didn't know and love that boy, he would be one of my biggest nightmares. That man is flat scary how silent he moves— like a whisper of fog in the night."

Shaking herself, she took a sip, and with a last look at the hall that Danny had disappeared down, she resumed her story. "So unbeknownst to Hooker, Manny basically had the same front row seat I had. In between radio checks, I filled him in about Hooker and Willie, and as much of Hookers back-story as I knew.

"Just about the time the sun is getting ready to pop over the east hills, Hooker is finally pulling the grade on Stupid Hill. Only, it wasn't stupid yet. Manny and Stella's was almost the only house on the hill back then." Dolly glanced back through the front window as if she could see the lines of tacky houses that now blanketed the north side of the hill.

"In the half light of Christmas morning, they pulled up out front, and Manny was standing in the upper driveway. Being the gentleman he is, Hooker got out to open the door for the girls. As they get out, heading for the house, they leaned over on both sides of the kid, and plant a big kiss with fresh lipstick on his cheeks. Stella says that he was redder than a tomato.

"After the girls had said their 'thank you' and gone inside, the men start the dance about getting paid or in this case, not. This was Hooker's only tow for the evening. On commission, it's his choice to charge or not.

Manny and Hooker just stood watching the sun come up. It was Christmas morning. Manny said he guessed Hooker wouldn't accept a tip either, but would he take a Christmas present they had got for him?" Johnny noticed the reflections on Dolly's eyes were wetter.

"Hooker figured because they didn't know him, he was safe there. He didn't know Manny, either. Manny reached in his pocket as he told Hooker that Stella had gotten it for Hooker the year before, so Manny was just holding it for him. He pulled out a money clip with a few bills in it. When Hooker started to take out the bills, Manny instructed him there are two places you don't count your money—at the poker table, and in front of the person giving you a present. Hooker only saw the five dollar bill facing out, and felt he was okay with it and let it go."

The kid laughed. "But... he didn't know Manny." Stella nodded and they both laughed.

However, the joy, mirth, and camaraderie of the day were not shared seven miles away. Ivory chopsticks moved by the slender fingers of a killer as they carefully inserted a stack of sixteen 1958 San Francisco minted dimes down into a shotgun shell, one dime at a time. Each dime was like a bead on a rosary, receiving a ritual mantra prayer. A latex-sheathed index finger slid in, as the whole was picked up ceremonially and tamped back down on the table. Sixteen times before the top was crimped back over and sealed with a spot of wax from a burning votive candle.

Carefully, the especially loaded shell was placed in a hollowed out space in the pages of a book. The killer slowly closed the Bible on the six freshly re-packed shells. Kissing the first two fingers on the right hand, each pad was placed on the chests of the two young men in a small framed photo on the nightstand. The drawer was opened and the Bible, likewise kissed, placed inside and the drawer closed. The night's ritual of revenge was done—just in time for vespers.

27

"I had a long talk with Box last night, but he isn't talking either."

"Squirt, sweetie," Stella turned toward Johnny and placed both of her hands on the sides of his face, patting the right hand slowly. "In life, there are things you want to know, and can't. There are things you need to know, and don't. There are even things you know, and wish to hell you never did or even were in the same state as knowing. Hooker's relationship with his sister is one of those things that you can count your lucky stars that you don't know. It's bad enough that you even know about her."

The hard drawn lips on the young man were a tough thing for Stella to see, because it meant indecision and pain in someone she had come to care about. It's hard to be a mom or even a 'not-mom' when someone is hurting, and all you can do is just stand there and be with them. Throwing caution to the wind, she just went ahead and hugged him. By the slow count of five, and one deep sigh, she could feel the bristling steel melt into the soft stuffing in a favorite teddy bear.

"It's OK, honey. Things are just not very usual right now." She pushed back from him and holding his arms, she admitted, "It's never really 'usual' around here with Manny and Hooker and all of our extended family, but it can become a wonderfully boring routine… for a day or so." She smiled as a thought struck her. "Did those jeans fit OK?"

Taking a moment to shift from the one topic to the half a dozen pair of jeans, and a drawer full of underwear along with the dozen starched white t-shirts hanging in the closet that had rocked his world a couple of days ago. He tried to swallow the golf ball sized lump in his throat. "Fine," he squeaked.

Stella smiled knowingly as she patted her warm palm of a wrinkled life-worn hand on his chest then rubbed it back and forth. "Don't sweat the small stuff, kid. Life is short enough, and then we can't do for others, as we wanted." She quick hugged him for reassurance and grabbed his hand, pulling him toward his new bedroom and past the closed office door where the four other men were talking. "Come on. I want to show you something."

Hooker could hear them walk past as he was leaning up against the wall next to the door. Manny was on the phone and listening to someone he had called in Sacramento. It never ceased to amaze Hooker the names Manny could pull out of his Rolodex on his desk. If he had said that he was calling the White House or a personal line to President Ford at Camp David, Hooker would have just sat back and listened to the conversation, and asked how the president was after Manny hung up.

"OK, then, we'll see you when you come through

padre. Just make sure to give Stella some heads-up, so she can go to the market and buy some hot dogs or something. You know how she is." The man laughed with the person on the other end of the conversation. "You too, and have a great night with the Reagans next week." He nodded. "I'll pass it along. Thanks again and goodnight." He hung up the phone and silently sat studying it as if he didn't know what it was.

The antique Register hall clock ticked with a deep wooden drum sound in the quiet of the office. Manny's right ring finger tapped imperceptibly, keeping time with the clock. To think that his mental pace was in the same register would be to make a grave mistake. The mind was stirring then re-parsing the case from hour zero to the moment. The only things slow about Manny were the blinking of his eyes, and the beating of his still athletic heart.

"And?" Hooker wasn't as patient as the two older officers relaxing in the armchairs were.

Manny's eyes refocused and slid over to Hooker, who was leaning back in his chair against the wall with his hands out and palms up. "Don't lean the chair, it weakens the joints," Manny chided quietly as he turned to the police detective with the iron ridged flattop haircut the color of the aircraft carrier it was named after. "Do you know a priest named Father Damian Garza y Espinosa, Mike?"

"Sure, he's the new priest at Saint Mat's... hmm... about a year or so. Why?"

"The Archbishop said he is the only priest in the area that is under fifty, and only one other than Father McBride who saw military duty."

"But a Chaplin doesn't carry a gun or…"

"As Special Forces, Recon," Manny cut him short. The other three sucked in breath as one.

"Jesus," Chet Davis muttered.

"Something else." Manny paused, as both cops raised attentive eyebrows. Manny looked toward the PD. "The Archbishop confirmed your lab's suspicions. That oily residue was in fact not only holy oil but a very specific holy oil."

"Most of the holy oil the church uses is virgin olive oil made from green olives, with a trace of balsam added. The balsam of choice is camphor but due to cost, occasionally frankincense or myrrh is used."

Hooker twisted his face. "As in, the tree kings?"

Manny pointed his finger at Hooker. "Good boy, you've been doing your homework!" He rolled his eyes, and planted his face down in his palm. "Yes, one and the same.

"But our little dime shooter is using one of the rarest holy oils of all. It's made locally, and as your lab determined, the oil is olive oil made from the Russian olive, and the balsam is from the juniper trees up on Mount Madonna."

Manny leaned in. "But here's the kicker. There are only five parishes using that holy oil, and because it is only used for baptisms and consecrations, it is only handled by the priests.

"And, our boy Damian…" he stopped to check his notes, "…Garza y Espinosa, is one of those priests."

"But come on, a priest?" Chet held his hand out evidentially. "It just doesn't make any sense."

"I don't want to think he had anything to do with these killings, Chet. But, other than the oil, he has service in Vietnam as a Ranger where he would know how to make and use Foo Gas. I don't see any rational connection here. But when does murder, especially seemingly random serial murder, make any rational sense?" Looking down at his notes, and then glancing over at the pin boards, he concluded. "Right now, he's the best suspect we have. And as for fitting the profile, how many people would know anything about how to use Foo Gas as effectively as in the car?"

"Then why… I mean, why become a priest after you've done that job?" Mike scratched his head then slicked the rumpled single hair back into formation. "Usually, those kinds of guys go on to do sedentary things like working for other governments with trouble, or start racing stock cars around large dirt tracks… you know, safe and quiet." His sarcasm was syrupy thick.

"I don't know." Manny shook his head. "But I think I do know someone who may have a take on him," he said, looking over at a now properly seated Hooker. "Doesn't the Squirt need to have his stitches taken out today?"

"Probably, but I just figured I'd let Willie or Stella do it. They both have more experience than most doctors." Hooker referred to Stella's nickname for Manny as *Mr. Zipper*. He had more yards of scars from being stitched up, than all the balls in major league baseball and Little League combined.

Manny wagged his head. "No, I think you need to take him back to Valley Med."

"They don't do check-ups. You're supposed to go to

your regular doctor."

"And… Johnny has a doctor?" The old man gave him the questioning eye and a smirk. "Look, I'll make a call to Connie. Maybe she'll have to take them out herself, but I need you to have a reason to be down there. It's the one place we can all agree that Father McBride will be."

Looking at nodding heads. "And it is the one place and with you being the one person who can talk to him on his turf, as it were, where he would be willing to open up. You can tell him everything. We just need to know where this young priest is coming from and about his background." He hunkered in his chair like a coach with his fingers interlaced. "Are you up for it, or not?"

Hooker nodded. "OK, but I have to get rolling here real soon if I'm going to blow part of the payday in the Med." Hooker looked at his watch. "And speaking of which, I need to go check in with Dolly. She was holding some long commercial run for me."

Pointing his finger at Hooker, Manny finished with a reminder. "You need to get a new pan on Mae. Willie told me at the barbecue and it slipped my mind until now."

The Highway Patrol officer snapped his fingers. "I need to grab those dimes out of the pan and radiator before," jerking his right thumb at the other officer, "his evidence team has me forfeit at least a pizza lunch for being late harvesting evidence."

"Ah, it's OK, Chief, that evidence isn't going anywhere," Hooker laughed and waved his hand, looking at his watch again, "…for at least another two minutes."

The four laughed at the pressing nature of the evidence versus Hooker's need to continue working as they broke up. Manny grabbed his phone and dialed a direct line to the nurses' station on the third floor at Valley Med, as he called out to Hooker, "Grab the kid, but see me before you leave. Gentlemen, thanks for seeing me on my turf. I really appreciate it."

The officers waved as Manny started grilling one of his favorite nurses. Chief Davis turned quietly to Hooker. "I'll come out and get the evidence tomorrow evening when you break for lunch at Willie's. Hank told me that he'd show me how to do that sauce he had on the pig steaks Sunday, and I think Willie mentioned some nice cold beer or something."

Hooker smiled and slapped him gently on the side of the arm. "Yeah, sure. Barbecue sauce and beer, sure." He patted his arm patronizingly. "Let's face it, Chet. We both know you're coming out to see if the Speedwagon is ready for a test drive." The two smiled large at the man's love for older trucks. "And, if I know Willie, he's probably busting his hump right now trying to make that happen just for you."

Laughing, and heading down the hall, Hooker stopped, thought a moment, and smiled deeply. Turning back, he added, "And I wouldn't be surprised if there wasn't a cute little-butted moonshine-running someone all greasy and sweaty going elbow to elbow with him… and she might even be out there tomorrow night." He smiled as the other man blushed.

"Now you're just teasing me." Chet coughed as he grabbed at the imaginary steak through his heart. "You are just a cruel person, Hooker—toying with a man's heart."

The two laughed as Hooker headed back down the

hall. "Squirt! Go time."

Reaching the young man's room and finding it empty, he was confused. Checking the bathrooms, he found all empty, making him even more confused, so he headed for the deck. Stepping through the sliding glass door, he looked around the basketball court sized three level deck, all of which stood empty. Then he noticed that Box hadn't taken the opportunity to slide out through the door toward the small knoll of grass, so he must be with the kid. Leaning on the railing he called out, "Hey Squirt? Stella?"

"We're down here in the garage, Hooker," Stella's answer drifted up from under the deck.

Closing the glass door against the heat, Hooker walked over to the pantry and sure enough, the secret door stood wide open. Grabbing a jar of home canned pears, he headed down the stairs opening the jar and fishing out a pear-half with his fingers. "What's up, guys?"

The two turned where they stood between a 1963 Corvette and a 1966 Dodge Dart GT. Stella spied the fingers in the jar reaching for a second half. "How many times do I have to tell you that when you open a jar, there might be other people who want some, and using your fingers is not the most sanitary option?"

Hooker walked up and offered the jar to her. "Want some, Stell?"

"Oh course," as she grabbed the jar and fished out a half, and passed the jar to the kid. "You into pears from our garden?"

The kid didn't have to ask, nor did he need to be pushed. He understood that this was the test, the trust that only comes from fingers stuck in a jar and drinking milk directly from the gallon jug passed around true friends or family. Stella warned him laughing, “Just don’t use your bunged up hand.”

They laughed as they finished off the jar, while leaning against the cars.

Squirt wiped the back of his arm across his mouth. “My, gosh, those are good.”

“Come this August, you can help us put up a couple of hundred more jars of them,” Stella recruited him. “We usually take a week and can about 1,200 gallons of donated fruits and veggies from around the valley, and we can use all the help we can get.”

Hooker leaned conspiratorially and stage whispered, “She’s not joking. Run—while you have a chance!”

The kid thought about the number of jars that would be. “What do you do with all that food?”

Hooker and Stella both pointed at a set of double doors along the wall of the fourth car bay. “It’s all in there,” Stella started, “or what’s left from last year. Mostly empties in there now, waiting for the harvest.”

“But you can’t eat that much?”

“No, no, that’s not for us. Well, some, but most of it goes to officers who are hit with some hard times and need some food to tide them through. And then there are other people we find out about that need some extra help. A few jars here and there aren’t much, but a single jar of handmade preserves will always be worth more than a case of store-bought junk. It’s the love that goes into the jar that counts.”

The kid looked askance at Hooker as Hooker held up his hands. “Don’t look at me. I usually take some long hauls or hide out with Willie during their cook the jars fest." Hooker lolled his head in the Zombie roll and winked at Stella as he smiled.

The woman slapped at his shoulder and confided with the kid. "Hide out my Aunt Judy's patootie! Those two hauled most of the fruit up from the lower valleys. Then they would dip and peel into the middle of the night while Willie would sing the worst sorry sounding cowboy love songs." Holding her hand on the kids shoulder, she continued. "If Willie ever starts singing in a *twangy* sort of voice – run! Because to stay around is to risk wetting your pants from laughing too hard."

They turned and were headed for the stairs. "So what were you two doing down here?"

The kid snuck a peek back over his shoulder at Hooker. "She wanted to know which car I wanted."

Hooker laughed as they headed up the stairs. "I'm taking you to the hospital to get your hand checked, and then we need to make some money before you even consider owning a car like either of those two."

Stella commented at the top of the stairs as she reached the pantry, "I don't know about the Corvette or Dart, but I do know he's going to need a car to get around." She thought a moment. "Manny is never going to use them again, and I certainly can't drive either one of those monsters, so why not?"

"Why not what?" Manny asked as they emerged from the pantry.

Stella turned. "Let the kid use one of the cars."

Manny thought about that. "I'll tell you what: you drive the Dart to San Francisco and back without a scratch, and no ticket, then say that again." The serious look on his face stopped the conversation and any possible argument.

The kid leaned over to Hooker. "What's so special about an old granny car?"

Hooker smirked. "The old granny car, as you so ignorantly put it, was built by Willie." Knowing that meant nothing to the kid, he continued. "Willie stuffed a 340 Hemi that's twenty thousands over and a twitchy five-speed transmission and posi-traction rear end." Seeing the blank uncomprehending look on the kid's face, he finished. "It's a ten-second car."

"What's a ten-second car?"

"It's a car that can run the quarter mile drag in ten seconds or less."

"Is that fast?"

Hooker gave him a blank stare, and then said, "About a hundred and fifty miles an hour, but that is just in the first quarter of a mile, then she opens up…"

As the kids eyes grew, Hooker reminded him that they needed to leave. Turning to Manny for a situation report, he called for Box.

"The good father is there, just got back from lunch, so he's in for a long run." Pointing toward the kid, he said, "Drop Johnny off with Connie, she'll take care of him and pump him for information about how bad you have been abusing him. So just go talk to the good Father."

The two men and cat were out the door and across the plaza under the watchful eye of Stella as she slowly closed the door. She knew better than to call after them something like 'be careful' or 'watch yourselves'— she had been married to Manny too long, and knew it wouldn't do any good. The door quietly clicked shut, and she held her hand flat against the edge with her other on the handle, a short quiet prayer. Turning, she looked at the man she had shared life and death with too many times to count. He pulled his hands up out of his lap, and wiggled his fingers for her to come and sit in his lap. The two stayed that way until long after the sound of Mae had faded down the hill with her head resting on his large shoulder, his safe arms around her.

Finally, she quietly spoke. "We were looking at the apartment downstairs. Squirt thinks it would be more than enough room for his sister. She wants to study to be a nurse."

The silence from Manny was a reassurance that he was actually thinking about what she was saying, and knew that the story about the car was just about pulling Hooker's chain.

The low rumble in his chest preceded his speech. "You're right, it's time to sell the cars. The space could be used by something a lot more useful." He petted her hair. "I'll talk to Willie and make some arrangements."

The afternoon sun was starting to pour into the sunroom, and the urge to take a nap in the warm breeze coming in through the lower apron windows moved the two. It was one of those little things that the two liked about the house… a house made for naps.

28

"Look, Manny isn't stupid." Hooker continued the argument about why Johnny wasn't getting a car. "Neither is Estella. She's just going through one of her 'new mother' stages." He looked over at the kid who was studying a bug on the windshield very hard. "Look, relax. You're around a week, and you already have new jeans that I bet you wish she'd washed first." The comment drew a tiny smirk and a bump up in the body, or just a lump in the road, but only on the kid's side.

Hooker softened. "Look, tomorrow we'll load it all in a go bag and shimmy it over to Willie's and let him do the laundry. Of course, if you wear boxers, his heavy hand with starch and the military crease down the two cheeks will really make you remember him."

The chuckle started low, and with a lot of resistance, built to a full on foot-on-the-dash-so-you-don't-fall-over belly laugh. Even Hooker almost passed a little yellow VW under the wheels of Mae before he gained control.

"She means well, but she has no idea why Manny even had those cars."

"Why did he?" Slowly getting some control back.

"To keep Willie alive." Dead serious, Hooker glanced over at the kid.

"What was he dying from?"

Hooker thought about that for a few minutes as he wound his way through the south end of Willow Glen. He wanted to see if something was still there. The streets were all residential, and as a tow truck, he was marginally OK to be there—but if a cop wanted to be hard-nosed about it, he could get a ticket for what he was doing.

They turned a left corner and Hooker pulled over to the side and parked along an empty lot where two houses had burned down the winter before. He set Mae down on a low loping idle and turned in his seat. Leather draped over the seat back-rest, across the open window and over to the steering wheel as his left first fingers bounced a stiff finger tap dance on the French ivory wheel. "Speed. He was dying from speed, as well as a love he had but couldn't have."

"Huh? I don't…"

Hooker held up his right hand in a stop. "You have now met Maddie under two conditions. Drunk off her butt and ready for a Sunday barbeque." The kid nodded. "The Maddie you haven't met is the one he is madly in love with. The one he would have married if things had been a lot different."

Hooker looked about the old burn and sniffed. The smell of the gelatinized gasoline was still gooey in the air, even months later. Putting the truck back in gear and heading for the hospital, Hooker thought about how much it smelled just like the burned out car in the IBM parking lot, but he also knew the bomber was dead. He swung the giant beast right onto Winchester Boulevard, and shook the chill in his spine.

Looking over at the kid, he remembered where he was in the story. "Back in the day, her father and three brothers were the biggest moonshiners in the entire upper central coast. They even ran a fair portion down as far as Bakersfield and Wasco to the Kentucky and Arkansas transplants, all who had come out during the dust bowl, but still had a taste for White Lightning. I don't know if it's true or not, but the story goes they were always getting stopped just outside of Stockton by the same cop, four times a year, for the same three cases. Rumor had it that those bottles stood on the top of the liquor cabinet within easy reach at the Governor's mansion in Sacramento. Maddie will only tell you 'whatever you heard, is probably true.'"

"The other more public side of the family business was racing. They were the fastest rogue racers in Central and Northern California. If it ran on wheels and gasoline, they drove it in a race—even Maddie. When it came to iron and hot grease, it was spread thick across the five of them. Their mother had died with Maddie's birth. Her father never even tried to be a mother to a little girl. She was just thrown in with the other three boys.

"Willie used to hang around their garage almost as much as the boys and Maddie, so he was kind of like the fifth boy, except he was a little different. As girly as Willie is, Maddie was a tomboy. I don't know if she likes girls or men, but I do know that if you see a dress on one butt in the air, and bib-overalls on the other, with the upper bodies down in the motor area of an old car or truck… the bibbies are the only butt connected to female parts."

"But what's that got to do with Manny saving Willie?"

Hooker uncrossed his eyes that had wandered into looking at something that was only a memory. "The Corvette – right." Gathering his story, he continued. "Willie built the 1963 Vet from what was called a *Killer Engine*—it was a 375 horse powered, 327 cubic inch engine. By the time Willie was done, it was up over 500 horses, ported, polished, and strapped to a matched gearbox and positive rear end. The car could tear up a drag strip or dance down the freeway. He tried to give it to Maddie as a gift."

"And… ?"

"She wouldn't take it. She said that no self-respecting librarian would be caught dead driving to work in such a flashy car. So he built her the Granny Car."

"But that car is just as fast?" The kid was resting his tousled hair in his hand sticking out of the leather jacket that was a mirror to Hooker's.

"Faster and lighter." Hooker looked out the front windshield at the hulking concrete and glass mass of Valley Med. "Much faster." Turning back to the kid, he finished the story. "One night, they ran down to Monterey for dinner, and they were on the way back. They told the police they were only doing about eighty, but the twirling skid marks for almost a quarter mile told a much different story… and luckily, ended up two-hundred yards into a soggy freshly plowed field." Nodding at the large building in front of them, "They both got here by helicopter."

Hooker stared at the gray building that housed so many stories.

He turned back to the kid. "It took Maddie almost a year to walk again with a cane. Willie was only a little luckier."

"So Manny offered to buy the cars." The kid was beginning to understand the family dynamics. "But wasn't the Granny car wrecked?"

"Not that much. But by the time Willie got around to fixing it, I was in the house, so things changed pretty quickly. By the time the Granny was up and running again, we already knew Manny and he had bought the Corvette and had his eye on the Dart."

Hooker turned in the seat toward the door and rolled up the window. "I don't think Manny even drove the cars more than a few dozen times before he got the bullet in his back and ended up here, too." He looked down at his hands for an answer that wasn't there. Quietly, he looked up, and then at the kid. "Let's go and get your hand taken care of."

As they climbed out of the truck and locked her up, the kid complained. "I still don't see why I can't just take the stitches out by myself. It's not that hard."

Hooker braced him in front of the truck. "It's not about you. You are just the excuse and diversion here. What Connie says you need, you seriously need. If she says x-rays, you get x-rays. If she says enema, you get two of them – you hear me?" The kid was nodding. "Until I come back for you, you do everything Connie says for you to do: except talk to little Miss hair-to-her-ass Loretta Lynn at the front desk. If she asks you anything, you just tell her I'm beating you, working you all hours of the night, and I make you sleep in the puddle of oil under the truck. You got that?"

The kid snickered. "There's no pool of oil under Mae. She wouldn't allow it."

Hooker snarled. "Pretend there is."

The kid nodded and shrugged, and as they started walking off toward the ER entrance, he turned his head back toward the truck, and in a very bad John Wayne imitation said, "Sorry Mae, but a man's gotta do what a man's gotta do."

They walked about another hundred yards, and just as they were about to get to the entrance, Hooker growled out of the side of his mouth. "You're a really weird kid. You know that? You know? You are really weird."

"Yeah," the kid agreed. "I get it from my sister and you."

Hooker clipped the top of his head with a slap. "Don't be bad-mouthing your sister. She's nowhere near my class of weird." He followed it up by flipping his foot up and slapping the kid's new jeans in the seat. The kid laughed.

The force of a busy morning at the ER hit them full on as they walked in at four in the afternoon. Many of the brain and parts donors had been there since the wee hours of the drunk-shift, or when the bars closed and the stool drivers became Mario Maladroit. This would back up the morning catastrophes, which blended into the after-lunch industrial fell-asleep-into-the-machine crap that would fill the void until the late evening.

Hooker motioned the kid to follow him and wound his way through the walking death traps and sick people. As the mass moved in a slow drunken dance, the way to become noticed was to either shoot off a gun or just stand still within the eye range of the person whose attention you needed to attract. The blonde sensed the calm in the stormy sea of humanity and jerked her head up.

At first, she was trying to remember who the kid was, then she notice the shit-eating grin next to him with the tight thin beard wrapped around it. "Oh jeez, what now?" Turning only half way, she kept her eye on Hooker as she called for back up. "Connie, we have trouble."

Connie exploded out of her stupor of going over charts and shuffling schedules. She grabbed the doorjamb to stop from continuing out into the typing pool. *Hooker*, she thought, and then stepped back into her office for a clipboard that, although it contained nothing but blank paper and used up forms, made for good cover. She waved towards the end of the long desk of typing stations, as she whispered out of the side of her mouth. "We'll be back in operatory Number six."

Cynthia whipped around. "We don't have an operatory Number six – we have only five. Connie Lynn Nichols, what are you up to?"

The head nurse ignored her as she split the crowd like a battleship on a mission, and then turning to Hooker and the kid. "You two, come with me." At the end of the hallway, they turned down another smaller hall stopping into an exam area to grab a blue cloth wrapped roll of triage supplies. Shooting the nurse a hard glare to stop any protest, they continued down the side hall and into a small break room where a large nurse was stuffing the first of three donuts in her mouth as she scanned through the latest trashy tabloid.

Connie leaned over and took the two donuts from the box and shoved them into the two gaping mouths of Hooker and the kid. Then spinning around before the nurse could make a sound, she braced her with her eyes. "Weight Watchers wouldn't approve of your diet, and neither do I. Be glad I didn't take the one out of your mouth, too." The nurse's eyes bulged at Connie's audacity. "And your break was over almost twenty minutes ago. So now you get to run all over this hospital looking for Father McBride." Putting up her hand with the index finger up, she snapped. "Now scoot! I want him in here in less than the time it takes me to remove these stitches."

The nurse had disappeared before the chair had bounced off the floor, or the half of a donut had bounced a second time on the plate. Hooker stuck his head out the door, watching the sizable woman make a sizable amount of haste.

He stepped back into the room as Connie gently pushed the kid down into a seat, and took a seat, too. Hooker peeked back out the door, and then looked at Connie. "Could you talk to Mae West that way, when you get a chance?"

The head nurse ignored Hooker as she started removing the bandage. "Shut up, Hooker, your truck is fast enough as it is." She began to hum to herself as the bandage came off and she could view the stitches. Muttering to herself as much as to the kid, she complimented his hygiene and care of the wound. Occasionally, she would look up with one eye cocked and give a hard look at Hooker. But she kept humming as if she had all the time in the world. When two nurses started to bubble their way into the room, they took one look at her and went back to work.

She chuckled softly to herself as she commented, "I ought to bring my work in here more often. Seems there would be a lot more staff on the floor."

Father McBride strolled into the room, and without acknowledging anyone, went straight to the coffee urn as he decanted a large mug. Taking a hesitant sip, he relaxed and turned so he could lean up against the counter. "I haven't removed stitches since I left the old neighborhood." His brogue fell from his lips a little thicker than usual.

Connie raised one eyebrow and looked at the old friend, then smiled broadly, as she opened her arms and spread them, draped back across the chair and table. With a very good thick imitation of the man's affected accent, she asked, "And tell me, Father, would that be Dublin or Boston?"

Caught at his own game, "Nay, that would be lower west side… Berkeley. Well, Emeryville." He smiled his warmest smile at a shared jest. "How can I be of help?"

Connie jerked her head at Hooker. "For all of the sakes involved, talk to this man honestly and spare nothing."

The priest looked at Hooker and then Connie, and understood the gravity of the conversation to come. He nodded his head and the mug of coffee towards the hall. "Let's take this down to the Chapel. I can almost guarantee we won't be interrupted there, unless it's a couple of Connie's hot-blooded nurses having a little rendezvous."

Twenty minutes later, having shared their thoughts

and concerns about a priest who fit the killer's profile right down to the use of Foo Gas, Hooker had more than his answer, but less than he wanted.

"The traces of holy oil are worrisome, I'll grant you that, but I'm positive that you gentlemen are barking up the wrong tree." He slowly scratched his head of thinning white hair. Looking up, his eyes pierced the air between them. "Look, son, if I knew more, I'd tell you. I know you think Father Damian could be this person they are calling the *Dime Load Killer,* but I really don't think so." He reached out and placed his wrinkled hand on Hooker's knee. "I'll tell you what. Do you still have lunch at that place up on Winchester Boulevard?"

"Sure, almost every night."

"Let me go talk to the young priest and explain the circumstances. At worst, I'll come buy you and the kid lunch. It's the least I can do."

"It's a date, sir." Hooker stood and held out his hand. "I'll see you there about eleven tonight."

The Father remained seated, but shook his hand. "I'll see you there." Nodding towards the small altar, he made his apologies. "I'd walk you out, but I think I need to have a bit of a conversation here right now."

Hooker looked at the cross. "I understand. Just don't let Him get the upper hand."

The old man chuckled. "Son, He always has the upper hand."

Hooker, looking back, watched the man. With his body riddled with arthritis, he took a while to get down on his knees, and then began to talk to his boss. Hooker looked about the room and felt the silence of peace – so very different from his world.

Returning into the insanity of the ER, he looked around, and then headed down the hall toward the break room. Just before he entered, he could hear the kid's voice talking about how his sister and he had gotten to San Jose. Hooker smiled inwardly. For all the iron tough and brass Connie pushed around, she could also get to the heart of a story faster than anyone Hooker knew—other than the interrogation sisters, Dolly and Stella.

Hooker cleared his throat as he walked the last several feet to the doorway of the break room. As he turned the corner into the room, Connie was standing and cleaning up the small mess they had made of eating something. "Well, it's about time you got back, this young man has work he needs to get to, and it doesn't include lounging about in some chapel swapping lies with an old man in his dotage."

Hooker looked at the kid who looked a little like his hand was still in the cookie jar. "If she says we're good to go, we're gone." Turning to an equally caught red-handed Connie, he continued. "Thanks for this, I think we got more than we came for," looking back at the kid, "in many ways." Turning on his heel, he strolled back out the door and down the hall, paying attention to, but ignoring the sound of starched white uniform hugging leather and a mumbled votive of assurance. *Jeez mareez, this kid gets more mothering than I do.* Hooker smiled thinking it was starting to be a good day.

He was wrong. So very wrong.

29

The chopsticks methodically pulled apart the roll of extra-fine steel wool. The killer had become adept at using chopsticks with both hands at an early age while helping cook. Working at pulling out wisps of steel wool, then inserting them into the plastic 2-liter bottle, was child's play.

A web of half-inch holes drilled in the bottom of the bottle. A staggered double row of holes stitched their way down the four sides of the green plastic cylinder. The web pattern in the end creates a barrier for the steel wool, but not the dimes. It would break away easily, and be destroyed with the third shot. A fourth shot would be lacking the silenced effect of the contraption, but couldn't be helped. It was unnecessary. The rows of holes along the side were pressure relief for the expanding gasses pushing out the air between the steel wool. The term 'silencer' was a misnomer. It should be called simply a 'muffler' as it just muffles the sound of explosively expanding gasses by rerouting and slowing them down until the concussion shock sound wave is diminished as close to nothing as possible.

The sound of the old record played so softly in the background as to not be heard by the other residents in the building. Jefferson Airplane's *White Rabbit* would have been severely frowned upon. Lips followed each word carved indelibly in the killer's heart along with memories of a happier time, and also the beginning of the horror.

The click of the four chopsticks working to tear apart the puffy cloud of warm steel wool echoed the sound of the tiny click as the needle slid back and forth in the never-ending loop of the finished record. Both hands moved adroitly pulling and pushing the wool.

The final piece of wool is inserted, and the chopsticks are all brought together and carefully laid to rest in a case with an extra pair. A set of three ivory chopsticks with three names hand engraved in the sets. A thoughtful gift brought back from Vietnam, an offering of family and love from a place of horror, hatred, and destruction. The delicate two right fingers, index and ring, were ritually kissed, and then placed on the photograph, each finger in the middle of the bare chests of two young smiling males bracketed with arms draped across the shoulders of a younger happier killer. The fingers lingered—much happier days.

The killer slowly tried the snug fit of the bottle on the barrel of the shotgun. The new form used to warm and expand the mouth of the bottle had worked perfectly… lessons learned so many years before… with a different gun, and a different kind of bottle.

Hunting close range at night was so much different from hunting long range in the light of day; so much different.

The latex-clad right hand slowly slid the bottle off the barrel and set it aside. Wrapping the bottleneck to the barrel with tape would come later that night after prayers. There would be plenty of time before the midnight meeting. All the time in the world.

30

The two priests sat at the back of the booths, quietly talking shop. They were dressed in black with small white squares at the throats of their rabbinical shirts. The small number of neighborhood denizens sat scattered like leaves tossed about by a gust of breeze. The two waitresses didn't really mind having their quirky customers scattered about, or as the ladies would say *separated,* it was easier to maintain the peace that way.

The various diners stole surreptitious glances at the men in the back booth. Some were not sure as to why these two were here on their turf. Others just worried about the diner becoming a soup kitchen where they would have to listen to some preaching just to get a meal. A few just stared drunkenly slack-jawed at the apparition that they knew were just 'vapors' of their breath.

The glass doors swung open as the two leather clad, almost twins, walked into the diner and headed for their section of the counter. Jerry, who was always in seat 107 (seventh seat along the counter) looked up in his best Annie Greensprings fortified wine sort of way. "Hey

Hooker…" and was then stuck for any more scintillating conversational contribution.

Hooker spotted the older priest waving from the back booth, and walking past the counter crustacean, patted him on the shoulder. "Hey, Jerry, good to see you up and around this side of the dirt blanket. You holding your own on that Thunderbird diet?" He continued toward the back.

Dazed and confused, Jerry tried at a response. "No… ah, um, Thunderbird, Hooker…" Then he realized that he was talking to himself, so he returned to his original conversation. It seemed to be more personally meaningful anyway.

"Hooker." Father McBride stood up leaving the younger seated. "So very good to see you. And this must be the young man that I have heard so very much about." Reaching over, he shook the kid's hand. "Johnny, isn't it?"

"Umm, yes, sir."

"Please, no 'sir' here, just us padres, or Father Mike, if you want." Turning to the quiet young priest still sitting, he introduced the man. "Hooker, Johnny, I'd like you to meet the newest member of our clergy here in San Jose, Father Damian Garza y Espinosa." Looking hard at the young priest, he asked, "I did get that right, didn't I?"

The young priest nodded his head as he reached across himself and the table with his left hand as he leaned slightly forward to shake hands. "You did fine, Mike." Turning to Hooker and Johnny, "Please, you can call me Damian or Dan. I just don't respond well to being called late for dinner."

The kid leaned in and shook the offhand clumsily.

"Squirt, everybody just calls me Squirt."

The young priest smiled a small smile then grew a larger one as he asked, "Is that because you were small once, or because you're the fucking new guy?"

The term was like a grenade in the silence that stopped the other three men dead in their tracks. Candy, who was walking up to their booth, was also silenced. Then she shoved her brother into the booth and hip-checked Hooker out of the way. "Yup, same as you, Dan, but for stunning the words out of Hooker's mouth, the pie is on me tonight. You can pay tomorrow night."

The young priest laughed. "You have a deal, Candy. Make mine that French apple."

"It's called Dutch. Dutch apple pie."

"Mmm, it's all European and delicious to me."

The other men settled in and placed their orders, all as Hooker kept sneaking looks at the waitress, trying to figure out what was going on. The left-handed shake had also unsettled him, but he wasn't going to say anything yet. There was just too much at stake.

The waitress read back the order. "OK, then, I have one chick plate mashed with ranch, a burger with a salad for the growing kid—no fries, four coffees and two pieces of Dutch apple pie." She looked up from her book to see if there were any other items she had missed. She nodded and spun on her heel, as she smacked the book on the top of first Hooker's head, and then backhanded her brother. "Behave you two, you are out to dinner with some nice guys." Then she caught one of the other regulars doing something. "Fester, I have my eye on you. I'll cut you off for a week if you don't sit back down and behave."

Father McBride watched her as she worked the room full of less than desirable customers, and did so as if she were their mother—a firm yet caring hand. He smiled at some inner thought or memory, and then looked at Johnny. "Now I see how you have survived."

The kid glanced at, as much as listened to, his sister, "Yeah, she's hard sometimes, but she's soft where it counts, I guess." Then realizing what he had just said turned beet red. "I… I didn't… I meant…"

Hooker put his hand on his arm. "We knew what you meant." But it didn't mean that they couldn't laugh at his expense. It was as good an icebreaker as was the young priest busting him with the rougher street vernacular of the term FNG.

Turning to the young priest, he tried to be subtle. "So Father Dan, what brings you to San Jose?"

The priest looked Hooker in the eye measuring where to go with everything he knew about why he was there, and about Hooker's place in the entire scheme of things. "I had a calling, and then I was assigned here." He said this with a blank straight face that he had learned in the seminary, but had perfected with real life experience in the military. "But then that is not what you meant, is it?" He didn't blink. It wasn't so much a challenge, as it was a notice that he knew what was going on, and wasn't shying away from addressing things as they landed on the table.

"Hooker," Father McBride interceded. "I took the liberty to confide in Dan what this is all about. He is here to help to the fullest of his ability."

"I wasn't intending to ambush him…" Hooker tried to explain himself.

"Look," the young priest reached across his body and rested his hand on Mike's arm. "I'm not a child. I can look after myself." Patting the arm. "It's OK. I'm a big kid now."

McBride looked him in the eyes, and the young priest engaged him and nodded. The older man turned toward Hooker and rolled his eyes. He raised his eyebrows, and pressing his lips taut, he smacked his tongue against his teeth with a click. "OK." He jerked his thumb at the other man in black. "He's all yours. Have at him."

The young man sat back as Candy brought the coffees. "Jeez, I didn't mean to let him just shoot me in the booth. At least give me a running start."

Candy put the coffees down and looking at the young priest quipped, "No can do, Kemo Sabe. You no can run anymore." This raised a smile on the priests' face.

Hooker pointed back at the retreating waitress. "You know Candy from before?"

"This is my parish, Hooker. So, yeah, I know her from before." He leaned forward with his hands in his lap. "I know all about you and how deadly you are with an unloaded fork, too." He smiled as Hooker's eyes popped open even wider. "Yeah, you're kind of famous around here in the middle of the night."

Hooker started to ask a question but was stalled as the 'w' froze on his lips as his open pointing finger stopped in mid-air. His mind was chugging along, but the gears weren't engaging. He literally didn't know where he wanted to go in gathering information.

The young father continues. "What shift do I come in on? I roll in here about the time Jerry sobers up enough to go home, and Mac decides the worms in the parking lot will leave him alone for one more night. About two-thirty or so in the morning, when I wake up with cold sweats from being back in Vietnam, and don't dare go back to sleep." He took a bite of the pie and chewed slowly, savoring the fruit flavor, and then pointing with his fork at the table. "This is my assigned table. This is my library, and I'll be here reading for a couple of hours while she does all of her side work."

"The Bible?"

He turned an eye on Johnny, then a quick glance at the older priest who was smiling and looking at his pie, purposely ignoring him. "Not usually. Mostly science fiction or trashy magazines about hot rods and street machines," he said as he looked at Hooker.

Hooker didn't know if he was being set up or just getting his chain yanked, but he did like the man's style. "Big block or small?"

"Truth be known, I'm kind of a die-hard Mopar kind of guy. There has never been an engine that will out endure and perform like a Hemi." He smiled as his eyes hooded with memory. "Personally, I would go for a Dart stuffed with a 318, six-pack, and Max Wedge front clip with a shaker hood."

"Not exactly a typical priests ride." Hooker smirked, thinking about the convertible granny car in Manny's garage.

"Yeah, but it would be grand to drive that kind of car again."

"Speaking of cars, what about Cadillac?"

The man turned serious but quiet as Candy arrived

with the plates of dinner for Hooker and Johnny. As she placed the plates, the young priest took another small bite and chewed slowly.

"OK, two tow driver dinners," as she poured refills on the coffee, "and everyone is fueled up. I'm going to go take a fast break, so no fist fights or stabbing small children while I'm gone." The men all smirked and nodded their devotion to her directions.

As she left, the young priest put down his fork, thought a moment, and then looked at Hooker. "Didn't you really want to know about shotguns and Foo Gas?"

Hooker took a bite, as his stomach turned over like a large fish rolling in the sun of his abdomen. He realized that there was not one punch this man wouldn't pull, so he thought about how he could ask anything that didn't sound like he was judge and jury. He thought about the background that he knew. "Experience?"

Relived that the conversation was now out in the open, the priest took another small bite and dabbed at his mouth with the napkin at the end of his right arm. The silver glint off the pincer hook was not lost on Hooker. The conversation just took a huge leap sideways. The young priest missed nothing—the change in Hooker's eyes told him everything he needed to know.

"If you look over there in the shadows, that's my ride. I had Candy put it over there out of the way." Hooker could see the wheelchair. "After I lost my hand, some of my hearing, half my guts, one leg just below the knee and the other at the ankle, I spent a lot of days in the hospital thinking about what I had done, and why I was still alive. It wasn't self-pity, it was soul searching to figure out where I would go from that bed and into the future.

"There was a padre who came to Letterman Hospital every day. One day I asked him if he could just shove me out the door, so I could look up at the Golden Gate Bridge. He ended up pushing me to the middle of the bridge and asking me if I wanted his help in shoving me over the side. I couldn't say a word after that for about an hour. I had never thought about suicide, but he knew that somewhere inside, I was weighing that option.

"We ended up doing a lot of talking in the next year as I got my rehab, and learned to walk on the plastic legs and sticks. These days it's just easier to ride," he held up his hook, "even with this little gem."

Hooker put down his fork across his empty plate and wiped his mouth. Clearing his throat, he thought about what the man was saying… or what he wasn't. "I don't know what to ask anymore. I mean, obviously you couldn't have been standing on that berm and shooting a shotgun at me with your right hand."

"But I do know a lot about guns, and more importantly, Foo Gas." The man mirrored Hooker with his fork and wiped his mouth. The napkin returned from his lap, but was deposited on top of the plate with still half a piece of pie underneath. Seeing Hooker's quizzical look, he explained. "I wasn't joking about losing half my guts over there. I can only take so much food at one time, and sugar is even more restricted. I'll be paying all day tomorrow for that little bit of heaven."

"That munches the big one."

"Yeah, but then it is what helps me maintain this girly figure." He smiled. "But seriously, getting back to the Foo

Gas. Did they ever get the spectrum analysis back on what was in the gasoline?"

"You can check with Manny, but I'm pretty sure it was Styrofoam."

The priest became pensive. "Describe the set-up, or can you?"

Hooker looked at the kid who had been silent the entire time, as he looked up at Hooker who nodded at the priest. "Walk him through it, newbie, same as you did for Manny. No analysis, no thinking—just what you saw."

The kid nodded and it was almost as if his eyes rolled up in his head. He wasn't in the booth, but was back at the scene. His description was scarily accurate, and so exacting that Hooker could smell the burned out car and cremated bodies. Hooker hadn't remembered that the kid had gone over the mechanism so meticulously with Manny. But he had something then, and was doing something now, which Hooker had never seen done before—exacting total recall of what he had seen.

About halfway through Johnny's recall, Candy quietly walked over and touched Hooker on the shoulder, and motioned him to follow her as she put her hand up to her head with the little finger and thumb extended. He had a phone call. As they walked away, Hooker asked her if she had seen the kid do that kind of detail recall before.

"Sure, that's the problem. He does it in his sleep."

"And why is that a problem?"

"Because what he sees, he never forgets. Trust me, there's a lot of shit he should forget." She handed him the phone. "There's a lot I'd like to forget also. It would do us both a lot of good."

Hooker nodded in understanding. “This is Hooker.”

“I’m sorry to have to break up your little love fest, but CHP needs you right now above the Cats, about the five-mile curve with the bad drop off. They have a set of doubles jack-knifed, and the cab is over the edge…” Dolly quit talking when she realized she was talking to a dial tone.

“Excuse me, but we’ve gotta go,” Hooker rushed as he reached over the kid and grabbed his jacket. “Can we pick this up in the morning or something?”

“Sure. If I’m not here between two and four, Candy will have my phone number. Just call, I’m two blocks away. He wiped his mouth. “And Hooker, it sounds like Special Forces, but with more of a second hand domestic twist to it. I’ll kick around what I might be able to help you with.”

Hooker stuck out his left hand as an offer of peace. “Thanks.”

Father McBride interjected. “I’ll get the check, Hooker. You be the Samaritan.”

The two leather jackets were racing for the door as Hooker called back, “Thanks!”

The doors, key, brake, clutch, silver button, seventh gear, and they bounced west out onto Winchester Boulevard. Grabbing back at the microphone behind his ear, Hooker keyed the red button as it passed his head on the way to shifting up into ninth. Pulling it back, he checked in. “1-4-1, 10-8 for the Cats.”

“10-4, 1-4-1, dispatch shows you 10-8 at twenty-three forty-two. CHP is advised. You’re free to rock and roll. Your cross over will be at the pass-through at the south end of the reservoir. They would suggest Summit Road and then backtrack the mile, but things are already wall-to-wall. See Officer Schwindler. Chief Davis says if you need to remove any center fence, try to keep it less than sixty feet this time. Cal Trans seems to be having a little fence budget problem lately."

"10-4." Hooker hooked the mic back on the slide mount and reached to drop the two gears as he slid around the corner onto Hamilton Avenue, goosed the power, then used the Jake brakes down around the cloverleaf to the mid-point, and then it was gas and gears all the way up to 'rock-and-roll' speed. Hooker loved the middle of the night in the early part of the week. One car went past on its way back into San Jose. Slowly, Hooker rolled the window down and settled into eighteenth gear, which would take them up the lower part of the Highway 17 mountain pass into the Santa Cruz Mountains. Hooker's right hand dropped down as it turned up the eight-track, and then fondled Box's ear. As his fingers found the top of Box's head, he could feel the purr that was a mirror image of the throbbing coming from under the hood.

Go time. Hooker's drug of choice, and Box would second it.

Hooker glanced over at the kid chewing on something as he watched the world fly by through his open window with his leathered arm cocked out the hole. "What are you thinking?"

Without really looking at Hooker, the kid gave it a moment to gel, then supposed. "I think he may know something." The kid looked out the open window to the side, watching the city end and darkness fill the night.

Turning he finished, "As I was talking, I could feel him going through a mental check list. Then… I don't know, his face maybe, it changed… something I said, hit the bell for him."

Hooker glanced over as he took the transmission down to lower gears. "We'll stop by when we're finished with this mess and see what he thinks."

Shifting down again for the grade, Hooker saw the reservoir off to the left and knew the pass-through would be coming up soon. He reached back to the mic and keyed it at his cheek. "1-4-1, I'm 10-97 at the reservoir. Was there going to be an officer standing by at the pass-through?"

"They didn't say, Hooker."

"10-4." Hooker knew that it would most likely be something he would have to feel for in the dark. CHP rarely had the extra manpower in the middle of the night to stand by at a pass-through for a tow truck, or even an ambulance, for that matter. As he reached back to hang the mic, he glimpsed a lone flashing red light, and as he got closer, a matching yellow light in the back seat of a cruiser. He shifted down three more drops, and gently threaded the needle and waved at the officer who had the forethought to help. He would have to put in a good word with the Chief.

31

The night breeze blew the dust, bits of waste paper, and leaves, in a swirl behind the darkened car sitting backed into the dark far corner of the parking lot. The black Buick La Sabre sat, the engine compartment still ticking as it cooled down. The swirl of dust stopped and seemed to settle behind the car trunk. The occupant looked in the rear view mirror, seeing nothing but the lights in a building two blocks over through the trees. The two hard locust trees bent over the car had helped confuse any glancing eye that may have strayed its way, much like the duck blinds and deer perches of the killer's youth.

The sound of the giant yellow tow truck were still fading as the killer silently pounded slender fists on the steering wheel, seething at the missed opportunity with the stupid tow truck driver.

Calming down, the killer leaned back against the headrest, right hand searching for, and then softly stroking, the hand carved stock of the shotgun. The delicate fingers found the tiny lines of the aged black walnut that had come from the yard back home. The light of a turning car triggered the memory of the lightning that had hit the tree and split it down the center all the way to the ground. Their father had cut out the blanks for four matching shotguns. Then, two years later, he began to carve them. This gun was the oldest brother's, the first to shoot and the first to die. The hand rubbing on the wood was like a calming blanket. The strokes became slower and shorter as the killer remembered everything that had been lost, and the reason for being here tonight.

The light breeze stirred the leaves and dust, but one pile of dust stayed behind the car—painstaking writing, letter by letter and number by number, with a nub of a pencil found years before on the northern end of Stevens Creek Boulevard. The paper delicate, and easily punctured, but the dust was the epitome of patience, each letter, and number exacting in the detail of an engineer writing the most important notation of his career.

Slowly, the dust and dirt swirled and collected in the space of the dark of the trees. The dark was protective, and the tiny touches of fingertips felt the way, guiding the eyes that needed to see and to gather that which was needed by his friend. The shreds of the night hung from the dust's shoulders and head, the perfect blending of the night. The wisps of what could have been, blending with the shadows of what was impossible in the dark of imagination gone rapidly beyond the usual. In the middle was the calm of the man who lived his life in a calm that was anything but calm.

Slowly, with the wind and movement of shadows, the dust moved, bobbed, and weaved as the eyes, missing nothing, took in the shotgun, the bottle attached at the end, the extra shells, and the hair of the killer, as well as the unusual clothes. The dust now knew the identity of the killer and the possible reason for tonight's vigil. The dust was making connections like he hadn't in many years. Why, just now, he had written like he hadn't in so many years? Something he didn't think he would ever do again, but this was for his friend.

The driver suddenly realized that the dusty shadow of the night was a *human being* and quickly muffled a scream. In this startled state, the killer started the car, slammed it into drive, and shot across the parking lot lurching out into the boulevard and racing away. Just when the front doors of the diner opened and a wheelchair emerged.

The young priest turned to the elder and smirked. "Hmm, I didn't know we were powerful enough to drive the devil away in a Buick." The two chuckled about working in mysterious ways as they crossed the lot toward Father McBride's twelve-year-old Ford Falcon.

Stopping at the side, the elder padre patted the old friend on the rear quarter panel. "If only we could instill a little more fire and brimstone in old Lazarus here. He's been a good trooper, but at nigh-on hundred and twenty thousand of the long miles, he's asking for a deeper rest than I can grant at this time." Turning to the younger priest, "and you, we should find you one of those new vans with a power lift or something, so you can get around."

The seated man waved his last hand. "Mike, that is why I have this small parish. My wheels can make it to anywhere I need to be, even down to your bulwark, the medical center." Shaking his head. "No, I haven't a need for a van, or even a car. Any time I have needed to get around, I have a list of volunteers that will be willing to take me anywhere but Heaven's gates."

"But that isn't the po…" He hesitated, looking up at the apparition approaching them from along the bush line. He bent and squinted as he wasn't sure what he was seeing, and if it were real or imagined? "What have we here…?" As his Irish burr thickened, his heart started beating a bit faster than usual.

"What is it, Mike?" Father Damian pushed back away from the car so he could see a broader view of what the elder was looking at. Looking along the bush line, his well-trained eyes caught the slight movement, and then, in the slightly lighter patch of dappled night, a face among the dirt and trash carried with the shard of a defensive life on the streets.

"Peter?"

"Hmmm."

"Peter, meet Father McBride. He's a very close friend of mine." He palmed a stay motion to the elder padre as he carefully started rolling toward the street urchin. "Peter, Peter, are you alright?"

The small voice in the bushes was pained as well as frightened, "N…nnn… no."

Damian stopped.

"Ho… Hook… Hooker is… oooohhhh," the man wailed pitifully as if in pain.

Damian edged closer, and spoke lower, "Hooker is what, Peter? Hooker was just here,; but he had to go somewhere and help people who needed him."

"Y… yes, Hoo… Hooker helps p… p… people."

"Yes, he's a very good man."

"But… but he… he, he is in danger."

Damian edged the last ten feet and stopped within an arm's reach of the man. Quietly he asked, "How is Hooker in danger, Peter?" He folded his hand and hook together and leaned forward in supplication. "What do you know about Hooker being in danger?"

"The d… dev… the devil!" The man was clearly agitated, and Damian had never seen him shudder and stutter so much. A small cloud of dust vibrated and floated about him. Clearly, something had happened, and it had him very upset.

"What did you see, Peter? What about the devil?"

"She was he… he… was here."

Ignoring the 'she' reference, the padre bore in. "Where was the devil?"

The man licked a finger and made some kind of a sign, or wrote something in the air that only made sense to him, and then pointed at the dark back corner of the parking lot.

"It was in the trees?"

The man nodded, "Sh… she… she was parked. Parked in the dark. Parked in the dark with a dog no bark, watching for the cat with no hat – leather. She waited with hell, ready by her hand, for the Hooker come walking to send to the promise land."

Damian sat stunned. He had never heard the street urchin say more than a few words at a time, much less spew out a string of words in a rhyme that precluded his agitated stuttering. "You said that the devil was a woman?"

"Y… yes, ev… yes, an evil woman." The man was

looking around everywhere but at Damian as he reached out with a cigarette in his extended fingers. “Evil… evil woman with a dog no bark.” He waved the cigarette, “M… m… mus… must Hooker. Must tell Hooker. Mu… must warn Hooker. Devil.”

Damian took the cigarette that Peter offered as he did most nights. He knew that Peter bummed the cigarette off Hooker just so he could give it to him a couple of hours later. It was their ritual, a touchstone for common ground. “Yes, I know this came from Hooker. Thank you.”

“N… no… not that one.”

Damian realized he was holding a filtered cigarette, not a Camel straight. He looked closer. There in pencil, inscribed by a very finely trained hand, were perfect letters and numbers written in the font used by engineers. Reading the series, he realized what he was looking at. “Peter, is this the license plate number of the woman’s car?”

The man nodded. Strangling to be talking so much, but torn by his emotional ties to what he had left, and with a touch to humanity he croaked, “M… must warn Hooker. Sh… she… she has a dog with no…wi… with no bark.”

The meaning slid in from Damian’s past as he remembered that some of the guys in Vietnam had referred to their rifles as their *dog,* and if it jammed or the sights got mangled, about how *that dog don’t hung,* but he couldn’t understand the term of not barking. “You mean she had a gun. Yes, we know about the shotgun.” Then it dawned on him. “You mean the gun had a silencer on it, don’t you, Peter?”

The man nodded.

Looking at the cigarette with the license number, he looked up. “Do you know what kind of car it was?”

Father McBride spoke quietly from his car. “Probably the black Buick tearing out of here like the devil himself was after it.” Licking just the center of his lips, the man sadly added, “But I guess it was the devil *herself* driving.”

Damian turned back to look for confirmation from Peter, but Peter was gone. All they had were the numbers penciled on a cigarette… a cigarette that Damian so much wanted to smoke at that moment. Turning back and deferring to the elder, he held up the cigarette. “Who do we call about this, and how do we explain my friend Peter?”

Father McBride thought for less than a second then waved the young priest back towards the diner. “I believe I know just the person to call, who can handle all of the bases at one time,” and as he opened the glass door, he turned and pointed at the young priest, “and, if you plan to stay in this town for very long, someone you need to know.”

As they walked back into the light of the diner, Candy came walking out of the back. “Candy, my dear, I need to trouble you for the use of your phone. We need to call Dolly.”

Candy’s right hand came out from behind the prep station holding the phone.

32

"Hooker?"

The whisper carried like a deathly smoke across the highway from the external speakers, and fell down the side of the embankment. The two young men covered in dirt, mud, and other fung, looked up at each other. It sounded almost like the wind calling Hooker's name. Hooker thought a moment, *Sweets*. The last thing he needed right now. If Sweets were calling him now, there was trouble, and he didn't think he wanted to know about it.

"Hooker? If you are out there, you need to be careful. The evil is on the move, and it is full, man, so very full." The voice melted over the rocks, and oozed down into the soul. Hooker shivered.

Johnny looked at Hooker and saw the slight blanching along with the light flush of green just below the tightly trimmed beard and jaw. "He's right, isn't he?"

Hooker nodded. "It's what he does."

"Creepy."

"Even when you get used to it." Hooker reached over and buckled the snap hook around the cable. "Done. Now let's go pull this bad girl back to the land of the safe."

They climbed the embankment to the highway. "Why are they always female?"

"Why are what always female?"

"All the wrecks we recover. You always call them a female."

"No, I don't."

"Yes, you do. They are 'bad girl', or 'sweetie pie' or even a 'prom queen' – every one of them."

Hooker dodged the truth, realizing he did, and he knew why. He shrugged it off. "I don't know…"

Scowling, he thought about needing to be as honest with himself and the kid, as he wanted the kid to be with him. He drew his lips tight across his teeth, looking over the entire set-up as he held the winching controls. Focusing on the cable strung in a curved configuration that would twist the tractor as it pulled it up to the highway, he suddenly thought about Box. He could feel the cool ear between the knuckles of his right hand. He knew it was just a transit thought, but he knew what it meant… so as he pulled the levers out, which made the controls live, he glanced over at the kid and confided. "Maybe I'll tell you about it sometime," and pulled the levers up and started the winch pulling.

Thirty minutes later, the tractor was sitting righted on the side of the highway, and the first trailer was following Hooker like a fish on a short line. They would stash the trailers, first in a parking lot where they looked innocent, and go grab the tractor, and start the first of three tows back to San Jose and the Fly's yard.

"Why spend the time stashing the trailers? Why not

just leave them on the side of the road?"

Hooker smiled as he thought of an incident in his early years. "There was a guy, several years ago, who moved a trailer to the center dirt divider out on one-oh-one, while he hauled the tractor back to his yard. When he got back an hour or so later, the trailer door was open. The broken lock just hung there. Nine black and white TVs sat in the trailer, but not a single one of the one-hundred and fifty-three of the color TVs. The cops found no truck tire tracks, just several dozen car tire tracks."

"Whoa. Fast."

"A gypsy bob-tail is faster. It would take less than two minutes for a lone trucker with no trailer to just back right into a trailer, raise the airports, hook up the air, and be gone."

"So we just go hide the trailers."

"Yup, in plain sight, but logical, like where they're an empty trailer waiting for pick up… such as the Safeway down here." Hooker pointed towards where they were headed. "That's why it's so important to know where things are. The right business with a large lot and some trailers or cars that park overnight are prime places to stash two or three tows that you can do in a few minutes to clear a wreck.

"Knowledge is the power to get your job done. For my territory, knowing all of the back roads and ways to get around a wreck or another way in is crucial. I cover over five-hundred square miles down here. Only about thirty or forty of that is what we would call city streets. There's a popular motor boating lake down here called Calero Dam. Most people get there from the south or north on one road.

I know all five ways to get in there.

"If I can get in fast, while everyone else is taking the long way around, I can get the tow. If I can stash a tow and get back before any other driver has gotten there, I might get two or three tows on a large wreck. Know your roads, and where you can stash a paycheck, and you're in business."

"Meanwhile the chips are still working the wreck and clearing the traffic…"

"… And, watching over my other trailer." Hooker smiled at how quick the Squirt was learning.

"That is pretty slick."

"I didn't think of it, but learned it from the Ace himself."

"Ace? The guy at Dolly's dinner?"

"The very same."

"Who did he learn it from?" They unhooked the trailer behind the Safeway.

Hooker chuckled as he lowered the cables and settled the trailer on its landing gear. "From the people who stole all of those TVs."

They were still laughing as they climbed back up into the cab of Mae West. Striking the large red button that released the air brakes, Hooker reached back and grabbed the mic from behind his head. "One-four-one, 10-8 for second trailer."

Hooker eased the clutch and started rolling.

"10-4, Hooker. Be advised that we have a description and license number of the car the shooter is now driving, and she is armed with the shotgun and soda bottle silencer."

Hooker looked over at the kid in surprise. He slowly brought the mic up to his mouth and thought a moment with a frown before depressing the red button. "Ayah, ten-nine?"

"I said—we know who she is, and what she's driving. It's a black sixty-six Buick La Sabre."

"She?"

"She." Dolly's tone was one of *and don't argue*, a tone very familiar to Hooker, so he didn't.

"10-4." Hanging the mic, he looked at nothing out of the windshield. "Well, that is weird."

Johnny had big eyes as he looked forward. "Man, I'll say… about as weird as it gets."

He was wrong.

Dolly was back after a few minutes. Hooker knew she had weighed who might be on the air, and then Dolly being Dolly, threw caution to the floor, stomping on it, and pickled her lollypop mic. "I doubt you would have any reason to know her, but it's Sister Mary Margaret Joseph at the Holy Redeemer." She keyed off, then back on with a bit of motherly nudging. "Just watch for a Buick with a nun in it, and be very careful out there, Hooker."

Hooker almost bit his tongue, but then she would know he was concerned anyway, so he shrugged and said it anyway. "You threw me out of the nest years ago. Don't start reeling me in now, momma." It was the closest to a hug he could muster over the air.

The return double click rattled around the cab like a dog snapping his teeth—cold and hard, but with meaning.

Dina keyed in on the yellow radio quietly, but with her teeth clenched. "I am so going to smack the back of your head if you don't behave. And if you get yourself killed, I'll… I'll kill you myself."

Johnny looked over at his boss with a refreshed light. "Boy, they sound pissed off."

"Worried." Hooker downshifted and threaded through the pass-through as he waved to the officer still standing by with his rotators lighting the way.

Johnny looked back out the side window hole as he checked the mere inch or three that Hooker had cleared the fence post. Reflecting about the two comments, he dittoed. "Yeah, that's what I said."

Both worked the next hour in their own silence. Hooker a couple of times started to direct Johnny, but turned to find the kid already doing what was needed, or the next thing. *There's hope for this kid yet, but I'd kick his ass if he settles for tow driver,* Hooker thought.

As the tractor followed along backwards, with a slight cock due to the need for the belt to be tied off with the steering wheel slightly out of center, they headed for the yard. Hooker was pretty happy the rig had some tin damage, but not real serious stuff. An easy turn with some good profit would mean a nice commission back to Hooker in the form of a full set of tanks or more, as he was thinking about some of the paint chips on the working bed.

"We could just make a diner stop before Candy goes off shift," Johnny offered.

Checking his watch, Hooker figured the time they would need to also retrieve the two trailers. "As long as we make it sort of quick. Those trailers need to go up to Palo Alto, and I want to do it before the traffic starts to build on the 280, much less the 17 crush."

"Actually, I just wanted to tell Candy something before she goes home. Food can wait."

"How about you go visit with your sister. I'll run back up and grab the first trailer, and then pick you up on the way back through. The north ramp is right there, and Hamilton has that sweeper ramp that would make it easy to get off. I'll just blow the horn from across the street, you can run out, and we'll be in the wind."

Jumping out of the rig twenty minutes later, the kid turned. "I'll give it about forty-five then have them make you up a sandwich or something to go."

"Great." Hooker cleared his mirrors of traffic behind him. "Just have her put it on my tab."

As the door clicked shut, Hookers left leg rose as he eased down on the gas. Mae West roared down Winchester Boulevard past Sarah Winchester's house that sat quietly waiting for the hundreds of tourists that would wander it's halls with their mouths hanging in stark wonder.

Hooker's eyes scanned the instruments lit up on the dashboard. The head temperature had been a little high earlier but was back down to her usual location of the needle. Hooker downshifted and turned onto Hamilton and then cranked down around as he corkscrewed the cloverleaf on-ramp to Highway 17 and back out to Los Gatos. Slowly easing his right hand forward, he turned up the eight-track a few notches more and slipped in a new tape by Elton John. The cab filled with the song Hooker was hoping was going to play first as he and the giant yellow missile rocketed down the freeway.

The wind was a gentle chill as it blasted through the open window where his elbow was cocked out and resting on the sill. The needle on the big dial flirted between the seven and the zero, as Hooker reached back and flicked the switch to broadcast on the side band of the radio. Keying the mic, he reached out to Sweets and Danny.

"It's OK, kid. He understood when you didn't answer that you were probably working."

Hooker downshifted as he approached the off-ramp for Los Gatos, a nice sweeper that he wouldn't have to stop on. "So did he share what he's been seeing?"

"No, man. You know how he gets about that stuff."

"OK. Well, tell him I have to hook this trailer, and I'll call him back in about fifteen minutes."

"Will do, Hooker. Stay safe." The big man signed off.

Great, Hooker thought as he hung up the mic and switched it back to the Dolly side, *now even Danny is worried.*

A few miles away, a black Buick slowly drove through a residential neighborhood. Slender self-manicured fingers drummed a tattoo of irritation on the steering wheel. The right hand slid for the fifth time in two minutes back down to check the custom stock of the old Mossberg pump shotgun. The fingernail traced the fine crack that had been there since it had fallen out of the tree with the young boy as they tried hunting pig with a solid-slug shell. The recoil of a quarter pound of solid lead was something her brother had not expected. It had dislocated his shoulder as it knocked him off the small perch in the elm tree, dropping him to the ground sixteen feet below, and in the path of a very pissed-off wounded 300-pound European sow protecting her brood of suckling piglets. It was the pig's rampage that had cracked the black walnut stock and put her brother in the hospital for a couple of weeks. Not the fall.

The sister thought about her two brothers more than the nun did about god. Even as a novice in the convent, her rosary was not beads supposedly blessed by the Vatican, but beads she had made herself out of rolled tissue paper glued together by the blood of her brothers. Over the years, she had collected the tissue paper used to stop their bleeding as she sewed up their cuts and scrapes and had then secretly made them into hard beads. These beads had become her personal rosary of the two brothers she loved more than anything. As she drove slowly, looking for the small house, her left hand thumbed and fingered the beads as she named each brother. She touched each bead that was made of their blood. "Timothy, pure of heart, Matthew the protector, Timothy, pure of heart, Matth… ew…" She had found the house.

It had taken her months to find out which officer had stopped the car that night, and which had pulled the trigger. The officer who had pulled the fifteen-year-old car thief over that night had been taken care of first.

The power of the simple black dress and coif of a nun had always amazed her. How trusting trained police officers and county clerks were, people who were trained to ferret out truth, and to be untrusting. She had learned the true power of the habit several years before when she had hunted down the recruiter who had enlisted her older brother, than talked him into serving, not only a second, but a third tour of duty as a Special Forces LURP, or Long Range Reconnaissance Patrol, a duty from which he had never returned. He had stolen half of her life, so she had stolen all of his in a bathtub in a hotel that charged by the hour on the seedier side of Monterey.

As she sat in the idling car, in the early light of the day, she thought of their growing up. Their father had taught her and Matthew, and later little Timothy, how to hunt for food. Their practice training had been carefully walking up to deer in the southern Santa Cruz Mountains, and touching them on the nose, or slapping them on the rump. She had almost always been the better of the three at the game, and at the frontal approach, she was the master. Unassuming, unthreatening, just another plant in the meadow or forest. A trick she had found even easier with humans once she had graduated from the convent.

Her pulse rate was slowing. She focused on the surroundings of the neighborhood. The light was still on over the porch. She knew that if she went up and rang the doorbell next to the oak and glass door, there would be nobody coming to answer the door. There was nobody home. Her prey was still running for several minutes more. Only when the officer returned from his daily five-mile run would he open the front door, turn off the porch light, and enter the small light green depression era composition shingled bungalow with the yellow trim. Exactly thirty-eight minutes later, the long-divorced officer would step out of the house, lock the door, and drive off in his duty cruiser. She knew that he owned a private car, but it didn't run very well… not since she had poured lapping compound in the fuel tank a couple of months before.

As she sat there, she watched the cross street three blocks ahead, and also checked her side mirror, specifically the cross street two blocks away. The officer had fallen into the worst trap of complacency – routine. From watching and following him over the months, she knew he ran only four routes, all of them exactly five miles from his front door. She would kill him at that fifth mile, just as he had done to Timothy, shooting him at mile marker 5 on the Watsonville highway. The image of the grainy black and white photo printed in the Mercury News of a small crumpled body seemingly wrapped around and hugging the mile signpost, burned forever in her mind.

She saw everything else through that image, much like looking through sheer drapes to the world outside. You can see the world, but it is always filtered by the veil of the drape. Only her training as a nun, and losing her older brother years before, had prepared her to not react other than a mourning sister over the tragic loss of her brother. Retribution would come later, and as she glanced in the mirror, she saw the gray sweat suit clad man turn the corner. He had run course number C, and her lips pulled back in a small mirthless smile, as she knew that retribution was at hand.

The elder officer plodded along, one athletic shoe in front of the other. The five miles each morning cleared his head as he first ran and then jogged around certain courses. Each had its purpose. One had hills to work his upper legs, and then stretch his shins. Even though it killed him for an hour after, the net gain was a more limber leg set, which was something he didn't get behind the desk. Today had been what he called his *heart through the chest run.* For the first three miles, he wound down through the southern tip of Willow Glen known as the Hollows. It didn't seem like much of an elevation change until near the end of the third mile, when he turned up a forest trail that climbed the thirty-eight floors of elevation in less than three blocks, and then there was the last mile left to run back to the house. All of the routes were exactly the same five miles that represented the five years of happiness he had enjoyed in his marriage before the fighting had begun.

Five hundred feet from the front door, across the final street crossing, and as he made the little jump over the water running down the gutter as the sprinklers at the yellow house ran out of control and broken with five geysers fountained in the yard, he scowled with his eyes as his mouth hung gaping open, sucking the air as he jogged past the corner, and turned his attention to the street in front of him.

The quiet of the neighborhood was what had attracted him. The early morning, in a community dominated by retirees, was his personal silent gym. Even the many dogs seemed to be retired, or at least didn't care, as the slapping of his rubber soled shoes padded by each and every day. As he trotted past the driveway of the house three doors from his own, he noticed the black car idling at the curb across the street from his house. Somewhere buried in the fuzzy grey of runner's hypoxia an alarm bell was sounding. An alarm bell that should have awakened the neighborhood, but was more of the sound a gopher makes as he scurries along in his holes under the lawn.

The door of the black car opened as Chief Davis made his way past his neighbor's driveway and sixteen feet before Chet would turn left up his walkway and take the last eight steps in a faltering pace reducing to a walk. The gopher stopped as time telescoped for the gunmetal grey-haired officer.

A nun was exiting the black car, but it wasn't a Bible that she was carrying in her right hand.

A police car with flashing lights silently slammed around the street corner ahead. Chet knew there should be a sound of screaming tires, protesting against sliding sideways fast enough to produce smoke as the car slew right in his vision.

The sunny day had become a dimmed moving tableau of grey as the scene before him moved with the precision of a large watch ticking off each second. As the scene slowed down for each facet to be examined, sound became nonessential.

The nun raised the shotgun with some large object on the end that looked more like a small watermelon than something that could be life threatening. As the gun came up, the cop car came to a halt and an arm extended out of the window. Sound erupted back into Chet's world as the police revolver fired and the yellow flame licked out three feet from the end of the barrel in the morning light and drove birds from their safe roosts in the trees. The second shot galvanized the nun as she swung the barrel of the rifle toward the car forty feet away, and fired. Sound had stopped again. There was no sound other than something that sounded like a grunt at any gym. The large green melon on the end of the shotgun burped bloated, and the sound returned as the windshield of the cop car exploded.

Chet felt the doorknob in his hand before he realized he had taken the last twenty feet to his door. Hitting the door with his shoulder as he turned the knob, he slid in past the oak planking as fourteen dimes found their last burial in the grain of the hardwood door.

Stumbling past the small table near the door, he reached into the drawer and grabbed the Colt 45, the one his father had carried in the *War to End All Wars*. He pulled the slide as he took the two steps across the large front window that exploded in shards right behind him. Turning, he aimed in the general direction of the black car and fired five fast shots, not thinking about the house across the street or anything else. He was fighting for his life.

The window jam near his head exploded, and the shards and dimes peppered the side of his face, chest, and shoulder. As he fell, he finished the clip in the general direction of the black car.

The colors around him fuzzed and lost shape as they turned grayer and grayer and Chet heard the car door slam. The squealing tires were reassuring as his world turned black. The model 19 fell empty to the floor. Silence settled back down on the street, and even the dogs, of which there were many, seemed to be retired and uncaring.

33

"Sugar in the sunshine!" Hooker cursed.

"What?" Even Box looked up at Hooker's uncharacteristic outburst.

"We forgot to grab your stiff-as-a-board pants and shirts to wash."

Johnny thought about how uncomfortable his new jeans and starched t-shirt had been that day, or was it night. "Screw it. I'm too tired to care at this point."

The large ball of gaseous fire blazed over the east hills and seared their unaccustomed eyeballs. "I really need to just break down some day and buy a pair of shades to leave in here." Hooker reached forward and pulled the visor extender down, which only tempered the heat of the spotlight, which they were driving directly into.

The kid fumbled with his, and looked at Hooker's—there was no extension on the passenger side. "Yeah," he grumped as he leaned back and just closed his eyes. "Speak for yourself."

Chuckling with more than a bit of punchy sleep deprived humor, "I just did." Hooker giggled, and then slapped his right hand over his mouth. *Thank goodness,* he thought, *it's time for bed.*

The sweeper down on to Southbound 101 was as clear as he could expect for the early morning commuters. Most of the commutes had shifted to the northbound since Silicon Valley, as they were now calling it, had moved most of the jobs away from IBM, and had grown exponentially in Santa Clara along the new expressways. Hooker drifted the giant into the second lane as he closed on a slow moving high-cube box pulled by a Peterbilt. The older truck was having a struggle keeping up with the flow of traffic. The black smoke pouring from the top of his twin stacks told Hooker that the rig didn't have much farther to die. He chuckled as they swept past, and the kid looked at him and jerked his chin askance.

"Old truckers never die," Hooker explained, "they just get a new Peterbilt."

The kid either didn't get it, or was too tired to laugh. Whichever, Hooker didn't care either.

"Hooker?"

Hooker reached behind his head and grabbed the mic. He didn't like the sound of Dolly's voice and glanced at his watch. She should have gone home an hour ago. "Yeah, baby."

The squelch couldn't hide the tattletale of her grabbing the lollypop mic too hard. "Do you have your No-No radio on?"

"No, baby, I'm behaving myself."

"Well, stop it. Turn it on, and turn it up. The bitch just shot Chet."

Hooker almost hit the Dodge next to him, but

recovered. Both drivers were wide awake now. Reaching over, he turned on the police band radio—highly illegal, but sometimes very useful.

Making sure he wasn't about to hit some other car, he keyed the mic. "It's warming up. What bitch and when did she tag Chet?"

The police band surged into activity as Dolly answered. Hooker turned the police down, and asked, "10-9… the other radio walked all over you."

"About twenty minutes ago." He could hear the quivering in her voice. "PD had sent a cruiser by the house, but he was out for his morning run. The cruiser went looking for him, but had a bad feeling and came around the corner as the bitch was about to plug him. The officer got off some shots, but she riddled his car and him with dimes. The guy got the call in, but he's going to be touch and go for a while."

"So who's the … female?"

"I told you, a nun, or someone in a nun's habit."

Something wasn't connecting, and the important ends were hanging in front of Hooker's mental eyes, but he couldn't see how to put it together. "Do they know where she went?"

"We're trying to follow that, but it doesn't make much sense. They're chasing her down the Almaden Expressway."

"But that is pretty much a dead end… oh shit."

"Hooker…"

"Sorry." He let go of the key. He needed to think. If she really knows the territory, she might know about Hicks Road. . .

The map played out in Hooker's head. He knew every square mile of his fiefdom. Technically, the auto club said his territory was only forty-seven square miles. But Hooker knew he was the only rig to call for many of the recovery jobs in an area more like *six hundred* forty-seven square miles with well over a thousand miles of freeways, expressways, streets, lanes, roads and tracks from highly maintained Cal Trans freeways to dirt tracks that were at one time either logging or fire roads left to return to nature.

Hicks Road was one of the more interesting back ways few people knew about, and even fewer actually used. Where Almaden Expressway with its almost straight smooth four lanes ran out, Almaden Road took over as a twisting snake, sometimes slowing to twenty miles per hour through little shanty towns of recluses. The extremely rural road ran through deep forest, tiny horse properties, and other falling down shacks that were barely surviving better than the road. Where it dead ended was at Hicks Road, where she could turn right and wind up and over the twisting dragon run of the pass to Highway 17—not far from where they had been all night. At that point, she had a choice of running down to the coast or back into San Jose.

If she turned left, she would be at the 101 freeway in less than twenty minutes, and could run north to Frisco or south to any choice of locations on the freeway, including the giant of all hiding places, Los Angeles. The other option, but not the most likely, was to go over the hills to the central valley. Everything was about what or where she would feel comfortable running to, and what roads she knew to take. Hooker only needed to know which choice she was making to hopefully get there first. He downshifted and slowed the truck as he too was rapidly approaching his decision point.

He raised the mic and keyed it. "Dolly, how close are they following her?"

"Aren't you listening to the radio?"

Hooker looked bug-eyed over at the kid who just rolled his eyes and then closed the lids and laughed. "I can't talk to you and listen at the same time." He off-keyed, took a deep sigh and keyed back. "How close are they? Do they have her in sight?"

"Yes," she confirmed, and through her open mic, Hooker could hear she was listening to their scanner. "It sounds like she's got a fast engine in her car, because she is slowly pulling away from the officer."

Hooker upshifted again as he triggered all of the flashers on the front of Mae. This is when he wished he had a siren. And seeming like he had the power to snap his fingers and get his wish, a siren started wailing to his right. A CHP cruiser dropped down the on ramp as Hooker went by. He couldn't tell at a glance, but with luck, it would be Micha now closing on his tail.

Hooker hoped the cruiser wasn't closing on his six to write him a ticket, because it just wasn't in the cards today. The low-slung, specially rigged chippy pursuit cruiser sidestepped over two lanes and was now in the center or hot lane, and moving up rapidly. The simple fact that it was one of the few hot-rodded pursuit cars almost guaranteed it was Micha. As the cruiser came along side of Hooker running at eighty down the freeway, the officer keyed his outside speaker. "Hooker, go to Tack three," blared across the lanes of traffic—it was Micha.

Hooker leaned over and switched the selector on the radio that was a match for the radio in Micha's cruiser. He clicked the key twice.

Immediately the radio responded, "Hotel 1-4-1, this is Charlie 3-4."

Hooker now had his call tag. "Hotel 1-4-1, go ahead Charlie."

"1-4-1, you are apprised of the situation?"

Remembering Dolly, Hooker returned, "10-4. Stand by one."

He keyed the other mic. "Dolly, I need to know if she takes McKeon Road or goes on down Almaden road to Hicks."

"10-4, Hooker. She's approaching that point now. Stand by."

As Hooker raised the second mic, Micha called back, "We need to get to Bailey Road or Morgan Hill, stay behind me, but keep up." Hooker double keyed the mic and shifted up another gear, thinking to himself, *Keep up?*

There was a snort from the other seat, "Keep up?" Johnny observed. "Does this person even know you?" He snorted again. "It's more like, 'Please don't run me over!'..."

Dolly's voice came across. "She took McKeon, Hooker."

He raised the mic. "OK. This is the important part. The officer needs to stay with her no matter what." He reached over and danced his way into the top tier as they flirted with 90 mph. "The next decision point is Bailey Road at Calero. If she stays on McKeon, then it will become Uvas. From there, she only as two real options—

she turns at the Chesboro reservoir or stays on Uvas and heads for Watsonville highway."

Grabbing the other mic, he passed the information and game plan. "Charlie, suspect just turned on McKeon. The pursuing officer is falling behind but we need to know if she turns on Bailey or heads for Uvas or Chesboro. Tell that Chip to man-up and keep up."

"10-4, Hotel. We will head for Bailey and wait." The pursuit car pulled a small bit ahead until Hooker eased down on the pedal, and shifted one more time. He still had four more open gears in the box.

"Where do you want to catch her?" Johnny was sitting up and cinched his belt tighter for the fifth time in fewer minutes.

Hooker, out of habit, checked his mirrors for anyone trying to keep up. The tiny smirk on his face was more about the kid and his belt than it was about anyone who could hit a flat hundred on the 101 south at this time of the day. He was sure if any drivers in the light traffic ahead of them looked in their rear view mirrors, they weren't going to argue with a Highway Patrol wailing down the highway. Especially one being followed by an even larger truck with flashing lights looking like a shark chasing a small tuna for lunch as the freeway portion of the 101 ran out onto the Monterey Highway, more commonly known as *Blood Alley*—a two lane cluster fuck anytime of day.

The old highway worked fine for its first seventy years when two lanes handled the farm traffic just fine, but now the two flashing and screaming vehicles couldn't maintain the high-speed. Micha dropped to a reasonable seventy. The new slower speed made Hooker antsy.

The morning traffic heading south was scattered along the edge of the highway under the row of trees on the dirt shoulder. The heavy northbound commute was separated from this by only a little asphalt and two highly effective lines of paint less than six inches wide. A look of fear was plastered on almost every face as the high-balling freight train of car and truck barreled past at a wind rocking speed made all the more scary by the keening of the siren.

The cruiser started to slow, and then resumed speed, as they blew past the turn for Bailey Road. "Hooker, she's still headed south. Let's just hope that Strombeck can grow a pair for the curves ahead."

Hooker thought about the sweeper curves on McKeon-Uvas Road. They weren't exactly treacherous, but they could take you by surprise when they weren't banked right or worse, not banked at all. *Maybe we'll get lucky and she'll pile it into one of the sand hills down near Casa Loma Drive, or spin it out into one of the many small farm fields or pastures,* Hooker thought to himself, but he knew with a car like that, she most assuredly knew how to drive it.

He muttered out loud to himself as he reached back for the microphone, "Who the hell is she?"

"Dolly?"

"Hooker."

"Has anyone found out anything about this nun?"

"All they know is she is local somewhere."

Hooker knew who would know. "Have Dina call McBride, but you call the Archbishop." He snapped off the mic and was immediately back on. "Please."

"That's my boy, I have the card right here, and I'm

half dialed."

"Hooker?" The wane voice seeped through the cabin from the secondary two-inch tweeter that monitored the non-active band of his personal radio behind his head. Hooker wasn't even sure Sweets was even on the radio. He should have been home in bed with this much sunshine.

Flipping the switch to change the active band, he keyed the trigger on the mic. "Go Sweets."

"I've got a bad feeling, Hooker."

"Sweets, at a hundred miles an hour, I'm kind of busy here."

"Hooker, I keep seeing motorcycles, leather jackets, and an angry mob. It doesn't make since, but I also see a nun."

Hooker keyed the mic and then released it. Thinking about angry mobs and motorcycles and what it could mean. He keyed the mic. "Where is the nun, Sweets?"

"In the middle of it all," Sweets moaned that ethereal voice that Hooker knew he was seeing it all now. "She is in the middle, but it's not about her—she's connected, but she's not touched by it, just standing there… in the middle. It's just raging all around her, the mob and flames. Hooker, they are taking the town apart."

"Who is, Sweets, who's destroying the town? He looked over at the kid and back down the highway, as he shifted down again as the daily traffic was building approaching Morgan Hill. If it weren't for the start of the bypass at Tennant Road, then by Gilroy they would be doing good to maintain an even fifty.

"The leather crowd on the motorcycles."

"It's a gang?"

"I don't know. I don't feel that."

Hooker swore internally at being stumped. So close, and yet a grey fog. "Do you see anything else, Sweets?"

"Just the water towers."

Hooker jumped on the information. "What's it say on the tower, Sweets? Those towers always have the name of the town on them."

"Nothing, my man, nothing. Just the two gray towers standing out in a field." Sweets moaned in that far off but coming back way of his that meant he couldn't see anything more.

"OK, thanks, Sweets." He keyed off. "Shit!" Hooker wanted to just throw the microphone through the window, or at least do some bodily harm. He hung the mic behind his head and danced down to the next lower tier of gears. The farm traffic of Morgan Hill wasn't going to let them just fly low down the two-lane highway of Blood Alley.

"Where do you think she might go?" Johnny asked, still white knuckled with his right hand on the door handle.

Hooker was thinking the same thing. "Dolly said local, and most people will run to where they feel safe, where home is or was."

Hooker's right index finger beat a fast tattoo on the ivory of the steering wheel, his eyes blinking and almost keeping up as he tried to see the answer. *But which town?*

"She didn't go for Hicks Road, so I'm thinking that she's running south. If she takes the Chesboro turn onto Oak Glen, she's coming out to the highway to get lost in the city streets or hit the freeway and run flat out. I'm guessing with the mill she's got that we may not be able to keep up with her."

Squirt was learning on the fly. “And if she doesn’t take the turn?”

“Then she is headed for Hecker pass and over to Watsonville.”

The Squirt frowned out the front window. “What’s in Watsonville?”

“Nothing but a clean shot at the Coast Highway and all points south, including the one-oh-one or the coast highway.” Hooker dropped a gear and kept the motor revved higher.

“Which means…?”

“We’re screwed. We can’t get from here and up Hecker pass fast enough. We’d have to know where she is headed first.” Hooker was thinking divine intervention, but he knew something that was almost as good.

Grabbing the mic from behind him, he checked that the selector switch was toggled correctly. “Momma, how we coming with that divine intervention?”

“Nowhere, Hooker. He’s in a meeting and can’t be disturbed.”

“OK, I need you instead.” He snapped the mic down onto the shifter and dropped another gear. “What town got torn apart by bikers in leather?”

The silence was the longest three ticks of a second hand Hooker ever wanted to experience.

“I’m assuming there is a point in asking about old movies?”

“Movies?” Hooker was confused.

“Marlon Brando and the *Wild Ones,*” she retorted.

“Who?”

“Smart ass… Marlon Brando… *The Wild Ones* was a

movie about bikers tearing apart Hollister back in the late forties.

Hollister! Hooker lightly banged his fist on the steering wheel. Keying the mic. “Do they have twin water towers?”

“I don’t think so, but they do have a lot of grain silos.”

Of course, silos. They would be just naked concrete cylinders that Sweets would confuse for water towers, but they almost never have the name of the city—just who owns them or an old ad for Mail Pouch tobacco.

He grabbed for the lower mic under the dash, “Charlie…” forgetting what the call numbers were, “…whatever. Micha, she’s headed for Hollister, so she will have to come out on Chesboro and head south on Oak Glen, or whatever the road is at that point. We can take Tennant Avenue, and it runs right into it.”

“You’re right. Strom just called, she’s coming out.” The cruiser surged a bit ahead as the traffic was lighter and the road was straighter, allowing people to see the cruiser’s lights from farther away.

Hooker pushed the gears to the higher, and his right hand dropped in habit to the lower side of his seat. The furry head was braced full upright. Box loved a good fight, even if it was from inside the hulking truck. Hooker scratched the top of his partner’s head and fingered the ear. “Box, you need to be in the sleeper hole, buddy.”

The orange cat understood the sleeper hole command, no matter how it was given. Bouncing off the side of Johnny’s leg, Box hit the large archway leading into the sleeper. Hiding over in the one corner, was a padded hole slightly smaller than his box. Hooker and Willie had built it as a bed, but the cat had dragged a cardboard box up into the cab for his continual use. The other was for just when things might get rough.

The cruiser's brake lights flared as Micha braked for the hard right turn onto Tennant Road. Hooker steered for the left side of the two-lane highway and downshifted in preparation to drift the eleven-tons of truck. "Grab on!" as he snapped the wheel left then pulled hard right as the rear-end's eight large tires broke away from the hold on the asphalt. Wailing like a large pack of injured dogs in heat, the back end slewed and came around, lining the truck up facing west on Tennant Road. Hooker stomped on the gas, and danced with the gears to keep his giant chrome bumper mere yards from the back of the wailing cruiser and his friend.

"Hooker, the Archbishop just called back. The nun, Mary Margaret Joseph, grew up in Hollister."

Thank you, he thought as they ran down the middle of the four-lane street, *but you are just a few minutes late.*

Sadly, Dolly added, "Her real name was Anna Rose Stillman."

For some reason that name rang a bell, but he was a little too busy to try to remember why. As it was, it wouldn't matter anyway.

The radio burped. "Timothy Stillman was the kid that Chief Davis killed this last winter after he blew up that ATF guy and his family in Willow Glen."

The dominos began to fall for Hooker.

The kid had blown up or burned an ATF officer that had been investigating several pockets of anarchists and other right-wing extremist nut-jobs living up in the hills. The groups saw themselves as the last hope of the dying America. They dealt in growing marijuana, running moonshine, and dealing in illegal guns and explosives. The kid had learned about bomb making from his older brother who was a decorated soldier that died in Vietnam. Hooker was sure that everyone else, same as he, had forgotten the quiet mousy nun, hands clasped in her lap fingering a long rosary wrapped in and around both hands, praying continually. She had been as easily ignored as the potted plant in the corner—until today.

Hooker double keyed the mic and slid it back behind his head.

34

Anna Rose was beyond caring who knew her or remembered her. The events of the last eight hours, one accidental intervention after another, made her guts seethe as she threw the car around the tight bend in the road. The same bend in the road she had spun out on ten years before as her big brother had taught her to drive the hot-rodded Buick.

She could hear Matthew's calm voice as he guided her through the driving, shooting a gun or making a bomb—all of it was the same to Matthew. Everything was a preparation for the inevitable, the crumbling of society when every family would have to fend for themselves. Except that wasn't the way things turned out. Anna Rose fingered the Rosary of blood and tissue that was wrapped around her arm and hand and fed through her fingers.

Matthew was supposed to return home from that far off land of heathens, having served his country's masters for a third and final time. He had learned much, and in turn, taught it all to her and Timothy, so that they would all be ready. But who is ever ready for a mere child, a girl of six or eight with a live grenade in an outside bar in downtown Saigon. She fingered the Rosary faster as she chanted her mantra, as engrained as breathing for her now.

The Buick with its reworked 340 engine roared down the pass road towards the stop sign. Anna Rose glanced in the rearview mirror for the CHP officer who dogged her since Willow Glen. How they had figured her out and prevented her from removing the last person on her list was beyond her, but right now she was looking back up over a quarter mile of empty asphalt and she was happy. Happy, but not enough to worry about running the stop sign. For just one moment, she considered running the sign over, but she knew the dangers that could stop her meant caution and attention to details.

She slid the medium sized car around the corner as if it were the bicycle that Matthew had trained her and Timothy to ride. The large twenty-six inch balloon tires turned only a couple of feet from her face as she rode down the dust-laden back roads of Hollister—home.

They say home is where the heart is, but for Anna Rose, it was where the soul was. It was where the gang of motorcycle hill climbers tore apart the town, and the older deputy sheriff, her grandfather, had tried to stop them. His widow had followed him, but only after a long interlude being a mother. First, while she raised their daughter, and then again, when her grandchildren needed her in 1961. Three orphaned children after their parents were taken from them by a hail of bullets from a posse of revenuers' intent on shutting down all of the stills in the upper central coast area.

The new decade had been only days away when Anna

Rose lowered the guiding light of her life into the family plot next to her husband. And then it seemed like she had just clapped the dirt from her hands, and she was digging again for her older brother, and then once more only a year later. Now, just one more space remained in the family plot, and she was determined to leave it empty for as long as she could.

Unknown to her, eleven tons of destiny rolled only six miles away—and closing in fast.

The giant engine was just hitting the power band as Hooker pulled the mic out from between his legs. Keying the mic, he reached out to the car in front of him. "Fall off, Micha. You can't go head to head with her and survive, but I can." He danced the gears up another notch and closed on the police car's rear end.

Hooker heard the officer key his mic, and say nothing, then watched as the car snuggled right and out of Hooker's way. Hooker mouthed a small grunt of satisfaction. *Nobody argues with twenty-two thousand pounds of steel and chrome—nobody!*

As Hooker pounded up into the next gear, Johnny squealed in a high girly voice, "You can just let me off anywhere along here is fine."

Hooker shot him a look of question and amazement, to which the kid just waved his two hands in a forward shooing motion as he chunked out in a newfound husky voice, "Kidding, just kidding."

The time for kidding was rapidly coming to a halt.

Tennant Road takes a slight rise before it turns into another name that nobody ever cared about, but today, as Hooker cleared that rise and made that almost imperceptible veer to the left, he looked ahead along a tree line of old oaks for any movement. As the large truck settled down from the low rise, a fast moving shadow among the morning shadows of the trees alongside Oak Glen road caught his eye. Hooker knew that the fast moving car was no granny out for a Sunday drive. Morning sun flashed a Morse code off the glass and chrome of a black Buick La Sabre, and Hooker began to adjust his speed.

The slightly curvy section of Oak Glen would keep her from moving faster than about ninety, whereas the straight-shot of the road Hooker was on would allow him any speed he needed for the next ten seconds and closing.

To have two vehicles meet from a right angle, the cars need to look like they aren't moving. It's an optical illusion that occurs and has fascinated many who forget how it culminates. But the final culmination was what Hooker was looking for. A permanent stop to the Buick—and he wanted it at the intersection.

Time telescoped for Hooker as his foot feathered back and forth taking commands from the eyes and brains as they raced for the end of Tennant Road where it *T'd* with Oak Glen. Where Hooker was sure minutes were crawling by, the tenths of seconds were flying past. Johnny now understood what he had signed on for, and where it was headed. Reflexively, his hands sought to pull just a tiny bit more slack out of the belt that was already restricting the blood flow to his legs.

The intersection was just out beyond the end of the giant hood.

In her side vision, she had caught the flicker of a large

yellow truck. For hundreds of yards, she refused to admit that it could be the pesky tow truck. But as they drew closer, the blue flames were more than distinct enough to know that her Moby Dick was highballing down the very road she would need to use, unless she continued for about a half mile more and went around on Sycamore Road. Every second counted, but the road had just straightened, and so she pushed the gas pedal to the floor. The 340 engine, which had been rebuilt as a 455, growled and surged.

Out of the corner of her eye, she knew she was too late as the chrome grill and giant bumper loomed large, and then was the cause of a sickening crunch as the rear half of the car was sheared away and collapsed sideways, much like an origami construct under a large hand slapping it to the table.

The world spun for Anna Rose. The strike was little more than a tug for Hooker and Johnny. The truck took away the back half of the car as it made its way into the field of torn-up grass and little stakes with orange ribbons. Mae started to become mired in the soft mud as Hooker spun her steering wheel to make headway back to the road before they became totally stuck.

Throwing mud balls, streamers, and any other form of yuck and guck in a soggy field, Mae fishtailed around and reached out for the safety of the asphalt. The front tires had just touched solid pavement when the truck halted suddenly. Hooker's will, gas, jockeying gears to rock her—nothing would move the truck.

Hooker sat back as he put the gears in neutral and pulled the large red button that set the brakes. He looked down on what had once been the front half of a Buick La Sabre. Everything behind the back of the front seat was gone and now sat in the middle of the field. The shearing force had been so almost perfect that only a hacksaw and a lot of sweat could have done a cleaner job. An older car with a frame and body would have created more of a crumpled mess, but the unibody construction had sheared away at the swipe of the massive bumper and eleven tons of avenging angel. The front seat now sat a couple of inches above the asphalt where it had spun to a stop.

Reaching for the door handle, Hooker kept his eyes on the front of the car. Nothing was moving except the now released driver's door sprung open with no post left to latch onto. In the distance of the small valley, Micha's siren ricocheted about the hills and forest as a dull keening wail from a dying beast.

Hooker slipped his feet out of the door and jumped down to the roadway as Johnny started out of the other side. Hooker, as if in a daze, cautiously started for the backless car. He could hear the kid get back in the cab and tell Box to stay in the hole. Some part of him wondered why after such a wild ride the cat couldn't get out and prowl in his favorite turf of tall grasses.

He blinked, and another piece of the rapidly changing scene clicked into place, but seemed unimportant as the habitual side was already turning his body to tell Johnny to let Box out. The mind is an amazing item—sometimes it's in control, and sometimes it goes on vacation. The bee sting at his neck, back, and butt, also didn't make any sense.

The leather clad man flying out of the door eight feet

in the air only made sense if this was a comic book and he were Superman. But then, that wouldn't explain the shotgun that was aimed at just above Hooker's head when a buck-thirty came blazing out of the end of the barrel. Time was collapsing, and Hooker's hearing was starting to synchronize with his shock-stalled brain.

The elongated "Noooooo!" from Johnny was punctuated by four explosions, but Hooker only saw two come at the mouth of his shotgun as the Squirt pumped the second rack of change down the retribution-pipe. As the second flare of heat, fire, and silver slid across the air by Hooker's head, the bees that were stinging him were unrelenting as they picked him up and twirled him about, stinging his shoulder and side as he lost his battle to remain standing.

The flying body of the avenging new kid was rapidly becoming twisted into a non-returnable, no-refund heap of meat chewed through with silver tumbling through avenues where there shouldn't even be pathways. The mass, missing the body it was intending to knock out of harm's way, rebounded off the asphalt a couple of skidding times and came to rest just past the body of the man he had tried to protect.

Leather oozed red life into the cracks of the warm spring highway. The sound of birds had stopped many long seconds before, as silence except for the incessant cry of a siren now harmonizing with three more in concert across the small valley.

Too late, much too late.

A few dimes lay about where they had spent themselves beating off a hard surface and bouncing back to die from use. These would now become just evidence.

A Raven glided overhead, a symbol of the end of life. The morning sun was warm on the black leather and denim crumpled in twin heaps along the pitted macadam of Oak Glen Road where it was met by a road nobody remember except that it was the last part of Tennant Road; a fitting meeting for the last part of a brief but explosive event.

The door on the Dodge Polaris characteristically screeched its hard wail of steel on steel as the tall California Highway officer stood up stunned from his seat. The sunlight twinkled off the high polish of his calf-high boots with their military spit-shine. His right hand rested on the butt of his service revolver as he cautiously stepped around his door and approached the puddle of black cloth that had once been a nun, a pistol-gripped pump shotgun with the tattered remains of a green plastic soda bottle taped to the end still clutched in her right hand.

Standing over the body, Micha reached forward with his boot and kicked the shotgun several yards away. Routine, but by looking at the missing parts and what was left of the head, he knew that the ‘SOP’ was a ‘WOT’, but then a lot of standard operating procedures were just a waste of precious time.

The officer looked about the silence of the scene. Since the day standing in the rain behind his friend cradling the prom queen, he had never felt so useless. The officer and friend fell to his knees and wept.

35

The high-pitched squeaking of white rubber-soled shoes on polished linoleum floors were almost the only sound that changed in the room. They would approach, pause, and then fade away, leaving only the soft hiss of the oxygen in the nose, and the occasional tick of a monitor. The turning of another page was regular like the step of the minute hand on the large wall clock over the head of the bed.

The soft sunlight fell lightly on the tipped up blinds that held the room somewhere between dimmed and almost lit. The low ambient white noise of the pulsing city, washing the glass of the window, ebbed and flowed as the day followed its course. The clock ticked, the page turned, a monitor blinked, and the soft breathing rose and fell almost imperceptibly as the man waited.

The approaching footsteps were not that of a nurse. The footsteps slowed and stopped outside the door. The sound of the chart being turned and shuffled through then returned to the chart rack by the door indicated a doctor or an intern. The black clad man stepped into the door.

"Damian, I'm going down for some coffee, son. Would you be up to joining me?"

The young priest moved his marker, and closed the book and laid it on the small table. For some reason, the trashy action novel just wasn't getting his attention or enjoyment. He looked over at the form lying in the bed, unmoving. Inwardly intoning a short prayer, he turned toward the other priest. "Wail," he intoned a truly awful fake imitation of his friend, "as long as the good father is buyin', 'ho am I ta be sayin' no?" He pushed on the wheels in his own special way with two appendages of disparity, but nonetheless, propelled the chair toward the door.

The two chuckled softly as they progressed down the hall of the intensive care unit. "Any change?" Father McBride looked down in hope. The other shook his head.

"Nothing yet, at least from where I'm sitting." He thought as they turned the corner and stood waiting for the elevator. "But you know, I was in a coma for over six months, and they weren't really sure I was going to ever wake up."

The steel doors opened and a young woman started to get off, but stepped back. "Well, if it's both of you, then it must be time for the morning coffee" Candy reached over and pushed the large button with the 'B'. The coffee urn they all knew they were headed for wasn't in the cafeteria, but rather in the basement, and was the personal fiefdom of Walter Green himself. Janitor coffee is always the best in the house. She looked at the two men's faces, but they didn't have to say a word. At times like this, it was always a waiting game.

Three floors above, a warm hand took the slender

hand of the young man, and carefully started clipping the fingernails. The clucking of the tongue was the ticking of a clock as she finished the one hand and moved to the left. "Umm mmm mmm, amazing how time does fly when you lazing about in a bed," Stella hummed to herself as she slowly moved the large soft nail file over the freshly cut nails. Her left thumb rubbed gently over the four tiny pink dots on the back of the hand. "At least those are healing nicely."

"Is there a sponge bath in the offering, too?"

Stella didn't have to even look up or turn around at the voice she had listened to all her life. "I hope you at least put some shoes on this time."

Dolly let go of the door-jam and wandered into the room looking for a place to settle. "I certainly did not."

Stella leaned back and caught a glimpse of the ubiquitous flip-flops, which to her sister were the closest to footwear you would ever get her to don. She knew that when she died, Dolly was to be buried barefoot, but with a pair of flip-flops in the coffin, just in case there was a dress code at where ever she ended up.

A large black woman in blue scrubs came through the door pushing a very oversized wheelchair. "Miss Dolly, I am so very sorry. I didn't expect you for at least another hour."

Dolly turned around and raised her arms for a hug, "Katie Did. Honey, how have you been?"

Muffled by the large hugging the larger, "Great, and you?"

"Hmmm, you know—same old day, just a different shift." She gratefully eased herself into the chair. "How is that Marvin of yours?"

Laughing, "How in the world should I know? You talk to him more than I do."

Dolly gave her a look of question. "How would I talk to him?"

"He's working nights for the county now. I think his call number is Alpha thirty-two, or something like that." She tossed her hair about. "I don't keep up on that detail stuff, you know. He goes to work, and I cash the checks," laughing.

"Alpha 3-2 … but wait." She adjusted herself up on one elbow. "That is a guy named Mark or Marcus, or something like that."

"Marcus Ulysses Nims. We just called him Marvin Gardens like in Monopoly, because his momma did. She loved that game, always winning, too." Touching Dolly on the hand, "Listen honey, I love chatting with you, but I need to get back down to the ER. We are full of brain donors today." Pointing at Stella, "How's the boy today?"

"No change."

"It be OK, trust me. That boy is a fighter. He is no donor," and she was gone in a blue whirl of scrubs and squeaking white shoes.

The two ladies sat quietly, each humming and reading their own brand of trashy novels. Stella liked the manly swashbuckling science fiction of discovering other planets, whereas Dolly was more down to this earth and was rereading James Michener's *The Drifters*—something she never did, nor had the desire or weight to do.

"Where's Box?"

Dolly looked over at her reading sister. "At Willie's."

Her sister looked up. "What's at Willie's?"

"Box." She looked at her sister's questioning face. "You asked."

Stella laid the book down into her lap and gave her sister a hard look that only a sister could give and get away with. "Have you been smoking bat shit again?"

Her sister mirrored her with laying her book on top of her chest, which was on top of her belly, which was filling her lap. "I am not being batty. I was sitting right here and as clear as day, you asked where Box was."

"I certainly did not."

"I did."

The two women looked at Johnny. Dolly, always being the *Dolly-who-never-cut-a-driver-slack-when-she-didn't-have-to*, snapped, "Shut up, Squirt. My sister and I are having an argument here!"

"OK, but can I get something to drink here first?" The whisper was weak and scratchy, but the fight was good to hear after two weeks of coma, five surgeries, and two shunts in his head.

"Anything you want." Stella was by his side and patting his left hand.

"Anything he wants, that is, except moonshine. Maddie and Willie are down in Bakersfield racing that car or truck, or whatever it is." Dolly's voice was starting to crack as she struggled to get out of the wheelchair. "Oh, hell, just ring the damn buzzer, would you."

Laughing, Stella held up the plunger for her sister to see.

"It isn't working fast enough!" Dolly stormed. Facing the door, "WE HAVE AN EMERGENCY HERE!" she bellowed loud enough to make the deaf in the ER jump.

The little blonde nurse came skidding around the corner, expecting to see blood and mayhem, or something equally traumatic, but only found two women and a patient. Looking from one woman to the other, "What's the emergency?"

The woman standing next to the coma patient nodded her head towards the patient. "He's awake, and would like to know what you have to drink…"

". . . As well as a couple of steak dinners," her sister finished. Then as an afterthought, added, "…and some Jell-O for the kid."

The nurse approached the bed and took the right hand, all the while watching the monitors. "But the main monitors at the nurses' station didn't register any changes in his heart rate or breathing."

The face swathed in gauze quietly responded. "Yeah, I'm sneaky like that. But, when you're finished holding my hand, can I get something to drink please?"

The nurse was flustered, but Stella calmed her down with a quick, "He did say *please.*"

The nurse gave up trying to find a pulse and rushed out.

Dolly settled back with a satisfied smile. "Well, that ought to change the look on the day."

Stella patted and rubbed Johnny's hand. "It is such a shame that Hooker couldn't be here to see this." A lone tear crept out of the inside of her left eye, the matching one on the right wasn't that far behind in falling.

36

"Hey, Squirt, wake up and smell the coffee."

The blinds were still dark, and the dim blue night light that shone all night was still on. The hallway was still in the dimmed night mode so as to not wake the patients as the nurses and staff came and went in the rooms, checking vitals, swirling thermometers in the ice water before taking rectal temperatures and other things that go bump or squishy in the night.

Johnny looked around the room and saw the dark figure sitting in the darkest corner. Slowly, the figure glided out of the corner, pulled by the barefoot single leg not in a cast. Hooker took shape.

The bottom of a hospital gown, barely hiding the required dignity, peeked out from under the black leather jacket over the ubiquitous starched and ironed white t-shirt. The left arm of the jacket hung empty and impotent while the arm rested in new surgical wrapping and a sling under the bulging leather jacket. The silly grin was optional with Hooker.

"At least you're growing the beard back," Johnny

croaked. "You looked really creepy without any hair on your face and head."

Hooker ran his palm over the half inch of new hair and beard. His fingers picked up the empty patches where the scars would grow instead of hair. "Yeah, I considered going Yul Brenner for a while, but then it might be a little cold during the winter and ice cream season." He continued to push and pull the wheelchair closer.

"So what is with the wheelchair?" The kid was sensitive to the various changes that he and Hooker had both been going through on the road to recovery.

"It helps with your birthday present, dufus."

"But my birthday isn't until Octo…" he paused, trying to do some mental math.

"Don't even try it Einstein… today, it's your birthday." Hooker got close to the bed and unzipped the top of the zipper that had been almost to his neck. Reaching into the jacket, he pulled out a pint bottle with no label. Reaching into his jacket pocket, he produced two small jelly jars. Handing them out to the kid. "Here, hold these a second." He handed them off then unzipped the rest of the jacket to reveal a large patch of orange fur.

Box's head popped out from under Hooker's arm and looked at the kid in the bed. Nobody had to tell him twice where he was to go. Hooker stood up as the cat stretched out and lightly jumped onto the bed, purring like Mae West after a bad tune-up. Hooker unscrewed the cap and poured a couple of fingers worth into each jar. "Maddie says *hi.*" Replacing the cap, he laid the bottle on the bed and reached for one of the jars. "Hmm what should we drink to? If it's not your birthday, we need something to celebrate."

"How about the fact that we're both alive?"

"Nah, we were that before."

Johnny sniffed at the moonshine. "How about friends?"

Hooker thought a second. "How about, here's to friends who look after you when you can't."

"I'll drink to that," as the kid raised his jar to his lips and sipped his first taste of moonshine. Hooker watched over the edge of his jar as he sipped from his. The show was well worth the admission. He imagined that he was looking at something similar to his face at age sixteen when Willie had finally let him try a sip of Maddie's best. It's truly amazing that a human face can make those kinds of changes in such a short time.

The kid's voice was strained and sounded more like chalk on smooth steel, "Smooth."

Hooker laughed and reached in his jacket and pulled out an envelope that was as thin as one piece of paper can get, and laid it down in the kid's lap. "Maybe the second sip will be rougher."

"What's this?"

"Just an offer..." Hooker sat back down in the wheelchair. "...that you might want to consider."

The kid looked at the envelope, then placed it in his lap as he took another sip of the moonshine and thought. Letting the fire subside a moment, his hand lowered into his lap with the jar as he leaned back into the hospital bed and pillows propping him up in a semi-sitting position that relieved the pressure of the eleven wounds where the dimes had entered, and the longer scars where the doctors had done the same, chasing all but two of them. Quietly as his left hand stroked Box curled beside his uninjured leg, he tipped his head back and asked the ceiling and Hooker, "So, why would a nun kill people she didn't even know?"

Hooker sipped on his jar. "That was the problem. She did know some of them. Chief Davis and the first CHP officer had been the ones who had stopped her little brother this last winter, and killed him in a firefight at the IBM parking lot. Everyone else, it seems, was just collateral damage along the way."

Johnny slowly rolled his head forward and took another sip as the medicinal factors of the clear liquid were starting to take effect. "For what?"

"Remember that burned out lot in Willow Glen?" The kid nodded. "One of those had been the home of an Alcohol, Treasury and Firearms agent's and his family's home, along with their neighbor's home. The agent had been getting too close to his operation of selling stolen guns and running moonshine, so he killed them in the middle of the night with a Foo Gas bomb."

The kid frowned with his swollen left cheek scrunched up. "But a nun?"

Hooker shrugged and his eyes rolled large as he looked down at the moonshine, thinking about another woman who had come from a local family of moonshiners, but had seemingly turned out for the better. "It seems that the family wasn't all that stable anyway. The older brother had volunteered into the Army and served three tours of duty in Vietnam, just so he could learn more about guns and explosives. When he was home, he put his sister and the little brother through the intense training that he had learned the previous year."

The kid thought about things he knew, and things he thought he knew, but didn't have much of an equation of an answer. He swallowed another tiny sip. "So she..." he squeaked, and then cleared his throat, "so she was really only a nun from the clothes out."

Hooker nodded and took another sip, and then poured them both some more. "It would appear so."

The night duty nurse walked by, then stopped, and returned. Coming into the room, she whispered, "Visiting hours were over several hours ago, young man." She came around and saw who was sitting in the chair, and as she was about to say anything else, her eyes adjusted as she saw Box and the bottle.

She turned and walked toward the door, adding curtly, "There better be a little of that left for me when I get off in another hour."

"Oh, there is plenty of Box to go around, if he'll let you touch him."

"That is not what I meant, young man!" She stopped and returned to the door, asking quietly as she looked back down both ways of the hall, "Does the third floor know where you are?"

Hooker nodded. "Uncle Willie and Maddie are up there directing traffic."

She stepped in the few steps to rub Hooker on his good shoulder. "It's good to see you two finally moving about." She kissed him on the largest pink scar on his head. "I'll be back for some of that bottle in an hour."

Hooker chuckled. "Bring your own Dixie cup, Celeste."

"I will honey, I will," and she was gone down the hall.

Hooker looked back at the kid who was looking at the letter, but not understanding what his eyes were reading. He even started rereading it with his lips moving, but the two short paragraphs still meant nothing to him. Or, maybe they did, and it was the damp eyes that were the problem.

The kid put the letter down, and looked at Hooker. "I don't understand."

Hooker shrugged the leather jacket against the large itchy bandages, which weren't covered by the lightly starched t-shirt, and tipped his patchwork head of shaved surgical scars and hair. With the quirky little smile of his when he was having fun, he grumped warmly, "It basically says your family: Dolly, Manny, Chet and others, think you should wait until you're physically able to enter the academy, but you've been accepted to the Police Academy for San Jose Police or California Highway Patrol—your choice. It means you get to be a cop."

The new scar rippling along Hooker's cheek and running back to his ear made him a matched set with the cat snuggled by the kid's lap. Smiling until the scar buckled, Hooker thought to himself, *the kid is really going to have to work on that goofy stunned look.* It just wasn't real cop potential. He sat back and enjoyed another sip. *So much for having a free employee.*

SNEAK PEEK

COMING SUMMER 2014

Cover Design for NIGHT VISION by
Pat Erickson at pat-erickson.artistwebsites.com

Night Vision

Sidelined

In the dark of night, red looks black and the white of freshly exposed bones are gray. Nothing is truly black and white. All is a varied palette of grays. The evil things that humans do to each other are likewise in the palette between, and rarely at the extremes—except, when they are.

There is an old tale about a man wandering in the wilderness with a staff and a lantern. The lantern had no candle, and yet, there was light. The light, it was said, could illuminate the darkest corners of a man's soul. Ancient story, but that was for an ancient and simpler time. Today it might be as simple as the light from a passing car spilling between the slates of a freight car shoved off on a siding, sitting, waiting to be used again. Or it is simply the crucible for unspeakable acts against another.

In the dark night, a truck rolled to a stop at the stop sign at the highway. The driver looked across the highway. The side field was broken up and seldom used. Its sporadic tall grass clumps were like an audience to the faded old red-brown freight car verged on dilapidation. He had noticed it Monday night as he headed for work at the

Gilroy's spice plant. He didn't remember the door on the side being open.

"Kids," he thought as his right hand reached across the metal dashboard. The cigarette lighter popped back out from the hole in the dashboard and into his waiting yellow stained fingers and thumb. The red glow from the hot metal end, flared as he lit his cigarette. His eyes were on the door across the highway as his right hand found the hole in the dash from years of habit. The smoke seared sweetly as he took the first deep draw of the morning. His wife had never liked him smoking, but his truck was his kingdom. He confined the habit to his work commute each day where there would be no dispute.

He fingered the turn signal from habit, and slowly eased the fifty-two Chevy pickup out onto the empty highway. Turning left, he headed for work on the graveyard shift. The rail car was no longer even a memory as he turned up the radio. The sounds of Tennessee Ernie Ford sang to his truck driver's soul as they crooned together about another sixteen tons of coal and being deeper in debt.

The light had swept along the walls, and then faded in the night of the railcar. What had, a second before, been a Rorschach of bright red bloody flesh and neon white bone around the silent scream and wide pinpointed blue eyes frozen in horror quickly faded to gray on gray. The high pitched whistle of air ebbed and flowed from the slit in the throat. Life giving air pushed and pulled by lungs that would soon no longer be needed in the journey from life into death.

The slender claw of a hand weighed the thin long

bone with human hair bound to it at the end. The slow movement was like the scale balance of life itself being weighed.

The brush dipped again into the dark cavity of the body that was pinned like a bug to the walls of the railcar. Small crescent cuts opened into cups to pool the blood, marching down both sides of the torso. As one fountain congealed, a new one was cut to renew the flow.

A low melodic hum was almost the silence, but contentedly not. Feeling the added weight of the loaded brush, the strong boney hand carefully moved to the wall, and continued the curious twists and turns, creating the night terror's tableau. Drawings and glyphs stretched around the walls of the rail car. Quarts of blood turned into a maniacal scribe's ink or an artist's paint.

The gibbous moon played hide and seek with a handful of late summer clouds. Far in the distance, a lone coyote howled his tortured call of alone desperation. The body of late summer crickets was ominous in their silence.

The killer gave a last little giggle at the final pass of the bloodied brush. Throwing the now useless tool over his shoulder, he sat down on the floor to watch his latest life drain away, and to feel the essence of the spirit as it flowed from one vessel to the newer more deserving.

His left hand silently withdrew the short bladed knife from the scabbard on his belt. His right hand dreamily plucked a hair from his head. The point edge of the sharp blade slid along the hair in the moonlight. A slender portion of the hair, peeled back like the skin on a carrot.

Without thought, his right hand placed the hair in his mouth, as the left hand returned the knife to the scabbard.

His right fingertips danced slow and delicate along the edge of his left Killing Boot in delicious anticipation. He could feel the stirring of his penis as the time drew near.

The killer eyed, with satisfaction, the lacey fringe that hung from what was once a face. Every slice had been a symbolic stripping of the identity. Every other strip had been a part of the killer ingesting the power and strength of the victim's essence. Each strip sucked of its delicate copper and salty nature before being swallowed. Every finger pad had been a delight of sensual touch on the tongue.

The hollow whistle of the shallow breaths now drew shorter, and more rapid. Soon, the killer knew, they would catch, stop, and catch again. This one was strong. This one might actually take a third try.

The moon slid behind another cloud as the white blue eyes grew flat and dull. The fourth and final catch in the breathing rattled for the last time. The killer smiled at the strength and determination that resided in the heart and spirit.

The dark eyes flared with a red heat. The eyelids covered the up-rolling eyes as the killer reached release. The chest fluttered with the rapid breathing. Then the final low moans…

Out in the field, a lone cricket rubbed its legs with the heat of the night. A fast hand pinched it to silence and then passed it to a faster death between yellow and black molars. The juicy tiny feast was much smaller than the Master's, but no less satisfying. The small figure shifted back into the small gully and became the tufted grass in the night.

The silence of the night was complete.

Most in the South Bay Area slept—but tonight one was dying as another renewed his power.

To be continued...

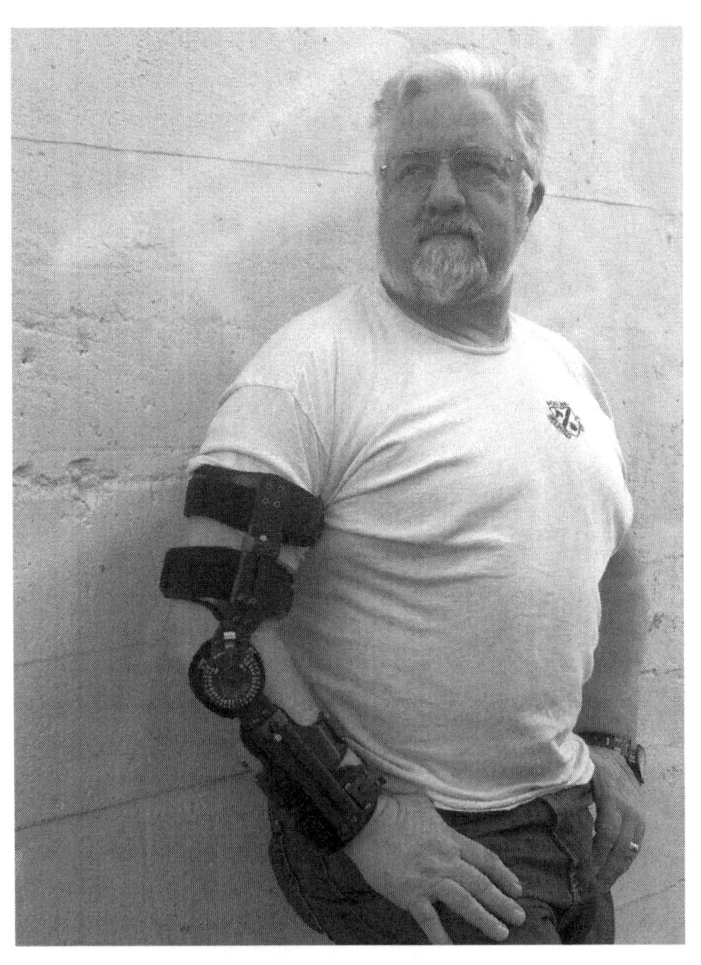

BAER CHARLTON

About Author

Baer Charlton graduated from UC Irvine with a degree in Social Anthropology, monkeyed around for a while, and then proceeded onward with a life of global travel, multi-disciplinary adventure and meeting the memorable array of characters he would come to describe in his writing. He has ridden things with gears, engines, and sails and made things with wood, leather and metal. He has been stitched back together more times than the average hockey team; his long-suffering wife and an assortment of cats and dogs have nursed him back to health after each surgery.

Baer knows a lot about a lot of things in this world; history flows through his veins and pours out of him at the slightest provocation. Do not ask him what you may think is a simple question, unless you have the time to hear a fascinating story.

8685761R00271

Made in the USA
San Bernardino, CA
21 February 2014